Praise for
red-hot

"Harte has a writing style that rivals Nora Roberts."

—*Romantic Romp* for *The Troublemaker Next Door*

"If you haven't had a chance to read this series yet, get it on your TBR list."

—*Night Owl Reviews* Top Pick! for *How to Handle a Heartbreaker*

"The characters are engaging and so endearing that readers will have no choice but to root for them."

—*RT Book Reviews* for *Ruining Mr. Perfect*

"Packed with sass, sensuality, and heartwarming emotion…an absolute delight!"

—*Romance Junkies* for *What to Do with a Bad Boy*

"High-octane chemistry keeps the pages turning and your engine revving!"

—Gina L. Maxwell, *New York Times* and *USA Today* bestselling author, for *Test Drive*

"This is truly a must read!"

—*Night Owl Reviews* TOP PICK! for *Roadside Assistance*

"Readers will swoon at the romantic gestures and fan themselves during the steamy love scenes."

—*RT Book Reviews* for *Roadside Assistance*

"*Zero to Sixty* is a savory romance that blends humor, heart, and heat to deliver a top-of-the-charts performance. It's love at first sight."

—*Night Owl Reviews* TOP PICK, 5 Stars, for *Zero to Sixty*

"A blazing hot, emotionally intense love story."

—*Kirkus Reviews* for *A Sure Thing*

"Playful banter and steamy sex scenes add up to a satisfying romance."

—*Publishers Weekly* for *A Sure Thing*

"Another exceptionally red-hot romance by Marie Harte with a strong yet sweet hero!"

—*Harlequin Junkie* for *Just the Thing*

Also by Marie Harte

The McCauley Brothers

The Troublemaker Next Door

How to Handle a Heartbreaker

Ruining Mr. Perfect

What to Do with a Bad Boy

Body Shop Bad Boys

Test Drive

Roadside Assistance

Zero to Sixty

Collision Course

The Donnigans

A Sure Thing

Just the Thing

The Only Thing

All I Want for Halloween

MARIE HARTE

Published by Sourcebooks Casablanca, an imprint of Sourcebooks, Inc.
P.O. Box 4410, Naperville, Illinois 60567-4410
(630) 961-3900
Fax: (630) 961-2168
sourcebooks.com

Printed and bound in Canada.
MBP 10 9 8 7 6 5 4 3 2 1

Dedicated to D & R. I love you.

And for everyone who asked about J.T.'s story, this one's for you.

Chapter 1

Late Friday evening, J.T. Webster stood behind the counter in his tattoo studio and stared at the stupid nineteen-year-old waiting for an answer. Young and dumb and itching to prove himself to his posse of wannabe bangers watching from a few steps behind, the kid smirked and tugged at his flat-brimmed ball cap. Yeah, because nothing said menacing like the Seattle Seahawks.

"Well?" the kid drawled. "You have the balls to do it or not? I'm for real, man." The little punk shot J.T. the finger, then lifted his shirt and pointed said finger at the gun tucked into the waistband of his jeans. "I'm not playing. I want the tat. Or is that too much for you to handle?"

His two friends snickered. A bunch of rich kids slumming in the rough section of town, no doubt. Their clothing appeared to be of high quality, intentionally gouged with holes and made to look worn. Every one of them seemed well fed, no signs of hunger or desperation on their faces. And J.T. hadn't missed the pricey sneakers worn by two of them.

Mr. Armed and Annoying continued to mouth off. "Yeah, you look big and talk tough, but you're just a scared poseur. All muscle, no guts. And what the hell kind of tattoo artist doesn't sport any ink?"

J.T. sighed. He'd wanted to close early; but Grim

was still finishing up with his client. And honestly, he welcomed an excuse to delay a Webster family dinner. Normally he loved hanging with his family. His dad had found an amazing woman, his cousin always made him laugh, and he loved his bossy little sister. But lately his father was on his ass to find a girl and settle down, God forbid. So J.T. welcomed any distraction to put off more of his father's haranguing.

Even threats from a kid more likely to shoot off his own dick than hit anything in the shop with that crappy toy tucked in his pants.

God, give me patience. "Look, man, regardless of your toy gun, I'm not tattooing 'pussy magnet' on your neck. This isn't a customer-is-always-right kind of place. Here, I'm in charge. I've dealt with my share of customer regret. You don't look that bright, but there's always the chance you might grow a brain and realize you're not going to score with the word 'pussy' creeping up your neck."

The kid's eyes narrowed. Behind him, his friends waited, looking less than amused.

"And let's be honest. The jackasses behind you in the Power Rangers shirts—"

"It's anime, asshole," one of them fumed.

"—and Bieber haircuts are no more threatening than that pistol you're trying to pretend is a real gun." In the next instant, he yanked the kid over the counter, removed the weapon, and shoved the kid back.

He checked the mag, found out the shithead was carrying—*for real*—then removed the magazine and cleared the chamber before tossing it all into the trash can behind him. The kids looked confused about whether to fight or leave as J.T. hustled around the counter and shoved the gun-toting punk up against the wall.

Infusing his low voice with menace, he growled, "How about instead of 'pussy magnet,' I tattoo 'dead and gone' on your forehead?"

The kid thrashed as his face turned red. He gasped for air while J.T. held him off the floor with little effort and pressed his forearm into the boy's neck. A glance over his shoulder showed the idiot's friends, frozen and scared.

J.T. scoffed. "I can take care of all of you before anyone asks about the noise. And guess what? No one will have seen anything down here. Yeah, there's a reason we set up shop in this part of town." Because the rent was damn cheap.

Just then, Grim opened the door. Six five, his head shaved on the sides with a mass of dark-brown hair combed back, Grim sported a trimmed goatee and tattoos all over his body from the neck down. He wore a perpetual glare that said he'd rather kill you than talk to you.

His client didn't look much nicer—a large biker who'd recently gotten paroled. The guy took in the scene without blinking. He looked down at his forearm. "Good work, Grim." He nodded to J.T., then left.

The kids not pinned against the wall took one look at Grim, another glance at J.T., and made a mad dash through the door.

Grim stretched his neck. Bones cracked. "New clients?"

"Dickheads with a death wish." J.T. glared at the boy about to pass out. *So* not worth his time. He stepped back, and the boy fell to his hands and knees, gasping for breath.

Grim joined J.T. and stared down at the quivering mess of badass. "Want me to get rid of the body?"

Obviously Grim had heard more than he'd let on. Or so J.T. hoped. With Grim, he was never quite sure if the big guy was joking. The locals left their place alone due to the staff more than their clientele. And more than half the guys J.T. worked on had done time at one point or another.

The teenager looked ready to wet himself; his eyes held a suspicious shine.

J.T. crouched to stare into the kid's soul. *Oh yeah, I'm e-vil. The big, scary mother with a score to settle.* "We still got that vat of acid out back?"

"I think so."

"I'm s-sorry," the boy burst out. "Just a j-joke, man. Kidding."

"Yeah? I got a gun and bullets in my trash can that say otherwise."

"They're blanks. *I swear*."

J.T. leaned closer. "Get the fuck out, and don't come back."

The boy crawled away and nearly clocked himself running out the door.

Grim walked around the counter and plucked the gun, magazine, and ammo out of the can. He stared at it, then looked to J.T. "I'll take care of this." He grabbed his duffel from under the counter and dumped the contraband inside. "I'm outta here. Later, boss."

J.T. had learned years ago not to ask Grim questions. "See you Monday."

Grim had the weekend off, and J.T. had decided to take some time off as well. He was booked four months out. Considering he did custom work and commissions by appointment, he didn't worry about missing a weekend for possible walk-ins. One of the other artists could handle that.

J.T. took great pride in the studio. He'd built it from scratch with money earned by hard work and sweat. He'd sacrificed by selling his soul... Or at least it had felt like it, slaving for his father in his dad's garage. While working full-time, he'd put himself through tattoo school and a two-year apprenticeship to *the* Edward S.K. Dude had since retired, but he was a legend in the business and picky about who he took under his wing.

Now the studio had a steadily growing clientele. Plenty of repeats, a growing number of celebrities, and people who were serious about body art. Unlike Pussy Magnet.

J.T. chuckled to himself and locked up, setting the security. His smile faded as he dragged his feet toward his Charger and stared up at the cloudless indigo sky. The late July weather remained pleasant, probably hitting the high sixties later.

The perfect evening to share a meal with the Webster patriarch and family.

He told himself tonight would be different, that Liam wouldn't be on the love warpath, and forced himself to drive. Good old Dad had the sense to at least let his girlfriend do the cooking.

Much to J.T.'s surprise, the normal traffic he encountered when driving anywhere in Seattle seemed to have vanished, and he made the trip across town to his dad's in half the time it usually took.

He parked in front of the two-story house aged by time and weather and grimaced at the sight of his sister's '69 GTO. He loved Del like crazy, but she could be so annoying when with her behemoth of a husband. Now married and all lovey-dovey about relationships, she was as bad as his dad, constantly on J.T.'s ass to quit his "playboy ways and grow up into a real man." Such inspiring words. It was a wonder he didn't already have two ex-wives and six kids.

Shaking his head, he left the car and remembered the way his sister used to be—obnoxious, angry, and bitchy. She was still all that, but now she smiled all the damn time. Which was cute but annoying and, honestly, a little scary.

He'd barely rung the bell before the door was yanked open and his cousin dragged him inside.

"You're late," Rena snapped.

So it was going to be like that. He groaned for effect. "Rena, honey, I've had a hell of a day. Can you believe a guy brought a gun into the shop?" He blew out a breath. "I just can't handle any more drama."

Her expression transformed from raging to horrified. Then, being Rena, caring.

Such a soft touch. He fought a smirk.

"Oh my God. Tell me."

"Tell *us*," Del chimed in before taking a swig of beer and wiping her mouth on her forearm. "It was a client, right? Or your latest one-nighter, more likely."

"My clients love me." He glanced around and, not seeing the rest of her family, asked, "Where's the ball and chain? The kid?"

"Home having a boys' night." Without missing a beat, she added, "Had to be a girl, then. Who you bangin' this week? Gina? Tina? The Farley twins? Not Sue."

"Please. I'd never date any of the chicks at Ray's.

Mess up hanging at my favorite bar? That's just stupid. I like my beer flat and cheap but spit-free, thank you."

Del grinned.

Rena glared. "I never spit in the beer I serve." She paused. "Though I have purposely confused orders sometimes and maybe spilled a beer or two on rude customers. Mostly women, surprisingly. The problem guys tend to be drunk but nice."

"Because they want in your pants." Del snorted. "She's still delusional about men. Must be all those romance books she reads."

"You'd know." He slid his sister a sly glance. "How's Mr. Sexy, anyway?"

Rena sighed. "So dreamy. I can't believe you married Mr. Sexy. Voted the hottest cover model *ever*. He still hasn't signed all my books."

His sister marrying an ex-romance-cover model was about the funniest thing ever. To look at Mike McCauley, you'd never know. The guy worked construction, had huge muscles, and glared if you so much as mentioned a book or his embarrassing past making women swoon.

Del laughed. "Mike hates that you know about that. It cracks me up that he gets embarrassed."

"Which makes my life worth living."

Liam boomed from the kitchen, "Is that my wayward son I hear? Has he finally come to visit his dear old da?" he ended in a pathetic attempt at a Gaelic lilt.

"Since when are we Irish?" J.T. murmured to Del, who shrugged.

Rena chuckled.

"Liam, stop shouting and go talk to him like a normal person," they heard his girlfriend, Sophie, scold.

Del and Rena shared a smile with him. Sophie was the best thing to happen to his father in forever. A sweetheart who didn't tolerate Liam's crap but loved him for it all the same.

Yet another strike against being here, though. Between Rena, who ate romance books for breakfast, happily married Del, and his father and girlfriend all swoony in love, there were way too many people trying to make sure J.T. found happily-ever-after. Frankly, he was fine with a happy ending, but try telling that to the women in his family. No one understood sex could satisfy, whereas commitments never did.

He'd been drooling over one particular honey for months. Had she been anyone else, he'd have made a real move, not the small flirtations he'd managed on those rare occasions when he saw her. But she was related to those blasted McCauleys. Such a waste of a fine blond.

Liam was grinning when he joined them in the living room. "Ah, J.T., my boy. Where've you been hiding?"

"At work. Not all of us can sit back on our fat asses, old man."

Liam didn't take offense. If anything, his grin widened. "Jealous?"

"You know it." J.T. accepted the bear hug his dad gave him. Though most wouldn't see it, J.T. recognized the familiar bone structure he shared with his father. He had his mother's brown skin and smile—according to Liam. But J.T.'s larger-than-life personality he'd inherited from the big mouth hugging the breath out of him. Even at sixty, Liam Webster remained a powerhouse.

"Dad, try not to hurt him," Del said, sounding as if she cared. "You know how frail he is."

J.T. glared at her over his shoulder before turning back to his dad. "Don't mind Del, Dad. I've heard when women are pregnant, they get all hormonal."

"I'm not pregnant, doofus," Del shot back.

"Oh, sorry. I just thought...with that belly...you, um. How awkward." Considering his sister still looked athletic and toned, he had no reason to think she'd take him seriously.

So when she blushed before turning to Rena to ask if their cousin thought she looked fat, J.T. could only blink in surprise.

"No, Del. Honestly. J.T. is just being himself. A jerk." Rena stuck her tongue out at him, her bouncy golden curls accenting the cocoa brown of her face. So pretty, she looked just like her mother, only softer. And thank God Rena didn't seem to have the track record with men her mother did. One drama queen in the family was enough.

Liam frowned. "You seem a bit annoyed—well, more than usual—with your brother. What's going on?" He stalked to Del, took her chin in his hand, and swiveled her head back and forth.

"Dad."

"No, you're different." He stepped back and looked her over. His eyes widened. "Holy shit. She *is* pregnant."

The room turned as quiet as a graveyard.

"She does look a little off," Rena commented after a lengthy pause.

"I am not." Del tried to wriggle away from their dad, but he refused to let her.

"Fess up."

Del turned even redder.

J.T.'s jaw dropped. "Holy fuck."

Del groaned. "It's too early to tell anyone yet. I'm not even really sure. I mean, I did one of those stupid tests, and it was positive. Then negative. Then positive again. I see the doctor tomorrow."

J.T. snatched the bottle from Del's hand. "No beer for you."

"It's root beer," she snapped.

"Oh." J.T. took a closer look, saw he'd been mistaken, and handed it back. "So I'm going to be an uncle? Again?" Del had married into a husband and child. Colin McCauley, her stepson, was a cute troublemaker whose pranks made the whole family proud. And knowing the McCauleys, who all seemed to take the word *family* to heart, Del being pregnant with Mike's kid would be a huge celebration for months to come.

J.T. asked, just to stir his sister, "Is it Mike's?"

Del narrowed her eyes on him. "You're an asshole, you know that?"

"Wait, who's an asshole?" came an amused, husky voice from behind him. The same voice he dreamed about, had naughty fantasies about, and generally obsessed about as he drew picture after picture of the smokin' blond.

He turned slowly. *Damn.* Hope Donnigan. Sophie's niece and a McCauley family cousin. Here, within arm's reach.

He gave a slow smile, thinking dinner tonight might not be so bad after all.

She saw him, and her eyes widened, the golden brown the same color as the honey he wanted to drizzle over her body, then lick off, bit by bit.

"J.T.'s the asshole, as if that really needed explaining," Del muttered. "What are you doing here?"

"Nice." Rena frowned at Del, then turned a welcoming smile Hope's way. "Your aunt said you needed a break from your mom. Welcome to the beginning of a great weekend. I don't know if you remember me, but we met at Del's wedding. I'm Rena."

Hope nodded, her gaze now suspiciously avoiding J.T.'s. "Sure, I remember you. Hi, Liam. Del."

"Hey there, girlie." Liam gave Hope a hug, taking the petite blond off her feet. Since he and his dad were the same height, J.T. figured Hope to be maybe a few inches over five feet, if that. Small but curved in all the right places. She'd fit him *just* right.

J.T. cleared his throat. "Hey, Hope. Remember *me*?" he teased. "I'm J.T."

Her gaze returned to his and stuck.

She knew who he was. He just wanted to see her sweet blush before she stammered her response. When she said nothing, he frowned. "You doing okay? Seen Greg lately?"

~

Hope couldn't find it in herself to blink, focused on God's gift to womankind. Her aunt's invitation to dinner had come at the perfect time, giving Hope an excuse to avoid her mother's weekly nagathon. Since her idiot older brothers had hooked up with the loves of their lives, her mother had deemed Hope fair game again. So much for their pleasant détente, when Hope had stopped blaming her mother for her many issues and Linda Donnigan had stopped getting on Hope for breathing wrong.

Yet Hope hadn't anticipated seeing J.T. Webster. He hadn't been at the last two dinners Aunt Sophie had invited her to. "Greg?" she asked, her mind on other things.

Like how incredibly J.T. filled out a simple T-shirt and jeans. The man had the prettiest chestnut-brown skin. She could stare at him for hours.

Hope swallowed a sigh.

Liam was white, and she knew J.T.'s mom had been black. She also must have been gorgeous, because J.T. had his dad's height and brawn, as well as the face of an angel who liked to sin. A lot.

She swallowed a sigh and continued to visually eat him up, wondering if the size of his hands and feet could be correlated to the size of other things.

God, get your mind off sex, Hope. His father is here! Aunt Sophie is here! And you're off men, remember?

"Yeah, Greg," J.T. said, looking concerned. "Gas Works Park ring a bell?"

Geez, she'd seen Greg and J.T. just last week. "Oh, no. No problems on that front." To Liam, who studied her a little too intently, she explained, "Ex-boyfriend. A jerk I ran into. No biggie." She shot J.T. a look, pleased when he kept quiet.

Last weekend, Greg, a guy she hadn't dated or seen in over four months, had accused her of using her brothers to bother him. But Hope hadn't thought about Greg the Cheater since she'd dumped him, so she knew her brothers couldn't care less about the guy. When Greg had tried to get a little gropey at the park, she'd taken him down, courtesy of the self-defense classes her brothers taught.

J.T. hadn't had to do more than watch her take Greg out. She'd been so proud of herself…when she'd been able to tear her imagination away from what J.T. would look like naked.

Those images played over and over in her head. So sad.

"Right." Liam stared from her to J.T., a question in his eyes.

"So who's pregnant?" she asked, hoping to shift attention away from herself.

Rena squealed. "Del is! A tiny little bun in her McCauley oven."

Del looked embarrassed, which was funny, because Del could outswear the mechanics she bossed around on a daily basis and took *woman power* to the next level. She had arms covered in tattoos, funky ash-blond braids, and icy-gray eyes that seemed to look *through* and not *at* a person.

Hope could see a faint resemblance from brother to sister, despite their different skin tones. Both J.T. and Del had eyes shaped like their father's and the same stubborn chins. Only someone as obsessed with J.T. would have noticed that, she realized, and felt like a moron for being so enthralled with the man.

Fortunately, Liam and Rena started badgering Del for details, letting Hope off the hook.

Since she hadn't yet greeted her aunt, Hope started to turn and found J.T. suddenly in her way. "Oh, sorry."

He put a hand out to stop her from bumping into him. And *sweet baby sexy*, she felt the touch go from her arm all the way through her body, centering between her legs. *Oy*.

"Sophie's in the kitchen." Which was about four

steps behind him. "I'll take you." He wrapped his graceful fingers around her arm, his large hand spanning her wimpy biceps with ease, and tugged her gently away from the others. "You look good."

Her face felt hot, her entire body like an inferno next to his manliness. "Oh, uh, thanks. You too."

He chuckled, and that deep rumble had her quelling a shiver. J.T. was huge, his body corded with muscle. His square jaw and high cheekbones—in addition to that dark-eyed stare that seemed to see everything—made him look more like a predator than an even-tempered artist. Though she could totally see that he'd earned his reputation as a ladies' man.

"This old thing?" J.T. glanced down at his T-shirt. "Took me forever to pick it out. I mean, I want to look perfect for family."

They'd entered the kitchen, and Aunt Sophie overheard him. She smiled. "You always look handsome, J.T. I'm glad you came for dinner. Hope, you too."

He left Hope to give Sophie a kiss on the cheek, his big body totally engulfing Sophie's smaller frame. "What's for dinner?"

"Always thinking with your stomach. Just like your father," Sophie teased.

Hope had always loved Aunt Sophie, especially because, like Sophie, Hope didn't fit the mold her family expected of her. Unlike Sophie's two older sisters, Sophie hadn't married and had children right away. She'd traveled the world, fell in and out of love, and enjoyed an art career that had spanned several decades.

She'd always been the fun aunt, with stories that pulled Hope away from life in dreary Seattle and took her into far-off castles and cafés, living through Aunt Sophie's escapades.

To see her aunt so in love, at her age, gave Hope, well, hope. If her aunt could live a full life without a man by her side, then choose to find someone later in life, so could she. Unfortunately, Hope didn't have a career she loved or grand adventures overseas. After earning a business degree, she'd bounced from job to job in Seattle for years until finally settling into a cozy role as an administrative assistant at her cousin's financial firm.

She liked it. She'd become good at it, and she thought she might just have a head for organizing and money matters. Yes, Hope could be just like Aunt Sophie. She *wanted* to be just like Aunt Sophie.

Yet for all her positive thinking, the job didn't fill that loneliness inside her.

"Right, Hope?" Her aunt was looking at her with a bemused expression.

"Oh, sorry. I was thinking about something else. Say that again?"

"I was telling J.T. that this recipe is a family secret."

Hope raised a brow. "Really?"

Sophie gave her a mock frown. "What does that mean?"

"I, er, hadn't realized our family had secret recipes. Mom doesn't cook, and Aunt Beth is so-so in the kitchen…but don't tell her I said that. Since when are you into cooking?"

Sophie blushed. "Liam's not much good in front of the stove, so I decided to take up a new hobby. We take classes together."

J.T. stared. "Classes?"

"Cooking classes. It's fun." Sophie smiled. "You two

should try it. Besides, cooking is cheaper than eating out all the time."

Which her aunt could well afford. Hope thought the woman just liked cooking for her man. It must be nice to do fun things together. Yet she had to admit she couldn't see big Liam wearing an apron and taking instruction on how to flambé.

She shared a look with J.T. that told her he thought the same. Wisely, they said nothing.

J.T. squeezed her shoulder. "I'd better go rescue Del from Dad. Did you know she's pregnant, Sophie?"

Sophie's green eyes twinkled. "I heard. I'm so happy for her."

J.T. grinned, and Hope steeled herself to stop mooning over the man. After he walked away, she turned to see her aunt watching her. She prayed her ogling hadn't been too obvious.

"So, what's new with you and your mother?" Sophie asked. A familiar topic.

"You don't want to know."

Sophie patted her arm. "Don't worry, sweetie. My mother and I used to argue like cats and dogs too. But as we got older, we put our differences aside. She mellowed out, and we could finally just accept each other for who we are." Hope just stared at her aunt…who sighed. "Yeah, I don't see your mother relaxing either. She's a lot more like our father than Beth or me. You know, I used to think Beth was the worse of the two when I was growing up. Linda used to be the nice one. But as she grew older, she grew more…"

"Aggressive? Hostile?" Hope paused. "Domineering?"

"I was going to say 'determined.'" Sophie laughed.

"Of the three of us girls, she was always the most ambitious." Her smile faded. "I know you two seem to butt heads more often than not, but honey, she really does love you. She wants the best for you."

"I know." Which was what made Hope's feelings for her mother so confusing. "The problem is she thinks she knows what's best. But she doesn't care what *I* want."

Sophie nodded. "And that's the million-dollar question, isn't it? What *do* you want, Hope?"

Hope shrugged, feeling the dissatisfaction she'd been trying to deny for months. "I wish I knew, Aunt Sophie." Because anything had to be better than feeling so lost all the time.

Chapter 2

Hope sat through the rest of the dinner, smiling with the others while remaining adrift, like an observer—watching but not exactly taking part in the group dynamic.

More than lonely, she felt...empty. Something was missing, and she had no idea how to fill that void. Men sure the heck hadn't been the answer. She'd stopped dating nearly five months ago, tired of picking up loser after loser. Greg had cheated on her, then turned verbally abusive. Before him, Jim had been a sleaze, hitting on anything with boobs. Rob demanded she obey him to the letter, and Brian had firm rules about what and how to do everything.

Hope wanted to think she had enough smarts to steer clear of trouble. But in retrospect, Greg was one in a long line of mistakes she continued to make.

Laughter distracted her, and she tuned back in to the conversations around her.

Rena and Del teased each other with affection. J.T. joined them while continuing to watch Hope out of the corner of his eye, which made her jittery. And Liam and Sophie looked so happy together, their joy should have been contagious.

But all Hope could feel was a kind of emptiness as she tried to ignore the self-pity threatening to turn her inside out. It felt as if everyone she knew had found love and happiness. Everyone except her.

Even as she thought it, she wanted to smack herself. She had a job she actually liked and a terrific boss. Cam was a genius when it came to money matters, and she enjoyed being his assistant, taking care of the administrative tasks as well as being the bright face that welcomed clients to his swanky firm.

Hope genuinely loved her cousin and his wife and baby…

Hmm. Maybe that's the problem. My biological clock is tick-tick-ticking away.

She'd wondered about the possibility, but she didn't feel desperate to conceive.

J.T. leaned close to whisper, "Hey, you still with us?"

She took a sip of water, embarrassed to have been caught zoning out. *Again*. "Yeah. It's been a long day. Sorry."

"Nobody noticed but me."

She turned. A mistake, because they sat nose to nose, so close she could see the warm brown of his irises, see his eyes crinkle when he smiled. A crazy part of her wanted to stroke his cheek, to see if he felt as sexy as he looked.

His smile widened. "You're so pretty."

Not sure how to handle such blatant flattery, she blinked and regrouped. Her face felt hot, and this close to J.T., she couldn't think.

Then she gathered her wits, reminded herself she was taking time off from relationships, and gave him a grin. "You're pretty too."

She turned her attention back to the table and made small talk with Del about life with the McCauleys. Finally, some genuine mirth melted the ice around her heart, and she was able to enjoy herself despite sitting way too close to J.T.

Dinner broke up, and Hope departed with sincere thanks, hustling away from more talk of weddings and babies. And J.T. He'd been a little too intent watching her, as if he could sense her turmoil. Too attractive and not what she needed in her life.

She drove herself home to her tiny apartment in Fremont, far enough from her parents that they couldn't walk over to drop in. After parking in the garage, she headed to her unit, locked herself inside, then flopped onto her couch.

When all was said and done, she decided to stop lying to herself. She *knew* why she was unhappy. And it wasn't just a case of loneliness.

The antithesis of her mother, Hope had never dreamed of earning millions and being the best of the best at her workplace. Fighting to get to the top didn't appeal. She'd never been overly ambitious about a job.

A degree in business and the intention of going to law school had seemed to satisfy her parents. Keeping them off her back for four years, when she'd had no idea what she wanted to do, had made sense at the time. But school grew tedious, and business bored the crap out of her. With law school out, a few years of working in cubicles and staring at spreadsheets had made her reconsider the worth of her degree.

Realizing that business had been a mistake, she'd gone in the opposite direction. A stint in retail had been fun yet ultimately unsatisfying.

More jobs working for other people had been both good and bad. She'd thought she'd found her dream job working for a unique company that tried to make people's dreams come true, setting them up on dates and arranging for fantasies to come alive.

But her boss had been a nightmare and the catty employees too much to handle. After so much chaos trying to find the right job, the perfect opportunity had fallen in her lap. A chance to work for her cousin, a genius investor on everyone's radar. She had benefits, a boss she literally loved, and a steady paycheck. The job didn't have much in the way of advancement, but she liked the work and enjoyed the daily challenges of managing Cam's busy schedule.

Still, all that was just a way to make a living, not the totality of what made Hope tick.

It had taken her twenty-nine years to figure out what she really wanted in life—true love. Period.

Hope liked working, no question. She didn't want a man to provide her with nice things. She'd buy them herself. And someday she'd figure out what she wanted to be when she grew up, she thought wryly.

She had her mother's looks—blond hair and a curvy figure kept toned by regular trips to the gym. She didn't lack male attention as much as she attracted the *wrong* attention. Hope didn't understand it. She was no one's doormat, so why did she keep dating men who treated her so badly?

After some soul searching and a hard talk from her oldest brother, she'd decided to forget about guys and focus on herself. She'd taken a self-defense class at the gym, joined a book club, and started watching foreign films to broaden herself intellectually.

Unfortunately, she kept falling asleep during the

movies. She couldn't read one more piece of prize-winning literature where the man cheated on his wife and they all died at the end. And the self-defense classes she loved had ended all too soon.

She'd tried discussing her weird funk with her best friend, Noelle. But Noelle could talk about nothing but Paris, where a mutual friend was currently honeymooning. Yeah, Noelle was a bona fide crazy Francophile now taking French language lessons and a French cuisine culinary class. The woman had made escargot for Hope a week ago, and it had been a slimy disaster.

To make up for it, Hope had insisted they watch a cartoon about racing snails. Noelle had pledged to never eat another snail again.

Hope chuckled as she got ready for bed, needing that burst of amusement to shake her from yet another pity party. She was done feeling sorry for herself. Her mother might not realize it, but Hope actually did have a lot in common with her. Determination. Intention.

She focused and did a few minutes of meditation, clearing her mind of everything except feeling optimistic.

I'm smart. Healthy. Heck, I'm almost thirty, and I'm living on my own with a great job and good friends and family.

Wait. Thirty. She blinked her eyes open. God, just another three weeks, and she'd hit the big three-oh. Thirty and single and...

"Stop it. I'm great. No need to panic because I'm dateless and childless." *Ugh.* Saying that out loud sounded awful. "I mean, I'm independent and man-free...by choice." Yeah, that was better.

Bucking up, Hope resolved to be productive during her weekend. She had plenty to do to keep herself busy. Needing to reset her attitude into that of the positive, can-do girl she wanted to be, Hope went to bed and envisioned herself having pleasant dreams about her very happy life.

Instead she had nightmares—sexy dreams about J.T. and all the things she really shouldn't be doing with the man.

~

Saturday passed without incident. Hope took refuge in keeping busy—doing chores, working out at the gym, and forcing herself to watch yet another foreign film, this one about a talking horse in Spain who found his soul mate in a starfish on the beach. Weird, but she liked the animals and the concept of a happily-ever-after, even though she decided to take a long break from indie films for a while. Keeping busy had perked up her mood, so she felt ready to tackle Sunday brunch at her parents'. She could do it, could get through a meal with her mother without wanting to stab the woman with a fork.

It helped that golden boy Landon and happily in love Gavin weren't able to attend. She loved her brothers deeply, but she felt lacking next to them. She'd at least kept a job longer than Theo, though, so she had that going for her. Goofy, lovable Theo would turn twenty-one in another month, and if she had issues with her life, he had them in spades. She felt for him. Trying to figure out what to do with life after high school wasn't easy.

Her father opened the door on her first knock, then took her in his arms and hugged her off the floor. Van

Donnigan had a laid-back, almost hippie-like attitude about life. He was all about being Zen and stress-free and doing what felt right, living the dream. Hard to believe he'd retired from the Navy as a corpsman, or that he now worked for a major pharmaceutical company making big money. He looked and acted decades younger than his sixty-three years.

Van had a head of dark hair just starting to go silver, gray eyes, and glowing, sun-kissed skin due to a healthy regimen of eating right and daily runs.

"Hope, my baby girl. I missed you." He kissed her cheek.

Man, she loved her dad. "I missed you too. Even if it's only been two weeks."

"Two weeks too many." He slung an arm around her shoulders and tugged her inside. In a lower voice, he confided, "Your mother's in a mood. She lost the Hosterly listing to Trina Blackwell, and she's not happy."

Hope groaned. Linda Donnigan sold million-dollar houses. She had skill, panache, and a web of contacts throughout the city that fed her information night and day. Hell, Linda made Google pale by comparison. She knew everything about everyone, and she took losing as a personal affront.

Vacillating between love and irritation with her mother, Hope settled instead on pity. She could lose with dignity and a smile. Linda didn't know how to handle second place.

"Should I go?" Hope asked. "I don't want to set her off."

Her father sighed. "No. She needs your support. And I need you to act as a buffer for me when she starts throwing knives," he teased. Then he cleared his throat and changed the subject as they entered the kitchen.

While her dad chatted about what his work friends were up to, Hope absorbed the wonderful smells coming from the oven. For as long as she could remember, her father had been a genius in the kitchen. Linda had no problem ceding him the task of feeding the family, and he enjoyed experimenting with food, so their system worked.

Her parents truly complemented each other, for all that they were opposites in so many ways. Her mother had often shaken her father back to life when he'd get too introspective, and Van could charm Linda out of a bad mood with his killer smile.

She found her mother finishing with the place settings at the dining table. Linda's disappointment vanished when she saw Hope looking at her. Her mother, so good at masking the bad with forced good.

"Hi, sweetie. So glad you could make it today."

Determined to be nice no matter what, Hope donned a mantle of fake cheer. "Wouldn't miss Dad's famous French toast casserole." Truth.

Linda grinned, and Hope wondered if she'd look as good as her mother in thirty years. Her mother's white streaks only made the blond of her hair look lighter, more golden. Daily workouts kept her trim, and Hope had the uneasy feeling that if they actually raced, her mother might win.

Her father stuck his head out of the kitchen. "Oh, and I stole the recipe from the Food Network. Don't tell anyone." He winked.

Linda sighed. "I'll feel guilty eating all this, but I

don't care." She sat with Hope and waited for Van to join them. As usual, her father got the head of the table, and Linda sat to one side, Hope on the other.

"Is Theo coming?"

"No." Her father placed the casserole on the table, joining the carafe of coffee and a jug of juice already there. "He's working."

"Still at the coffee shop?" Every day that Theo kept a job counted as a win. Her little brother—not so little really, since he towered over her—had to deal with Van's grilling the same way Hope normally dealt with her mother's. Hope still didn't understand how Landon and Gavin had managed to avoid the wrath of their parents.

"Yes, he's doing well there," her mother answered. "Better than me with that screwed-up listing."

Since her mother had brought it up, Hope found it a safe topic to broach. She fortified herself with caffeine before asking, "So you learned you'd lost the listing this morning?"

"I had a bad feeling yesterday. It was confirmed today. Trina's double-talk and connections to the mayor won the Hosterlys over." Linda huffed. "She used her looks too. Jeff Hosterly is a total lecher. That cosmetic surgery really worked to bring out Trina's *ass*ets." Linda seemed less upset about Jeff being a creep than that Trina's enhancements had scored her the listing. "I wonder if I—"

"No." Van shook his head. "You're beautiful and smart, and if the Hosterlys couldn't see that, then they deserve what they get with Trina."

"A four-point-two-million-dollar house," Linda

griped. "I could have gotten it for them for four-point-one-three." She sniffed. "But live and learn. Next time I'll make sure to hire a trustworthy assistant."

"Assistant?" Hope asked, confused. "What does that have to do with Trina?"

Van winced. "Oh boy. So it was Cathy feeding her information, then."

Linda nodded. "Yes, so I'm once again without someone I can trust at my side. I mean, Kelly's good to step in while I'm searching, but he's not Cathy. She was so good at keeping me organized." Linda turned to Hope, her gaze a little too intent for Hope's peace of mind. "Would you like to—"

"No, Mom."

"But honey, you don't know what I'm going to say." Linda gave a light laugh that didn't fool anyone.

Hope's father made a mad dash to the kitchen to grab everyone more water. Coward.

As much as Hope felt for her mother's loss, she had her own sanity to protect. *Be nice. Mom's having a bad day. Smile to take the sting out of no.* "You want me to step into Cathy's role. Sorry, Mom. Been there, done that two years ago." *And got the migraines to prove it.* Hope shook her head. "I love you, but we can't work together. We're not a good fit."

"Well, that's true." Her mother looked her over. "You know, I stopped by Cam's last week and saw you typing madly behind your desk." Linda paused. "He doesn't mind what you wear to work?"

Hope counted to ten in her head before answering. "I always dress professionally. Cam likes us to be business casual. I'm pretty sure I wore skirts all last week." Which day had her mother been in? She couldn't remember. Not that it mattered, because Hope had never had issues with her appearance at work.

"You had one on." Linda nodded. "But it seemed short to me."

Riiiggght. And you saw that from your position on the other side of the desk while I was sitting? Count to ten, count to ten…

Van stuck his head out from the kitchen, looked at both of them, then ducked back inside. "Forgot my glass. Be right out."

Hope gritted her teeth, then forced herself to relax. "I don't wear miniskirts to work, Mom. And since Cam didn't complain, he obviously thought it was fine." Though, what if he hadn't liked it but didn't know how to tell her? Or he was trying to decide how to tell her? Or if—*Argh*. He didn't care. Hope wore business clothes, nothing revealing or inappropriate. *Linda strikes again.*

"He has no taste." Her mother sighed. "I would have thought marriage to Vanessa would have helped him. Now there's a girl who has it all." Her mother pointed a spoon at her. "Top of her accounting firm, a partner even. She has a beautiful baby girl and a decent-enough husband to boot." She chuckled. "I'm kidding. I love Cam. He's the smartest of Beth's kids, you know."

"I know." Linda had only said that a million times.

"Graduated college early and is already making a mint with his own firm. I realize it's just temporary work for you." Or so her mother continued to remind her, because in Linda's mind, if there was no room for advancement, the job didn't signify as worthy.

Hope heard her father's sigh from the kitchen.

"I'm good, Mom. I love my job." Hope forced herself to drink her juice and not respond to her mother's clucking. She cleared her throat and in a loud voice said, "Man, Dad, this French toast is awesome."

Linda frowned. "You've never been one for numbers, despite that degree."

So much for dear old Dad coming to the rescue. "And you want me to work for you?"

Linda talked over her. "You know, when you were younger, I thought maybe you'd be good in fashion. Not retail, but design. You do have an eye for it. I still think you'd be amazing selling houses. I can teach you so much more than that brief bit you learned a while ago. You're beautiful and smart and fast on your feet when it comes to conversation. I really think you should give being a real estate agent another shot."

"No thanks. I'm good where I am."

Linda blew out a breath at the same time Van returned with a pitcher of water and three glasses balanced in his hand. He gave Hope a big smile and nod, and she refrained from arguing with her mother.

"Well, then, if I can't convince you to look elsewhere for satisfying work you can grow and advance in, tell us what else is going on with you. Are you dating again?"

"No." *Jesus, kill me now*.

"Why not?"

"Linda…" Van gave her the first warning, which she ignored.

"What? I'm interested in my daughter's life. With the boys all set and Theo finally talking to the recruiters about boot camp, we've only got Hope to worry about."

"Why does Theo get a pass?" Hope asked, though

she knew she shouldn't have. No point in throwing her younger brother under the bus just because she'd been targeted.

"He can't commit himself before going away," her father answered. "I mean, I got lucky with your mother. But there were a lot of hard times for us back then. Distance is no way to start a relationship."

"Which is why I think you and Steven would hit it off," Linda segued with a smile at Hope. "He's a doctor. Alice Cooper's son."

Hope blinked, familiar with the name. "Isn't Alice Cooper some rock star?"

Van snorted. "*Some* rock star? You're so young. Alice Cooper is the godfather of shock rock."

"He's a guy? With a name like Alice?"

Linda frowned. "Obviously it's not *that* Alice Cooper. Van, honestly."

Hope smothered a grin. Her father laughed outright.

"Alice is Steven's *mother*," Linda explained. "Steven moved here two months ago. I sold him a house, that nice one on Taylor Avenue."

"Oh, right. The stonework with the red door." Her father nodded.

Linda beamed. "Yes. It's a beautiful house. He's a very nice man. Hope, I think the two of you would hit it off."

Her mother's matchmaking had been disastrous in the past. Hope preferred her own awful exes to her mother's snobby missteps. "No thanks. I can find my own dates, Mom." *Take a breath; she's had a bad day.*

"What would it hurt to meet him?" Linda sighed. The put-upon mother. "He's a nice man, has a great job, and clearly has money. Take me out of the equation, and you'd date him in a heartbeat."

"No, I wouldn't. There's more to a man than money and a good job."

Van focused on his plate. "Man, am I a great cook or what?" he asked in an über-cheery voice.

Her mother was on a roll and didn't notice. "Well, it sure wouldn't hurt for your future boyfriend to be respectable. The last man you dated was awful. Didn't Greg fix heaters and air conditioners?"

Hope gritted her teeth. Granted, Greg had been a jerk. But she hated her mother's prejudices. If a date didn't fit Linda's preconceived ideal of the perfect man with the perfect job and perfect bank account, he didn't rate. When younger, Hope had broken up with many a boyfriend instead of dealing with her mother's disapproval. That she'd been weak enough to allow Linda's influence still bothered her.

"It doesn't matter what Greg did. He's gone now." Hope paused, recalling Greg's odd complaint that her brothers had messed with him last week. "Did you ask Landon and Gavin to talk to him?" She wouldn't put it past her mother to interfere.

"What?"

Sensing genuine confusion, Hope shook her head. "Never mind. Mom, I'm sorry you had bad news about your listing. But I'm good. I'm happy being single, focusing on my career."

"A career with no possibility for advancement. No way to move up or even laterally in the company. But at least you dropped that idea about making dreams come true." Linda huffed. "I'm sorry, honey, but you sounded like you were opening a prostitution ring. And I never understood how Greta Hampton ran her business without being arrested."

"Mom." Hope flushed. "Greta still runs a successful business, you know. Even if the woman is psycho." When Hope had tried to start her own fantasy firm, the woman had gone nutty, threatening her with lawsuits and even bodily harm. "Wanting to make people's dreams come true, for me, meant arranging perfect dates and outings. There was nothing illegal about it." Though she'd petered out on the concept, tired of trying to think of ways to make everyone else's lives better while being envious on the sidelines.

"Yes, well, running your own business takes time, energy, money, and know-how. You told me you had no interest in going back to school for your master's, so it was a smart move to forget about that dreamer thing."

"Nope. I'm done with school for sure."

Linda sighed. "Hope, can't you see that this job is going nowhere for you too?"

Broken record, meet Linda. "I'm happy where I'm at."

"Where you are," Linda corrected.

Annoyed and desperately trying to hold on to her patience, Hope counted to fifteen in her head. Ten obviously hadn't done the job.

"You know," her mother continued, "if Steven won't suit, I have another friend. Evan's an English professor. He's single, maybe ten years older than you are, and a lovely man."

"No."

"You'd like him. I know your taste, and he's someone

you'd find handsome. He's a teacher, so he's not too *rich* for you," Linda said with a bite. "God forbid you like someone who can rub two nickels together."

"Seriously, I'm fine. I don't need help finding a man." For some reason, J.T. Webster and his sexy smile popped into her mind's eye.

"Really? Honey, you're nearly thirty. If you don't find a man soon, you'll turn into Sophie. Don't get me wrong. I love my sister. But don't you think she'd redo her life if she could? No children and no husband and she's fifty-two already. Way too late for babies."

At mention of her aunt, who'd only ever been supportive, Hope lost her cool. "You know what? I *am* dating someone." The words started coming, and she could do nothing to stop them. "I didn't mention him, because he's someone you'd hate. He's blue collar, an ex-con, and he comes from a broken home," she said sweetly. "No pedigree to impress you, for sure."

"Oh?" The arched brow did it.

"Yeah. Did I mention he tattoos people for a living?" Her mother's passionate disdain for body art was a known fact. "You should see the crowd he hangs out with, Mom." Hope gave a pretty shrug. "Not one of them has a nickel to rub, let alone two. Just think, if you're lucky, you can have a poor son-in-law who's got baby mommas all over town."

God, stop. You can't go there. Not with him. But her mouth continued to ignore her. Hope would have brought up the mixed-race angle, except the one thing about Linda Donnigan Hope had always admired was that Linda was color-blind. A true woman of the people, Linda didn't care about race, sexuality, or religion. Hell, she'd have done cartwheels of joy to have a gay daughter, so long as Hope dated a rich lesbian.

Linda narrowed her eyes. "You're lying. You're gun-shy since Greg, and you should be. Talk about a poor choice."

Hope fumed. She *knew* she'd made a mistake, especially with her mother always there to remind her.

"I'll call Steven. Let me fix this for you, since we both know you can't see fit to fix yourself," her mother added with a grumble. "He's a doctor, for God's sake. You can't get much better than that."

"What you mean is *I* can't get much better than that."

Linda frowned. "That's what I said."

"No, you meant—Forget it. I don't need you to fix me, Mom. I'm good the way I am." *With or without a man.*

Hope gripped her fork and focused on not jumping over the table and stabbing her mother with it.

"Linda." Hope's father, ever the eternal peacemaker, covered Hope's hand and squeezed. "Let's just have a nice meal and forget about all this." He turned to Hope and smiled. "Hope's just fine the way she is."

But Linda had a bone to pick. "Bah. You baby her too much. No. The girl needs a reality check. Life isn't going to get better as she ages. She's pretty and young now. The world is her oyster. But it won't be that way forever. Tell you what, Hope, why don't you bring your new *boyfriend* to dinner? I'm happy to meet him…if he exists." Linda snorted.

Hope frowned. "What does that mean?"

"Just that it's convenient you have a boyfriend all of a sudden, one who seems to press all my buttons."

"He exists, all right."

"Ha. Sure he does."

"He does too." *Not. He does not. And why can't I stop sounding like a rebellious eight-year-old? Hell, might as well roll with it.* "You know, he's an amazing artist. Maybe I'll talk him into that tattoo I've been thinking about getting."

Linda's eyes narrowed. "You will not."

"I'm twenty-nine years old. I can do what I want."

"I'm still your mother, young lady. You want peace between us, you follow a few simple rules."

"*Simple rules?* Date rich men and work for you, living the Linda way? Is that it?"

"Well, you're not getting any younger," Linda snapped.

"You know what? I'm full." Hope stood. "I'm finished with brunch. Thanks, Dad."

"Hope..."

Her mother glared. "Say and do what you want. You always do...no matter how poor those choices might be."

It was as if Linda heard nothing but her own voice. Live by her direction. Date who she chose. Pop out a kid or two to round out Linda's idea of how Hope should live her life.

Well, screw that. Hope now had some plans to make, and one tattoo artist to see. With any luck, he'd done jail time.

She couldn't wait.

Chapter 3

Monday evening, J.T. was finishing up a client when Suke stuck her head over the high partition separating his station from the others.

"Sorry, but there's a hot chick here to see you."

"I don't have anyone scheduled after Dan."

Dan tensed as the needle dug into a tender spot.

"Yo, man, relax. I told you, we're nearly done. You're doing great."

"Sorry, sorry." Dan drew in a breath and let it out. "I friggin' hate this part." He'd had a similar tattoo drawn over his left wrist, so he knew what to expect on his right.

"Yeah, the parts that aren't as fleshy hurt more. But you wanted it."

"Hell yeah." Dan chuckled and remained still, his arm stretched out on the table extension, unmoving under J.T.'s hand.

J.T. once again put pressure on the foot pedal, the quiet of the rotary machine a welcome relief from the older, louder equipment he used to use. The days of the loud drilling noises, cigarette smoke, and metal music gone wrong no longer existed. Now he tattooed his clients to some chill bass vibing the studio.

"The chick?" Suke said again. "I told her to wait."

"Yeah, sure. Fine. I'll talk to her when I'm done."

Suke nodded and left.

It took J.T. another half hour to finish with Dan.

After covering the tattoo in ointment and plastic wrap—because he knew Dan would just rip a bandage free to show off his new tattoo—he walked the guy out.

"Remember, any problems, call me. You didn't scab last time, so I'm thinking you won't this time either. Give it a week and a half to heal, then I want you back in so I can take some pictures. That is one wicked reaper, Dan."

Dan grinned. "I know, right? You're the shit, J.T. Love you, man." He did the perfunctory half chest-bump on his good side and cradled his tattooed arm like a baby. After paying Suke, he left with a promise to return.

J.T. sighed and rolled his head on his neck, then stretched his shoulders. The session had been three hours long, but so worth it. He'd done excellent work. He glanced around, pride in his efforts enforced by the artistic feel of the place. *His* place.

The funky lobby of Tull Paint & Body had been done in dark colors, the floors a clean gray cement. Original artwork decorated the walls, using photos of designs the guys and Suke had done in the studio. A few Tull T-shirts and mugs sat on a rack by the counter, where whoever manned the desk would catch walk-ins and take payments. Where their apprentice, Daisy, would have been if she hadn't left early to run some errands.

"J.T.?"

He froze for a moment, feeling déjà vu. He kept hearing Hope Donnigan's voice in the weirdest places. Although she *had* actually been at his dad's on Friday. He turned to see her standing by the wall-mounted screen to his right. Huh. She was really here.

"Hope?"

She wore open-toed sandals showing off dainty, blue-painted toenails. Shapely legs disappeared under a knee-length, floral sundress. A cropped sweater hid her shoulders. She looked like the essence of summer, and he wanted to kneel down in worship. Innocence radiated from her in waves, as if begging him to muss her a little.

He should have felt dirty for wanting to muddy that innocence. Instead, he grew more aroused. *Hell.*

"Hi." She smiled at him.

His heart raced. Damn, that dimple slayed him every time.

"He says hi back," Suke said dryly. "I'm Suke, one of the harder-working artists around here. I take it you know J.T.?"

Hope nodded. "Great place. I hadn't realized it was down here."

As she and Suke spoke, J.T. watched them interact. Hope didn't seem to care that Suke had tattoos up and down her arms, piercings in her nose and lip, and spiked black hair in a dare-to-be punk style. Nor did she seem to mind the way Suke was eye-fucking her.

"Hey," he growled; *he* minded.

Suke grinned. "I'm leaving for the day. You need me to stick around and lock up? Maybe walk Hope out to her car?"

"Go."

Suke chuckled and left.

"She's nice."

He laughed. "Suke? She busts our balls on a daily basis, but we love her. Now what brings you to the lion's den?"

Hope grinned. "Is that what this is? The sign outside said Tull Paint & Body."

"Yeah, a play on Auto Paint & Body, like a car paint shop. I worked for my dad before I opened the place, and some of him stuck." Jesus, he was babbling.

"Tull?"

He shrugged, searching for calm. "My dad is a big Jethro Tull fan. Sounded cool when I was twenty-five." He paused, shoving his hands in his pockets. "What's up, Hope?"

She flushed, now looking uncomfortable. "Ah, this is kind of awkward. I have a favor to ask." She didn't say any more.

She looked so damn adorable. He couldn't help himself. He had to mess with her. "Okay. So you want a baby without the commitment. I get it. You want to make one right here or in the back room? Do you have some paperwork for me to sign first? You know, about rights for the kid?"

"*What? No.*" She blinked at him. "Have you done that before?"

"Nah, but I can't think of a more awkward conversation. So now that I know you're not here to use and abuse me, what can I do for you?"

"Ah, actually..." Her face turned bright red.

He gaped. "Shit. Really?" He took a step closer. "You want to abuse me? I'm game."

"J.T." She blew out a breath. "I have a problem. And I kind of dragged you into it."

"Color me intrigued." He led her to the high-backed purple leather chairs by the coffee table, on which a print portfolio of their work lay, along with some tattoo mags.

"Sorry," Hope apologized. She crossed her legs to sit demurely in the chair, and his heart threatened to leap from his chest. He wondered if she felt the same sexual chemistry he had since the first time he'd laid eyes on her.

Probably not, since she didn't seem affected by him. She was shy, gorgeous, and could have any guy she wanted with the crook of her finger. He couldn't imagine why she needed his help, but whatever. He was game. And truth be told, he felt protective of her. She was a weird extension of family his sister had married into.

"Hope? Just tell me."

"It's my mother. She's such a pain." Hope glared, and he was taken aback by the fierceness from a woman he'd never seen be anything but pleasant. "She was on me about dating some rich guy. A doctor this time. Then she was riding me about my job, my lifestyle, being boring. You name it. She jumped on my nerves and ground them to nothing."

"Ah, sorry." He still didn't see what part he had to play in this.

"So I mentioned I was dating someone. A tattoo artist who had baby mommas everywhere and had done time. Have you done time? Because that would be good."

He blinked. "Huh?"

Like a steamroller, she continued, "I need you to pretend to be my boyfriend the next time I have to go to dinner at Mom and Dad's. And you need to be awful."

He didn't like the tone of this drama. "What? Play the big, bad black man to scare your lily-white mom?"

She snorted. "Please. If only it was that easy to scare Linda Donnigan."

He relaxed, more than glad to know she couldn't care less about his skin color. "Then what do you need, exactly?"

"My mother loves people of all races, genders, and sexual persuasions. But she's a snob. It's all about money and success with her. If you're not dying to be president, you're nothing."

"President as in…?"

"The top of whatever your career is, or the actual POTUS. With Linda, it could be either," Hope said wryly. "I have no drive to be more than Cam's assistant right now. I work at my cousin's investment firm, and I'm basically a glorified secretary. But I'm okay with that."

"You don't sound okay." She sounded frustrated.

"I am. Mostly." She sighed. "Look, none of this is your fault. I needed someone I thought my mother wouldn't like."

"That hurts." He wasn't lying.

"It's not personal. She doesn't know you, J.T. But she's not a fan of tattoos at all. And you look tough. So I thought, who do I know who would freak my mother out?"

"Me?"

"Yes." She smiled. "I just need you to pretend to be my new boyfriend a few times. Then we can 'break up,' and she'll never know."

"I have met your mom, you know. It was brief, at Del's wedding. She might remember." He frowned. "Then again, she was drinking that night."

"She likes champagne." Hope leaned closer and grabbed his hand.

The feel of her smaller palm against his caused sweat to break out on his forehead. He stared into her honey-gold eyes and felt himself nodding.

"Dinner will be delicious, because my dad's an

amazing cook. But it might be uncomfortable because Mom will grill you."

"Why not just ignore her and do what you want?"

Hope's face set in a charmingly militant expression, though he doubted she'd be happy with the description. "It's the principle, J.T. She thinks she can tell me what to do, how to act, where to work. I'm tried of it. Tired of her always thinking I suck at everything. So I lashed out, acted like a spoiled teenager, and now I'm stuck backing up what I said, or I'll look even stupider than I already do."

"Isn't it *more stupid*?"

"No, it's *stupider*." She looked hard at him. "Don't tell me you're a grammar nazi."

He flushed. "Ah, sorry. My one vice."

"You only have one?" She raised a brow.

"Funny. But at least lying to my mother isn't one of them."

She said nothing, just looked unsure of herself.

"Oh, now see, that's probably awkward. Me mentioning my mom, who's dead and all." Which she would know, being so close to her Aunt Sophie.

She just stared at him.

"What? She died when I was four. I barely remember her." Sad but true. What he knew of her had come from watching his father grieve for the woman for nearly *thirty years*. He cleared his throat. "So this dinner. You want me to come and act all thug-life for your mom?"

"Yes. No. It's dumb."

It was an excuse to spend time with her. Why the hell was he trying to talk her out of this? "I get it, Hope. Your mom is making you feel like you don't know your own mind, and you're trying to show her you do."

"I told her I might get a tattoo, and she went off." She smiled. "I'm not proud of it, but annoying her was the highlight of my day yesterday."

He laughed with her. "Big of you to admit. Hell, why not? I'll go to your dinner."

"Thanks. I don't know when it will be. In a week or two, maybe." She gripped his hand, and he wondered if she was aware of him holding on to her with no intention of letting go anytime soon. "About what I said before... Forget all that. Just be yourself. You won't scare her, but you'll show her I can make up my own mind."

She started to pull her hand away, and he tightened his hold. "Now wait a minute. What's in all this for me?"

"A great dinner?"

"Hmm. No. I was thinking of something else."

She grew guarded. "Like what?"

"How about a real date? You and me go have fun together. Like out in public somewhere," he said so as not to scare her. "Your choice."

Her eyes widened. "You want a real date?"

"Did I stutter?"

"Um, well, okay."

"Why so surprised?"

"I don't know." Then he saw it. That flutter of nerves, of desire, as she stared at his mouth.

Oh hell. He had little discipline when it came to Hope Donnigan. Knowing she wanted him back would make dating her a very bad idea. Yet he couldn't help himself.

"Come on. I'm a safe guy to be with. My sister will kill me if I screw you over, which I wouldn't anyway. But she wants me keeping the McCauley ecosystem steady."

Hope's slow smile was blindingly beautiful. "McCauley ecosystem?"

"Yeah. There are all these relationship ties between the McCauleys and you Donnigans. Then add in us Websters, and Rena, the guys at the garage, 'cause they're close like family. The gang at Ray's..."

"I've always wanted to go to Ray's Bar."

He paused. "It's kind of a rough place."

"All the more reason for me to go. Okay, J.T. You'll have your date. I get my dinner. And it makes sense to hang out a little, because my mother will interrogate you. We really do need to get to know each other better." She looked a bit nervous when she added, "But, um, no kissing or sex or anything, okay? I'm coming off some bad relationships, so I'm staying away from men. But you won't count, because this is pretend."

"I don't count?" Now she'd irritated him.

"Not what I meant. I meant—"

"I get it." But he didn't like how fast she was to dismiss him. "Okay, deal. We go to Ray's for my date. We go to your place for your fake dinner."

"My parents' place, but yeah."

"Shake on it."

"You have my hand."

"A hug then, since you're practically family." He tugged her to her feet, then pulled her into his arms and sighed at how perfectly she fit. "You are tiny, aren't you?"

She withdrew and glared up at him. "I'm not a child, J.T."

"Trust me, I know." He kissed her before she could reject him. A quick peck on the lips was all he intended.

But the moment their lips met, they both froze.

He meant to pull away, knowing he'd gone too far. Then Hope softened under him and gripped his arms, her fingers trailing down to knead his thick forearms. She made a tiny growl and opened her mouth.

When her tongue slid between his lips, he forgot himself and yanked her closer.

And that was all she wrote for the next several minutes of his life.

Hope lost herself in J.T. He smelled like an invitation to sex and tasted like candy. Good Lord, but the man knew how to kiss.

The moment he'd touched her lips, she'd forgotten her own advice to steer clear of men and latched on to him. And now she could do nothing but enjoy a real man concentrating on her.

He moaned, slanted his mouth at an angle that gave him deeper access, and followed her tongue with his, dipping into the recesses of her mouth and stimulating every damn cell in her body.

He was hard. *All over*. His broad chest swelled. Arms that she could barely fit her hands around tightened. As did the rest of him when he drew her into his body.

She felt caged in his embrace, totally controlled by a man much more powerful than herself. But she sensed nothing but arousal and safety, oddly enough. Nothing overbearing, like what she'd experienced with a few of her exes.

A smart woman would put a stop to the kiss. Especially when he put his large hand at the small of her back and pulled her closer still, allowing her to feel the impressive bulge between his legs. Their disparity in size was evident, especially that big part of him she felt all too clearly when he rubbed against her belly. She gasped, caught between his kiss and his shocking dimensions.

He trailed his lips down her cheek to suck at her neck.

She moaned, tilting her head back, doing her damnedest to find the will to push him away. But her body had other plans.

Her breasts ached. The place between her legs throbbed. And the rest of her tingled, every part of her needing to lie down on the nearest horizontal surface so she could spread her legs in welcome…

"No." She pushed weakly at his chest.

J.T. froze, panting. "No?" he choked out.

"Yes. I mean, no. We can't do this," she managed between large intakes of breath.

He slowly put her away from him and stared at her from under hooded lids. All she could think was that he looked kissable.

"Stop."

"Huh?" She shivered.

"Don't look at me like that."

She licked her suddenly dry lips, and he glanced away and swore.

"L-like what?"

"Like you want me to… Never mind." He blew out a harsh breath. "Yeah, um. Good idea to stop that. We're just pretending, right?"

"Huh?"

"About dating. So we can fool your mom if we have to kiss in front of her to be believable."

"Right. Yes. Uh-huh." *Think, Hope. With more than your ovaries*. "I'm sorry. I didn't… I wasn't trying to put out the wrong signals." *That I want you? That sex with you is on my must-have list?* "I told you I had some tough relationships in the past." She swallowed the lump in her throat. "I'm trying to do better and be focused on me right now."

"Sure. I get you." He nodded and tucked his hands in his pockets, which did nothing to mask the raging hard-on under his fly. "Smart move. I met Greg. I feel you."

She sighed. "Yeah."

They all started out nice, then slowly morphed into monsters. J.T. seemed amiable, sexy, safe. What would he turn out to be in the end?

"Okay, then." He cleared his throat and guided her toward the front door. "We won't do this again. But we know we can pull it off for your mom if we need to."

"Right. I really do appreciate you doing this for me." She stopped and faced him, feeling bad for pulling him into her mess. "You don't have to, you know."

"Um, yeah, I do. Where else will you find a tattoo artist with several baby mommas and jail time on his résumé?"

She stared. "Really?"

"Well, no. That's not *all* true." He winked at her. "But to find out which parts I'm lying about, you have to buy me a beer at Ray's."

She gave him a smile, unable to help herself. Charming should have been his middle name. That and handsome. "It's a date."

"Wednesday at six work for you?" he asked. "It's a little less crowded in the middle of the week, and less scary for a first timer."

"I won't be scared." She'd heard from her brothers about the rough types who hung out around the place.

"Honey, *I* was scared my first time. And my second, my third..." They shared a laugh. "Ray's is good people. Tough, but good. I'll pick you up. Will that be okay?"

She thought about it and realized she didn't care if he knew where she lived. "You're practically family," she teased. "I trust you."

She couldn't read the look he shot her as he walked her to her car and waited for her to belt up. Once all secured, she rolled down her window. "Okay. What's with that look?"

"Just remember, Hope. We *aren't* family." He shook his head and bent to stare her in the eye. "Because I'm not down with kissing my family like I kissed you." He stroked her cheek, sighed, and straightened. "Now go home before I forget why I shouldn't give you what you're asking for."

Heck, *she'd* been the one to say no earlier. But when his eyes narrowed, she obeyed. Better to keep him happy since he'd agreed to help. Plus, she trusted what she knew of him. If he thought she should leave, she'd go. Because if she stayed any longer, she might assault the man and have her wicked way with him. And that would pretty much shoot her independent, no-men stance all to hell.

Turning on the radio, she sang all the way home, feeling better about life than she had in a long time.

The next day, Hope arrived at work early, in a cheerful mood. She wore a business casual outfit of dress pants, heels, and a silk blouse. Even Linda would have trouble making an issue of her clothing, styled hair, and makeup.

Instead of annoyance at thoughts of her domineering mother, Hope smiled, recalling J.T.'s warmth, the feel of his firm yet soft lips guiding her. Melting her. She sighed as she took the elevator to the office on the second floor. "Dating" J.T. would prove to be a challenge, because everything in her wanted to be with the man for real. To see if he could make good on his reputation's promise as a marvel in bed.

She'd been off sex too long, was all she could think. But J.T. was so much more than a hot body. His smile seemed to light up his face. His sense of humor and work ethic, as well as his artistic skill, made her want to know more about the fascinating man. For all that his sister and father could be hard cases, J.T. seemed so much mellower. No temperamental artist, but an even-keeled, fun guy who could soothe the savage beast (of his sister, in particular) with a joke or two.

She'd liked being part of their family at dinner Friday night. As much as she'd liked seeing J.T. in his workplace. The designs she'd studied while waiting for him had stunned her with their intricacy and true workmanship.

Hope had been prepared to see the typical skulls, roses, barbed wire, and the like. But the art his crew did was so much more. His work especially had captivated her. What did he see when he looked at the world? So much more than she did, apparently. Which made her wonder what he saw when he looked at her.

She stopped at the locked office door and stared at the vase of flowers in front of it. No doubt a surprise gift from Cam to his wife. He did that sometimes, though he normally had the flowers delivered to him during working hours. She took the vase inside with her and started her day. Powering on the computers, the lights, and most important, the coffeepot.

She might have thought Alex, Cam's assistant and an all-around nice guy, had received the flowers, because Alex's partner loved the stuffing out of him. But Alex had gone east to take care of a family matter and wouldn't be back for three weeks. The poor guy's brother had passed, and Alex needed to attend to his estate.

She missed Alex's snarky sense of humor, as well as his gourmet beans. He was a coffee snob and insisted they use the beans he chose. And he chose very well.

After she'd gone through some emails and scheduled a few appointments, she studied the bouquet, curious as to why Cam would send flowers to the office so early. Were they an apology to Vanessa for a fight they'd had? A secret romance to surprise his all-knowing, all-seeing wife? Or were they for someone else? Cam had occasionally received flowers from a few of their more amorous clients, which Hope found hilarious.

She nosed through them and spotted a card. She frowned, decided to open it on a whim, and read. A peek at the card didn't tell her much.

To add to the beauty behind her desk.

She stared. *Her* desk? The flowers had been sent to Hope? But by whom? Her thoughts immediately went to J.T. But their kiss last night had been spontaneous, and he'd agreed to keep their relationship friends-only.

She didn't have any other admirers. And she frankly couldn't see Greg ponying up any cash to give her something nice. Not unless a spider or thorns lay buried beneath the blooms.

At the thought, she set the vase on a table away from her desk.

Cam arrived soon after. "Good morning, Hope." He smiled, dark-haired, blue-eyed, and handsome like his father, but with his mother's warm disposition. "Flowers, hmm? Who's the lucky guy?"

"I was going to ask you. I thought they were for you until I read the card." She handed it to him. "So these aren't from you to Vanessa, then."

He shook his head. "Nope. I wonder if one of our clients has a crush." He winked.

Since he saw no harm in the gift, she figured she shouldn't either, though it creeped her out a little. Hope wasn't one for secret admirers. She wanted badly to text J.T. to ask if he'd sent them, but she'd feel beyond stupid if he said no. If he'd sent them, he'd probably mention it at some point.

"They look nice on the table by the chairs." Against the far wall, away from her desk.

Cam must have caught her unease. "You want me to get rid of them?"

"Can you just make sure there are no bugs or surprises in the vase besides the bouquet?"

"Ah, sure." He looked and shook his head. "Nothing but pretty flowers."

"Okay, then." Hope smiled, determined to enjoy the colorful surprise and start in on the day's work. "Your first appointment this morning is with Carol Knopf at ten. You have her electronic file, and I've printed out a paper copy of her investment summary that you can give to her."

"Great." Cam gave her a hug. "Have I told you how glad I am you agreed to work with me?"

With, not *for*. *Take that, Linda*. "Have I told you how glad I am I accepted?"

They smiled at each other.

"Oh," she said, remembering what else she'd meant to tell him. "I brought the sugar substitute Carol likes. I'll have it on the tray with the coffee and beignets." High-end clients received high-end treatment. "You aren't wearing cologne, are you?" She sniffed him. Subtle, yet there. "Cam, you know Mrs. Knopf can't handle scents."

"Crap. I forgot. I'll wash it off." He turned toward his office, then stopped. "You look really nice today. Just thought I'd mention it. Next time, *I'll* get you flowers."

She smiled. "Promise, boss?"

Chapter 4

J.T. HAD KNOWN IT WOULD BE TOO GOOD TO BE TRUE NOT TO run into anyone he knew at Ray's Wednesday night. His cousin, Rena, manned the bar. Guys from Webster's Garage—more Del's place than his father's, what with his dad semiretired—were playing darts. He recognized the pair and Heller, who wasn't supposed to be back yet.

J.T. considered Axel Heller, owner of Heller Paint and Auto Body, a true friend. The poor guy had recently lost his mother to cancer, and J.T. had intended to pay his respects the moment Heller returned from Germany.

Sam and Lou were amazing mechanics who worked for his sister. For that alone, they deserved praise. The guys were a lot of fun, decent despite looking like street fighters, and he considered them friends.

"Do you see people you know?" Hope asked from beside him. "You can go talk to them if you want. I see Rena waving me over. And there aren't too many people here giving me dirty looks, so I doubt I'll get into a fight," she teased.

He'd warned her to be cautious at Ray's. She'd smartly worn a pair of jeans and a casual pink T-shirt, her hair pulled back in a ponytail. Nothing fancy. Yet she still drew every male eye in the place.

Gruffly, he said, "I'm going to say hi to Heller. Guy lost his mom recently. I hadn't realized he'd come back already."

"Oh, I'm sorry." She put a hand on his arm, and J.T. felt her touch to his toes. Warmth trailed, and not just the sexual kind. Hope had a way about her, doling compassion that made him feel as if she truly cared about *him*. Not just because she was a nice person, but because she felt for J.T.

Stupid to think that. She clearly didn't want a relationship. But she cared. And that mattered.

He seated her at the bar and warned her and Rena to watch out for assholes, which had both women rolling their eyes at him. Then he promised to return once he'd talked to the guys.

He reached their table and gave Lou the stink eye.

Lou shrugged. "Sorry, amigo. I had no idea he'd come back until he sat down next to me."

Next to him, Sam nodded. "Yeah. He's not lying. This time."

Lou shot him the finger. Sam arched a brow and told him to do something anatomically impossible.

Next to them, Heller regarded J.T. with blue eyes so dark they looked black.

"You okay, man?" J.T. asked and sat on the other side of him.

"*Ja*. Life and death coexist," Heller said, his German accent thick. "We cannot have one without the other." Six five, blond, and typically scary as fuck, Heller intimidated those who didn't know him. But the guy had a soft spot for artists like J.T. and Lou. And he was a genuinely nice person under all the anger and aggression he often showed.

Lou, Del's paint specialist, shook his head when J.T. would have commiserated.

Instead, J.T. slapped his grieving buddy on the back and nodded at the dartboard. "Who's winning?"

Sam sighed. Almost as big as Heller but now more mellow since he'd found love, he didn't fight nearly as much as he used to. A crying shame, in J.T.'s opinion, because watching Sam mop the floor with the idiots at Ray's could be entertaining as hell.

Lou grinned. "Like you have to ask. Heller's ahead by thirty. I'm hanging in there. Sam sucks."

"Shut up."

J.T. chuckled. "Like old times, except the gang isn't all here. Where are the others?"

The mechanics from Webster's were a family, usually thick as thieves. But now that the others had all gotten girlfriends, the guys didn't get together as much. A shame, but J.T. knew they had to grow up some time. *They* had. Not him, though. He'd learned from his father's example too well.

Sam answered him. "Foley's with Cyn. Dinner at her folks'. Johnny and Lara are doing whatever the lovebirds get up to when they're not around. Probably playing nurse." Lara was close to completing her nursing degree, and the guys loved teasing Johnny about it. "But the real question is what the hell are you doing with a Donnigan? I recognize the blond from Del's wedding party. That's Hope, right? Mike's cousin?"

As one, everyone at their table turned to see Hope laughing with Rena. Then the guys turned back to him. Lou raised a brow. Sam smirked. Heller just stared.

"What? We're just friends. She wanted to see Ray's, and I'm not a moron. I brought her here on a mostly empty night. She's stubborn enough to come on her own."

Lou winced. "Yeah, not a good idea."

"I know." J.T. saw some slick asshole approach her, say something, then leave.

"I brought Ivy here once," Sam said. "Never again."

Lou snickered. "That's because you're an idiot. You think I'd bring Joey to this place? No way in hell." Lou's girlfriend seemed too innocent to hang out at Ray's. Yet for some reason, J.T. didn't think Hope would have a problem here.

"Rena works here." J.T. felt the need to defend the bar. Okay, so Ray's wasn't superclean or finicky about their clientele. So they had no dress code, frequent fights, and a few police raids now and then. J.T. liked the place.

"She's a hard worker," Heller added. "I think Ray's is fine."

"Whatever. You just want the bartender," Sam muttered. Heller turned icy eyes on him, but Sam wasn't deterred. "We all know it. Hell, *she* knows it. Make a move, Romeo. Take advantage of that sympathy she keeps shooting your way when you're not looking."

Heller sat straighter in his chair. "She's looking here?"

"Yep." Lou fought a smile. "Maybe you should get us another pitcher."

Heller left the table in a rush.

The guys laughed at him, J.T. included. "Sucker."

"Okay, look. He's in a rough place," Lou said. "Might want to check on him in a few days. I've been keeping an eye on him, but my paintwork finishes tomorrow, and I'm scheduled to be back at Webster's as of Friday. He's not doing so good."

J.T. sighed. "I know. His mom was great. His dad's an ass and, I bet, making trouble for him?"

Lou nodded.

"But enough about Heller." Sam *thunked* his glass on the table. "What's up with you and the hot blond?"

"I told you. I'm showing her Ray's."

"Uh-huh." Lou's smirk was annoying.

"Watch the tone, Cortez."

"Or what? You'll insult me to death?" Lou snorted. "Hate to break it to you, guy, but no one is afraid of your tiny fists."

J.T. looked from his own graceful, artist hands to the guys' blocky mechanic ones. "Not my fault I care about my art. But push comes to shove, I can hit back. I mean, I was raised with Del. Among the wolves, man."

Sam tilted his head, considering.

Lou chuckled. "Good point. But don't change the subject. I saw you drooling over Hope at Del's wedding. You had it bad then. I'm wondering if you're gonna try to make a move now that you've got that McCauley connection going for you."

J.T. cringed. "It's like a curse, that name." The guys laughed. "But seriously, Del is so happy lately." And pregnant—but that was something *she* needed to tell the guys. "Mike's a dick, but he's great to my sister. Their whole family is. And with Dad hooked on Sophie…I'm thinking there might be another wedding down the pike."

"Seriously?" Lou blinked. "Liam taking the plunge? Damn."

"Yeah, well, don't count on wedding bells yet. The old man is scared but trying not to show it. I'm gently easing him into his 'I do's.'" J.T. grinned. "If he lets

Sophie get away, I'll personally kick his ass. He's so much nicer with her around."

"Agreed." Lou nodded. "We don't see him all that much anymore. But when we do, he's always in an up mood. It's nice to see."

Sam frowned, and J.T. wondered what the guy had to be bugged about. Did he not like Liam being happy? Then he said the words J.T. had dreaded. "Ah, you might want to head back over to your girlfriend. Trouble ahead."

J.T. swung around to see Fletcher sneering and mouthing off. "Damn. I thought Ray kicked his ass out." He hurried to Hope just as Heller punched Fletcher in the face.

And the night got more interesting…

Hope stared in shock as a scary giant of a man, who'd seconds ago been staring at Rena with adoration, smacked an obnoxious racist in the mouth. The guy's head snapped back, and the giant followed with a punch to the racist's stomach that felled him to his knees.

Before Hope could move, J.T. pulled her back behind him. "Stay there."

Like he had to tell her twice. She watched in shock and awe as the giant—Heller, according to several onlookers—took out two more rude men, both of whom could have used a bath several times over.

When a fourth man would have attacked Heller's blindside while he dealt with the others, J.T. calmly decked him, a clean kick between the man's legs. The sneaky guy went down with a groan.

"Ow, that's gotta hurt," someone said from behind her.

"Rena, you good?" J.T. asked his cousin, who remained behind the bar.

Unlike Hope, Rena didn't seem fazed by the violence. She poured more beers and handed them out. "Fine. J. and Earl are coming."

Two men not quite as tall as Heller—but large, angry, and wearing black T-shirts with the word BOUNCER in bold white letters—collected the injured.

They dragged the defeated brawlers away, gave Heller a look and a warning, then returned to their posts near the main door.

"I am sorry if you were scared," Heller said to Hope in a gravelly German accent. His deep voice startled her into taking a step back. "But they were not going to go away because you said no."

"Oh. Yes. I see." She swallowed. "Thank you."

J.T. roped an arm around her shoulders. "Hope, meet Heller. Heller, this is my friend Hope."

"Hello." The giant, Heller, glanced from her to Rena. "You are Rena's friend too, yes?" Taller than J.T., with huge muscles and menace dripping off him in waves, he seemed a little too much for a girl to take. Handsome, yes. But too overpowering for Hope.

Not like J.T.

She subtly stepped back once more, so that she was nearly on top of J.T. "Yes, I know Rena. She was making me laugh when those guys came over. The one, Fletcher, said some rude things to her." Hope frowned. "Some racist things. I'm glad they threw him out."

From behind her, Rena said, "Ray let him return on a probationary basis. But now Fletcher's permanently banned." She sounded smug, took a look at Heller, and made a sad face. "Oh, Axel. Come here. Let's see those knuckles."

The huge man meekly followed her into the back, and Hope could see his unabashed admiration for his makeshift nurse.

"I like her," she told J.T. "She's so sweet and funny."

"Yeah. We all have a soft spot for Rena." He tugged her with him away from his friends at the other table, who had yet to take their gazes from her and J.T., and sat with her at a different table. "Rena's mom and my mom were sisters. When mine died, my aunt stepped in to help with me. Well, when she wasn't running from one guy to another. Unlike Rena, Aunt Caroline is not good with men or money." He sighed. "Mama with drama, that's our Aunt Caroline."

Hope tried not to smile.

"What?"

"You're funny. That fight was crazy, but you're still so calm. You kicked that man in the… Well, between his legs. He went down hard. But you barely blinked, and now you're here with me, talking about your mama-with-drama aunt." She shook her head. "Ray's is just like my brothers said it was."

"I'll bet." J.T. paused, studying her. "You don't want to leave?"

"Heck no. We just got here."

He sighed. "Of course you want to stay." He muttered something she couldn't make out, but she was having too much of an adventure to care. Hope had been sheltered all her life. She'd never seen a fistfight before. Not one other than between her brothers or that had been scripted for a movie or TV. Had her mother called her staid? Unadventurous? Hope wished Linda could see her now.

Except that wanting to stay at Ray's wasn't a way to get back at Linda. She liked it here. "Do you get in a lot of fights?" she asked her rescuer.

J.T. shrugged his massive shoulders and waved at one of the waitresses. "Hold on. Hey, Sue. A pitcher of Coors and some nachos?"

The waitress, a woman with muscle, tattoos, and lots of piercings, nodded.

"I did her Chinese dragon," J.T. mentioned. "Hell, I did artwork on a lot of the guys who come to Ray's. But to answer your question, no, I don't get in a lot of fights. My hands are my livelihood, and frankly, I'm old enough to know better."

"How old are you?"

He grinned. "Thirty-two. How old are you, Miss Nosy?"

"Twenty-nine." She sighed. "I'll be thirty in a few weeks."

"Why the sigh?"

"Because I'm not married, don't have kids, and have a job with no potential, according to my mother." All of which were true.

"So what? You don't have to be married with kids to be happy, do you? I mean, I'm not. I've got a job I love. I'm sitting with the hottest girl in the place, and I don't have to worry about having an active social life because I don't have a kid at home waiting on me to play daddy."

"Good points." Her cheeks felt hot because he'd called her the hottest girl in the place. *You're so easy, Hope*. "It's just hard when all your friends and family are moving on to a different stage in their lives and you aren't."

"Tell me about it. My sister is happily married. Even my dad's getting all clingy with Sophie. Not that I think that's a bad thing, but it's weird. All the guys at the garage, who I used to hang with a lot more than I do now, are hooked up with women. And Heller's always mooning after my cousin. It's like all the happiness of being single has been taken over by these *couples*."

The disdain with which he said that had her laughing. "God, I feel the same way. I went to a wedding last week. Remember? I was wearing that awful pink dress when I met Greg on that hill."

He nodded, his gaze intense. "I remember. I was thinking, man, she looks sweet. Pink was my new favorite color. Then I saw Greg starting to hassle you. Before I could get close enough, you had him on his ass." He chuckled. "It was freakin' hot how you handled him."

She blushed. "Thanks. I just did what I was taught. I took my brothers' self-defense class."

"Good thing you did." He paused as Sue brought their pitcher and some glasses, then darted away with a promise to return soon with food. "Seems like the class was worth it."

"Yeah, it was." Hope watched him pour them beer, taken with his huge yet graceful hands, his long fingers, the corded strength of his forearms and biceps.

"Ah, you mentioned a wedding?"

She took a hasty sip, found it palatable, and took another. "Yeah. A friend of mine got married. It was a beautiful wedding." She sighed. "Except for the bridesmaid dresses, it was awesome. She and her husband are honeymooning in Paris. Now my best friend won't stop talking about all things French."

He chuckled. "I dated a French chick once. Don't believe all that talk about the French making the best lovers. She was boring and hated kissing. It was weird."

The woman had to have been nuts, because the one thing Hope could attest to was that J.T. could kiss. "I'm not sure what to say to that."

"Not much to say." He shrugged and drank his beer. The waitress dropped off the nachos, and he pushed them toward Hope. "Ladies first."

"Oh. Cheese. Yum." She took a large bite, not caring that she wouldn't appear dainty or ladylike while she gobbled down nachos slathered in sour cream and guacamole. Normally, she did her best to try to impress a date, but since this one with J.T. didn't count, she didn't bother.

He didn't either. They fought for the few black olives in the dish, as well as the cheesiest chips.

"Hey, back off, woman. That's mine."

"Please. You need to watch your figure. I'm doing you a favor."

He blinked. "Watch my figure?"

"Yeah. You don't want to get all bloaty from the dairy, do you? Especially since that table has been eyeing you all night."

He groaned. "I'll talk to them. Sam and Lou are such a pain in my ass."

"Are Sam and Lou girls? Because I'm not talking about your friends. I'm talking about them." She nodded to the girls making eyes at J.T. the moment he turned.

Hope wanted to be above catty jealousy, but it

annoyed the heck out of her that the "ladies" at the table couldn't see J.T. was with her.

"Oh." He blew out a breath. "Sorry. I dated one of them a while ago. She wants to get back together."

Surprised at his honesty, she nodded, hoping he'd continue.

"But we're too different. She wants babies and marriage. I want to stay swingin' single."

"Right." Hope refused to feel an ounce of disappointment that the man she refused to date didn't want permanence. "Swingin' single is where it's at."

"It is when it comes to psychotic exes," J.T. mumbled and leaned closer, his voice low. "She was talking about dating exclusively ten minutes into our first date. And she..." He blinked, flushed, and pulled back. "Let's just say she was willing to do anything to get an agreement out of me."

Hope frowned. "Please tell me you didn't date her for sex then dump her."

"That was our agreed plan," he said, being shockingly forthright. "She wanted some lovin', same as me. I don't try to scam my way into a girl's heart. See, when I'm dating someone, we both go into a relationship with the same goals in mind. Fun, pleasure, and parting our separate ways. Trish...well, she tried changing the rules from the get-go. I tried to let her down easy."

"Uh-huh." Enjoying herself, because the insight into his character amused her, Hope continued the interrogation. "I'm sure you rejected her advances and sent her home with a polite *not interested*."

He smiled. "Well, now. I wouldn't say that. I'm a gentleman, Hope." He ignored her snort. "I didn't want to upset her. So I shared myself, spreading joy. And even…hope."

She groaned.

He laughed. "Kidding. I mean, I did make her happy. And that wasn't a euphemism for sex. I tried going out with her, keeping my intention of casual fun clear. She seemed on board when I told her I refused to date her and only her. But after a few weeks, she got weird. I bailed. I've tried to be nice, but—"

"Hey, J.T." The woman stood behind him.

Hope had watched her approach and wondered how he'd handle it.

He crossed his eyes, and Hope had to work not to laugh at his annoyance. "Oh, ah, hey, Trish."

"Hi, baby." She shot a cold-eyed glance at Hope. The girl was pretty. Long, dark hair, dark-red lips, dark eyes. She had curves and dressed to show them off in a short skirt, a belly-baring top, and heels. "Who's this? My replacement?"

"I have a feeling nothing I could do would replace you," Hope said, trying to sound complimentary. Sadly, as curvy as she was, Hope would never fill out the clothes Trish wore. And with her luck, she'd kill herself in stilettos that high.

The woman blinked. "Huh."

J.T. tried to bite back a smile, but Hope saw it. "This is my good friend Hope. She's never been to Ray's, so I'm showing her the place." He blew out a breath, then added, "She's my new girl, Trish. Be cool, okay?"

"Oh. It's cool here." Trish put a hand on J.T.'s shoulder. "Very cool."

He tensed, and Hope felt for him. As much as she

thrilled at being in her first *He's my man* altercation, she'd never been in a situation where she had to fight over someone. But feeling the animosity growing and wanting to live on the edge for once, she raised her chin and gave Trish the stink eye.

"Yeah, cool." Hope pointed a finger at J.T. "He's mine now, Trish."

Trish frowned, most likely not having expected Hope to be anything but perky.

J.T. just stared at her.

"Well, okay. But don't hog him forever." Trish let J.T. go. "He never stays long, you know."

Hope nodded. "That's his appeal. Have a great night. And I have to say, you're really working those heels."

Trish laughed. "I know, right?" The woman sashayed back to her table and was soon joined by a pair of rough-looking customers.

"That was impressive." J.T. guzzled his beer and poured another. "But I was really hoping for a girl fight."

"Please. First of all, it would have been a *woman* fight. I doubt Trish was a girl even when she was five. More like a brawling preteen. And second, is it wrong if I was hoping for a little sparring match while I'm here?" She laughed, joyous and excited and feeling alive for once. "Man. That's never happened to me before. Ray's is awesome. I'm definitely coming back here soon."

J.T. put a hand over hers. "Not without me."

"Well, okay. I guess."

"Don't guess. Say it."

Her laughter fled as she looked into eyes darkening with authority. She nodded, her throat dry. "Not without you."

He didn't smile, but his satisfaction was clear.

Feeling strange and now a little unsure, Hope tried to take charge of their date again. "Okay, I told you about the wedding. Now you tell me. Do you have a lot of kids with a lot of different mothers? Have you done jail time? And do you have tattoos I haven't seen?" *Yet.*

Oh God. I am in serious trouble with this one. I need to end this date and not have another.

But she couldn't stop herself from moving her hand so it now rested on top of his. She gripped him, once again tingling from their contact. "Answer the question, J.T. Or I'll have to get mean."

"Promise?"

Chapter 5

When J.T. dropped her off at her place, Hope had tried to leave the car and him behind. But he'd been raised better than that. He walked her inside her building to her apartment, waited for her to unlock the door, then watched as she stepped inside.

She turned, her hand on the doorknob. "Thanks for a fun night."

That she meant it made him want to shout with joy. Stupid reaction.

"Yeah, sure. No problem." He studied her, aware she watched him as well.

The tension between them grew, each not moving, looking into the other's eyes. He stepped closer, and she tensed, her breathing loud.

Not smart, but screw it. He ran a finger down her silky cheek. "I had fun tonight. You're okay, Hope Donnigan."

She gave a slow smile. "So are you, J.T. Webster." Her smiled faded when his finger grazed her lower lip.

"Maybe we should go out again. We didn't share too many personal details. I'll probably fold if your mom grills me too hard."

She nodded. "Yeah, that's true. We should figure things out."

Surprised she'd agreed without any persuading, he waited for her to suggest a time and place.

"Does Friday work for you? We could go bowling and talk over strikes and spares." She paused. "Can you swing by to pick me up here? Would that be okay, us driving together?"

Her place, then in the close confines of his car, in private. Together. Cinching the straps of attraction even tighter. No way in hell was he that stupid. "Sure. It's a date."

Two days later, J.T. tried to lose himself in his art, drawing a siren that started taking on familiar features as thoughts of Hope continued to intrude on his day. In just four more hours, he'd be sitting at the bowling alley, staring at her ass, and trying to act like the thought of them having sex had never entered his mind.

He sighed. *I am such a moron.*

The date at Ray's couldn't have been better. Hope had not only proven to be bloodthirsty under that veneer of blond, ladylike manners, she'd also been funny and a hell of a darts player.

They'd paired up and taken Sam for twenty bucks, Lou for ten. Heller, fortunately, had bowed out, too busy mooning over Rena. Though the Websters kept a protective eye on Rena, no one had a problem with Heller wanting to court her. J.T.'s dad thought it amusing that the brawny German was getting nowhere fast with the girl. Del didn't mind, and J.T. had never considered Heller a threat. The poor bastard was head over heels for her, and Rena refused to let him into her soft little heart.

A lot like how Hope was refusing to let J.T. into hers. No, but she'd let him into her apartment later tonight. In just three hours and fifty-nine minutes. No, fifty-eight minutes.

He sighed again, baffled at his reaction to the woman. Shit. He felt butterflies in his stomach, his nerves of steel more like nerves of putty at the thought of her soft skin, that golden hair, her ripe, red lips… J.T. breathed in deeply and let it go, needing any release he could get.

"Swear to God, you need an inhaler or something. What the fuck, man?" Vargas glared at him from across the room at his station. While cleaning up after his last client, the cranky tattoo artist gave J.T. his infamous death glare.

Unlike Grim, who looked like a human version of the Grim Reaper, or Suke, who screamed tough chick at a glance, Vargas looked almost normal. He had the requisite sleeves of tattoos and artwork creeping up his neck. Sandy hair cut conservatively short, jeans, a buttoned-up short-sleeved shirt, and a pricey watch made the guy seem more yuppie than grunge.

Until he spoke. Then the attitude came pouring out. A basket case of nerves and emotion Vargas churned into artistic talent. The guy specialized in blacks and grays, and he had a waiting list almost as long as J.T.'s.

"Problem, V?"

"*You*. You're my problem. What's with all the sighing? It's getting on my nerves."

J.T. grinned. "Nicotine patches not working anymore?"

"Hell. I quit using those two weeks ago. Thanks for noticing."

Daisy walked in, saw Vargas steaming, and walked back out.

"So if nicotine's not your problem, what's up your ass, then?" J.T. looked at his buddy and noticed the absence of candy wrappers. "Ah, so no sugar?"

"Bad enough I'm off smoking." Vargas ran his hand through his hair, causing sections to stand on end. "Marci told me I had to quit with the candy," he snarled. "She's on a fucking diet."

Grim left his station to lean against J.T.'s partition.

"What the hell are you looking at?" Vargas barked.

Grim blinked, looked to J.T., who shrugged, then wisely walked away. Despite having both height and brawn over the lanky Vargas, Grim knew better than to taunt the guy. Vargas fought dirty, had a mouth that didn't quit, and possessed a seriously scary knife collection.

"So because Marci's all set on losing an extra ten pounds—because her girlfriend's getting married and insisted Marci be her maid of honor—I'm suffering."

J.T. stifled a grin. "Sorry, man."

"No, you're not. I can see you trying not to laugh at my misery." Vargas moaned. "I miss my Snickers."

"So do we," Grim said from his station.

Vargas snapped back, then moved in Grim's direction to continue the fight.

J.T. chuckled, pleased to see the team working together—just another day at the office. Vargas pissed because he continued to abstain from the pleasures in life. Grim making smart-ass remarks. Daisy hiding in the front while J.T. puttered with new designs.

Well, he *should* have been puttering. Instead he was consumed with Hope Donnigan. He probably would have been done with her if she'd been what he expected. A pretty blond who looked down her nose at the hardworking stiffs at Ray's. Instead, she'd proven how truly nice she was, and she'd sparkled with enthusiasm. She'd loved it there, hanging with the guys, messing with Trish, talking to him.

He knew he'd disappointed her by not having a hard prison record. His nonexistent kids and relatively low drama when it came to relationships—Trish notwithstanding—hadn't done him any favors either. But Hope had made allowances for his nonproblematic upbringing.

Then again, he hadn't told her the whole of it, not wanting to scare her off before… Before what?

He wished he knew what the hell he was doing with her. He liked Hope a lot. Lusted after her, no question. And he wanted to help her out with her mom, because he could tell that underneath her jokes, her strained relationship with her mother bothered her.

Friends.

Yeah, he and Hope were and would be friends. Period. He just wished he could convince his body of that fact. And his stupid heart. Because it raced like crazy at just the thought of her. His dick spiked any time she entered the same room. And his appetite and concentration were all out of whack.

Making a follow-up date hadn't been smart, but he'd done it all the same. What really surprised him was that she'd accepted. She seemed to have shocked herself with her hasty agreement, but they'd both played it off as though another date meant nothing.

"Because it doesn't," he said under his breath, then readied for his client arriving in an hour. No harm in being prepared early. He needed to get his head in the game. Clients came first. *Tattoos should be permanent works of art and skill, not a permanent mistake.*

"Yeah, yeah, Eddie. I remember," he said to himself, repeating the words of his mentor.

Vargas approached him, apparently done schooling Grim. "Talking to yourself. Yeah, man, you need help."

"If I give you a Twix, will you shut up?"

Vargas held out a hand.

J.T. gave him the last of his precious stash.

They had peace for all of twenty minutes. Then Suke showed up bitching about the crappy VW bug in her parking space, which they all knew belonged to Vargas. And another argument heated up. J.T. and Grim watched from the sidelines until their next clients showed.

The moment the door chimed, the dispute ceased as if it had never existed. Suke and Vargas got back to work. Grim and J.T. penciled a few designs.

J.T. glanced at the clock and knew he had it bad. Because now there were two hours and thirty-seven minutes left. And it felt like forever. Even after his client showed.

Hope waited nervously, wishing she hadn't suggested bowling, of all things. Such a lame second date—that wasn't a date. Her parents had been in a bowling league years ago, and they'd always claimed it was so much fun. She didn't know why she'd mentioned it.

It was safe, though. How much trouble could Hope get into with the man in a public place surrounded by ugly shoes, bowling balls, and waxed lanes?

She'd called the bowling alley to verify their hours,

only to find out they were closed for renovations. Great. So she called her backup place and learned it was a league night and closed to individuals.

"Now what?" She ran a hand over her hair, annoyed that she'd brushed it a bazillion times so it shone. That she'd taken care with her makeup, striving to look fresh while carefully applying just the right amounts of mascara, eyeliner, and blush. Her jeans cupped her butt and made her legs look longer than they were. And her T-shirt showed off her waist without clinging to her chest too much.

That she'd so carefully chosen what to wear should have set off alarm bells. Why did she give a fig what J.T. thought of her? He knew what she looked like.

Yet she didn't want to look less than her best for this date that wasn't a date.

For all that J.T. acted mellow and pleasant, she'd seen his rougher edges, how fast and easily he'd taken down that jerk at Ray's. How intense he could get when staring into her eyes. Handsome and aware of the fact, J.T. fascinated her. Even more so now that she knew he could turn on that meanness she'd sensed but had never seen until a few days ago.

She had to don some semblance of metaphorical armor, even if it was tied to her clothing.

Well, at least she wouldn't be wearing ugly shoes tonight. What to do instead?

She should have called the alley before. But—

A knock at the door interrupted her train of thought.

She took a deep breath, focused to stop being so darned nervous, and looked through the peephole to confirm his identity. She hadn't gotten more flowers since Tuesday, and since J.T. hadn't mentioned them, she was pretty sure he hadn't sent them. But she couldn't shake the feeling there was something off about receiving them.

Seeing J.T. standing outside, she opened the door, glad she'd taken care with her appearance. The lady-killer devastated in black jeans and a collared shirt. The top two buttons of his dark-blue shirt were left unbuttoned, revealing a tempting breadth of muscle and a hint of chest hair.

Mr. Manly. Figured he'd hit all her buttons. Geez.

Hope was seriously irked that she couldn't find one thing not to like about his appearance.

"Ah, you going to stare me to death or what?" he asked with a smirk, as if he knew why she was annoyed. "Kidding. You look irritated. Been talking to your mom?"

"Um, no. I haven't talked to her since brunch on Sunday." She wished his biceps weren't so thick, his chest so broad. Some women liked legs and butts. Hope was a sucker for muscular arms. A solid upper body flipped her switch, big time. Unfortunately, J.T. had it all.

Hell. Even his smirks turned her on. So pathetic.

"You ready to go?" He patted his chest. "You'll note I've got my bowling shirt on. I'm ready for some strikes."

"That's not a bowling shirt. That's a regular collared shirt."

"Hey, it counts." When she made no move to leave her apartment, he groaned. "Okay, out with it. What's wrong?"

"We can't bowl tonight."

He frowned.

"A's is closed for renovations, and the Bowl-a-Rama has league night."

"Bummer. I was looking forward to trouncing you."

She had an idea. It wasn't a great plan, but they did need to get their ducks in a row before dinner with Linda. "Why don't we stay here? We can play a board game or something and take notes on each other."

"So, like, a study session with games and beer? And food? You do have food, right? I can't study without food."

"Were you like this in college?"

"Didn't go to college. Just high school. Well, and tattoo school, but I don't think that counts."

"There's a school for tattooing?" She hadn't known that.

"So can I come in? Or did you want to frisk me first, to make sure I'm not carrying?" he taunted.

Her ideas of frisking wouldn't help them remain platonic friends. Because she totally knew what he was packing. She'd felt it when they'd kissed and—"Come in." Not wanting to go down *that* particular memory lane, she hurriedly stepped back from the door and forced herself not to look below his neck for at least thirty seconds. He entered, and she locked up behind him.

"Scared you, didn't I? Relax, Blondie. I'm harmless."

She followed him down the short hallway into the living room. "Yeah, right. I saw what you did to that guy at Ray's."

"Well, mostly harmless. And to answer your question, yes, there's such a thing as tattoo school."

"Really?"

"Yep. There are different ones all over the country.

Some are pretty serious, and some are a waste of time. The one I went to was pretty deep into biology and art classes. So you had to be able to draw more than a stick figure to graduate." He looked around and nodded.

"Does it pass muster?"

"It's you." He pointed to the tidy space of her living room. "Everything is stacked and organized. Your knick-knacks all arranged in rows on your bookshelf there tell me you like control. I bet there's no dust either." He wiped a finger over a shelf, and it came back clean. "Oh yeah, you have a neat fetish going on."

She frowned.

Before she could say anything, he held that clean finger up to silence her. "Now hold on. I'm not criticizing you. I have a neat home too. Well, it's organized. A little dusty, though." He continued to move around, taking in her leather sofa and accent chair with an ottoman. She had pillows to add color, in blues, yellows, and orange tones.

Hope admitted she had a bit of clutter, but she kept it neat. She collected doodads from the places she visited. A set of plastic, oversize dice from Vegas. A small wooden bear sculpture from Portland. Some funky maracas from her one brief family trip to Mexico years ago, when she'd been a teenager. Mostly pottery or sketches and paintings from small towns in the Pacific Northwest.

"Do you like to travel?" she asked him.

"When I have the time. I moved around a lot back in my early twenties. Saw the country, tried to avoid jail and my many baby mamas."

"J.T."

He laughed. "Sorry, couldn't help it. Yeah, I traveled.

But honestly, I missed home. I like Seattle. My dad and sister are here, and now I have a business that's all mine. I'm not looking to take off for Aruba anytime soon." He gave her a once-over that unnerved her because she liked the attention. Too much. "Although if you promised to model a few bikinis, I'd make the trip."

"Ha ha." She ignored her racing pulse. "Well, when you're done psychoanalyzing me through my furniture—"

"What? No way. Just because you're organized doesn't mean you're anal-retentive...or have mommy issues or anything." He laughed at the rude gesture she gave him. "Not so nice either. Hmm. I'll have to add that to my list."

"I'm trying to tell you I have no food in the house. I need to go grocery shopping." She scowled. "I hate grocery shopping."

"Yeah? I love grocery shopping. It's like an ancient ritual, gathering instead of hunting. And I get to mingle while doing it. A win-win."

"Some of us don't go to the veggie aisle to find a hookup." She could too easily see him chatting up women over tomatoes, making dates over yams. A new girlfriend at each visit. *Yep. Time to let reality sink in.* J.T. was handsome and sexy but not boyfriend material. She had to stop thinking about him in any way but as a friend.

"I'll order pizza," he offered. "You do have something to drink, though, don't you? Besides water, I mean."

"I have some sparkling water and juice."

He made a face. "Fine. I'll order a two-liter while I'm at it. Any preferences on the pizza?"

"I'm easy." As soon as she said it, she clamped her

mouth shut. The laughter in his eyes didn't help. "Oh, shut up."

He smiled wide and ordered a giant pizza—hold the onions.

Either he didn't like onions, or he hoped to get lucky tonight. She hoped for the former, because despite telling herself in *so many ways* that he wasn't good for her, she still hadn't convinced her hormones to take a backseat to her brain.

After he ordered, they stared at each other until she threw her hands in the air in surrender. "Okay, I'll get the game."

"Wait. So we're really going to play a game?" He looked disappointed. "This isn't a ploy to get me all to yourself in your cozy little apartment? You're not going to show me your etchings?"

She tried not to but couldn't help laughing at the sad face he made. "No, no etchings to see. You can help yourself to a self-guided tour. Just stay out of my dresser."

"Got it. No panty souvenirs. You're not getting a good Yelp review, I'm just letting you know."

"I'm heartbroken."

He sighed and left her. She heard a door shut and a toilet flush a few moments later, so she knew he hadn't been rummaging in her bedroom. She hoped. She hadn't done laundry and could only be glad she'd done a haphazard closet toss of the clothes on her floor. Clean, dirty, she'd sort them out later.

Between laundry and grocery shopping, she had a tie for *most-loathed chore* she continually put off until she was out of clothes and food.

Once J.T. returned, she set out the Rummikub game,

one of her favorites involving number tiles and rummy-like rules.

J.T. frowned at the setup on her kitchen table. "What's this? I have to do math? You are such a sucky host."

She bit back a smile. "This will be fun. You'll see."

Fun for her. She went through the rules with him twice but refused to be nice to him while they played. Time to let the insults fly. "Let's go, princess. Play a tile or pick up. I think I just turned forty waiting on you."

His eyes narrowed. "You're not that nice, are you? Who knew you turned into a witch when you get competitive? You weren't like this at Ray's."

"I was trying to be nice for your friends."

"Bullshit. You almost made Sam cry with those bull's-eyes."

"Yes, but that was skill, not trash talk," she said primly, forcing herself to refrain from gloating over her winning hand. Since the tiles in her tray faced her, he had no idea she was going to cream him. The poor sucker hadn't even laid one set down. "Once you get the hang of it, we should play for money."

"Oh-ho. A gambler. You're a real competitor behind that sharklike grin."

"Flatterer." She showed him a toothy smile, and he gave a pretend flinch.

The pizza arrived, interrupting them. They ate while they played, though she stuck to her soda water and juice while he guzzled half the bottle of soda. Gross.

"That's all sugar, you know."

"I know. But after watching Vargas twitching over a Twix, I decided to save myself from becoming too healthy."

"Vargas?"

"One of my guys. You met Suke. I work with four artists full time, and we have occasional guest artists work with us when they swing through town. There's Grim, Vargas, Suke, and Nao. I love 'em, but they took some getting used to."

"I'm sure you're just a prince to work with." She wasn't kidding.

"Yep. Just call me Mr. Easy." He winked. "I'm the boss. They work on commission, but I get a small percentage since I pay for the building. I also supply the aftercare products and facilities, including all the furniture. It was a hefty price at the beginning, but totally worth it.

"The application equipment and ink is theirs unless they want to buy from me. Suke can be a pain in the ass about her ink, but that's expected. She's really into the details. We all are, but she takes it to an obsessive level."

"Huh." Hope had liked Suke, having spent her time talking to the woman while waiting on J.T. At first, Suke's attention had been a little forceful, but once she'd realized Hope had no interest in going on a date and wasn't going to flip out by standing near a gay woman, she'd turned off the attitude and been surprisingly pleasant. The woman looked like she had enough brashness to break J.T. in half, so to find her almost sweet under the piercings, tattoos, and gruffness had been an eye-opener.

As if reading her mind, J.T. added with a sly glance, "Suke thinks you're hot."

"I am. She has good taste."

He paused in the act of taking another bite of his slice, set it down, and laughed. "Every time I think I have you figured out, you throw me for a loop. You're shy and arrogant. Sexy and demure."

"Demure? Who uses words like 'demure' in everyday language?" An artist and poet, her J.T.

No, not mine. *Just J.T.*

"I'm deep, what can I say? I have many layers, Ms. Donnigan. Peel them back, and you'll see." He winked and devoured the rest of his pizza. "Okay, now that I'm pleasantly full, and you've trounced me for the fifth time with this stupid game, how about we talk about you and me?"

"You and me?" Hope repeated, her voice cracking. She cleared her throat, ignoring her heated cheeks. "Sorry. Scratchy throat."

"You and me," he repeated. "What do you like to do? Your favorite color? Cats or dogs? Tell me something only a lover would know." His voice deepened, grew huskier.

She was glad they sat at her small kitchen table, because if they'd been on her couch, she feared she might have leaned forward to kiss that smirk off his lips.

"Um, well, I like shopping, walking at night under the stars, and I love old Doris Day movies. My favorite color is red, and I prefer cats over dogs."

"Something a lover would know?"

She'd been hoping to avoid that one. "Let me get back to you on that."

"Uh-huh." He stood, cleared the table, and instead of returning to the kitchen, walked into the living area.

She panicked. "Where are you going?"

"To the couch to get comfortable. Want to join me?"

Chapter 6

Could he be any more of an idiot for leaving the safety of the kitchen table that had separated them? Did he need to sit on the couch and show her how hard he was—just from being near her?

Watching the blasted woman make love to her food instead of eating it had driven him insane. It wouldn't have been so bad if she hadn't kept licking her lips after each bite, then giving him subtle, hungry glances, as if wondering what it would be like to eat *him*.

He stifled a groan, his body heavy, aroused, frustrated.

It wasn't like him to go without for too long. J.T. had a healthy sex drive, one he kept sated with a lot of safe sex. Yet meeting Hope had put a kink—and not the good kind—in his plans for months. He knew better than to pursue her. His sister had spoken the truth about the fragile McCauley ecosystem. Imagine if he and Hope hit it, and it was amazing. Then she'd want to be with him all the time, looking for boyfriend material, because God as his witness, nothing about Hope Donnigan screamed one-night stand.

Nah. She was a commitment type down to her sexy blue toenails.

She'd cry when he broke it off, beg him to stay, and family events would grow awkward when the Donnigans were invited. If his dad married Sophie, then *all* family events would be tough.

No way in hell he'd make life weird for Del or Liam. Nope. No way.

Hope swallowed, her attention on his crotch before she yanked her gaze back to his face. Well, hell. How was he supposed to be good when her nipples beaded against her T-shirt? She had beautiful, full breasts that would fit perfectly into his palms.

His pulse raced, and his cock swelled, hampered by now-tight jeans.

Hope, however, seemed determined to ignore her arousal.

If she could, so could he. He laced his fingers behind his head and focused on her face. "Well? You going to tell me all about Hope Donnigan? More than that surface stuff you mentioned?"

She grabbed a notepad and pen and tossed them to him, getting no closer than the plush chair next to the couch. *Smart girl*. "You might want to write this down."

"Good idea." He carefully—painfully—crossed his ankle over his knee and propped the legal pad over it, effectively hiding his erection.

He could almost hear her sigh of relief and wanted to growl with frustration. *Must be nice to be aroused and be able to move around without hurting yourself*. "It's still hard, Hope."

She gaped. "*What?*"

"Writing this way." He gave her an innocent expression. "It's still hard to do, even with the pad propped on my knee."

"Oh, right. Well, just do your best."

"I can rearrange it, I guess. It's more comfortable if I shift it left, actually, so it's not squeezing between my legs." Oh yeah, her big, brown eyes grew nice and wide. "It's not easy to sit like this, especially with you leaning forward like that." He deliberately stared at her nipples. "You hard too?"

She crossed her arms over her chest, her cheeks pink. "Excuse me?"

"Hard of hearing? I asked if you were going to tell me all about yourself, Blondie. Now you're supposed to answer. Try this. 'Why, yes, J.T. I will tell you all about myself. I love pink, shopping, and big cock—"

"J.T. Webster!"

"—tails like the ones in that picture near the TV." He nodded to a photo of her and one of her friends sipping from a monster margarita. He ignored her red face, having too much fun. "And I like my men like I like my coffee. Dark and sweet." He batted his lashes. "Did I get it right?"

Her eyes narrowed. He clutched the pen in his hand, digging the tip of it into the legal pad hard enough to push through the paper. Hope in a snit was the hottest thing. Her eyes darkened and her lips parted, as if ready to lean close and plant a punishing kiss on his lips. Or other places.

He bit back a growl. "Well, sweetheart? I'm waiting. The sooner I get this info, the sooner we can schedule dinner with Momzilla, and I can get back to my regularly scheduled dating life." He might have said that with a little too much hostility, because, well, his dick felt ready to fall off, he was so hard. All he could think about was bending her over that freakin' chair and pounding into her until she screamed his name.

"Oh, sure, J.T. No problem. Let's chat." She sounded

breathy and had a mean look in her eyes. The damn woman stood up and walked to the couch.

And sat right the fuck next to him, so close their thighs touched and their breath mingled when she drew closer. He dropped the pen, and the notepad wobbled between his legs. She reached for it, and he jerked back instinctively, shocked at how badly he wanted her hands on him.

But Hope only grabbed the pad, stared into his eyes, and smiled.

Warnings flashed at the mischief on her face.

Despite being ready for her, he froze when she reached down again, searching for the pen that had unfortunately fallen onto the couch and rolled right under his crotch.

"Hope," he choked. "Ah, I—"

She dug her hand deeper and grazed his fucking balls as she retrieved the pen. But she didn't blush, and she didn't smile. "So, something a lover would know? How about the fact I can tie a knot in a cherry stem with my tongue in under thirty seconds?"

Chapter 7

OKAY, NOT SMART, AND NOT NICE, BUT J.T. WAS ASKING FOR it. *Still hard, my ass.* He knew exactly what he'd implied and took great pleasure in teasing her, only to then get bitchy. He wanted to go out and relieve his arousal? *Join the club, buddy.*

As if she were at fault for his problems.

She'd done her best to stop staring at the man. God, knowing he was aroused and growly turned her way on. She liked her men a little mean, probably why she kept picking assholes, but whatever. Now she had *this* asshole to deal with.

She'd never been so forward before, but he deserved it. And it wasn't as if she'd grabbed him by the balls. She'd simply reached underneath him for the pen.

She sat back, clicked the pen a few times, then wrote down a few facts, ignoring the way he gritted his teeth and glared at her.

"I like white or milk chocolate but can't stand dark. It's too bitter. I'm a cat person. Dogs are okay, but I'm not a fan of the slobber." She gave him a look. "I like them drool-free—like my men. I prefer a man who can control himself." She gave his crotch a dismissive glance, seeing his scowl out of the corner of her eye. Doing her best not to laugh, she continued. "I appreciate kindness and manners. Pink is not my favorite color.

Red is. I also like purple. I prefer skirts over dresses. I don't like high heels, but I love pumps. And sadly, I've given up foreign films."

She stopped writing and handed him back the pad. "Any questions?"

With him sitting so close, it would have been impossible to miss the large man suddenly looming over her like a dark cloud. A dark, sexy cloud.

"You want to play, little girl?" He moved closer, at an angle as he sat facing her, and she leaned back into the couch while pretending to remain unaffected.

"Ooh, I'm so scared." Well, maybe a little. He was big and tough and making it difficult to remember why she shouldn't jump his bones. "Hey, you started it. 'Still hard.'" She snorted. "Right."

"Let me tell you about me." He moved so fast she had no time to adjust. One minute she'd been sitting up, the next he had her back flat on the couch. He tossed a back cushion to make room for his big body and now straddled her middle. Though he sat up on his knees, she still felt some of his weight over her.

Not good, because when she tilted her head up, she came face-to-face with Mr. Still Hard.

"J.T., get off."

"Pay attention. Here, I'll take notes for you." He started writing while talking, leaving Hope nowhere to look but up at the ceiling or at the mouthwatering package displayed inches from her face when she lifted her head. "I like a sweet, submissive woman. She should be able to cook, think I'm great, and give amazing head." He lowered the pad to look at her. "That isn't a euphemism. I mean I like a good blow job."

"Didn't you say *amazing* head?" she asked, growling at him.

"Good point." He lifted the pad and crossed through what he'd written, then added to it, continuing to talk as he wrote. "She should like sex. A lot. And she should be hot for it a few times a day, to keep up with me."

"Gee, this is great information I can share with *my mother* when she asks. Because I'm sure she'll want to know how many times we do it in a given day."

He peered over the pad and nodded. "Feel free. I'm happy to share."

"Keep going. I'm all ears." And nerves, apparently. Their sexy banter had gone a little too far, but she was loath to be the one to cry uncle.

"Oh? You want to hear what gets me off? Or would you rather see me lose it?"

"You're going to give me a show? Really?" She paused when she saw him unsnap his jeans. *Oh my God he's going to whip it out! Danger, danger!* "You're just reinforcing what I said before about guys having no control."

He tossed the notepad and glared down at her. But at least he left the snap of his jeans alone. "Yeah? Well, I'm not the one who reached between your legs, Ms. Grabby."

"Feel free. I've got nothing to hide. I can control myself."

"Is that right?" With impressive speed, he blanketed her fully, leaning up on his elbows so as not to smash her. His feet had to drape over the end of the couch, he was so tall. His height didn't dampen their connection, though. They pressed together, hip to hip, and she felt that large, solid essence of him all too firmly against her belly. "Well, let's just see how much control you think you have."

"Go for it, Webster." *What am I doing?* She couldn't stop herself from daring him to...what? Touch her? Feel how wet he made her just by existing?

Before she could call a halt to it all, he unbuttoned her jeans with slow, measured movements. J.T. stared into her eyes, and it was the sexist thing ever. His breath heavy, his eyes dark, his lips firm. He used one hand to angle the zipper down, then moved to the waistband of her panties. "Soft," he whispered.

She tilted her chin. "And red. And lacy."

He looked down and stopped moving, his big hand poised to delve beneath the fabric. "What am I doing?"

"Good question."

He didn't pull away, as she'd thought he might. Instead the blasted man left her to kneel on the floor and yanked her to a sitting position on the couch while shoving the coffee table out of the way.

He'd effectively positioned himself kneeling between her legs. "I couldn't see from on top of you. This is much better." He gave her a wicked grin and tugged her jeans down to her thighs.

"Hey, you can't—"

"Can and did. Just tell me to stop, and I will. I mean, since you have something to hide, apparently." The naughty hunger in his gaze drove her to insanity. Reason and rational thought went right out the window when he pulled her jeans completely off.

"Do your worst." She gave a fake yawn. "Wake me up when you're done."

He gave a low laugh, and she tensed, shocked to feel his breath over her abdomen where he'd pulled up her shirt. He planted a kiss on her belly button, and she shuddered.

"I like your taste in panties, Hope." He pulled back, his eyes dark with desire.

She squirmed, embarrassed and annoyed to feel herself slick, arousal causing the need gathered between her thighs.

J.T. didn't give her room to move, his large hands on her thighs, controlling her movement. He widened her legs but didn't pull her thong down. She didn't know whether to be annoyed or grateful and decided on irritated when he stroked her hips, skin to skin, unencumbered by her tiny panties.

She waited what felt like forever and stared at him. But his gaze remained on her red thong. He didn't remove it. Instead he pulled it to the side, exposing her sex.

"Oh fuck. You're wet."

"I, ah, well—"

He slid a thick finger between her folds, and she nearly shot off the couch. J.T. had big hands, mother of—

"Easy, baby. Let's see just how slick you are. How sweet," he murmured, and before she knew it, his mouth replaced his finger.

J.T.'s mouth felt like fire, an inferno that continued to build as he stroked her with his tongue.

"*Oh, oh, J.T.*" She arched into his mouth, aware he now held one of her breasts while the other hand kept her thong pulled aside. The playboy molded her breast, then played with her nipple, pinching and tugging. And all the while he lapped her up like he had nothing else in the world he'd rather do.

She shot toward a climax before she could stop. "I'm coming, wait," she tried, not wanting him to stop but needing him to. He let go of her breast, only to fit a thick finger inside her while he tongued her to orgasm.

She cried out while he pumped his forefinger in and out of her, the ecstasy more than she could bear. The climax lasted way longer than it normally did and left her panting, incoherent, when he finished. He licked her again, and she shuddered, overcome.

J.T. put her thong back in place and her jeans back on her, awkwardly tugging them up over her hips without fastening them. "Well, that answers one question," he said, his voice like gravel.

It took her a moment to fashion a response. "What's that?"

"You're a natural blond."

J.T. did his best to come back to earth. What the fuck had just happened? They'd been talking, then flirting, then heavily teasing. From pizza to a board game to oral sex so amazing he'd come in his jeans, grinding against the couch while he ate the sweetest pussy he'd ever had.

No, no—oh fuck, yes. Again.

The no's should have been winning, but her scent and taste lingered, and he licked his lips, wanting more.

She slumped against the couch, blinking at the ceiling, her expression one of repletion, a foggy pleasure he felt all too well.

He stared at her panties—a fucking *thong*—pleased with the damp spot in front. God, but she'd been wet.

Still was. He could imagine sliding inside her, his fat cock fitting so tight, locking in her body.

He should have been too tired. But his dick jerked, and he wondered if trying again would be pushing it. *Yeah. Probably.*

"You said something about an answer?" She slowly sat up, not caring that he knelt in front of her. She had yet to button up her jeans, and the knowledge she was so close, just a thin strip of silk between her and him... "To what?" she asked.

"Huh?" He rubbed his hands over her toned thighs, squeezing and convincing himself he'd done enough damage for one night. He should go before he did something really stupid.

"Never mind." She stretched, let out a kittenish moan, then sagged back against the couch, thoroughly pleasured.

He felt more than a measure of pride to have exhausted her. "Guess I should probably go."

"Um, yeah. Might be best."

He stood, by sheer will not grimacing at the sticky mess in his pants. Then he walked to the door and paused before leaving. "So we both know who lost, right?"

"Lost what?"

"Control, sweetness." He winked at her, pleased to see that woke her up. "Of the two of us, who came all over my tongue?" He waved. "See you soon."

She stood and wobbled on her feet. Having finally realized her pants were open, she hurried to button up. Blushing so hard it looked like it hurt, she stalked over to him and poked him in the chest. "You still owe me a round of bowling."

"I do, hmm?"

She narrowed her eyes at him but took a step back. "Yeah. And another chance to show you I'm just as controlled as you are. It's not my fault it's been a while. You were handy."

Hmm. Someone sounds defensive. "Handy, was I?" He had to smile.

"Oh, go home. And come back tomorrow. We're bowling, buddy. And the loser is not going to be happy about it. I can guarantee you that."

He crooked his finger at her, delighted when she stomped closer once more.

"What?" she snapped.

J.T. kissed her before he could think better of it. "You taste damn good. See you tomorrow. Same time?"

She scowled. "Yep. Six. Don't even think about being late. We have a score to settle." Her face still bright red, she added, "We're not having sex, and no more kissing."

There was kissing, and then there was *kissing*. "We didn't have sex, Hope." He'd come close, but he hadn't affected the ecosystem.

"You're darned right we didn't. And we won't." She mumbled what sounded like, "I'm making good choices now," then turned to glare at him and in a louder voice stated, "I'm off men."

The thought of Hope with another woman flooded his mind with X-rated images, none of which she'd find titillating. "Right." He cleared his throat and winced at the return of his arousal. That's all he needed, to sport another erection around the woman he could barely keep his hands off. "See you tomorrow. And no sex." To needle her, he added, "No matter how much you beg for it."

She slammed the door behind him, and if it wasn't for feeling cold and funky in his pants, he'd have claimed victory. But he had to hand it to her. Even unknowingly, she'd brought him to his knees.

With any luck, he'd manage to convince her to get to *her* knees. He groaned at the images accompanying that thought all the way home.

Hope spent her night replaying the evening with J.T. Through the rest of her Friday and into eventual sleep, where she yet again dreamed about him. She woke up with J.T. on the brain and wanted to slap herself for her lack of control with the man.

Staring at the ceiling, trying to concentrate, she again wondered how things had gotten so out of hand. She'd been trouncing him at a board game. Shared pizza, good times. Laughter. And then…he'd gone down on her? On a dare? A challenge? How exactly had she lost sight of her pledge to put herself first?

Well, technically I focused on me. I mean, his lips and tongue were on me. It was my orgasm, not his.

She flushed, needing to talk to someone. But as Saturday rolled around, she had no idea who to talk to. Ava, her brother's fiancée, had provided useful advice plenty of times. As a clinical psychologist, Ava knew what she was talking about. But Ava knew J.T. as a friend, and Hope felt funny about sharing her feelings about him.

Mostly because she didn't know how to define her emotions. She liked J.T. She was attracted to J.T. And… what? Confused, alarmed, shocked at how easily she'd fallen prey to his seduction. She still couldn't pinpoint when she'd lost control of the situation.

Yet she couldn't deny she felt a heck of a lot more relaxed since having had an orgasm. It had been too long since she'd been with someone else, and it had felt good. For once, a man hadn't gotten off and left her to fend for herself. No matter what J.T. might think of their evening, she'd won in the end. Because that man packed a punch when it came to sex.

The safe thing, though, would be to keep her clothes on and her legs together. A bowling alley was just the thing. She'd interrogate him tonight, see what made him tick. Maybe figure out why she was so susceptible to his charm.

Yet, she didn't just want to get one over on her mother with a pretend relationship. Hope wanted to know about J.T. He was her friend. A casual friend who'd seen her panties. Sure. But since they were done messing around, the friendship would continue to develop.

After making plans to talk to Noelle tomorrow—after Noelle's big date with some French guy she'd met during her language classes—Hope spent her day doing chores, finally getting her laundry washed and dried if not folded. She showered and dressed, then waited for J.T. to arrive.

Nerves plagued her, and she couldn't understand it. That same flirty need to get him to notice her reared its head, and she shoved the stupidity back down, where it belonged. J.T. had agreed to help her deal with her mother. Period. No dating, no sexual relationship, no longing for something deeper.

God. Why did she always *do that* with a guy? Start

wondering what tomorrow would be like with him by her side?

That was her problem. A need to be partners with someone. Standing on her own two feet the past five months had been good for her. She'd grown. And not around her belly, thanks to workouts at the gym, and thanks to an emotional maturity that had come from being alone and being okay with that.

She cringed, remembering Greg and her other exes. Noelle liked to say that no one made mistakes; they had episodes they learned from. Apparently Hope had learned not to date the Gregs of the world. What would she learn from J.T.?

He rang the bell, startling her, and said through the door, "It's me."

She took her time opening it, because she didn't want to look as if she'd been ready and waiting for him for the past forty-five minutes. *Desperation be thy name*. "Hello."

He smiled, a grin that told her he knew something she didn't. "Hello, Hope. You ready to bowl?"

"What? No button-down shirt tonight? Slumming, are we?" He slummed so well. The T-shirt he wore had shorter sleeves, showcasing the definition of his *huge* biceps.

She made her own muscle, stared from it to J.T., and sighed.

He laughed. "Don't worry. I promise not to show off my glorious manliness around your tiny biceps."

"Thanks so much."

"Come on. We should get to the bowling alley." He looked past her to the couch, then gave her a knowing look. "Where it's safe."

She felt foolish for not wanting him to come in any farther. But honestly, she worried more about her willpower than his restraint. “Safe? From what?” She snorted. “Your colossal ego toppling me over?”

“Oh, I’d like to topple you. Right over the back of that chair…” He sighed. “You have a great ass.”

“Seriously? This is you reining it in? Us just being friends?”

His amused expression turned into something more thoughtful. “Good point. Come on. Let’s go bowl a few and share some fries. In public. Fully clothed. Okay?”

He just had to keep picking at her. She blushed at the *fully clothed* comment, unable to forget he’d not only seen her in a thong, but he’d seen and kissed under it as well. Hope wasn’t the type to give it away on the first date. Not that she minded what other people did, but she’d never felt comfortable being so intimate so fast.

Until J.T.

“What color?”

“Hmm?” She followed him to his car and buckled herself in. “What did you say?” The look he was giving her didn’t do her raging libido any favors. She prayed her shirt hid the effect his nearness had on all the standing points of her body. “J.T.?”

Chapter 8

J.T. NEEDED TO RETHINK WHAT CAME NEXT OUT OF HIS mouth. Asking what color underwear she wore tonight didn't seem smart. Not if he planned to steer clear of the danger zone. And going down on Hope definitely counted as an iffy maneuver. He started the car and headed toward the bowling alley.

"Ah, what color ball do you like to use?"

She gave him an odd look. "I generally use a twelve-pound ball. I don't really care what color it is."

"Yeah." He fiddled with the radio, needing to fill the silence so he could ignore the raunchy thoughts filling his head. Most of them involving Hope and that sexy perfume she wore, her rubbing it all over him, naked body to naked body.

"Did you do any tattoos today?" Hope asked.

He glanced at her, not surprised to find himself wanting to smile. Something about the woman always put him in mind of growing things, vibrant flowers, and happiness. Even sitting, Hope seemed animated, full of energy.

"Yep. That's my job. Tattooing people."

"What did you draw?"

She was probably searching for a safe topic of conversation. Yet the more questions she asked, the more he thought she might really be interested in his job.

By the time they arrived at the bowling alley, he'd had her laughing at a few of Grim and Vargas's fights,

Suke's antics with Nao, and a client he'd turned away a second time for sheer stupidity.

"I swear, the guy comes in one more time, I might actually tattoo a pile of crap on his forearm and let him deal with the fallout of a pissed-off wife forever. A poop emoji for a tattoo? Who does that?"

"A guy who wants a divorce, that's who."

He grinned at her, in complete agreement.

They bowled a warm-up game, and it amused him to see her so competitive. She'd complained before about her mother's inability to lose. Seemed like maybe Hope wasn't as different from her mother as she thought she was.

"So last night, we learned all about me," she said as he lined up to bowl. No doubt trying to screw up his spare streak.

"Oh, we learned *all* about you," he said, bowled, and ended up in the gutter, just like his thoughts. *Yeah, I learned how sweet that pussy tastes, how fine you look in a red fucking* thong*, and how your laughter makes me feel goofy good*. Nothing safe there that he could add. Though by the blush staining her cheeks, he didn't need to.

"Why is everything out of your mouth full of innuendo?" She bent over to grab her ball.

He groaned. "I'm sorry. It's not easy, okay? I'm doing my best to stop remembering last night." His voice lowered as he looked her over, from her lavender button-down shirt to the jeans that clung to her in all the right places. "I'm trying, but…I can still taste you."

She blew out a breath. "Stop."

"Okay, okay. I'm going to grab us something to eat. What do you want?"

She gave him a wobbly smile. "Surprise me."

He returned with a pitcher of root beer and cheese fries. Nothing that could remotely be considered nutritious. He'd have to work extra hard at the gym to burn off the calories. But unlike Lou and Heller, who seemed to think anything not on the food pyramid a sin, J.T. liked to indulge. It gave him something to work off when hitting the heavy bag or doing dead lifts.

Hope gave him a big smile and drank the soda he poured for her. "I'd be mad at your unhealthy choices, but one, this is a bowling alley. And two, I'm beating you."

He glanced at the score on the monitor above their lane to see she'd nailed a strike. He sighed. "Yeah, yeah, now shut up while I bowl."

He hit a few pins, his concentration shot. He'd gotten lucky earlier, but ever since he'd confessed to still tasting her, he found that no amount of root beer and fries could dilute her essence. It was like she was inside him, which was both crazy and scary and weirding him the hell out. Yet he couldn't stop himself from sitting right damn next to her while they snacked between bowling.

They finished the game and paused before their second.

"I won," she said in a singsong tone.

He glared. "Smugness does not become you."

She laughed. "Don't worry, I'll go easy on you in the next game. So while we're on a break, tell me all about you. Wait, let me amend that. Tell me the important stuff that has nothing to do with sex."

He feigned disappointment, which made her laugh again. That light, easy sound made his heart heavy. He wanted to just sit and stare at her for hours. *God, I need to stop acting like a teenager with a crush.*

"Aren't you hungry?" she asked, pointing at the mound of fries he'd put on a plate but hadn't touched.

"Yeah." He forced himself to eat. "So, um, let's see. I'm thirty-two, be thirty-three later next month."

"Oh? When? My birthday is the eleventh."

He smiled. "Mine's the thirty-first. So you're almost the big three-oh, eh?"

She didn't need the reminder.

"Hey, it's a good year." He shrugged at her frown. "What? It's just one year past twenty-nine. No biggie. I made it and am still going strong." He made a muscle, pleased when she fixated on it, then blushed and glanced away at her food. Hope liked the way he looked. *Hell yeah.*

"Okay, you're almost thirty-three. What else?"

"For the record, most of which you already know, I have one dad, Liam. My sister, Delilah. Try calling her that, and she hits you." He sighed. "Little sister, what can I do? Then there's my cousin, Rena, and my Aunt Caroline. I told you, she was my mom's sister. My mom died when I was a kid, and my dad married Del's mom, who was a bitch."

"Oh?"

"Yeah. Mean to me, meaner to Del. She was all about getting high and screwing guys not my dad." He shook his head. "But Dad wanted to keep Del, so he tolerated Penelope. Sad thing is Del looks a lot like her, but we don't tell her that."

After a moment, Hope said, "Liam's with Sophie now, so obviously it didn't last."

"Nope. Penelope left us after a few years. Died in a car accident. It took Del a while to get over it, but I was fine. Dad too. I don't think he ever loved her, to tell you the truth. He was so lost after my mom died that he wasn't himself for a long, long time."

And that had hurt. J.T. had lost his mother. He could only remember vague things after all this time, the scent of honeysuckle, her soft voice crooning a lullaby. But the melody never came together for him, and her face was a blur, the picture tucked away in a drawer at home his only reminder.

"I'm sorry." Hope stroked his hand, squeezed, then let him go.

He shrugged. "It's okay. It happened nearly thirty years ago. Hard to miss something you never had. Instead, I had hard-ass Liam Webster trying to keep me in line."

"What a chore."

He grinned. "No doubt. I grew up helping the old man around the garage. And I hated it. Unlike most boys, I didn't want grease under my nails. I hated playing with power tools. I wanted to paint and draw even back then. But I will say I've always liked girls." He batted his lashes, and she gave him a weak slug to the arm. "Ow. Quit trying to sabotage me for game two."

"Yeah, like that hit is going to sink you. Dream on. You suck all on your own."

"So cruel." He dabbed an invisible tear. "Anyway, that's pretty much all there is to know."

"Bull. So your dad had you working at the garage that you hated. You liked art better, and…?"

"And what?"

"Tell me more. About your childhood, growing up. Those hints about you being a baddie during your teen years."

"You like that, don't you? The tougher and meaner the guy, the better, eh?"

She grinned. "You know it."

He wanted to kiss her right then, right there, but refrained. Barely. "Right. So, ah, Aunt Caroline helped Liam raise me. She did her best, but I was a handful. And frankly, Dad ended up taking care of Rena and Aunt Caroline in between running off Aunt Caroline's idiot husbands. She's had five. Every one a deadbeat. And the guys in between were awful. Users, abusers, generally poor excuses for human beings. I have no idea why. Aunt Caroline is fine. She's funny and smart, but so clueless when it comes to men." Hope looked away, her discomfort obvious. "Hope?"

"I'm just like your aunt." She dragged her gaze back to his, embarrassment shining in her eyes. "I pick losers too."

"Aw, honey. No you don't. You're here with me, remember."

She gave a weak laugh. "You must be the exception. That's why I'm on a dating hiatus. I keep going out with guys who are all wrong for me." She took a deep breath, then let it out in a rush. "But that's another story." One he'd make sure they got to. "Finish telling me about you."

He had no idea what she was digging for. J.T. wasn't that deep. But what the hell. "I graduated high school, which was a miracle. I found it boring and knew I didn't want college anyway, not that we could afford it. I liked wrestling, did a little bit of football. But then practice started getting in the way of my social life. 'Cause I was a social butterfly back in the day." He wiggled his brows, and she laughed, relieving him that she no longer looked like she was going to cry. "I was done with school and started hanging with the wrong crowd. I might have gone to jail a time or two for being stupid. Some fights, a small count of shoplifting, which was BS because my buddy Troy stuffed a box of tampons in my jacket pocket as a joke and I got busted for it. Obviously not mine."

"Obviously." She snickered.

"I laughed until they locked me up. To say Liam wasn't happy is an understatement."

"Oh. Did he yell at you?"

"Ah, yeah. He yelled. And whooped my ass. Apparently eighteen is not too old to get spanked. My father is such a dinosaur," he said with affection, loving the old man.

She nodded, her eyes wide.

"Anyhow, I took some time to find myself. Kept drawing, kept working for my dad, then figured out I wanted to tattoo people for a living. A lot of Dad's friends had tattoos, and I was already thinking of ways to make them better. It took me a year of school, then two years apprenticing under this awesome guy. Anyway, that's boring stuff. I traveled the country, taking jobs in different studios that weren't too particular about licensing. My art got better and better, and I got serious. Came back to Seattle, started my own studio. I'm licensed here, all legit. Now I own Tull Paint & Body, and the rest is history."

It was gratifying to see her hanging on to every word, and a little unnerving. Hope listened with intensity.

"So no ex-wives or kids?"

"Nope."

"You didn't want any?"

"You seem pretty fixated on my personal life." He gave her a sly smile. "Interested?"

"Yes, because that's what my mother will want to know." She gave him a sly smile back. "I'm happy I won't be lying when I tell her you saw the inside of a cell." At his groan, she laughed. "I'm kidding. But I'm serious about the relationship part. What about that? You're still a social butterfly, huh?"

"Nah. Not anymore. You ask Del, she'll call me a whore. But then, she thinks dating more than two people in a year is loose. And not at the same time. I mean, one girl, then breaking up and going out with another. I'm a lot of things, but I'm not a cheat." He frowned. "I saw enough of that with Aunt Caroline's husbands. Not for me. When I'm with you, I'm *with you*."

She studied him. "Right. So, um, what else? What do you do for fun?"

He smiled.

She frowned and in a lower voice said, "*Outside* the bedroom."

"You're so much fun to tease." He chuckled. "I like a lot of things. Bowling, for example. I still draw for fun. I like movies, lifting weights. I'm not a runner, but I don't mind long walks, sightseeing."

"Wait. Long walks? Like hiking or camping?"

"Hell, no. If it's not a hotel or a real bed, I'm not interested. I'm talking about long walks in the city or a park. No tents involved. And not too much nature, or I'll be jonesing for city streets."

"Ah. Gotcha. Me too."

He nodded. "Not a fan of bugs and sleeping on the ground by choice. I mean, it's one thing if you don't have a place to crash. I lived out of my car for a few months when I first got started, back when I was traveling out east. But as soon as business picked up, I was renting a room with a bed and indoor plumbing."

She laughed. "I'm with you on that. What about your favorite food?"

"Caesar salad." At her look, he felt the need to defend himself. "What? I like the croutons, and I like it with chicken. I know, it's weird. Next question."

"Favorite color?"

He stared into her eyes. "Brown. Like, honey-brown. That golden color between yellow and mocha. I'm all about colors." He reached out and stroked her cheek.

"Stop." She didn't shy away, he noticed.

They sat that way, staring into each other's eyes. He knew it was beyond insane to kiss her again, but he felt himself leaning in…

"Well, well. Who do we have here?"

He and Hope sprang apart as his sister plunked her sorry ass at their table. "What luck! Mike and Colin and I were wanting to bowl, but this place is packed. Can we join your little party of two?" Del smiled at Hope, but her eyes narrowed on him with an expression clearly not friendly.

"Sure." Hope nodded. "We're on a break before our next game anyway. We can wait."

Mike and Colin McCauley soon joined them. They looked like the big and small versions of the same person. Dark-haired, blue-eyed, and smiling. They even dressed alike, wearing jeans and Chicago Bulls T-shirts.

"The Bulls?" J.T. asked.

Mike sighed. "From Grandpa. He's got this Chicago bug up his butt lately."

Colin smirked. "I'm telling Grandpa you said that, Dad. Oh, hi, J.T.!"

"Do it and die." Mike grabbed Colin and hung him upside down, then tickled him.

The boy shrieked with laughter. "Save me, J.T.! Save me!"

Del covered her face with her hand. "Mike, if you get us kicked out of here, I will personally geld you."

"What's gelding?" Colin asked between giggles. "Hi, Hope. Can I have some of your fries?"

Hope grinned. "Sure. Want some root beer too?"

"No," Mike said and walked away with his boy, still upside down and clinging to him like a monkey.

Del watched them go, then turned to study him with Hope.

"What?"

"You'd better not be on a date," she growled.

"Hey." J.T. took offense.

"Don't worry, Del." Hope smirked. "He's not ruining your ecosystem."

Del blushed. "He told you that?"

"I sure did." J.T. gave his sister a mean smile. "So did you tell them about the baby yet?"

"Shh. I'm going to Monday night."

"What the hell are you waiting for?"

"For the doctor's appointment, dumbass. I had to reschedule last Monday for this coming Monday. But I took a half dozen more tests, and they're all positive." She looked excited and nervous.

Aw, his little sister was gonna have a baby. He stood up, rounded the table, and yanked her into his arms. "I'm so happy for you, Del."

She hugged him back, and she was no slouch. His sister had plenty of muscle. When she pulled back, he saw tears in her eyes.

"Damn it, stop. I'm trying not to cry when I think about it. These are tears of happiness," Del said hurriedly. "So don't stress out just because of the waterworks. I'm super excited."

Hope smiled. "That's so awesome. Mike's having another baby. I bet Colin will be pumped. He's been wanting a sibling for a while. Cousin Jane isn't impressive. Not only is she too little, she's a girl. Cam told me Colin's hoping for a little brother someday."

Del laughed. "He's such a little punk. Just like Mike." She looked so happy, she glowed. Or maybe that was the baby. J.T. didn't know. He only knew that this was what he'd always wanted for his sister. Happily ever after.

And if Mike ever did anything to mar his sister's joy, J.T. would pound the guy into the ground and make sure no one ever found the body.

"So how's Jekyll?" The puppy Colin claimed as his own was now a huge bundle of fur and over a year old. Not so little, yet still young enough that he had more energy than J.T. could handle.

"He's still growing. Can you believe that? He's seriously almost as big as Hyde."

"Brody's dog?" Hope asked. Brody was her cousin, a pseudo-adopted McCauley.

"Man, there are just too many McCauleys and Donnigans in Seattle," he complained. "I mean, I'm bowling with Hope. You married Mike. Then Dad's dating Sophie, and Hope works for Cam... I could go on."

"Please, don't," Hope said.

Del laughed. "Yeah, don't. And don't even think of getting romantic with her," she warned him.

Hope raised a brow, and he watched her icy transformation with fascination, not having seen this side of her. "What if I want to get romantic with him?"

Del looked puzzled. "Why?"

"I don't know. Maybe I want to take a walk on the wild side."

"Hey."

Hope ignored him. "We're fully grown adults who can make our own decisions."

Del gaped. "Oh my God. You're so channeling your mother right now."

"That was just mean." Hope frowned.

"Ack. I'll be back with reinforcements. I can't handle Linda Donnigan when I haven't had dinner yet." Del darted away.

Hope groaned. "She just ruined my night."

J.T. grinned. "Yeah? She made mine. Hope, when you get all bossy like that, you make me..."

"I make you what?" She gave him that stare, and his entire body went haywire.

He quickly sat across from her, taking Del's spot. "Never mind. I suggest we shelve the getting-to-know-you conversation. Even though you pretty much got all my high points."

"Okay. But I reserve the right to ask one or two more questions."

"Sure." He nodded. "You earned them for taking on Del and winning. That girl has a mouth that doesn't quit. And you sent her running to her big, bad husband with her tail between her legs." He cupped his chin in his hand, his elbow on the table, and gazed at her. "My hero."

"Shut up."

He just laughed.

By the time Del and family returned, they had more soda and two pizzas on order, and Hope had added their names to the computer. Del studied her brother and Hope, wondering what his game was. He knew better. He'd accepted her marrying into the McCauley clan, and she knew he liked Mike, loved Colin, and respected her in-laws. Heck, he got along with all the McCauleys and their wives—he was right, there were a ton of them all over Seattle.

Colin idolized her brother, not that Del blamed him. J.T. had taken care of her for a long time. Her big brother had protected her from bullies, taught her to swear, to hold a wrench (though her father still claimed that he'd been the one to show her how to use one), and to deal with not having a mother.

Del couldn't have asked for a better brother. His one weakness—relationships with the opposite sex.

While Del had thought herself not good enough to marry for the longest time, J.T. had no delusions about his worth. Her cocky brother knew he looked good and capitalized on the fact. But he was a commitment-phobe, scarred, no doubt, by their father's inability to connect after losing Bridget.

But this... J.T. had always dated a certain kind of woman. People like the Websters—hardworking, street-smart, those who knew the score. Oh sure, the women he entertained wanted more than a few nights or weeks in the sack with him, but J.T. inevitably drifted away.

Here, with Hope Donnigan? Hope was different than his usual type. For one thing, she wasn't dressed in hooker heels, low-cut tops, and short skirts, which J.T. seemed to favor. For another, her brother charmed women. He seduced them, which meant dinner, followed by a night at the lady's place. A movie, maybe. A party, a night spent staying in, just the two of them. Not *bowling*, something J.T. did with family or the guys.

Del had heard he'd brought Hope to Ray's as well. And that the pair had been laughing, finishing each other's sentences, and in general looking good together.

Together—her brother and a Donnigan.

This had disaster written all over it.

And after she'd personally educated him on the McCauley ecosystem, which she thought the perfect way of describing their new relationships via her marriage to Mike.

Mike caught her eye, glanced at Hope and J.T., who were chatting with Colin, and glanced back at her.

Later, she mouthed. He nodded. Then he drew her in close and kissed her.

Every worry darted from her mind, and she sighed, so blessed to have found her soul mate, a concept she'd found corny as hell before Mike. She'd rather be tortured than tell anyone that, but he knew.

She pulled away, wanting this kind of love for her brother. Yet J.T. had to be ready for it. And he...

Was totally looking all moony and swoony at Hope.

"Oh my God."

J.T. turned to her with a frown. "What's your problem now?"

"Nothing." She felt Mike's pinch on her arm and slapped at him.

"Now, now, Delilah. No hitting in public. Set an example for the boy." He nodded to Colin.

"Shut it, McCauley." She gave him a mock glare, then pointed at J.T. "We'll talk later." She glared at Hope, feeling free to treat her as family. "You too."

"Ooh, I'm so scared." Hope scrunched up her face and put her hands in the air like fake claws. "*Grrr*."

Colin laughed and edged even closer to J.T., practically sitting on his lap. "Hope's so funny! J.T., show her how you can knock down all the pins. He's so good, Hope. You should see." Colin had a clear case of hero-worship for his favorite tattoo artist.

J.T. smiled. "Well, now that you're here, Colin, I can take the kid gloves off. You're in for it now, Donnigan. Colin told me to show you how good I *really* am."

"Yeah?" Hope snorted. "Bring it, Webster. If your ego doesn't get in the way."

"Oooh, fighting words," Colin whispered.

Mike laughed. "Your family is so dramatic," he said to Del.

"*My* family? You're kidding, right?"

They watched J.T. and Hope continue to taunt each other, with Colin getting a few insults in edgewise.

"Are you seeing what I'm seeing?" Mike said in a low voice.

"Yeah." But she didn't know if that was necessarily

a bad thing. J.T. seemed to be...more. Happy, alive, real. He used no gloss with Hope. No suave facade or player vibe.

As usual, women around them paid attention to her brother. The women in lane four. The older moms with kids in lane six. Her brother attracted the ladies without trying. So she could see Hope liking him.

Yet Hope wasn't dating, or hadn't been in months. Del had heard all about it from her mother-in-law, who'd heard it from Cam, who'd heard it from Hope herself. So was tonight an actual date? A meeting between friends with loose ties? Or something more?

Del wanted to know. And she knew how to get answers.

"Before you start grilling my cousin, I need to talk to you," Mike said. In a louder voice he added, "We'll be right back. Colin, stay with J.T. and Hope." He dragged her to a quiet area near the restrooms. The joy in his eyes told her he knew. *Damn*.

He crossed his massive arms over his chest. "So?"

"So what?" She felt nervous.

"Are you or not?" He scowled. Big, burly, tough Mike McCauley, Mr. Marshmallow to his kid and those he loved. And he loved her, of that she had no doubt. He looked nervous, hopeful, and scared. His first wife had died in childbirth. This would not be easy, but they'd get through it. Together.

She sighed. "How did you know?"

He shrugged and fiddled with his keys, unable to keep still. "I saw the trash overflowing with pregnancy tests, genius. Way to keep it a secret."

She wanted to be mad at his attitude, but his nerves

made her want to cuddle him, tell him they'd be okay. "I put that trash in the bin outside."

He sighed. "You didn't tie off the bag, like you're supposed to. We don't just dump trash in the can."

"Obsessive-compulsive much?" she muttered.

"What's that? Speak up, smart-ass. I can't hear you." He stopped fiddling and smiled, his blue eyes filled with so much love. "I swear if you are, I hope it's a girl. And she's just like you."

Del sniffed. She would not cry. "I might be."

"Might be?"

"I see the doctor on Monday."

"I'm coming with you."

"Fine."

"Fine."

They smiled at each other, and Del laughed. "I love you, Mike."

"I love you, Delilah." He kissed her, then hugged her until she squeaked. "Oh, sorry. Don't want to damage the goods." He rubbed her tummy, and she saw tears in his eyes. "I promise I'll try not to freak out for the next nine months. But Del…" He paused and glanced at J.T., Hope, and Colin waving at them to return.

"Yes?"

"I know how much you love J.T. Colin idolizes him, and he really wants a baby brother."

"And?"

"And as much as I'd do anything for you, I'm not naming my next kid Jethro Tull McCauley. Just sayin'. One J.T. in the family is enough."

She snickered with him. "And that's why I love you. We're so totally on the same page."

Chapter 9

Sunday afternoon, Hope waited for Noelle to show up at their favorite coffee shop. She still didn't know what to make of last night. Bowling with Del, Mike, and Colin had been so much fun. But mostly because J.T. had her laughing all night long.

She'd known he was funny. She'd enjoyed herself with him and his friends at Ray's. But around his sister and her family, he'd shared a part of himself she hadn't realized he'd been keeping separate.

He'd seemed more relaxed, were that possible, than he normally was. And he shone as an uncle. God, but Colin loved him. J.T. was the fun uncle, the one who swore, snuck Colin candy when Mike wasn't looking—though Del had encouraged him—and generally made anyone passing by smile when he laughed. Because his laughter was so genuine.

The entire evening had felt surreal, as if Hope was out with her own family. Included, amused, entertained. She hadn't had that much fun in a long time. And she'd gotten to know more about J.T. Not just his history that he'd shared, but seeing him take care of Del and Colin, and even Mike when her cousin wasn't looking.

When some belligerent guy had come near with words for Mike, who'd apparently once run into him at Ray's, J.T. had smoothly stepped in, intercepting the guy before he could ruin the tender moment of Mike helping Colin bowl, being all dad-like and supportive.

The angry man had left as suddenly as he'd arrived, but not without a fearful look in J.T.'s direction.

Hope sighed and toyed with the vanilla latte in front of her. She'd been worried that they'd go back to being flirty and a bit uneasy with each other on the drive back. Instead, J.T. had continued to be amazing, charming, and to-die-for sexy. He'd walked her to her door, then kissed her before she could go inside.

And the kiss…

"Man, I'm doomed." She stared glumly at her coffee.

The kiss had been tender, sweet, and all lips, no tongue. And it had shattered her conception of what he meant to her. Platonic? Just a friend? Nothing could be further from the truth. The man made her heart race and those ooey-gooey feelings rise. The kind that turned her into a blathering idiot who started throwing around words like *boyfriend* and *living together* and *relationship*.

"Excuse me, miss?"

She blinked into the concerned stare of one of the café employees. "Yes?"

He smiled apologetically. "I'm sorry to disturb you, but the gentleman said to give you this. Said it looked like you needed it." He handed her a plate with a sticky bun on it. Her favorite, and a treat she liked to give herself every Sunday she met with Noelle.

"The gentleman?" She glanced around.

"He left as soon as he ordered it. Nice guy wearing a hat."

She hadn't seen anyone in here with a hat. "Was he tall or short? White? Black? Deep voice, maybe?"

"Um, I'd call him average in size, nothing special about his voice. Average, really. He wore a sweatshirt. Sorry, but the hat hid his face. Not sure what he looked like. We were so busy I wasn't paying attention. I'm working the food counter today, not the register."

"Okay, thanks."

The employee left, and she stared at the treat. Had this same person left her the flowers? Should she feel creeped out or complimented? Why hadn't this person stuck around to give it to her himself?

"There you are," Noelle huffed and sat across from her. "You ordered already?" She took a piece of the sticky bun and ate it. "Oh, man, I needed this."

"Noelle, I have no idea who bought me that." She told her friend about the flowers too.

"Oh, a secret admirer. How cool!" The identity of the admirer didn't seem to bother Noelle, who continued to nibble at the pastry.

"Hey, get your own. I'll wait here." Hope rolled her eyes. "Mooch."

Noelle grinned and moseyed over to the pastry counter. Thirty years old, with a cap of short red hair, bright-blue eyes, and the build of a college basketball player—which she'd been when she'd attended Washington on a basketball scholarship—she'd glommed on to Hope years ago when they'd met working for a horrible boss at a boutique clothing store.

Since then, they'd become best friends going on… Wow. Six years now.

Hope waited for her to return, needing to talk. But the sparkle in Noelle's eyes demanded she ask about the big date instead. "So, last night?"

"A win." Noelle's grin warmed. "Jean-Luc—I swear that's his name—is my cooking instructor."

"Wait. I thought you met him in a language class."

"No. That was Pierre. Except his name is actually Paul. He just called himself Pierre to sound French."

"Ah, okay."

Noelle filled her in on the hot date. "Apparently French men *do* do it better in bed." Noelle laughed. "He was amazing. Or as I learned in class last week, *fantastique*. Man. I don't think I can go back to American men now."

"Wait. He's not from the U.S.?" How long could this relationship last?

Noelle went on a lengthy spiel about visas and work permits and Jean-Luc's employment in the States, for some big company that planned to keep him as long as they could.

At the end of her explanation, Hope pulled together the important parts. "So after just a week, you're in love."

"A week and four days," Noelle corrected, her tone lofty. She groaned. "I know. I feel stupid. Maybe it's just his accent. Or the way he used his tongue."

Next to them an older woman gasped, gathered her things, and walked quickly away.

Hope blushed and tried not to laugh. "Noelle, lower your voice."

"What? Oh. My bad." In a lower voice, she said, "So what's your deal? I know you've been down lately. I can see it, or I *could* see it. But you look a lot happier today. Is it the caffeine or something else?"

"Well, remember that guy I told you about from my cousin's wedding?"

Noelle grinned. "Oh right. The hot guy who looks like Dwayne Johnson? Except hotter, which isn't humanly possible? When do I get to meet this paragon? Because if he is the Rock, I can speak enough French for the both of us. He'll be Monsieur Noelle Katz before you can say *merci*."

"Dream on." Hope laughed. "But yes, I'm talking about J.T." She glanced around, made sure no one was sitting too close, and continued. "Let's call him Rocky, just in case anyone around here knows him."

"Oh, wow. Code names? This sounds serious. Tell me."

Hope explained the fake boyfriend plan she'd cooked up to get her mother off her back and J.T.'s willingness to play along. She also mentioned their many family connections, as well as their hot-and-heavy non-date on Friday.

Noelle's eyes grew huge. She leaned closer. "He was *oh God* good?"

Hope nodded. "Totally. And you know I'm not one for casual anything. He and I, we weren't going to go there. We have too much to lose if it goes wrong. He's so hot it's no surprise he's a major player. I mean, everywhere we go, women are eyeing him up like dessert."

"So? Guys look at you like that all the time."

Hope frowned. "They do not."

"Oh? Look at your three o'clock."

She did and saw an old man playing cards with his grandson. "Where?"

"Oh, sorry. My three o'clock. That's your nine." Noelle took a moment to confirm, then nodded.

"You're horrible with directions, you know that?"

"Yeah, yeah. So look."

Hope sipped her coffee and took a subtle glance to her left, only to see a cute blond man smiling at her. He winked, then turned back to his tablet.

She didn't see a hat or a sweatshirt on the guy, so she crossed him off her list of secret-admirer suspects.

"And the dude with the woman who sat down by the door. He's been staring at you."

"He has not."

"I saw him watching you while I was waiting to get my food. Is he still?"

Hope glanced over and saw the man talking to his girlfriend or wife. He looked over at Hope, saw her staring, and hurriedly looked back at his coffee companion. "Coincidence."

"My point is you're pretty. You can hold your own with a player."

"But I don't want to."

"It's time." Noelle sighed. "I was going to get a bunch of the girls together for a man-tervention, but now we won't have to."

"Excuse me?" Hope put her cup down, focused on her wacky friend.

"A man-tervention. It's something you have for a friend who's either dating too much, dating the wrong type, or not dating enough. You went a long time without, for you anyway. Most women can go half a year without dating, and it's no biggie."

"Where do you get your statistics?" Noelle could always be counted on for a laugh.

"But you're used to being with someone. And let's face it, you want a relationship."

"I—Crap. Yes, you're right. I do want a relationship. I want love and all the great couple stuff that goes with it." Hope sipped her coffee again, wanting the caffeine boost. "I finally faced facts. I've been kind of bummed out because I want true love, and I realized I've never come close. I came to that conclusion a week or so ago."

"You and every other single woman on the planet." Noelle huffed. "Heck, Hope. The last guy I dated turned out to be the king of boring. And he had no intention of ever leaving Tacoma. What a waste of a year that was. But I was like you, thinking it was better to have a boyfriend than be alone. Then again, I've been alone most of my life. It's hard to be tall and get guys."

"Whatever. You're beautiful."

"To you. But then, you don't want to do me. I don't think. Do you?"

Two guys at the next table swiveled heads toward them at the same time. The older one smiled at Noelle. The younger one raised a brow at Hope.

Hope quickly looked back at her dopey friend and hissed, "Would you *please* use your indoor voice?"

Noelle snickered. "Sorry…baby." She laughed louder.

Hope covered her face with her hands. "My face feels super hot. I'm blushing so hard I'm afraid I might spontaneously combust."

"Oh, come on. Let's walk and talk."

They gathered their drinks and Noelle's bag of meringues and left the coffee shop, heading for the Fremont Bridge. They crossed under a bright-blue sky, the sun shining high. Clouds moved along with the boats coming and going down the Fremont Cut as they passed from Lake Washington to Puget Sound.

Once across the bridge, Hope and Noelle walked along the trail, skirting bikers and runners all in a rush to get fit.

"Finally feels like summer." Like Hope, Noelle had dressed in layers. The jacket she'd worn into the coffee shop was now belted around her waist. "So tell me more about this J.T. What does J.T. even stand for?"

Hope shrugged. "No clue. But I do know he's handsome, charming, and really sexy." She paused, stymied. "I don't know what to do about him. His sister is right. We shouldn't date. It will end badly, and then the families will suffer for it."

"Dear God, the drama." Noelle put the back of her hand against her forehead, and Hope laughed. "Get a grip, Hope. So you like the guy. Date him. Have fun. Live a little. Why make it so serious?"

"Because that's how I roll, Noelle. Unfortunately. I always go a little too far too fast with guys. Except most of them are real jerks. J.T. seems different. Maybe that's the appeal."

"I say enjoy him. Reap the benefits, then go your separate ways later. At least keep him around to annoy your mom. That's what you and he are supposed to be about, right?"

"Right. Except I keep finding myself spending time with him, getting to know him, and it's got nothing to do with my mom. It's embarrassing. Like, I can't help myself around him."

"Oh, that's chemistry. I love when that happens. It's so rare."

"Yes, chemistry. And you're right. It is rare."

"Look, we both know that just because the sex is great

doesn't mean the guy will be great. I mean, remember Vincent? He was so good in bed. And a total douche every time he used his mouth for anything other than pleasing me. I cried when he left. Not because I missed his stellar company, but because I missed his golden phallus of joy."

A jogger running by whipped his head toward Noelle, missed a large tree root, and stumbled. After nearly face-planting, he righted himself and hurried away.

Hope bit her lip to keep from laughing.

"Was it the golden phallus comment that got him, do you think?"

Hope nodded.

"Ah, well. I still miss it to this day. But Jean-Luc is magical in *and* out of the sack."

"So you're going to marry him after knowing him for nine days. He'll use you for a green card, end up being the worst serial killer France ever exported, and I'll never know where he buried your body. But on the flip side, you'll be famous and your picture will be on every documentary they make of him. Plus, as a bonus, you'll be on Wikipedia when I click on his list of victims."

Noelle stopped in her tracks. "Wow. You just ran with that."

"Sorry. Saw a documentary on killers a few days ago."

"*Riiigght*." Noelle gave her a searching side glance. "Now that we've given your imagination a run for its money, I say go out with J.T. Irritate Linda. Sleep with him a few times, get it out of your system, part as friends, the end. It's only a big deal if you make it one."

The words continued to linger as Hope's Sunday evening drew to a close and Monday morning rolled around. She hadn't heard from J.T. and kept telling herself she wanted it that way.

Arriving at work at seven on the dot, she found another bouquet waiting by the door. A glance to her right and left showed no one about in the hallway, so she picked up the flowers and let herself in the office. This time, she locked the door behind her as she set up for the morning meetings Cam had scheduled. Only once she'd returned to her desk with a cup of coffee in hand did she turn to the new vase of flowers.

After a careful search, she found nothing dangerous. Just a lovely bouquet of irises, roses, lilies, and some white filler and greenery she couldn't name. The accompanying card said:

> *You're more than sweet and special. And honey-brown is my favorite color too.*

Hope frowned. That sounded like J.T., kind of. Except for the *too* at the end.

She pulled out her phone, uncaring of the early hour, and called him.

After three rings, he answered in a rough bark, "Yeah?"

"J.T. Good morning."

"Oh, hey, Hope." He sounded more relaxed. "It's early, damn." It was seven fifteen. "You okay?"

"Yes, thanks. I'm at work." She paused, studying the

note. It had been typed, not handwritten. "Did you send me flowers?"

"No. Why? Should I have?"

"Well, this is the second bouquet I've received at the office. But the note on this one sounded like you." A phone call to the florist after the first bouquet had been delivered had yielded little. The buyer had paid in cash, and no one there could remember who'd ordered what because they'd had a rush on orders at the time.

"Read me the note."

She did and worried about what it might mean.

"That's freakin' weird. A coincidence it mentions a favorite color, like we talked about at the bowling alley?"

"There's something else. Someone sent me a pastry when I was with Noelle at our favorite coffee shop yesterday. And it's the kind I always order when she and I meet. I think someone's been watching me. Boy, this is creepy."

"Are you okay? Is Cam there?"

"Not yet. I usually get the office going. He should be here soon, though. The door's locked. Don't worry."

"Smart. Okay. Do me a favor. Just let me talk to you until he gets there, okay? For my own peace of mind."

"Sure." A relief, because she hadn't wanted to feel alone waiting for Cam to show up.

"And make sure you tell your cousin about this. And your brothers."

"I will." Well, she'd tell Cam. He'd be calm about what to do. She would *not* tell her brothers. Landon and Gavin would launch into warrior mode, strategizing about how to deal with the enemy as if still in the Marine Corps. She could just imagine discussions on avenues of attack, mounting a defense, and ways to go on the offensive.

No, she'd be smarter to let the McCauleys help her on this one.

"And since you never called me yesterday like you were supposed to, we can talk tonight when I pick you up and take you to my place. That way you can give your mom details about my pad, and it'll all be true."

"Wait. I was supposed to call you?"

"Sure. You're the one pursuing me, aren't you?"

She frowned. "How's that? We're in a fake dating relationship, J.T. Hello?"

"Exactly. But since this show is for your mother, and you're taking charge, I thought, from a psychological standpoint, that you should run with that."

"What?"

"You know, taking charge. Being the man, the *wo*-man. That way you're not breaking your dating rules. That no-guy thing you've got going on. I mean, we're fake dating, right?"

"Right." Was it really? She was so confused.

"And if you take charge and keep making it all about you, then you're not letting some guy boss you around, making it like your past relationships. You're the one bossing me around. Make sense?"

"Kind of...not really. So I don't—"

"Exactly. You don't concede anything. You're still an independent woman. I'm just a dude helping you out of a jam with your mom."

Who went down on me and kissed me like it meant something. "Okay," she said slowly, trying to think. "So what are you getting out of this pseudo-relationship?"

"I'm hoping you'll want to use and abuse me some more. Like, maybe you need more orgasms or something. But we're not dating, and you're not into casual hookups, am I right?"

"Right."

"Exactly."

"I'm so confused." The doorknob rattled. Her pulse rocketed. "Someone's here."

"See who it is," he said, his voice clear, precise. "But don't open up yet."

The frosted door outlined what looked like Cam's frame.

Someone knocked. "Hope? Are you in there?"

"It's Cam." She let out a nervous breath. "Thanks, J.T. I have to go. But we're going to talk about this later."

"Sure thing. I'll swing by your office at five thirty. Now tell your boss about the flowers." He hung up before she could discuss him taking charge.

She scowled as she opened the door.

"What's going on?" Cam immediately asked. "Why was the door locked?" His gaze zoomed in on the flowers on her desk. "Again?"

She nodded, explained why she felt uneasy about the gift, and waited for his response.

He studied the card, turned it over, then tucked it into his pocket. "I'll make a call or two. But do me a favor. Stick close to the office today, and if you leave, make sure I'm with you when you walk to your car."

"Okay." She felt worlds better not to be the only one thinking the situation bizarre and a bit worrisome. "J.T.'s going to meet me here after work, though."

"J.T.?" Cam cocked his head. "As in, J.T. Webster? Del's brother?"

She blushed at his look. "Yes, but it's not like that."

"Like what?"

"You're giving me that big brother look of disapproval."

"Well, although I'm not your brother, technically, I am older than you by one year, so you have to do whatever I say, and not just because I'm your boss."

She rolled her eyes.

He nodded. "I'll just admit, it's nice not to be the baby of the family anymore. With you around, I'm not the youngest." His wide grin should have annoyed her but didn't. "And I don't disapprove, though I'm not sure what we're talking about."

So Hope found herself confessing her scheme to annoy her mother a second time in two days. But she left out all the sexy parts with J.T. that she'd shared with Noelle.

"Good luck with Aunt Linda," Cam said with a smile. "I always liked her."

"Yeah, well, you're the only one successful enough to be an honorary Donnigan." She couldn't help noticing he beamed at that. "Now let's get cracking. You have meetings all day, starting at eight with Brad Wheeler. After that you have the Lamberts, then Joe Gregory."

"No, Joe canceled. I have a new client penciled in, though. It's a meet and greet, so don't stress about information on him we don't have. Just get me a new client folder, and I'll fill it in as he and I talk."

"Sounds good. Now I'd better get through the emails piling up." It felt good to focus on work.

"Okay. What about those?" He gestured to the flowers.

"I say let's leave them where we left the others. On the table there by the guest chairs."

"Perfect. They do class up the office, you know."

"Yeah." Too bad they were freaking her out.

She and Cam settled in to work. When Brad Wheeler arrived twenty minutes later, Hope had almost forgotten about her earlier scare.

Brad offered her a shy smile. "Hello, Hope. Good to see you."

"You too, Mr. Wheeler."

"Call me Brad."

She smiled. "He's ready for you, Brad."

Brad noticed the flowers. "Oh, those are lovely. That reminds me to pick some up for my wife. Our anniversary is tomorrow."

"That's sweet. She's a lucky woman."

"I wish you'd tell her that," he grumbled, then walked back with her to Cam's office.

He left forty-five minutes later with a wave, and she spent the rest of her morning busier than she could have hoped. She had no time to worry about admirers, J.T., or her mother.

It was just as a handsome newcomer entered that she realized she'd worked through lunch, as had Cam. Too late now.

"Hello. Can I help you?"

"Yes, hello." His greeting held more than a little interest. Tall, dark, and handsome, the man should have been her type. But lately, if the guy wasn't a certain someone with warm brown skin, eyes to die for, and a killer smile, she wasn't interested. "I have a one o'clock with Cam McCauley. I'm Dr. Steven Cooper. And you are?"

"Hope Donnigan," she murmured. "I know your name."

"Donnigan?" He brightened. "Any relation to Linda Donnigan? She sold me my house."

Damn it. "Oh, ah, yes. She's my mother." Hope suddenly recalled exactly where she'd heard this man's name. Linda had wanted to set Hope up with this guy. This handsome, polite doctor who had the money to work with Cam. Her cousin didn't work with anyone but top-dollar clients.

"Oh, then it's doubly a pleasure." He reached for her hand, but instead of shaking it, he pulled it to his mouth and gave it a whisper of a kiss. The gesture touched her, until she remembered he was a product of her mother's machinations.

Hope gently tugged her hand back. "Let me take you to Cam."

She buzzed his intercom. "Cam? Dr. Cooper is here to see you."

"Great. Send him back."

To Steven, she said, "Follow me."

"Anywhere," he murmured.

She flushed and left him with Cam, who saw her and raised a brow in question but said nothing more than a hello to Steven.

Hope lost herself in work once more.

An hour later, Steven walked out with Cam, laughing and planning a follow-up meeting.

"Hope, set Steven up with an appointment two weeks from now, would you?" Cam asked.

"Sure thing. Dr. Cooper—"

"Steven, please."

"Steven, let's take a look at the calendar."

Cam left them, and she and Steven planned his return. "And maybe when I come back next time, I can take you to lunch." He smiled. "Your mother told me all about you." His grin widened. "She also told me not to tell you that, because you're stubborn and not happy with her right now."

Hope didn't sugarcoat it. "She's a busybody."

He laughed. "Who sold me a wonderful house. Look, I get it. She's doing what my mother constantly does to me. She's meddling. How about we go to lunch, talk, and get her and my mom off our cases? Because I have a feeling my mother talked to yours. Apparently being single nowadays is a cardinal sin."

Hope shook her head. "I know, right? I have to tell you, I'm not in the market for a man right now."

"What a coincidence. Neither am I."

He made her laugh.

"I'm kind of seeing someone, and even though it's not serious, it's about all I can handle," she told him.

"I totally understand."

They chatted a little longer, then Steven had to leave.

"Think about lunch," he said. "I'm new in town and could use a friend, but no pressure, and I mean that. I'll stop by early for my next appointment. You can let me know then."

"Sounds good." She thought she might just join him for that lunch. He seemed nice and polite. And he was funny too. Her mother, darn it, had been right. Take Linda out of the equation and Steven came across as a winner.

And he was no J.T. Webster. It might be good to get J.T. off the brain for a bit.

"You know what, Steven? Let's arrange to have lunch. You and me, and we leave our moms out of it."

He nodded. "I'll see you then."

After he'd gone, Hope returned to her reports. Before she knew it, five thirty rolled around.

J.T. came through the door just as Cam was calling it quitting time.

"Yo, Cam. What's up?" J.T. gave her cousin a wide smile and slapped him on the back. "How's my second-favorite blond doing? You keeping Vanessa in check?"

"*My wife* is fine, thank you." Cam blinked. "Wait. Second favorite?" He shot Hope an amused glance. "Ah, I see."

"They sure do make them fine around here."

Cam laughed. "Okay, Romeo. Keep my cousin safe."

"Will do." J.T. stopped smiling. "Cam, do me a favor and mention her 'admirer' to your brothers, would you?"

Hope frowned. "I'm right here."

"Oh, I already did. Told them not to tell Dad though, because he and Mom will no doubt blab to Uncle Van and Aunt Linda." Cam gave Hope an apologetic look. "You know it's only a matter of time before Landon and Gavin find out too."

"Cam. You can't tell them. They'll suffocate me with 'protective measures.' Once a Marine, always a Marine. And Theo's as bad."

"No messing around with your safety, Hope." Cam shook his head. "This whole mess is weird. I'll keep my eyes open."

"Me too," J.T. agreed.

"I'm. Right. Here." Hope glared at the pair of them.

Cameron kissed her on the cheek. "See you tomorrow, Hope." Along with J.T., he scurried her out the door, then locked up behind them.

"That's my job," she complained.

"Not until we find out who's behind the flowers."

"Yeah, what he said," J.T. had to add.

"You, hush. In fact, I have a bone to pick with you."

He sighed. "Follow me. I know just the place where you can yell at me all you want."

Chapter 10

J.T. BROUGHT HER BACK TO *HER* PLACE. SHE PARKED, WAITED for him to do the same, and preceded him through the building to her door. Once inside, she shut and locked it, then slid off her shoes.

"Okay, buddy. Let's talk."

He sighed, not sure he could resist her in her current pissy mood. "Where do you want me?"

Her subconscious glance at her hallway, which led to her bedroom, about killed him. "The couch it is." He hurried to his favorite place in the apartment and stared at the couch. "Ah, the memories."

"Stop it." Hope left him and returned with two bottles of water. She lobbed one at his head, but he caught it.

"What a great host."

"So what's the deal with you and Cam playing men who know better than the little woman? I'm the one feeling threatened by flowers and cinnamon buns." She paused, and he wondered if she heard how odd that sounded. "My point is, I should be taking charge of this."

"Fine. What do you want to do about it?"

She opened her mouth then closed it, saying nothing.

While she debated how to sound in charge, he studied her, in lust with her business attire. Hope always looked like a million bucks to him. But especially in work wear. Short, curvy, and classy, with her blond hair pulled back in a sexy chignon—he'd looked the style up after seeing her wear it that way once—her skirt formfitting and stylish, her shirt staid but hinting at the curves beneath. The whole package was pretty much his fantasy for being seduced by his hot secretary or boss.

As usual around Hope, his dick took notice, wanting to stand up and salute her. He opened the water and drank to distract himself.

She did the same. Just two pals hanging out together on a Monday evening drinking water. He grinned at the inanity of it.

"What's so funny?"

"Us." He shook his head and put the water down on a coaster. Then he spread his arms out on the couch cushions behind him. "Well? I'm waiting."

"Uh, right. Well, it's okay for my cousins to know, but not my brothers. They can get really pushy and wrapped up in Marine protective mode. They might both be out of the service, but it's always there. And with Theo signing up, he'll be just as bad."

He nodded, in agreement with the part about the service always being present in both her older brothers. He'd met them, and they were guys he wouldn't want to tangle with. Which was why he'd called them both to let them know about her secret admirer situation, a fact Hope would not like. At all.

But at least her brothers had agreed to let him take point, along with Cam, and gently ease Hope into their protection. So when they subtly showed up here and there, she wouldn't immediately boot them away.

They knew her better than J.T. did. Apparently Hope was still a little too trusting and naive, despite dealing with some pretty scummy exes. She had a big heart and wanted to think the best about people. J.T. knew that much about her too.

She seemed to deflate before him. "You agree with me? Good."

He watched her grab her cell phone from her purse, then dither over where to sit. When she chose to plant her sexy tush right next to him on the couch, he didn't know what to say.

"Now you sit right here and wait while I have a discussion with my mother. Then we talk."

Hope dialed her mother, who took her sweet time answering.

"Hello? Who is this?"

Hope pinched the bridge of her nose, conscious of J.T.'s scrutiny. "Please, Mom. Caller ID is a well-known fact of life."

"Oh, is this Hope? My only daughter? The one not talking to me? What a lovely surprise."

J.T. leaned closer to hear, so she put the call on speaker. "You're on speaker, Mom, so I can keep my hands free while we talk. Guess who I met today at work?"

"Who?"

"Steven." She saw J.T.'s eyes narrow and put a finger over her lips to remind him to keep quiet. He frowned but nodded. "What a coincidence that the same man you tried to set me up with at brunch just happened to find Cam and talk investments today."

"I'm so glad he went. Smart men take care of their money. Smart women too, in case you try labeling me a sexist." Her mother laughed. "What did you think? He's handsome and kind. Just your type."

J.T. didn't look pleased at all. For that she had her mother to thank. What a tangled mess.

"Yeah, about my type. I'd like to bring him to dinner. Not Steven. My tattoo artist boyfriend."

Her mother said nothing.

Hope grinned at J.T., who looked more bemused than annoyed with her. "Well? You said you wanted to meet him. Remember?"

"Fine. We'll have dinner this Friday evening. Six thirty. I hope this one isn't a vegan. Your father will be making steaks."

"Great. See you then." She disconnected and put her phone down on the coffee table, realizing that she was in for it now. No backing out of her fabrication anymore.

"So. Who's Steven?"

She turned to J.T., sitting so close. "I think the real question is, why did you think you could just take charge back in the office? I have a brain, you know."

"I know." The heat in his gaze should have bothered her. Instead, it only added to the sexual tension rising in her. "Believe it or not, I see beyond the curvy, blond bombshell to the savvy woman beneath. You're not just a pretty face. I get it."

A compliment, yet the part about knowing she was intelligent meant more.

He studied her. "You know, you and I couldn't look more different, but we're a lot alike."

"Oh?"

"Yeah." He settled into the couch, widening his seat and stretching out his long legs. Dressed in his typical business casual, he wore jeans, boots, and a black tee that clung to his body. Nothing at all wrong about liking the look of a man in his prime, she thought.

J.T. kept talking. "You see, you and me, we get judged on how we look all the time. Most people do, but we get it more. You get people thinking you're not that bright because you're blond and beautiful. Most guys take one look at you, and all they can think about is getting you alone and fucking you."

Blunt but on target. She just wished he wouldn't have used the word *fuck* because it put even dirtier thoughts than she'd been having about him in play.

"Then there's me. Most people look at me, see a big, black dude who looks mean when he's not smiling."

"And sexy."

He gave a half grin. "And sexy. And they think I'm all brawn and no brain. Chicks want a big dick. Guys either want to join my 'gang' or push me around to show they're not afraid of me. Or they are and they avoid me, because obviously a black man in Seattle is only in the city to mug and rape and maul people."

"Sadly, I think you have that right."

He raised a brow.

She frowned. "Oh, stop. I meant you're right that people stereotype us all the time. But I don't see you that way."

"I don't see you that way either."

"Right."

"Good." He sat there, his arms spread wide, his arms and chest begging her to touch.

She couldn't stop remembering what they'd done before on her couch.

A glance down his body showed he hadn't forgotten either.

Oh boy. She tried to calm herself, then thought to hell with it. They should probably just get a few things out of the way. "I think we need to stop making a mess of all this. So here's the deal. You and I are friends, correct?"

No hesitation. "Yeah."

"We care about our families and don't want to screw up their lives with entanglements and regrets and you never calling me the next day."

He smirked. "Yeah, right. More like you seeing me in the street and pretending we never met."

"Sure, because most women look at you and run the other way."

"Well, when you put it like that, you're right. You'd never ignore me. But you wouldn't be shouting from the rooftops that we slept together."

She huffed. "Because I do that with all the guys I sleep with. I announce it to everyone. Oh hey, Big Brother Landon. Guess what? This is Greg. He and I had a sixty-nine, and it was gross."

J.T. cringed. "Okay, bad example."

"Gavin, meet Rob. He thinks our sexy times should begin with him ordering me around the room in a drill sergeant voice. And he always wants me to salute and call him *sir* before bending over."

"Please, stop."

"Oh, and Theo, I know you're not yet twenty-one, but did you know Brian thinks having rituals before sex is a turn-on? Wash my hands and feet twice, then put the nightgown on, then take it off and fold it in half four times, place it on the chair, and wow. I'm so in the mood."

J.T. covered his eyes with one hand. "You've made your point."

"Finally." She snorted. "Because sadly, I could go on. Anyhow, you and I are friends who find ourselves attracted to each other. There's no point denying it. I think you're sexy as hell, and you have a hard-on anytime we're alone together. Unless you're always thinking about something else."

"No. This is embarrassing. I usually have more control over my body. But you mess me up."

The feeling is mutual, believe me. "There's nothing wrong with us being honest about it. And we shouldn't be embarrassed. We just, um, seem to hit it off. Physically."

He put his arm back along the couch. "I agree with everything you've said. So what's your point?"

"My point is we're not going to do anything to ruin things. So we had fun the other night. I'm not demanding marriage, and you're not acting all macho about my mother trying to set me up with another guy." She dared him to object, saw him swallow, and when he said nothing, continued. "Yes, Steven is a handsome doctor and seemed interested. I'm not. I don't want a new boyfriend. I'm tired of finding all my Mr. Wrongs." Tired of always being hurt.

"Okay." His gaze softened on her. "I get it. I'm tired of all my Ms. Wrongs too. You're not the only one not wanting to go through another breakup. You want the truth? I'm not a commitment kind of guy. My dad went through hell twice. First when my mom died. Then when he married Del's mom. I lived with that for a long time. I don't want it. Do I want a wife and kids?" He shrugged, and she had a feeling he was being more honest and open with her right now than he'd been with anyone in a long time. "The idea is nice. Sure. I look at Del with Mike and Colin, see how happy she is, and I think that would be cool, to have something like that. But I've dated a lot, and I just don't see that future in the cards for me."

She answered with her own truth, because J.T., of all the people she knew, understood. "That's me. I mean, I watched my older brothers fall in love. And I've seen my parents together, happy and successfully married, for my entire life. By the time my mom was my age, she already had a husband and three kids, and a career she was getting off the ground. But me? I'm nowhere near having the perfect family." She shrugged. "So it's easier not to date and pretend I'm okay with it. I'm not, not really. But I'm finally happier on my own than being part of a couple. I refuse to rush into anything because I'm almost thirty."

"Yeah, when is your birthday, again?" he asked.

"August eleventh."

He nodded. They watched each other with new understanding. "So what now?"

Despite all her talk about keeping some distance, she didn't want it. Not tonight. "I'm hungry. I say we get something to eat. After."

He frowned. "After what?"

"After I take charge of our plan to thwart my mother."

His frown eased, and he chuckled. "You sound like a supervillain."

"Sure, why not?" She scooted closer and put a hand on his thigh.

J.T. tensed all over. "What are you doing?"

"I'm coordinating with my evil henchman." She stroked his thigh, amazed at the muscle on the man. Then, because she couldn't help herself, she put her hand on the bottom of his shirt and dragged it higher. "Wow. You have a total six-pack. No, wait, is that a twelve-pack?" She ran her fingers over his taut abdomen, enthralled with the soft skin overlaying such rigid muscle. Man, she'd kill to have a stomach that flat. And he had the softest brown skin. She wanted to lick him all over.

"Um, Hope?" He sounded hoarse.

She smiled, feeling empowered. "Look, we laid out the ground rules. We both feel the same way. I'm just trying to even the score. You did something to me the other day, and I've been curious ever since."

His body was like a rock under her hand. So pretty, and right now all hers. She had a feeling J.T. wouldn't mind a little experimentation.

He cleared his throat. "You, ah, you go right ahead."

She glanced at his splayed arms, his hands gripping the back couch cushions for dear life. A perfect way to end her Monday. She rested both hands on his belly and slowly dragged them higher, learning the feel of him as she moved.

Breathless, she traced the contours of his chest, grazing his nipples, which tugged a groan out of him. She feathered her palms over the hard buds, and he shifted on the couch, clearly aroused.

Then she leaned closer and breathed in the scent of him, a hint of cologne and man that made her ravenous. She tugged his shirt up to his neck and kissed him there, right over his heart.

"Christ, Hope..."

She let the shirt fall back down and leaned over him, kissing up his neck to his cheek, pleased when he tilted his head to the side to give her better access. She kissed her way to his ear and whispered, "You seem so tense. Can I help you unwind?" Then she nipped his earlobe, saw him jolt, and heard a few swear words she didn't think usually went together.

"Yeah, yeah. Help me. Any way you want." He continued to hold tight to the couch, his eyes closed, supplicant to whatever she had planned.

Hope wanted to play, to touch and taste him everywhere. But then she'd end up losing herself in J.T., and despite all of this teasing, she didn't want to get in any deeper with the man.

So quit seducing him and leave him alone. Go get dinner, get back to being friends, and–

"Shut up," she muttered.

He opened his eyes and looked down at her. "What?"

"Nothing." She did what she'd been wanting to do all day and kissed him on the lips.

He parted for her immediately, and she gripped his shoulders and gave him a kiss that told him what she wanted. She thrust her tongue between his lips and ravaged his mouth, amazed a man could taste like sex and need and throw her desire into the stratosphere with little effort.

She had to kneel to reach all of him. Draped over his body at an awkward angle, she had to work to continue the kiss without sliding off him. But she wanted access to his pants, so...

He yanked his head back when she unfastened his jeans. "What are you doing?" He was panting, his eyes wide.

"Just checking to see how much control you have," she teased, recalling when he'd done the same to her.

"Fuck me." He slid his zipper down, then returned his hand to the back of the couch, out of the way.

She smiled at him, but he didn't smile back. All intensity and frustrated desire.

God, you are such a beautiful man. Hope kissed him again, this time with the feeling she hadn't wanted to have for a man, not for a while.

He kissed her back, passion and hunger there for the taking.

As she kissed him, she eased her hand beneath his underwear, grazing a long, thick shaft down to his balls.

Constricted by his underwear, she had to hold him tight, and he spread his legs wider, arching into her grip. Then he lifted again, and she left the kiss to look down, pulling his boxer briefs away from a huge, aroused cock.

She stared in awe at the sight of him, wondering if she was ready to take him inside her mouth.

J.T. was moaning her name and took the choice from her. He wrapped his hand in her hair and tugged her back for another kiss.

So she did what she'd been wanting to since getting her own happy ending on the couch. Hope started jerking him off. Her hand barely fit around him, he was so thick, and as she pumped him, she swore she could feel his heartbeat in the pulse of his arousal.

He kissed her like a starving man, thrusting with his tongue in ways that dampened her panties, readying her body for the treat in her hand.

Holding him tighter, she increased the strokes. Up and down, with firmer pressure, since he seemed to be seriously getting close, his kisses devastating to her senses.

Then he pulled from her lips and kissed the corner of her mouth, saying, "I'm gonna come so hard, Hope. So *fuckin'* hard."

She nudged under his chin and sucked a spot on his neck that made him shudder. And as she did, she jerked him off even faster. His groans turned to grunts, then a long moan as he came, jetting all over her hand and his belly. The orgasm lasted longer than she'd have imagined, as streams of seed landed on his shirt.

Yet he remained firm and erect in her hand, not softening even after he'd stopped releasing.

J.T. was breathing hard, his hand clenched in her hair while she kissed her way back up his neck to his chin. She started to pull her hand away when he wrapped his own around it, keeping her glued to his cock.

"In a minute," he rasped, breathing as if he'd run a marathon. "Oh, Hope. Shit. Damn." His vocabulary devolved from there, but she had to smile. She'd well and truly rung J.T.'s bell. And she couldn't have been happier, even if she was a little sexually frustrated. She really could have used that massive erection between her legs, though feeling him come had been amazing.

He wiped her hand on his belly, released her, and finally looked down at her. He said nothing, but his kiss had never been sweeter. And he continued to kiss her, stirring her up all over again.

She was aware of his naked parts hanging out, of the come on his shirt, of his seed still on her hand. The musky scent of him went straight to her head, and she marveled that nothing about J.T. had yet grossed her out.

Previous lovers had been less than fresh, too grabby, unpleasant after an orgasm with demands or a need to clean up right away.

J.T. acted as if he had all the time in the world as he made love to her mouth. And here she'd thought he'd be too tired to continue. She sure the heck had been after he'd rocked her world.

He pulled back and stroked her cheek, and the affection in her breast grew deeper. "That was amazing. Thanks, baby." He kissed her. "But I think I can do better than that. I mean, we're good friends, and we don't want there to be issues between us, right?"

She nodded. "Right, so why—"

He wrapped her hand around him, and she felt him finally softening. But not all the way. "I need some more. I don't think you drained me yet."

"Huh?"

"But this isn't enough."

"I, um, we weren't going to have sex, remember?" She felt stupid saying that, considering what they'd been doing.

"Oh, I remember." He grinned, and her brain took a snapshot of J.T.'s joy. Something she'd never forget, how beautiful he looked at that moment. Then he surprised her by lifting her in his arms and holding her over one shoulder with one arm while he adjusted himself with the other. "Now, time to *really* even the playing field."

She didn't know what he had planned, but at this point, she refused to argue. Especially because the man was carrying her over his shoulder, one arm over her waist to hold her in place as she dangled down his back, staring at his fine ass. He was so incredibly sexy. So strong.

She wanted to clap her hands and shout with glee that she'd broken him down, had him moaning and panting for her.

And then he had her on her back in her bed. He turned on the light on her nightstand and stared down at her.

She leaned up on her elbows. "What?"

"I want you naked. I want to see what I'm tasting."

She shivered. "I, um, okay. But only if you're naked too. But no sex," she blurted, as if abstaining from the final act would keep her heart safe. And really, what did she imagine might happen? They'd have a naked tickle fight? Man, she couldn't think straight.

He chuckled. "Oh, we're not gonna have sex... tonight." That *tonight* seemed tacked on at the end there. "But there's so much else we can do instead. Too bad it's not the weekend. I don't think we have enough time to get to what I have planned."

"Planned?" Just how much did he think they could do sans penetration?

He smiled and took off his shirt.

She stared, mesmerized. "You have a tattoo." He had tribal patterns in black over his upper left pectoral and part of his shoulder. Not what she'd expected. As a tattoo artist, she'd imagined he'd be covered in ink. That brief trip to his workplace had shown her even Suke had more.

"I'm picky. My buddy Eddie did this one. I've been waiting for inspiration to hit me for my next one." His voice lowered. "Gotta say I'm feeling pretty inspired now." He stepped out of his clothes, keeping on only his boxer briefs. "Now you."

She sat up, feeling almost shy, which she had never been. Though she didn't normally leap into bed with a man, she liked her body. But like most women, she felt she could do with losing a few pounds.

Hope stood and removed the sweater she wore to combat the AC in the office. Then she took off her blouse and skirt.

"Hot damn. Matching white lace? Nice, Hope. Very nice."

She smiled at him, and his eyes darkened. He stared at her body, and her nipples grew rock hard against her bra. She reached behind herself to unfasten it, then dropped it to the floor. J.T. stood as still as a statue.

"Now the panties," he said, his voice thick.

She hadn't worn a thong today, but the bikini panties were pretty and soft and made her feel feminine. She liked matching undergarments, especially her silky ones.

Hope stepped out of her panties, glad she'd done some landscaping that morning. She'd shaved all but a thin strip of hair over her mound. With the summer upon them and thoughts of dipping into a friend's hot tub, she had to be groomed for her bathing suit.

J.T. apparently approved, because he licked his lips and grinned. "Oh, I am gonna eat you right up."

"You are?"

"Yeah. I'm pretty hungry. Haven't had my dinner yet."

"Oh boy."

"Now lay back on the bed and spread those pretty thighs. We have a lot of no-sex to get to."

Chapter 11

Hope stared at her computer screen Wednesday afternoon, unable to concentrate. She should have been typing up one of the client's forms, because he'd changed an account and she needed to verify some numbers with him and his bank.

But she couldn't stop dwelling on J.T.

Monday night had been a dream.

He'd been an animal in bed. Then gentle, so tender he made her want to cry. And then she'd had another orgasm, and he'd coached her into trying something else. Where the heck did he get his creativity?

Despite not having had actual sex, she'd climaxed more in one night than she had in months. And he'd been right there with her. The man had stamina. And an ability to make her *want*.

Then, making everything worse, he had spent the night—clothed, next to her pajama-clad form—and slept with her in her bed. Her admirer hadn't bothered her at home, not that she'd thought anyone might. But having J.T.'s reassuring presence next to her, in addition to having had so many orgasms, had knocked her out. Instead of being anxious about sleeping with a man again, worrying she might drool, talk in her sleep, or scare him away the next morning with dragon breath, she'd slept soundly in his arms.

Of course he couldn't just slip out and leave the next

morning. After another round of heavy petting that turned into oral sex, which left her screaming his name, he'd departed with a smile and a promise to call her later.

And he'd actually called.

What to do about the man?

Her computer screen gave her no answers.

Fortunately, the door opened, giving her something else to think about.

Though Cam wasn't meeting anyone for another hour, he did get the occasional walk-in, referred through another client. He didn't advertise his services. No, her cousin was so good at his job that people came to him.

The edginess she'd felt on Monday after finding the flowers had faded. Cam was in the back room, and daylight made her fears fade. Plus, fear couldn't exist in the same space as Cam's wife.

Vanessa McCauley strode into the office wearing designer slacks and a chic blouse, her hair curled into a French twist. A fellow blond, Vanessa had never given off the dumb-blond vibe. One look way up into her frosty-blue eyes—she was nearly as tall as Cam—and you worried she'd stomp her heels all over your ego, your brain, and then your body.

Fortunately, she liked Hope.

"Well, well, her royal majesty has deigned to make her presence known." Hope grinned, appreciating that Vanessa's icy demeanor covered a warm woman inside, one who loved Cameron like crazy.

"Hello, peasant." Vanessa winked. "Is the royal jester in his office?"

"He is. Ah, and I see you brought him lunch."

"And you." Vanessa placed a bag of good smells on Hope's desk. "It's teriyaki chicken. Don't get it on your clothes, or it'll never come out."

"Thanks, I think."

Vanessa nodded and strode toward the back.

"How's Princess Jane doing?" Hope called after her. It was a well-known fact in the families that Vanessa and Cam's baby would no doubt be brilliant. Between his genius and hers, there could be no question.

Vanessa turned to smile. "She has two teeth and just called me Dada last night. I'm still working on that, but she's tracking and reading. Or at least, she seems to follow my finger when I read to her. And she gestures to what she wants. It's so exciting to see her learning what she likes and doesn't like." Vanessa's excitement turned from coldly beautiful to just lovely.

"That's so cool. I bet Cam's not letting you forget she called you Dada."

Vanessa sighed. "Why do you think I'm here bringing you two lunch? I lost a bet."

"Yeah, she did," Cam called out from his office. "Dada is the man!"

Vanessa muttered under her breath about impossible egos and left to join her husband.

Pleased to see her cousin in capable hands, and even more excited about lunch, Hope readied to go into the back kitchenette to eat when Brad Wheeler walked through the door looking frazzled.

"Hi, Brad. Are you okay?"

He sighed with relief. "I'm so glad I caught you. My wife decided to move around some money, and I wanted to make sure to drop this off before Cam changed things for us. Be nice to have money in the account before we move what doesn't exist."

She laughed. "No problem. He's having lunch, but he'll be done in half an hour. I know he was planning on working on your account later in the day."

"Oh, good." Brad deflated, noticed the bag on her desk, and straightened. "Let me get out of here. I'm sorry to interrupt your lunch."

"No, no. It's fine. I was finishing a few things before you came in anyway."

"Good." He smiled. "You know, I tell everyone I know about you guys. Cam and Alex are wonders when it comes to investments, and you're so organized. I always feel good when I leave, even if I'm nervous about some of Jenny's ideas about investing. Cam makes sure to look over everything. And don't tell my wife, but she's usually right about what she wants to do with our portfolio."

"You should bring her by sometime."

"I will." Brad smiled. In his forties, he had a competent air about him, and Hope knew he worked for an engineering firm downtown. She wished her mother could overhear the conversation and see her daughter interacting like a professional with a client.

Ah well. Linda would learn to eat her words soon enough. In just two more days.

"Um, Hope? Do you mind if I ask you a personal question?"

She shrugged. "Go for it."

"Are you seeing someone? I hate to ask." He blushed. "But Jenny's brother is moving back to town, and she wanted to know if I knew of any smart, pretty, *not crazy* single women. I hope that doesn't sound too forward. Jenny's family has a lot of money, so we've been trying to guide her brother toward a nice girl. His ex was…not so good."

"Sounds like my ex." She chuckled, but she felt for the guy. "Actually I'm seeing someone." A lie, but she didn't want to get involved with the clients in any kind of personal way. Yet another reason to steer clear of Dr. Steven Cooper. "He's a nice man, this time. I wish you luck with your brother-in-law, though."

He crossed his eyes, and she laughed. "Thanks. And I hope I wasn't out of line asking."

She smiled. "Not at all. Have a great week."

"You too."

Once he'd gone, she left her desk and hustled into the kitchenette to eat. She kept the door open so she'd hear if someone entered.

After wolfing down her lunch, careful not to spill on her clothes, she left the kitchenette and heard a thump from Cam's office. His door was closed, and she didn't dare ask what he or Vanessa were doing. Hope hurried back to her desk, smirking at thoughts of proper Cameron McCauley making out with his wife on his desk.

Vanessa left some time later, looking as put together as she'd been upon arrival.

"Thanks for lunch."

"Anytime." Vanessa smiled and closed the door after her.

Cam appeared, looking smugly satisfied.

Hope shook her head. "You're hopeless."

He straightened the cuffs under his sports coat. "I don't know what you're talking about." Then he sighed.

"When is Alex coming back? I had to cancel my racquetball time at the gym tomorrow to deal with more clients."

"Racquetball?" She would have made more fun of him if a floral delivery hadn't interrupted them.

Immediately nervous, she let Cam handle it.

"Delivery for Hope Donnigan." The young guy looked her way.

"I'll take them," Cam said.

The kid shrugged. "No problem. Sign here."

Cam signed a clipboard and took the vase full of yellow roses. Then he handed the kid a few bills.

"Thanks." The guy smiled and left.

Cam reached into the flowers for the small card, which was addressed to her. "You want me to open it?"

She nodded, feeling tense, scared, and annoyed with herself for getting so bent over flowers.

He read it and frowned. Then he looked at her.

"What?"

"Read this."

She took the card.

Flowers from me, finally. To my very good friend. And thanks for helping me keep the ecosystem clear. J.T.W.

The note was handwritten.

She smiled as happiness replaced her worry.

"What's this about an ecosystem?" Cam asked.

She shook her head. "Never mind. And yes, before you ask, they're from J.T. We're friends, Cam. Just friends."

"Uh-huh." He shot her a sly grin. "What do you think Del would have to say about your friendly flowers?"

"I can quit, you know. Then it would just be you here. By yourself. Making your own coffee and filing your own paperwork until Alex gets back. And he's worse than you with spreadsheets."

Cam blinked. "Ah, kidding. You know, I should get back to work."

"Yeah, you should." She watched him hightail it back down the hall.

Finding herself alone, she took a large sniff of the roses, not surprised to find them sweet, the petals soft, vibrant. So pretty.

Hope sighed. He'd gotten her flowers.

She set them on her desk and continued to glance at them throughout the rest of her day.

After work, Cam walked her to her car, and she texted J.T. to let him know she was leaving—and that she'd gotten the flowers. She'd decided to take them home, because she'd be better off mooning over him in private, and every darn time she looked at the flowers, she thought of him.

Once at home and ensconced in her favorite ratty pajamas, she had no intention of doing more than watching some TV before getting an early night's sleep. She'd been playing hooky from the gym lately, and her body felt sluggish.

Her phone dinged, alerting her to a text. Glad you liked the roses. They smell good. Not as good as you though.

She had to text him back. *Flowers from YOU? That's romantic. Hey, is this really J.T.?*

He sent her a goofy cross-eyed emoji. You're spelling correctly. Is this really Hope?

Ass.

Witch.

Speaking of...oh heck. I'm calling you.

Her fingers were getting tired. She dialed J.T., and when he answered, she said, "Speaking of *witch*, are you ready to meet my mom and dad?"

"You're going to hell for that."

"Probably."

They both laughed.

"We're not done prepping, you know," J.T. said. "Besides, you haven't seen my place yet. If we're dating, shouldn't you have been over by now?"

"Yes, but this is a fake relationship."

"Yes," he said patiently. "But a good lie has a lot of truth in it. So if you can describe my place because you've really been there, you won't trip yourself up too much."

"Good point." Not really. They both knew she didn't need to go to his house to prove anything. But she wanted to see where he lived, and he apparently wanted her there.

She kept waiting for awkwardness to drive a wedge between them. Not only had they fooled around many times, but he'd stayed the night. In her bed. With her.

Yet J.T. remained the same. No drama, tons of fun, and he made her laugh when not making her scream from pleasure.

She groaned.

"What?"

"You're kind of annoying."

"Kind of? I must not be doing it right."

She bit back a laugh. "Totally annoying. Aren't guys supposed to be clingy and need a lot of stroking? Not physically—get your mind out of the gutter. I mean, like, a lot of ego stroking?"

"I can't speak for all guys in general, but I know I love stroking." A deliberate pause. "The ego kind, I mean."

"Ha ha." She'd done a lot of that Monday night. They'd touched and kissed and touched some more. But she hadn't given J.T. a real blow job, and they hadn't technically had sex, involving penetration.

She had a feeling no matter how much she kept protesting that they refrain from taking that final step, that for all J.T. agreed with her, they were heading down a dark path. Well, a sex-filled path at least, because she was dying to feel him inside her. So much so that she'd started taking her birth control pills again. A very bad sign.

"Any other problems with your admirer?" J.T. asked.

"Nope. Not since Monday. I still feel weird about worrying, because it's just flowers."

"And a pastry. And watching you while we were bowling. Look, the bastard knows enough about you to know what you eat and when you eat there. He knows where you work too. It's okay to feel weird. I'm glad you're taking this seriously."

"Hey, I've seen enough horror movies where the idiot woman—and it's always a woman—goes into the basement of the abandoned insane asylum by herself. Then lo and behold, she's chased the entire movie by inbred mutants and dies at the end. No thanks."

"Hey, I've seen that movie. Except no one wore

pants, and it was called *The Nine-Inch Beasts of Sex Asylum 13*. Great flick."

She laughed. "Sounds awesome." She waited a moment. "Nine inches, huh?"

"Too intimidating for you? So I guess *we'll* never be having real sex, then?"

"Come on. Nine?"

"Every man has at one time or another in his life measured his cock. I'm no different. So maybe I'm eight and a half and stretching it. Get it? Stretching it?"

"Wow. Your jokes are getting worse. Sexual and just bad."

"Eh. It's late, and I worked on a huge pain in the ass today. Cut me some slack."

"What happened? And when can I come watch you work?"

"Anytime you want. But I know your boss is a ball-buster. If he's anything like his wife, you'd better watch your step."

She grinned, then remembered his comment to Cam about blonds. "What did you mean when you asked about your second-favorite blond? Did you and Vanessa date?"

He burst out laughing, and the brick of jealousy lodged in her brain crumbled and vanished. "Vanessa? You're kidding, right? I was into her for about five seconds, at the same time she was knocked up with Cam's kidlet. Nothing happened there. What can I say? I like blonds, and Vanessa is pretty. She's not you, but she's decent."

Flustered but not wanting to show it, Hope tried to change the subject back to his pain-in-the-butt client.

"Hold on," J.T. interrupted her. "If you can ask about Vanessa, I figure I can ask about your guy."

"What guy?"

"You remember, Dr. Steven, the guy your mom is trying to set you up with? What's wrong with him?"

"Besides being rich, handsome, and pleasant? Oh, and a doctor?"

"Yeah, besides that," he growled.

She grinned. "Nothing. He's nice enough, I guess. But he's got my mom as a referral, which I find a definite mood killer."

"Ah."

"And before you ask, I met him *after* the first flowers were delivered."

"Oh." He sounded disappointed.

"I told him I wasn't in the market for a man. That's why I'm with you," she added in a chipper tone.

"You're not that funny."

"I don't know. *I'm* laughing."

"That's because you're too far away from me to do anything about it." He chuckled. "If you were here, I—Hold on a minute." She heard him yell at someone, then what sounded like a door being opened. "Oh, hey, come in."

She heard a woman's voice, and once again jealousy reared its ugly head. *Stop it, Hope. He can have girl friends. Just not girlfriends. Ugh. I hate relationships! Even fake ones.*

He came back to the phone. "Sorry. Rena's here looking frazzled. I gotta go. Talk to you tomorrow, okay?"

Rena—his cousin. Hope's mood perked up again. "Sure."

"I'll come by your work at five thirty."

"Make it six. We have a lot going on tomorrow."

"Cool. Six, then. I'll trail you home, then drive you to my place. And Hope?"

"Yeah?"

"Bring an overnight bag. We have a lot of *cramming* to get done." His evil laughter didn't help.

She groaned. "That's enough out of you. Go comfort your cousin."

"Later, Blondie." He hung up.

Hope sighed. Wishing she didn't miss him already. This fake relationship was already better than any real one she'd had in years. Hell, it was better than any she'd ever had.

"I need therapy… And I'm still not talking to Ava about this." Because she didn't want to hear from a trained professional that she was making a mistake with J.T.

J.T. didn't like his cousin's puffy eyes and quivering lips. When his sister and Rena had lived together, he'd been close enough to feel like he could help if they needed it. Rainier wasn't a bad section of town, though it sure wasn't as upscale as Queen Anne, where Del now lived, or even Fremont, where Hope resided.

"Okay, tell me." He held out his arms, and she threw herself into them and started sobbing. "Hey, sweetie. Rena, honey, what happened?"

She cried until she hiccupped, and when she pulled away, she looked both sad and cute instead of just cute. Everyone liked his cousin, well, except the racist assholes who'd been plaguing Ray's lately. But from what he'd heard, Heller and a few guys who frequented the bar had been kicking a lot of ass. And Ray hadn't made idle threats either. The stupid white-power dicks trying to make a move on Ray's had picked the wrong damn place to set up shop.

"Does this have to do with Fletcher?" One of the worst offenders.

He had the sense Fletcher had a thing for Rena, but because she wasn't white, it was aggravating the shithead something fierce. The attention the guy had given her when she hadn't been looking bothered the hell out of J.T.

"Who? Oh, no." She pulled away in search of a box of tissues. Then she sat on the couch with him, holding the box, and frowned. "Did you clean up in here?"

He shrugged. "It was time. The dust mites were building condos in front of the TV. It was getting so I couldn't see."

She gave a wan smile and teared up again. "Darn it."

"Tell me before I go out hurting random people for maybe bothering you."

She sniffed. "It's the shop."

"The shop?" Not a guy harassing her, then. He started to relax.

She nodded. "The place I'd had my eye on, the one near the garage? The landlady told me it was mine. I'm so close to getting the money all together, J.T. My budget is nearly there. I swung by today, just to look at the place, and someone's in there." She started crying again.

"Rena, you'll find a better spot." God knew she'd worked her ass off for years trying to finance her own salon. Rena cut his hair. She styled the guys at the garage and a bunch of their friends too. It wasn't pity or friendship that had his buddies going to Rena, though.

The girl had skill and a smile that made you want to spend time with her.

"Look. You've saved. You've taken business classes, and you're one hell of a stylist. Everyone likes you. Even Fletcher, that shithead, though he hates himself for it."

She gave a small laugh and hitched her breath on a sob.

"You'll make it work. If that shop wasn't ready, then the right one is out there waiting for you."

"But it took me forever to find that place. It's perfect."

"It *was* perfect. The next one *will be* perfect. Let me help. I know people." And he knew one particular *people* whose mother was a real estate guru. Wouldn't Hope love him asking her mom questions about her job and being friendly? He could envision the rage in his curvy blond and already imagined the fireworks that might follow in bed.

Man, he had to get the woman there, then out of his head. She was driving him insane.

"How about you?" Rena asked, pulling back to study him. "How are you doing?"

Uh-uh. No way was he letting his gossipy cousin, whom he loved dearly, learn about his fixation on Hope. He'd never hear the end of it. Del was bad enough. "We're not finished talking about you. Now what's this about you and Heller? You finally put the bastard out of his misery or what?"

She blushed. "There is nothing between Axel and me. He just lost his mother, J.T. I feel so bad for him. We talk a lot, and he's so sweet under that cool, aloof, ah, I mean—"

"Serial killer–like exterior?"

She glared at him. "Axel is a gentleman. He's never been mean or rude to me. Ever."

"He'd better not be. I don't care how big and bad he is. I'll take him apart."

She patted his chest. "You're a good cousin."

"So are you." He patted her head, or tried to. She slapped his hand.

"Not the hair, unless you want to lose that hand."

"Well, that got you off your pity party, didn't it?"

"Jerk." She gave him a watery smile though. "So what's your deal?"

"My deal?"

"Please, J.T. The only women you hang with at Ray's should charge by the hour."

"Hey."

"Truth hurts. You dish it out, be prepared to take it." She blew her nose, sounding like a foghorn, and he tried not to smile to avoid hurting her feelings. "You were at Ray's with Hope Donnigan, the same woman you couldn't take your eyes off of at Del's wedding. The same woman who makes you nervous whenever you see her."

"What?" He scoffed. "You're dreaming."

"The same woman you barely took your eyes from at Uncle Liam's almost two weeks ago. You're into her big time, and we all know it. Plus, I heard from a certain bird that you were seen bowling with her and having fun. Smiling and flirting all night."

"Did this little bird have a big mouth? And was she possibly pregnant?"

Rena shrugged. "I've been sworn to silence."

He barked a laugh. "You? Silent?"

"Now who's being mean?"

"Oh, stop. I'm kidding." He wasn't. But at least Rena no longer had tears in her eyes, more intent on his crush than her lost salon space.

"You're different about Hope, Cousin. I've watched you. You really like her."

"Nah. I mean, she's great. We're just friends."

"Sure."

"We are. I'm helping her pull one over on her mom. That's all."

"Uh-huh."

"I'm getting the feeling you don't believe me."

"That's true. I don't."

"Rena..."

"You *like* like her. But you're too scared to make a move."

"Excuse me, but I've already made moves." *Shit. Hadn't meant to let that slip out.*

"Aha!"

"As in, I'm my charming self, and we've kissed a few times maybe. But that's it. Del doesn't want me screwing things up with the McCauleys if I sully one of their precious Donnigan relations. So I'm keeping my distance."

"Bull. Oh sure, you want to keep Del happy. But when, not if, you dump Hope, it'll be for the typical reasons you always give."

"I don't know what you're talking about."

"Don't you?" She patted his arm. "You are so messed up from what your dad went through that you've never let yourself truly fall for a girl. And you're thirty-two. Now that's sad."

"That's crap. I've had plenty of girlfriends."

"That you brought home for family dinner? That you hang out with for fun? That you go bowling with or bring to hang out with your friends? Not on hookup night at the bar, but to play darts with and just be yourself with?"

"Ah, well, that's different."

"Exactly."

He felt agitated. "You don't know what you're talking about. But you're upset, so I'll let it slide."

"Sure."

"And stop agreeing with me," he muttered, annoyed.

"Okay."

When he glared at her, she chuckled. "Sorry. No, I won't stop agreeing with you."

He gave a reluctant grin. "Come on. Want to watch a movie together? I can cook up some popcorn."

"Sure. What do you want to watch?"

He turned on the TV and flipped through channels. They settled on *The Cabin in the Woods*, one of his favorite flicks. Funny and horrifying, an homage to horror films. As they watched, he tried not to think about how much he liked the blond in the movie…if only she looked and acted a little more like Hope.

Hmm. That was something they hadn't done yet. A movie together. He wondered what she'd be into seeing.

"Stop thinking about Hope and focus on the monsters," Rena said before shoving a handful of popcorn in her mouth.

He flushed. "I am not thinking of—"

"Uh-huh."

"And stop agreeing with me!"

Chapter 12

Thursday evening, Hope stood in the foyer of J.T.'s home and stared. She hadn't expected such a nice place, though she shouldn't have been surprised. He was an artist, after all.

"Come on in."

"Have some candy, little girl," she added in a low voice, but he must have heard because he laughed.

"I promise, I won't bite. Yet." He snickered and grabbed her bag. "Don't worry. I won't pounce until after we've studied for the big test tomorrow."

She grinned. "It does feel like high school, doesn't it? Cramming for exams in your least favorite classes?"

"I wouldn't know. I didn't study that much."

"And still got A's though, didn't you? I heard Del making fun of you the other night. Suck-up."

"Hey. Not my fault I'm smart. The only class I deliberately tanked was English. I hated the instructor, but as a horny eighteen-year-old, I felt it was my duty to seduce her."

"You did not." She stared, wide-eyed. Then again, looking at J.T., she could believe he had.

"She was twenty-three and had really long legs. She sucked as a teacher but wasn't too bad in bed. Meh. I was young and stupid back then."

"Back then?"

He frowned at her. "But I also had a heart, and since

rumors went around that we'd slept together, I told her to give me a C minus so it wouldn't look like we'd been screwing for special favors."

"That's a lame cover."

"Yeah, well, they bought it. Of course, she got busted for sleeping with my buddies who did get A's in her class. Didn't help they failed everything else. I was the opposite, so the staff believed me."

"Wow. Nothing that exciting happened in my school. We had druggies get nailed and one teen pregnancy. That was it. Oh, and the science teacher and PE teacher got busted for having an affair."

"Nice." He grinned. Then he crooked a finger. "Hope, come closer. I promise, it'll all be okay."

"Stop." She felt silly for being nervous, but that duffel bag she'd brought signaled a turn she hadn't wanted to take with him. A sleepover at his house. A prelude to sex with J.T.—the sex she insisted she wasn't going to have.

"You know, we're not ever going to do anything you don't want to," he said in a serious voice, his expression calm. He stepped closer to her when she remained rooted to the floor and tilted her chin up so he could meet her gaze. "I swear, Hope. You're never in any danger from me. Remember, you're in charge of this."

"I am?"

"Sure. I'm the guy you came to use and abuse. Think of me as a prop."

"Stop saying 'use and abuse.'" She shook her head. "Wait. Think of you as what?"

"A prop. You're selling your mom one whopper of a story tomorrow, and I'm the best thing you've got to get her to buy it. I'm a prop."

"Like a prop dummy?"

He sighed. "I'm pretty sure the word 'dummy' didn't cross my mind." He brightened. "Think of me as a sex toy."

"Oh, that's helping."

"Yeah. I'm the super-deluxe model. I'm sexy and handsome." He flexed for her, and she bit her lip to keep from laughing out loud. "Plus, I'm hung like an elephant."

She did laugh then. "You win. I'm no longer nervous. Now I'm just embarrassed for you. Let's eat before I remember how annoying you are."

His smug grin only made it that much more difficult not to fall for him. She was halfway there already. What kind of guy agreed to help a girl out of a mess like Hope's with no expectation of repayment? No favor for a favor? Having sex was up to her. She knew he wanted it, but he would never force her.

Charm and fun were J.T.'s style. He made her feel comfortable and safe. A man with his size and looks could pretty much take what he wanted. But she doubted that would ever occur to J.T. A gentleman to his bones, he'd never do anything without his partner's consent. Integrity and honor were at his core.

Aside from the men in her family, J.T. Webster was the nicest man she'd ever met.

He looked wary. "Why are you staring at me like that?"

"I just realized something." She put her arm through the crook of his and let him lead her through the living area into his closed-off kitchen. "You're a nice man."

He pulled away from her, his expression horrified. "*Nice?*"

"Yes. That's a compliment."

"*Nice* is not a compliment. Nice is awful. Boring. Asexual."

She rolled her eyes. "Whatever. Hey, great kitchen."

"*Nice* is for Boy Scouts. I was never a Boy Scout. I'm badass. I scare people. *Nice?*" He set two plates down on the counter and continued to rant about better adjectives to describe himself.

While he wound down, she took a look around the townhome. The first floor was narrow but deep. She'd walked through the living area into an open kitchen. Behind them was a small dining area. He had an upstairs as well, and they'd passed the stairs to get to the kitchen. A powder room sat off the back of the kitchen, and stacked washer and dryer units had been curtained off inside it.

"Hey, are you listening to me?" he asked as he spooned chicken Caesar salad onto their plates. He'd also set out a few slices of stromboli from her favorite Italian place and glasses of water. It felt odd to know he remembered things she'd told him a while ago.

"Yes. My mistake. You're a complete asshole. I can't believe I'm spending time with such a narcissistic jerkwad."

"Okay, then." He nodded. "Good."

She laughed. "I like your house. It's clean and tidy, and your furniture is actually nice."

"When I first moved in, I had crappier stuff. But I've since traded a good bit for nicer pieces. Believe it or not, Tull is considered a premier tattoo studio in Seattle."

"I know." She smiled. "You're an artist, J.T. I never thought otherwise."

She'd discomfited him, and the surprisingly shy smile of pleasure on his face captivated her. Made him more human, less sexual deity needing worship.

"Now, let's study for the test."

An hour later, he'd committed her favorites to memory, and she'd pretended to relearn his. Sadly, she remembered everything she'd ever heard about the man. It was as if she had a J.T. section in her brain constantly greedy for information.

"Something else you should know," he said as he grabbed the cherry pie she'd brought with her, because she'd once overhead Del mention it was his favorite. He placed a big slice on her plate. "I'm clean. Like, no STDs, and I always use condoms."

She'd been eager to sample the pie until he said that. Her appetite fled, nerves replacing a need for sweets.

"What about you?" He didn't seem to have the same problem, put a large slice of pie on his plate, and dug in.

"Me?" Her high pitch embarrassed her. So she coughed to clear her throat and ignored the mirth in his gaze. "Um, I'm clean. Or at least I was when I had my last exam, which was right after Greg. But then, I haven't been with anyone since him except you." She frowned. "So if I have any issues, it's your fault."

"Oh, honey, you have a ton of issues, but you can't lay them at my door." He ate more pie. "Damn, this is good."

"For your information, Mr. Webster, I am a responsible, mature adult. I do have a few things I'm working out concerning my mother," she said primly, aware he liked to stir her up for some reason and unable to resist the bait. Especially with him laughing at her. "But one thing I am not is sexually irresponsible. I don't jump into bed with any dick." She glared at him to let him know that word applied to him, which he found hilarious.

"I hope you snort out a cherry," she said darkly. To which he laughed even harder. As usual, his laughter tugged at her to join in. "My point is that I don't sleep around. And I've always used protection. Well, in a new relationship. Only when I've been with someone for a long time do I rely on something other than condoms, and that's to prevent pregnancy."

He pushed away his clean plate and leaned closer to her. "You on birth control?"

"Yes." So they were really having this conversation. She took a deep breath and let it out, the charge in the atmosphere impossible to ignore.

"I've been with a lot of women. I won't lie. I also told you I don't cheat, and I don't. But because my relationships—the real ones, not like our fake one—don't last, I always wear a condom. Plus I'm not always a trusting guy, leaving birth control to the ladies."

"Good to know." She ignored the smirk he'd shot her when he said "not like our fake one."

"Right. Well, I'm letting you know I do one woman at a time."

"You do them?"

He waved away her pique. "*Do* as in relationships, Ms. Women's Libber. I respect women. Hell, I love women. By all accounts, my mom was an angel. My aunt is crazy with men but a real keeper with kids. And I love my sister and cousin. Period." His grin turned conceited. "I'm just letting you know how lucky you'll be when I'm giving you more orgasms…tonight."

She blew out a breath. "So you feel confident about tomorrow?"

"Yep. You wanting a tattoo, that's to mess with your mom? You never really wanted one?"

The change in subject threw her for a moment, and she had to think about what he'd said. "No. That part is true. I've always wanted a tattoo. Something special, something that's uniquely me. I've never gotten one because it's a big step, and I don't have an idea yet of what I'd be okay wearing for the rest of my life."

He had his elbows on the table, his chin in his hands, and studied her. "Nothing has to be forever. There's laser removal and modifications we can make for those who regret their decisions. But yeah, I feel you. I was the same way before I got mine."

"No one in my family has one, and my dad was Navy. My brothers were Marines."

"Huh."

"It would be cool if I was the first to get one. And of course, my mother hates the thought, so win-win."

He laughed. "You're too funny."

"Too immature, you mean." She sighed and slumped in her seat. "I know it. This whole thing with my mom is stupid. Really, really juvenile. But J.T., she's been on my case my whole life. I can never live up to Linda Donnigan's standards, no matter what I do."

~

The sad face she made turned their whole sexy vibe into something else. Not only did he want to make love to Hope, but now he started thinking of what he'd tattoo on that creamy skin if he had the chance. And it would have to be perfect. As much as he'd love to write *Property of J.T. Webster* on her hands, chest, and forehead, he had a feeling she'd reject the idea.

Hearing her being so down on herself didn't help either. Because when she hurt, he hurt. And that connection felt an awful lot like what his father had described having with J.T.'s mom.

Before he could have a major freak-out about his rampant emotions, the glitter in Hope's gaze stopped all panic. He needed to make her feel better first. He'd worry about himself later.

"Come here." He pushed his seat back and patted his thigh, as surprised as she was when she accepted and sat on his lap. She sat sideways, her legs dangling over his, her arms around his neck, and her head on his shoulder, her hand over his heart.

He wondered if she could hear the organ pounding. Holding her like this, sensing how *right* she felt in his arms, broke down another section of the wall he'd been trying to hold firm against her.

"You're fine. Your mom's the wacko."

She laughed against his chest. "She is, but so am I. I… J.T., don't tell anyone I said this."

"Never." He squeezed her tight.

"But I think I'm a lot like her. Sometimes it's like I have to be right, no matter what."

Not the news flash she thought it was.

"So what? We're all like our parents. I'm a lot like Liam. Stubborn, weird about dating. A hard worker."

"But those are good traits. Well, except the weirdness and dating part."

"Your mom has good traits too, right?"

"Well, yes. But I don't share those."

"What are they?" He kissed the top of her head and offered comfort, safety, assurance. But when he smelled the floral scent of her shampoo, his body stiffened—all over.

Hope didn't seem to notice. "Mom is tenacious, I guess. She's smart and funny, and driven. But that's not always a good thing."

"It is in this context. You're smart and funny and driven. You don't take anyone's handouts. Hell, you didn't even date the rich dude she tried to set you up with. I bet you've had a lot of guys want to buy you."

"What?"

"You know, like wine and dine you, set you up as their honey where you could just look pretty while they provided for you."

"Well, yeah. It's embarrassing to admit, but I used to get hit on a lot by older guys."

"Used to?"

She blushed. "Still do sometimes. And yeah, they're always trying to buy me stuff."

"You aren't someone who can be bought. That's a good thing." He kissed her head again and did his best to think pure thoughts. *Be there for her, dickhead. Don't push her for sex now. She's talking. Listen.*

"See? You're so nice, J.T. You have a big heart."

That's not all that's big...and getting bigger. "Stop squirming," he ordered, his voice husky. "I'm totally fine with trying to teach your mom a lesson. I'm having fun with you, so quit worrying."

She finally leaned back, which took pressure off his erection. He saw her big, brown eyes, full of concern. "It's not her I'm worried about. I don't want you to think badly of me for this. It was fun at first, but I'm better than this."

"Well, fuck. I'm not." He kissed her, and the tension leached out of her as she kissed him back, melting in his arms. He shifted her so that she sat over him, pressed groin to groin, her legs spread on either side of his. Somehow, he'd tangled his hands in her thick hair, and the feel of the long, silky strands added to the sensual haze fogging all his good intentions.

"Damn. Sorry, baby."

"I'm not." She dragged her mouth over his cheek, down to his neck, and bit him.

His blood pressure shot up a thousand points.

"This fake relationship is really working for me," she whispered and continued to kiss him up and down his neck. "You taste salty. Yummy." She moaned against his throat, and he found himself pressing them closer, one hand on her lower back, the other on her thigh, where he could manage the motion of her hips.

"Hope, I, uh..." He had no idea what to say. At some point his cock had taken over, leading him astray.

"I was scared to have sex with you, not because I'm afraid of you. Because I'm scared I'll like it too much and get clingy. But since this is just us getting to know each other and having fun, not dating or anything, I'm okay with it."

He couldn't make much sense of that. He had a feeling that, like him, she was rationalizing the need to fuck like rabbits, even while knowing it probably wasn't a good idea.

He didn't do committed relationships. She had being a wife and having two-point-five kids in her DNA. He ran a tattoo shop and had experienced jail firsthand. She'd gone to college, worked in finance, and her most rebellious phase seemed to consist of bringing him home to her mom and dad. His had been to steal a car and ram it through the wall of a guy giving his dad a hard time, back when Webster's had been teetering on bankruptcy and the banker assigned to his father's loan had tried to shake Liam down.

Fortunately, J.T. hadn't gotten caught that time. But the booze, the girls, and the occasional thievery could have gone sideways, had his father not stepped into his ass back in the day.

Hope had gotten good grades and acceptance to college as a result of *her* teen years.

He shook his head, trying to tell himself to end this before it began.

Then he realized it was okay, because none of this was real. And if he didn't do something soon, his dick might fall off from an overabundance of desire needing an outlet.

~

Hope felt him lift her, like the last time. For once, she liked the fact she was small enough to fit easily in J.T.'s arms. Though she still wondered if that impressive part between his legs would fit inside her. She didn't think she'd ever been with a guy that big before.

"I'm having a tough time thinking about anything other than getting inside you," he confessed, his voice low. Arousing. He took her up the stairs as if she weighed nothing. They passed a bedroom and a bathroom and entered his room.

A big bed frame, matching nightstand, and closet were all she made out before he lowered her onto a king-size bed. It took up most of the room, but as large as J.T. was, he'd need the space.

He didn't give her time to undress and instead took her clothes off for her. "Let me," he insisted.

Once she was naked, he just looked at her. "Fucking gorgeous. I have to draw you at some point, okay?"

She blinked and nodded, seeing the artist as well as the man.

Then the moment passed as he stripped naked. He froze, staring at her. "I'm going to slow down, because if I get inside you now, I'm going to ride you and come in two seconds. And I want tonight to last."

She stared at his cock, amazed at his size.

The thing bobbed when he walked to her, and he ordered, "Touch me."

Where she found the patience to tease him, she didn't know. "But won't it explode if I do? Or should I kiss it all better? You look a little…flushed."

He groaned. "You put your mouth on me, and I'll come. Do me a favor and grab some condoms out of my top drawer." He nodded to his nightstand.

She turned over and scooted toward it, but as she grabbed a few packets, she felt his hands on her ass.

"Give them to me. I'm going to calm down and give you a back massage. How's that?"

She handed the packets to him. "Are you sure you took an anatomy class, ever? Because your hands are not on my back."

He was kneading her glutes, and she moaned at how good it felt.

J.T. chuckled. "Such a smart-*ass*. Don't worry. I'm just slowing us down a bit."

"Whatever you want," she said and closed her eyes, her head tilted to the side. "Because that feels amazing. I still want to have sex, but now I'm thinking I want more of a back or butt rub first. Mmm."

He worked her glutes, her hamstrings, and back up to her lower back, rubbing out tension she hadn't realized was there. Then he slowly lowered himself over her, and they touched, skin to skin.

She hissed at the contact, feeling overpowered—and loving it.

"God, don't move." He groaned. J.T. leaned up on his hands and kissed her shoulders, her back. Then he kissed her cheek before whispering, "I'm wearing the condom. I want to fuck you so hard. Over and over."

He rocked against her as he said it, and her body went up in flames, anticipating when he'd turn her over.

"This first time will be quick, baby. I'm sorry about that." He eased up and pulled her into a kneeling position, on her hands and knees. He nudged her legs wider. "Our first time should be face-to-face. With me eating that golden pussy, licking you up, teething that clit. But I can't wait." He ran a hand down her flank and curled it around her thigh. His fingers slid through the dew gathered between her legs, her body slick and ready to receive him.

A thick finger eased into her, and she arched up.

"Easy." He was breathing hard, sliding that finger in and out, but so slowly. "Oh fuck. You're ready, aren't you, baby? Ready for a fast fuck."

"Yes," she moaned. "I really want you."

"Damn. I wanted to wait, but I can't." He withdrew

his finger, gliding over her sensitive clit. "Oh, you're hard, aren't you?" He gave a hoarse laugh. "But not as hard as me."

Then he was sliding inside her again—with something thicker and longer than his finger. He moved slowly, so big, and so incredibly filling. She was impatient to feel all of him.

She tried to shift under him, but he held her fast, continuing to penetrate with a torturously slow progression.

Until he was balls-deep and could go no farther.

"Oh fuck. Fuck. Don't move." He lifted up, and the motion pushed him deeper still. "I have to… I can't stop from…"

"J.T., fuck me already," she ordered.

When he pulled out and slammed back inside her, she lost all control.

The ecstasy of his taking couldn't be denied. She felt so close to him as her body clamped down, letting him get two more thrusts before she pulled him with her. He yelled as he climaxed, filling the condom and clutching her hips hard enough to leave bruises.

The tiny pulses as he jerked inside her set her off again, and for the first time in her life, she thought she experienced multiple orgasms. She couldn't stop coming.

When she could finally breathe again, J.T. slumped over her, still joined, kissing her wherever he could reach.

"Oh, baby. So damn good." He released a tremulous breath. "Fuck. That was out of this world." When he withdrew, she felt bereft. God, she wanted to cry. It had been a crazy surge of powerful emotion, a cathartic experience, even. As in, spiritual.

I'm losing it from great sex. So sad. She trembled on her hands and knees.

"Be right back." J.T. left the bed, and she collapsed face-first into it.

By the time he returned, she'd managed to roll herself over and stared at his ceiling. One of the bulbs had burned out in his overhead light. "You should replace that." She pointed.

"I'll get right on it." He leaped over her onto the bed, then rolled onto his side and leaned up on his elbow. "You okay?"

"Hold on. I'm trying to get the last brain cell I own working again."

He smiled, his gaze tender. "Me too." He stroked down her cheek, her throat, to her breasts and lingered, cupping her, petting her, then lightly pinching her nipples and sending streaks of fire to her core. She gasped, and his grin widened. "Sensitive there, eh? Me too." He leaned down to take her nipple between his lips and sucked.

"Oh." She clenched his head to her, then realized she was the one keeping him there.

He pulled back to watch her as he continued his sensual exploration down her body. He left no part of her front untouched, even caressing her toes.

When he returned to her face, he kissed her. "Hope, I just..." He sighed, leaned his forehead against hers, and closed his eyes.

"I know. Me too."

Neither spoke again for a while, but they didn't have to. Both knew something unexpected had happened. Not talking about it seemed the safest thing to do. They lay, him caressing her, her accepting his petting, for a while.

Before any awkwardness settled between them, J.T. nudged her with a returning erection.

"Um, I hate to ruin the mood, but I'm ready for round two."

"What took you so long?"

He laughed, and the emotional intensity of the moment gave way to joyous laughter once more.

Chapter 13

AFTER FINALLY MAKING LOVE TO HER FACE-TO-FACE, J.T. let her sleep for a few hours. He'd clearly tuckered the poor girl out, a fact he planned to throw in her face tomorrow. Well, after they succeeded at her parents'. He didn't want to super stress her out.

He'd watched her sleep for a long time. *God. He had it bad.* And what the hell was wrong with him, taking her from behind for their first time ever?

So romantic. She was lucky he hadn't pegged her ass and followed with an *I love you*. He snorted, but the thought of the l-word had him choking back panic, for real. J.T. had never been so close to a woman before. Oh, not physically. But emotionally.

He felt so in tune with Hope in so many ways. They had a lot in common. And he liked the fact that she was honest enough with herself to realize how immature it was to want to trick her mother. Yet she was doing it anyway to prove a point. Tenacious? Um, yeah.

Sexy, fun, adorable?

Yep.

She rolled toward him in her sleep, and he drew her closer to his chest, tucking her in tight.

That funny ache in his heart returned. He stroked her hair, loving the feel of her in his arms. Fuck, but he'd never had such deep feelings for a woman before.

Not romantic feelings, at least. He loved his sister, his cousin, his aunt. He loved his dad's Sophie too. Like a mom. But the need to protect, to care for, to help Hope was like a goddamn prime directive. He couldn't ignore it, and he kind of wanted to.

Fucking—no, *making love*—to Hope had been better than anything he'd imagined. She fit him to perfection. His second orgasm had been even better than the first. Not as desperate, and he'd watched her come when he did, the two of them staring into each other's eyes.

Romantic as shit.

He closed his eyes and groaned.

And that's when he felt clever little hands cupping his dick and reminding him that he had a naked and willing woman in his arms.

"Hope," he whispered. A glance at the clock on his bed showed two a.m. They'd both be tired tomorrow, but he could handle a fuzzy Friday. He had a bit of touching up today and some sketching appointments with clients. Nothing major.

She nuzzled his chest and kept stroking him with her hands. Her fingers moved down, soon cupping his balls, and he moaned and spread his legs wider, easing onto his back and taking her with him, now resting her on top of him.

"Hmm. Tasty," she said with a throaty chuckle. But instead of kissing him on the mouth, she proceeded to kiss a trail down his body, ending at his cock.

"Hope." He tugged her by the shoulder. "Turn around, baby."

She didn't listen and started licking him. Her lips

tugged at his cockhead before slipping over his shaft, taking him in her mouth.

He groaned her name and surged deeper, not meaning to, but his body had a will of its own. "So good. Oh yeah. Eat me up, Sexy."

She moaned and sucked, caressing his sac while she did. And his arousal grew fast and furious.

"Hope, turn around. Let's see who comes first, huh? Winner gives the loser a massage tomorrow. Winner's choice."

She pulled away to grin up at him. "You're on. Think I can swallow another mouthful before you do?"

"I can't wait."

He helped her turn, and then her pussy was in his face, her mouth over him once more, and he buried his mouth in heaven.

He licked and sucked, nibbled on her tight clit and prayed he had the strength to last. He'd already come twice a few hours ago. He'd had a long day and should have been tired. But she energized him, was all he could think. Because his cock was as hard as it had ever been, his balls tight and needing a release.

The thought of coming down her throat was enough to get him really going, and he increased his attention to her honeyed sex. She tasted damn good. J.T. knew a woman's body. He'd made getting to know it an art form. But he'd never had anything so fine as Hope Donnigan. Curvy, soft, yet toned in all the right places.

He loved the tiny moans she made as she neared completion. Loved the sweetness of her responses, the lack of artifice in her affection. Because every kiss and caress had meaning with Hope. None of this damn fake relationship was casual.

And the thought of having enough of her trust to go skin to skin helped get him to the edge. Especially when the sly woman used her teeth on that sensitive part of him, just under his cockhead.

He lapped her up and added a finger, pumping inside her with faster movements, his end too near to ignore.

He moaned a warning, unable to stop thrusting up while she bore down with those ripe lips. He ground her pussy against his mouth, trying to get more of her, to get deeper inside her.

He had half a mind to yank her off him and come up inside that hot pussy.

And he lost it. He cried out as he came in great bursts of pleasure, nearly blacking out as he drew her clit in his mouth while he came down her throat.

Then she was there with him, flooding him with an intense orgasm that seized around his finger like a vise.

Hope pulled away and keened, the waves of repletion now ripples as she eased into a euphoric glow. She turned around, still on top of him, and kissed him.

He tasted himself on her mouth and thought it the sexiest thing.

"I taste me on our lips," she said, as if reading his mind and mirroring the sentiment. "I like it."

"Not as much as I do. Your pussy is fine, baby. So damn sweet."

She blushed prettily. "Is this where I say I think you were right? It is nine inches. I measured."

He laughed. "Told you."

"Yep. Hung like an elephant. I think you bruised my

throat." She paused. "We should do it again until I get it right."

And right there. He stumbled again, one step closer to losing his mind and falling in love.

No amount of telling herself to relax worked. Standing with J.T. on her parents' doorstep, Hope tried to squash the bundle of nerves taking root inside her.

"Easy. We're not facing a firing squad," J.T. teased and rubbed her back.

She glanced at the flowers in his hand. "I'm still not sure that's a good idea."

"What? Coming as myself and trying to make nice instead of wearing a bandana and an eye patch, and smoking some weed to show them how badass I really am?"

"Not funny."

He laughed. "It is. Can you see me dressing all gangster—minus the eye patch, 'cause that's just stupid—and throwing down with your mom?"

She grinned. "Okay, that is funny. But I'd still bet odds my mom would pin you before you could say 'uncle.'"

"Nah. I'm king when it comes to wrestling." He leaned closer and whispered, "Like I pinned you early this morning. Remember?"

She blushed, recalling all too well their sexual marathon. Still unsure if sleeping with J.T. would end up being the biggest mistake of her life or the best sexual experience ever, she turned to tell him to behave and froze, caught by the strange look on his face. Not sexual or teasing, but intense…longing?

She cupped his cheek, trying to see what he didn't say.

The door opened. "Ahem."

She turned to see her father standing there.

Hope blushed and dropped her hand. "Oh, ah, hey, Dad." She leaned in to kiss him on the cheek. "This is my friend, J.T."

"Hello." Her father held out a hand, and J.T. shook it.

They stood nearly at eye-level, with her father a tiny bit taller but not nearly as broad. Dressed conservatively in a short-sleeved collared shirt and jeans, J.T. exposed enough muscle to be impressive. But then, she found him impressive with or without clothes.

Crap. I have got to stop thinking about stuff like that and get my head on straight.

"I know you," her father said as their hands parted. "J.T. Webster? Del's brother?"

"Yep." J.T. smiled.

"That's right. We met you at the wedding." He shot Hope an amused look. "Come on in. You have to meet my wife."

"Oh, joy," she muttered as they followed him inside.

"Hope, be nice," her father counseled.

J.T. smirked at her. "Yeah, be nice, or else."

"Or else what?" Landon barked.

"Well?" Gavin said.

Terrific. Her brothers. Just what she didn't need.

She turned to see Landon, Gavin, and Theo—who had yet to speak, his mouth stuffed with food—watching her.

"Oh goody, the gang's all here," she deadpanned.

J.T. coughed but didn't manage to hide all his

laughter. "These are for your wife." He held the flowers to her dad.

"That's nice of you. Hey, Linda. Hope and her boyfriend are here."

The word *boyfriend* gave Hope a start, but she hid it well. She still felt boneless from their time together. *Which is good*, she told herself. *That will make us seem more real*. She sure the heck felt like they had something going. Last night had been a turning point. Even J.T. was acting differently. He'd picked her up from work earlier and had planted a long, lingering kiss on her that started a slow burn that had yet to fade.

And the proprietary hand on her back, the arm around her shoulders, or like now, the hand holding hers as he held flowers out to her approaching mother. All gestures of shared intimacy and possession. But was he acting or being real? And why did it bother her so much to think he only played the part she'd assigned him?

Linda studied him, then slowly looked down to their joined hands. "So you're the boyfriend?"

He nodded. "And you're the mother." He mirrored her inspection. "Man, you sure are pretty."

Linda blinked, accepted the flowers with polite thanks, and turned without saying anything more.

"She'll put them in water and be right back." Van rocked back on his heels, and Hope had the feeling he was amused. "So you and my daughter are dating, hmm?"

"That's fascinating," Landon said. He stood next to their father, his arms crossed, wearing an attitude to match his *USMC Proud* T-shirt. The ex-Marine major could be a bulldog when he wanted answers. And he clearly wanted to shove his big nose in her business.

As did Gavin, the second oldest. Dark-haired whereas Landon was blond, he took more after their father in looks and disposition. He smiled but didn't seem as friendly as she might have expected. "J.T. I haven't seen you since the wedding."

"Can you believe my sister has been a Mrs. for over two solid months now? How crazy is that?" He squeezed Hope's hand. "Hell, I remember when she used to get me to braid her hair for her." He shook his head. "And we played fix the scooter with her plastic tools. Ah, the good old days."

Theo came up behind Hope and squeezed her in a hug that lifted her off her feet.

"*Theo*."

"Hi, big sis." He set her down and grinned. "Hi, J.T."

"Hey, Theo." J.T. smiled. "How's the flower shop treating you?"

"Good. I'm getting better tips. Since I quit the coffee shop, I have more time to look for a better second job."

Van frowned. "You quit the coffee shop?"

"Ah, can we talk about this later?"

Gavin sighed. "He broke up with his girlfriend, and it got awkward. There. No need for a convo later."

"Gavin." Theo glared.

"What? It was supposed to be a secret?"

Hope turned to J.T. "How did you know he worked at a flower shop?"

"I ran into Theo one day while I was picking up flowers for—"

"One of your many girlfriends?" Landon interrupted, playing the role of protective big brother.

J.T. answered, "I have a stable of about five of them,

and I rotate roses and lilies to keep my women straight." He snorted. "No, dumbass. They were for my dad for Sophie. It was supposed to be a surprise."

Landon scowled. "Dumbass?"

"I don't have girl*friends*. I have one girl*friend*, and you're looking at her." J.T. scowled back, not at all intimidated by her brother. She wondered if they went toe-to-toe, who'd win. They looked evenly matched. For all that her brothers excelled in the Marine Corps and taught self-defense, J.T. had a wealth of knowledge he'd learned on the streets growing up.

Hope grinned. "Ha. That's what you get."

Gavin and Theo chuckled, and Gavin said, "Told you so."

"Told him what?" Hope wanted to know.

Linda returned, the flowers now in a vase she set on the coffee table. "Dinner is ready if you'd all sit at the table."

Her parents set the food out while the rest of them sat down. Hope sat at the other end of the dining table, across from her father, who took the head chair. Her mother sat on one side of him, while Hope's older brothers sat on the other side. J.T. sat sandwiched between Hope and Theo, who sat next to Linda. With any luck, their current buffers would provide a bit of ease from the tension she could sense growing once more.

Landon and Linda kept staring at J.T., then looking at Hope, as if waiting for something. She didn't know what. Theo kept his head down, ready to shovel in the food, she was sure. And Gavin and her father joked about the gym where Gavin worked.

"So you think I'm getting puny, is that it, boy?" her father asked.

"Sorry, Dad. But yeah. Come down to Jameson's, and I'll work on bulking you back up." Gavin, a trainer at the popular Jameson's Gym, was the go-to man for everyone serious about health and training. Hope loved that he'd lost that wounded look he'd come back to the States with. After too many years fighting overseas in the military, Gavin had seen and done a lot to wound his soul. But now he'd settled, found love, and thought more about the future than the past. Zoe was good for him. And speaking of which…

"Hey, Gavin. Where's Zoe?"

"She and Ava are having a movie night. It was some chick flick I had no urge to see."

Well, at least Hope didn't have to deal with Ava's discerning gaze, because *Dr.* Ava would no doubt see through Hope's calm facade to the confused woman afraid of falling for her pretend boyfriend.

Who had no problem with his appetite.

J.T. tucked into the food her parents passed around. "You guys eat like this all the time? Because, wow. What a spread."

Linda looked down her nose at him.

Oh, goody. It was on.

"Really? You don't seem like a small man who's missed too many meals. Are you telling us you don't eat?"

J.T. smiled at her. "Well, with all my kids underfoot, I try to make sure they're fed before I get my plate. And you know, what with me in and out of jail all the time, I gotta see to the young'uns first."

Hope sighed. He wasn't sticking to the plan. His boasts were nothing so much as screaming they were lies. If he kept it up, Linda would never believe their carefully constructed story. Then Hope wouldn't be able to rub her nose it in afterward when they told the truth about J.T. being a decent, no-drama human being.

Her father wore a huge grin. He apparently wasn't buying any of J.T.'s nonsense. Gavin rolled his eyes, and Theo ate and laughed, another lost cause. But Landon, like their mother, seemed poised to pounce.

Then Landon ruined it by laughing. "You're so full of shit. Young'funs? Buddy, I know for a fact you're not a hick, and you sure as shit weren't raised *down South*."

Linda glared. "Landon, watch your mouth."

"Yeah," Hope said, hating to agree with her mother, but Landon was killing the mood before she'd gotten a chance to scam everyone.

"Oh, please." Linda huffed. "I know 'your man,' Hope. He's no more your boyfriend than he's a prison escapee. And I highly doubt Liam lets his son wander the country impregnating women left and right."

J.T. choked on his water. "You know my dad?"

"We've met. He *is* dating my sister." Linda shook her head. "I knew you were lying, Hope. But pulling poor J.T. into your scheme is beneath you."

"I'll tell you exactly what's beneath me. Or *whom*, I should probably say," she started, losing all sense.

~

"God, no," Theo sputtered.

"Stop. I can't hear this. I'll need even more therapy to be right again," Gavin whined.

Landon grimaced.

J.T. squeezed her hand under the table and took charge before her parents could get a word in. "Linda, you'll have to forgive us. Hope was annoyed with you and told you about us before we were ready. It was my fault, really."

"I don't—"

He talked over his *girlfriend*, knowing Hope would be annoyed, but he just couldn't go along with her scheme. Too many of the Donnigans knew his father, and J.T. had socialized with Landon and Theo a few times as well. Just in passing, but they'd know he didn't possess a poor reputation at all, unless it had to do with being a little too popular with the ladies.

"Hope is smart, funny, and beautiful. She doesn't need any help snagging a man. She's got great taste—she has me."

The others laughed, though Landon didn't seem too pleased, and Hope's mom still looked unconvinced. A glance at Hope showed her thoughtful instead of annoyed, so maybe he had a shot at getting home tonight unscathed.

He forked more steak into his mouth, wondering if he could keep Van when this was all over, because damn, the man could cook.

"Just to be clear." Linda enunciated each word. "You have not been in prison recently. You don't have a litter of children by different mothers, and you aren't a tattoo artist."

"No jail." Recently, she'd said. "I don't have any kids." *That I know of*. "But I do own the best studio in the city. Tull Paint & Body is my place."

"And they're amazing." Hope nodded. "You should see some of the artwork they do. Oh my gosh. J.T. is so talented."

He flushed, wondering why the compliment had gone

to his head when Hope was no doubt just gushing to screw with her mom.

"I thought about getting a tattoo," Theo said. "But Mom would have a hissy."

"Why?" J.T. asked Linda.

She ticked off each finger. "Infection. Scarring. It's permanent."

"Well now, that's all dependent on where you get your work done."

"And it's not something a professional would have on his or her body."

J.T. shook his head. "Not so. At least, not anymore. I know it used to be that having a tattoo pretty much meant you'd done jail time or were in a gang, but that was years ago." More like decades. "You'd be surprised at the variety of my clients. And they're not all men. A ton of women are getting tattoos as well. I just did a full sleeve on a woman who owns a small up-and-coming IT firm. It's beautiful, vines and flowers and lots of color. She wanted something that said growth but was techy, so I used her logo too. It's really cool," he said to Hope, excited about the project all over again.

"I would have gotten one years ago," Gavin added. "But I knew Mom would lose it, so I didn't."

"Well, I never wanted one," Landon grumbled.

Hope said in a loud whisper, "He doesn't like needles."

J.T. tried not to laugh at Landon's annoyance. The guys' dad had no compunction about hiding it though.

Amused, Van said, "Well, I for one am a fan of the arts. When I learned just who was dating my daughter, I looked at your website."

Linda frowned. "You did?"

Wait. Who had told her father about J.T.? He shouldn't have known J.T.'s name before she arrived.

"Yes. And for what he charges for his work, I don't think you can call him a hobbyist or an amateur. What he does is nothing short of inventive. Do you do all your own work, or do you sometimes do art that clients bring to you?"

"We have portrait artists in the studio. Most of my clients have their own ideas that I put into an actual image." He described his process and out of the corner of his eye saw Hope nodding, encouraging.

He clasped her hand on top of the table, then let her go when Theo nudged him with a new platter of roasted vegetables.

Linda remained quiet while Van and Hope's brothers asked him questions about his job and his associations with the people who hung out at Ray's. Apparently the guys had gone there a while ago to kick ass. Greg, Hope's ex, had gotten a tough talking-to.

"So you're really dating my daughter?" Linda asked as they were having dessert.

"Yes, I am." He couldn't look away from his plate. "This is some serious carrot cake." He stared at the thing in awe. "It has, like, five layers."

Van gave a bashful shrug. "Six, actually. I like to bake."

"Dad's the man in the kitchen." Gavin smiled. "I'm supposed to take a piece of anything left over home to Zoe. She ordered me to."

"Anything for Zoe," Van agreed.

"And Ava," Landon added.

"Her too."

"I don't understand." Linda seemed puzzled.

"What?" Hope asked, belligerent.

J.T. had sensed the discord under all the polite and not-so-polite chatter, but Hope hadn't been overly antagonistic. And frankly, her mother had been quiet but pleasant. He didn't see why Hope should be so aggravated with the woman. So she was protective of her only daughter? Liam acted like a wounded bear whenever Del had a hiccup, and she was meaner than half the guys he knew…on a good day.

"My daughter has a history of dating men clearly beneath her. She bragged about you being poor and basically bad dating material."

"Note the word *poor*," Hope repeated. "So yeah, I gave him some other bad character traits. To teach you a lesson, Mom. You can't judge a person just because they've had a hard history. And you really shouldn't judge a person for not being wealthy."

"Ah, I'm not exactly poor, I—"

"Please, Hope. J.T. is obviously good-looking. He's got character, a nice enough family. But he tattoos people for a living. He's not what you need."

"How dare you presume to know what I need? I'm not Linda Junior, Mom. I'm Hope, and I have my own wants and needs."

"What say we adjourn to the living room and let them talk it out?" Van suggested to J.T.

J.T. grabbed his plate and followed Van out of the room, doing his best to ignore the yelling. Her brothers joined them, obviously intelligent enough to realize it wouldn't be smart to get between mother and daughter.

"Do they always get along so well?" J.T. asked wryly.

Van sighed. "Lately, yes. My wife is a sweet woman,

but"—he glared at his sons choking on *Attila the Mom*, *ballbuster*, and *yeah, right*—"she has high standards she thinks her children should meet. She's always been harder on Hope than the boys for some reason. She nags from a place of love, but Hope has always felt as if she has to measure up. She doesn't."

"No, she doesn't." He felt for her. Some of the things her mother had said, and was still saying, had to hurt. Hope wasn't a loser for not meeting her potential. And she sure the hell had a great life, despite not making the money her mother thought she should. "Hope is a smart woman with different goals. I think she'd be happy if her mother could just let her be."

The others stared at him.

"What? Was I supposed to ignore the fact her mom is totally cutting her down? And it has nothing to do with me."

"It never did." Van smiled.

"Why are you so happy?"

"Because I like you. You're the first decent guy my daughter has brought home in a long time."

"Yeah, about that," Landon said, stepping closer to J.T.

J.T. kept his cool, though Landon was no one he'd choose to take on, if he had his way. And certainly not with Gavin so close behind him.

"What's the deal with the flowers and attention from her secret admirer at the office? You and Cam were kind of unclear on the message you guys sent us."

"What's that?" Van frowned. "Someone's been bothering Hope?"

J.T. wished Hope had told her family what was going

on. Still, the night wasn't a total loss. At least no one had tried to pound him for dating their precious sister yet.

"And don't think we're not going to talk about what you're getting up to with my sister," Landon added in a growl.

Hell.

Chapter 14

"Mom, just...enough. You're being ridiculous now. I don't need you setting me up with men. I don't need more criticism about the way I dress, my job, or how I'm not living up to your expectations. Jesus, do you love me for me or not?"

"Of course I love you," her mother snapped. "You're as annoying as I am when I do things my own way. Or so your father says."

Hope paused, not having heard that one before.

"You can be a real bitch, Hope. And I say that with love." Linda sighed, all the fight seeming to seep out of her. "It's a Donnigan family trait, you know, to think you know what's best for everyone. Oh, I know what you're thinking. Your father's not like that. But he is. He's just subtler about it."

"Maybe, but he doesn't make me feel like I'm stupid for doing things my own way. I have to make my own mistakes, Mom."

"It's just that you've made so many of them so often," Linda murmured.

"Oh! That's my point! You're always throwing my boyfriends or my job in my face. Honestly? I like working for Cam, but it's not my dream job. I don't have a dream job. Someday I'd like to get married and have a family. That's my dream job."

"I know."

"And that's okay, because that's who I am. I'm not you."

"I know."

But Hope was on a roll. "There is absolutely nothing wrong with J.T. He's the first guy in a long time I actually like. He's funny and smart. And he treats me well."

"It's about time."

"Yes, it is. He's not rich. I don't know how much money he makes, if you want the truth. But I don't care."

"You should."

"Why? You raised me to be an independent woman. I have a job. I buy my own clothes, rent my own apartment. Why do I need a man to buy me things?"

Linda frowned. "You don't. But he should pull his own weight. Do you have any idea how many friends I have who do everything? Janice has been working her ass off for twenty years, all so her louse of a husband can sit on his sorry butt and pretend to be looking for work. It's a joke."

"Yeah, and it's on Janice for putting up with it. I admit some of my exes weren't great, but I know that now. It helps that I have someone so sweet to show me the difference." Sweet? Well, J.T. treated her like…a queen, actually. Something to think about—in addition to the fact that she was as bothered about her mother dissing J.T. as she was about her mother getting on her case.

"I'm happy for you if you are, I guess." Linda shrugged. "But this thing with him seems sudden."

"It's a recent relationship. We just clicked." Truth. "Each of us is accepting the other person, Mom. I'm not trying to make him into Dad, and he's not trying to make me his next baby's mother," she teased.

"You do realize I couldn't care less if he's black, white, red, or purple. Your significant other should have decent employment and a need to better himself. Trust me."

"Oh my God, Mom. I'm not with J.T. for his money. I like him."

"You can't like a man who can support you?"

"I support myself," she growled, feeling like a broken record.

"Well, I admit I like this one more than the others. He was polite and dressed nicely, I suppose. I mean, I didn't see any holes or stains on his clothing."

Hope wanted to beat her head against the table. "Why weren't you like this with Ava or Zoe?"

"I didn't have to be. Ava has 'Dr.' in front of her name. And when I learned about Zoe's big job in the medical clinic, where your father has a few friends, I was satisfied. Both of them are lovely women. They found good men in your brothers. But frankly, Ava and Zoe aren't my daughters. You are."

Linda sighed. "I know you think I'm a snob, and maybe I am. But your father and I spent years working to provide for this family. You take for granted having food and a nice place to live. We didn't have that—all this—for a long time. And there's no way I'm going back to the way it was."

"So you're saying if Dad turned poor tomorrow, you'd leave him?"

"That is *not* what I said," Linda snapped. "I'm trying to have a discussion with you, but you're so difficult."

"I'm just like you."

"Please. I'm trying to tell you that while I think you

have your heart in the right place, you're not hearing what I'm saying."

Hope prayed J.T. was faring better with her dad.

"Linda? Hope?" Her father frowned at them from the doorway of the kitchen. "Are you two okay?"

Make that, faring better with her brothers.

"So let me get this straight. Three weeks ago, you catch my sister kicking Greg's ass."

J.T. nodded to Landon. "Yep."

"Man, I'd have loved to have seen that," Gavin said.

"It was pretty amazing. She's wearing this pink gown, and she's looking all pretty and girlie. Then Greg puts his hand on her. I was two steps from tossing him down the hill when she put a hurt on him." J.T. grinned. "Epic."

"And he was bothering her why? I thought they broke up months ago."

"You mean, after you two pounded him at Ray's? Yeah, I heard. Everyone heard about the two yuppies taking up for their sister. I hadn't realized it was you two until Rena mentioned Hope's name."

"Wait. Yuppies?" Landon frowned.

"They call everyone who doesn't hang at Ray's 'yuppies.'" J.T. shrugged. "Anyway, according to Greg, someone trashed his car, and he thought it was you two."

Gavin shook his head. "Why did Greg think it was us?"

"He said someone left him a note. I don't know any more. I didn't ask him any questions."

Landon and Gavin exchanged a look. "Thinking we should go talk to Greg again."

"Good luck." J.T. noticed that the yelling in the other room had died down at the same time Van had left. "What's up with your dad? He's so polite and nice. And he cooks like a god. Are you guys adopted?"

Gavin and Theo cracked up.

Landon sighed. "You'd think. I'm probably more like my mom. Gavin's like Dad. And Theo… *He* was adopted."

Theo rolled his eyes. Considering the guy looked like a carbon copy of his old man, no one was believing that one.

Landon stepped closer. "But now that we have some space to talk about it, what the hell are you doing with my sister?" Next to him, Gavin appeared relaxed, his arms crossed over his chest, but the look in his eyes told J.T. not to stir up too much around these two.

So the obvious answer to the question—*anything the fuck I want*—wouldn't work in this situation. He settled on the truth instead. "I have no idea." When Landon frowned, he tried to explain. "Your sister has issues with your mom."

"Tell us something we don't know," Theo muttered.

"But that's got nothing to do with me. I like Hope. A lot. She's beautiful, intelligent, and she's fun to be with." He shrugged. "She and I enjoy each other. What's the problem?"

"The problem is that you're known to be a bit of a man-whore," Landon said.

"He means ladies' man," Gavin said, as if to soften the blow. "Our sister's been through a lot, and we don't want to see her hurt."

"Yeah? What if she hurts me?"

"Not our problem." Landon didn't blink, his stare direct and intimidating.

But though J.T. liked to keep the peace, he didn't tolerate threats well. "Yeah? Well, you take one more step, and I'll make *you* my problem."

Before Landon could move, and he looked as if he intended to, Gavin stepped between them. "Great talk, guys."

"For the record," J.T. added in a growl, "I am not and never have been a man-whore."

Landon raised a brow but moved back when Gavin pushed him. "That's not what your sister says."

Friggin' Del. "She was trying to be funny. Look, not that it's any of your business, but I don't mess around. One woman at a time. I date a lot. That's not a crime. But I'm up front about what I want, and if the girl isn't into it, we don't date. Hope and I are on the same page." It was on the tip of his tongue to tell them the relationship was a fraud, but he couldn't do it. "How about respecting her choices and letting her deal? She's a grown woman, guys. Not like I'm robbing the cradle or anything."

"Oh, that's nice," Hope said from behind him.

He froze.

Her brothers grinned, Landon looking way too amused, to J.T.'s way of thinking.

"Come on, J.T. We're out of here." She stormed by him to the door.

He moved to follow and stopped when Landon put a hand on his arm. J.T. had had just about enough of Hope's high-handed brother. "You don't move that hand, I will end you, motherfu—"

"Save it." In a lower voice, Landon said, "You watch out for her, okay? We're going to look into this situation. But you keep her safe. You need anything, call us."

J.T. relaxed. "Yeah, I will. Cam's looking out for her at work."

Landon released him.

Gavin glanced at Hope by the door and whispered to J.T., "If we didn't know Hope would throw a hissy, we'd babysit her until this thing is over. But it's better if you're with her. She won't give you as much grief." He paused. "Then again, you did basically call her an old hag. So good luck with that."

"What? I did not."

"J.T., let's go. *Please*." Hope sounded annoyed.

Theo shook his head. "It was nice knowing you."

"Tell your parents I said goodbye, would you?"

Gavin nodded.

"We'll talk to you soon," Landon promised.

"I can't wait." He left Gavin and Theo laughing and joined Hope at the door.

They left in silence and continued not speaking on the drive back to her place. He didn't know what to say. She seemed a bit sad, angry, and—

"Well, that went well."

He parked alongside the street and turned to see her smile. "So you're okay?" Relieved at her mood and ignoring how much it meant to him that she be happy, he waited.

"I'm not great, but tonight went as expected."

They left the car and headed up to her apartment.

"Your mom bought that we're an item?"

"Yep." The sparkle in her eyes told him to stop

worrying. "For a minute there, I worried. You went off script." She slugged him in the arm, and he pretended it hurt to satisfy her.

"Ow."

"Oh, please. Your arm is a rock. Like your head," she muttered as they stepped through the entryway and locked up behind them. "I'm sorry if my brothers gave you a tough time. You didn't tell them we were faking, did you?"

Faking? "What? Orgasms? Are you telling me those weren't real?" He loved her blush.

"Stop. I meant that we're not exactly dating."

"Not exactly, hmm?" He stalked her, amused that she backed up until she hit the wall. Then he leaned over her, one arm braced next to her head. "So we're not dating. We're just, what?" He noted her quickened pulse, the rapid rise and fall of her chest. "Have I told you how much I love your work clothes?"

She wore another of those pencil skirts that hit her knees and a silk tank. This time, she'd left off the jacket, and he liked the way the shirt molded to her breasts.

"Um, J.T.?"

"Yeah?" He continued to lean against the wall over her, and placed a hand on her waist. They both shuddered at the contact. She felt so warm under that silk. He trailed a hand up her side and curved it over her breast. The nipple was hard, and he rubbed this thumb over it, back and forth, and saw her eyes darken. The notion she might want to call it all off since they'd done what they'd set out to do scared him.

"I, ah, thanks for being there tonight." She licked her lips.

"Sure." The thought of them being done unnerved him to the point he had to have her. Right now. Some way to convince her to continue the charade. Just until he'd had enough, whenever that would be.

He kissed her, burning with a need to take her taste inside him. So close, the scent of her hit him hard, light perfume and sultry woman mixing to bring him to his knees. He pulled her closer, feeling all those wonderful curves against his solid frame.

She moaned and wound her hands around his neck, brushing his nape with gentle fingers and driving him insane.

He was glad he'd brought condoms, because he had a feeling they'd need a lot more than one tonight. Though he'd been inside her just that morning, he felt as if he'd gone years without her, so hungry he couldn't wait.

J.T. unfastened his pants and pushed his underwear down. Her hot little hands grabbed him, and he moaned, kissing her hungrily as she stroked him. He ran his lips across her cheek to her ear and whispered, "I want you so much." He nibbled her earlobe, heard her moan, and pushed against her palms. "Let me inside a few times? I want to feel you skin to skin. Then I'll put on a condom. Okay?"

She nodded, and he didn't know if she'd really heard him, busy as she was, shimmying out of her panties.

He hiked up her skirt so she had room to move. Then he yanked her off her feet, against the wall, and positioned himself at her sex. "Lock those ankles behind my back. Oh yeah, feel me."

"J.T." She arched her head back, and he latched on to her throat as he slowly pushed into her slick heat.

"*Fuck.*" He wanted to ram deep, to fill her up and keep on fucking. Hope Donnigan was a dream he probably didn't deserve, but one a greedy man would take. "Feel me deep inside you, baby. So hot. God, I could stay here forever." But he couldn't, because he needed to move.

"You're so big," she gasped and gyrated against him, pushing him out so he could surge deeper.

They both moaned, and she kissed him again, drawing him closer. Her scent enveloped him. Her hands were busy around his neck, on his shoulders, like a kitten kneading his muscles, leaving her mark with each touch.

He knew he needed to stop and use protection, knew it was stupid to go bareback at all despite her being on the pill. But hell if he could think while surrounded by her wet heat.

Hope was grinding against him, now grabbing at his shoulders, trying to get closer. "More," she panted. "Harder."

He powered into her, loving that she wanted all he had to give. His cock felt huge, and the burning need to possess her boiled up from inside him. When she seized around him, crying out, clamping those ankles tight, he nearly lost control.

"Yes, yes," she whispered, her head thrown back as she jerked against his hips.

So much heat surrounding him, so much suction pulling him closer. He was going to come so hard.

With seconds to spare, he pulled out of her and pressed against her belly, releasing all over her. The climax left him breathless and dizzy, and he continued to spend as she kissed his cheek, his neck, and ran greedy fingers over his chest.

"Hope," he groaned, realizing what might have happened if he hadn't pulled out. What could have already happened if he'd come at all before he'd withdrawn. *Jesus, but he wanted so badly to come deep inside her*.

The ecstasy continued to drug him, letting him bask in the bliss of Hope. Worries and regrets could come later. Now he had a handful of condoms to put to use, and one sexy woman to destroy in bed.

Hope stared into J.T.'s face, knowing she'd never seen anything more beautiful than her man in climax. And that, right there, should have warned her to be wary. Those *her man* thoughts. *My boyfriend*. Pretending tonight had been way too easy, because she'd felt possessive and wanted to defend him. Not for her, but for him. Because everyone should know how amazing J.T. truly was.

But the dangerous sex they'd had... What if he hadn't pulled out when he had? What if he'd already come inside her before pulling out? The chance for pregnancy was almost nil, but what if...? A baby would be a disaster. And she still wanted to do it again. With him inside her. Their loving, so close, a part of each other, had been special.

And stupid, she kept trying to tell herself. Though the timing wasn't right for a baby, her birth control wouldn't be completely effective for at least a few more days. And even then she'd want to use the pill as backup for his condoms. She didn't worry about disease with him, but she did worry about pregnancy. As much as she dreamed about having them, she wanted marriage and a husband first, babies and a family second.

That the notion of accidental pregnancy didn't have her shrieking and running for cover told her she had it bad for J.T. Once again, falling for the wrong kind of guy.

But was he wrong?

He cupped her face and kissed her, the moment so tender it brought tears to her eyes.

"I owe you a new shirt," he teased as he pulled away. "And I'm sorry I lost it." He sighed. "I have no excuse. Next time, condom. I swear. You just get me so hot so fast..."

"I know. I should have insisted you wear it."

"Yeah, it's all your fault." He huffed. "Because I have no control around you." He took her hand and wrapped it around his cock, now wet with his seed. "This is all yours, baby. I just had you, and I want more. So much more," he said, his voice low. He kissed her, and she couldn't help squeezing him, feeling his heartbeat in the thick shaft.

When they parted, she stared into his soulful eyes, seeing a deeper affection there she hoped she wasn't imagining. "Bedroom."

He nodded.

They made their way to her bedroom, stripped and cleaned up, then lay on the bed, totally naked, open with each other. J.T. lay back and had her straddle him, setting her over his upper thighs, not quite meshing their parts together.

"If you're too close to my cock, I swear I'll end up sliding up into you, and then we'll have another accidental no-condom situation." He groaned. "I'm trying, but I can't not react, seeing you naked on top of me. You have any idea how many times I've jacked off to this image?"

She blushed and grinned. "Yeah? Me too."

His eyes widened. "Ah." He swallowed.

"That's it? Just 'ah'?"

"Hold on. My brain stopped working." He smiled at her laughter and raised his big hands to cup her breasts. "These are nice and big. A surprise on a girl your size."

"Hey, I'm tall."

He snorted. "You keep thinking that. But honey, your body is rockin'. You make a man want sex. A few kisses, and more sex. I try to be all sophisticated and modern thinking, but when I see you like this, all I can think of is how many ways can I plow that pussy?"

She frowned. "Crude." And sadly, such a turn-on.

"I know." He huffed. "I'm trying here." He massaged her breasts, and she soon forgot to be annoyed. "So pretty." He pulled her down to lie on top of him, but instead of going right for sex, he stroked her hair and talked to her. "I'm still not sure how we got here."

She laughed. "Me too. So confusing."

"I mean, I know I've wanted to do you forever, but I never thought it would become a reality. Between us being practically related through a few marriages, you being perky, blond, and all prom queen, and me being a big, black badass more comfortable in a bar like Ray's than in a Starbucks, I'd say it's still a mystery."

She tugged at his chest hair.

"Hey. Easy, baby."

"A few things you should know. Yes, I realize you're black. African American."

He grinned. "Black is fine, because black is beautiful. Although technically I'm also white, and maybe Portuguese, on my mom's dad's side, I think. So you figure it out."

"What you are is annoying," she muttered. "And beautiful and arrogant. Now shut up and let me talk."

"Yes, ma'am."

"I don't know how we got here either. We obviously share some serious attraction."

"I'll say. I've never before been with a chick where my dick buzzed every time I'm around her. I swear, it's like a compass always wanting to point in your direction."

She laughed. "Okay, that's funny. And I'm more than happy to be your guide." She kissed his chest. "Inside me, for starters."

"Hell yeah." He kept petting her hair, and she swore she felt him kiss the top of her head. The tender action brought tears to her eyes, which was just silly.

"We're not really dating, because we don't want to rock the boat with your sister and my cousins."

He paused stroking her hair, then continued. "Right."

"And it was all just to fool my mom, who bought that we're a couple."

"Uh-huh."

She leaned up so she could watch his expressions. "But I don't think we should stop yet."

"No?"

She shook her head. "I mean, to really sell this, we should probably keep going out. Or at least let people think we're still dating."

"No, you're right. If we don't at least look like we're dating, it won't seem real."

"Yes. Exactly. So we keep doing this—us together—for a while. I'm not seeing anyone else, and I know you aren't."

"Nope."

"But when you decide you want to go out with someone, you let me know, and we'll stage a fake breakup. Nothing too dramatic, but something final."

"Sure. Okay." He stared at her face and tucked a lock of hair behind her ear. "You are just so pretty. I mean, like, deep-down gorgeous. When you smile, I see you. The real you. I have to draw you, Hope. Will you let me?"

"Like this? Naked?"

His eyes crinkled. "No. You can wear clothes…if you have to. But I want this, your joy. You shine when you're happy, you know? It's like you bring out the sun, and I get all warm, basking in you."

She'd never had a guy say anything even half that poetic to her. "Wow."

He flushed. "Sorry. Sounds corny, right? But you make me that way."

"And here I thought I just made you hard."

He chuckled. "You do. But you bring out the softer parts of me too." He brought her down for a kiss that rocked her, because it expressed so much. Passionate, caring, sexual. J.T. aroused much more than her body.

She understood why so many women wanted a piece of him. And why it would hurt so much when he left. But she couldn't force herself to give him up. Not yet. Instead, she'd let him bask in her sunlight, and she'd revel in the rush of sensation from his touch.

Chapter 15

Hope kissed him with all the feeling she had inside her. He was so much stronger than her, his hands nearly spanning her back. But when J.T. cradled her to him, she knew she couldn't be anywhere safer. He kissed her, at first sipping from her lips with light, drawing kisses. Then he deepened the connection, the kisses growing hungrier, his body more insistent.

When he grabbed her hair and held her with a bite of force, she moaned, aroused anew. She loved how he could physically control her with little effort. He must have liked it too, because he grew a little rougher. He pulled her body up so that her breasts were over his face. Then he took a nipple in his mouth and sucked while his hands roamed freely.

Over her back, rubbing her ass, then those skilled fingers were seeking the heat of her, rubbing her clit with leisurely strokes while he continued to torment her breasts.

She was panting from need when he moved her so he could reach her mouth. She let herself slide down his body, over the thick erection prodding her belly. She trailed kisses down his neck and gave his nipples the same attention he'd given hers.

His moaning and shifting told her he liked her attention. And then she scooted lower, her lips making a path down his tight abs to the solid shaft thick against his belly. He was so big, so handsome down there. She'd never been a huge fan of the male anatomy. Oh, she liked a man in boxers, showing off his upper body. But she preferred some mystery in her lovers.

J.T. was just so beautiful, everywhere, that she had to *know* him. She studied him as she explored, first with her hands, then with her mouth. She loved the softness overlying such steely strength. His dark crown was broad and stretched her mouth as she drew him between her lips.

He arched up into her. "*Hope*. Oh yeah. Lick me there. Suck me." He moaned and swore, his entire body locked up as she moved up and down, learning what drove him crazy with each pass of her tongue and draw of her lips. Just as she'd gotten down a rhythm that aroused him to the point of grunts and moans, he stopped her.

Gasping, he yanked her up off him. "Wait. Condom. Now."

He handed her a packet from the nightstand, where he'd placed several earlier. As she put it on him, he shook, and she noticed the moisture beaded there, at his tip.

The moment she finished rolling it on him, he flipped her onto her back and mounted her. He nudged her thighs wide, and she welcomed him. But he didn't push inside her.

"Not yet." His voice sounded unrecognizable, so low, so gritty. J.T. kissed his way down her body, doing to her what she'd done to him. Her breasts had always been sensitive, but when J.T. bit her nipples, not hard enough to hurt but with enough pressure to stimulate, she felt an orgasm within reach.

He pulled with his lips, his tongue lashing each nipple until she could do nothing but moan his name and surge up and down in waves of lust. She clasped his head to her, mashing her pelvis against his belly, seeking more.

He didn't disappoint. J.T. traveled down her belly before putting an openmouthed kiss over her sex. He thrust his tongue inside her, then sucked her clit without stopping. She was coming before she knew it, and then J.T. had her ankles up on either side of his head while he thrust inside her.

Their gazes locked, and as he took her, she seized again, the pleasurable agony overwhelming. She would have felt more vulnerable, being open to him as he controlled her pleasure. But watching him come showed he felt the same things she did. His eyes narrowed, his breathing increased, and his chest and arms tensed, the muscles standing out in relief as he groaned and poured himself into her.

He continued to pump, his cock so thick and long he bumped that part of her that added yet another release. She felt herself let go, and the ecstasy burned into her brain. J.T. and all the best things in life in one glorious moment where she trusted him enough to put herself in his hands.

As he came down from his high, he slowly eased her ankles off his shoulders and withdrew. She immediately missed him inside her.

"Damn, Hope. You are the sexiest thing ever." She felt incredibly wet and worried that perhaps the condom had broken, so she asked.

But J.T. only smiled. "Nah, baby. That's all you. Come on. Let's get cleaned up before we snuggle."

"Snuggle?" She felt drained as he lifted her off the bed. Then the big lug carried her into the bathroom. "Wow. I feel boneless."

"Because I'm *the man*." He looked pleased and started her shower.

"The man?" she teased. "More like the sexy villain who seduced a poor, innocent girl out of her clothes."

He laughed. Hard. "Oh yeah. You're innocent, all right. About sucked my brain clean out of my head with those lips wrapped around my cock. And maybe I seduced you back, but Lord knows I didn't start this. It's not my fault you're a walking wet dream."

"I think that's a compliment. Maybe."

He smiled. "Oh, it is." He pulled her into the shower with him once the water temperature evened out. Then he did the oddest thing. "Hope?"

"Yes?"

He stared into her eyes, as if seeing into her hopes and dreams and worries. He cupped her face in those big hands. Then he kissed her, and she felt their connection in every part of her being.

When he drew back, she blinked her eyes open and saw what looked like love in his eyes. He turned them so they both felt the warm water cascading over their bodies. Then he hugged her and sighed.

"Heaven," he murmured, and she completely agreed.

They stayed that way until the water turned cold. And when she suggested a way for them to warm up, he was more than receptive.

J.T. didn't know what to call it, and neither it seemed

did Hope. So they enjoyed themselves and refrained from mentioning any more about their pretend relationship. How *pretend* could it really be when he spent half the night buried inside her?

With a grin, he decided it didn't matter. Unlike his sister and half the people around him lately, he didn't have to label shit to feel good about life. And since he and Hope were on the same page, it was all good.

At least, until they ran into trouble Saturday evening at a pizza parlor following a slick thrill ride of a movie. While arguing the merits of sex as a diversion versus just using an actual gun to keep the bad buys busy, an overly smiling couple and a little boy interrupted them.

"Well, well. Lookie who we have here." Brody Singer, one of those blasted McCauleys—if not by blood, then by association—stood right next to their table. With him were his now-pregnant wife, Abby, and Colin McCauley.

Colin beamed. "I saw you first and told Ubie and Aunt Abby we had to come. Hi, Hope." His eyes glowed when they settled on J.T. again. "Hi, J.T."

Hope bit her lip, but J.T. saw her grin. She knew how much Colin idolized him. Hell, everyone knew. The kid made no bones about wanting to be just like J.T. when he got bigger. J.T. wondered how Mike slept at night, knowing his kid had aspirations of following in J.T.'s footsteps.

He grinned, despite the interruption of a fabulous night. "Oh, hey. It's the coolest kid I know, the professional slacker, and the too-pretty-to-be-his-wife Abby Singer."

"Don't mind if we join you," Brody said and sat at their table without asking.

Abby sighed. "Sorry. You'd think I'd be used to this. I mean, I married him."

"Hey." Brody looked affronted, then winked. The family's con man—no doubt where Colin got it.

The blond goofball had been instrumental in helping J.T.'s sister hook up with Mike, and of course Colin had been a part of it. Between the three of them, they'd made sure Del ended up with a guy she truly deserved. So though J.T. might tease the guy, he liked Brody.

"Abby, you look prettier every time I see you." J.T. stood and moved around the table to kiss her on the cheek. "You're glowing."

She really was. The dark-haired beauty smiled, and he saw her bone-deep contentment. Yeah, every McCauley had hitched up with a woman who fit him. J.T. glanced at Hope, saw her raised brow and pointed glance at Abby, and realized she might not like him kissing another woman.

Well, how about that. A bit of jealousy on her part didn't annoy him, the way it had with so many of his past girlfriends. He *liked* the thought of her wanting him all to herself and told her so. "Don't worry, Blondie. I'm all yours."

"Oh, glad you were looking her way." Brody let out a relieved breath. "For a minute there, I thought you were talking to me."

Colin giggled, and Hope shook her head. "Such a McCauley."

"What's wrong with that?" Brody asked and winked at J.T.

"Yeah," Colin said. "I'm a McCauley."

"It's not your fault, Colin," Hope explained. "The McCauleys are known as the second best in our family. Except for you. You're one of us Donnigans, because you were so great at the prank wars."

"Prank wars?" J.T. asked.

Brody groaned. "Don't ask."

Colin gave Brody a thumbs-up. "I *am* awesome. I helped Gavin prank on his whole family. And then I got all of you." He gave Abby a sly grin. "Remember when you yelled at Brody for misplacing your papers?"

"Those were my edits, you little punk." Abby scowled. "Man, I looked for those *forever*. Typically I do everything online, but for that book, my editor had mailed my edits to me. I nearly freaked out for an entire day. Then they mysteriously appeared in Brody's section of the office."

"So that was you." Brody's eyes narrowed on the boy. "Good to know. Payback's comin', little man."

Colin snickered. "Yeah, right."

Hope looked at him. "You're seven, right?"

"Yep."

"Well, if you want to make it to eight, you have to learn never to confess what you did. Not until your uncles are old. Well, older than J.T., which is old."

"Ha ha." J.T. shook his head. "Colin, the one who's old is Hope. She's got a birthday next week."

"I'm three years younger than you, and isn't your birthday two weeks after mine, old man?"

He laughed, then stopped when he noticed Brody and Abby staring with fascination. "What?"

"Oh, nothing." But the smug look Brody shared with Abby was unnerving.

Hope frowned at J.T., then nodded at the married couple.

He shrugged.

"You know," Abby drawled, "all that body language isn't necessary. We're right here."

"Then what's with all the staring?" Hope asked and handed Colin a slice of pizza. The way she took care of the boy made J.T. feel she'd be a natural at motherhood, and the image of Hope looking after her own son gave his chest an odd pang.

Brody leaned back in his chair. "Oh, we're just curious. Dating is so different these days. Back when Abby and I got together—"

"When I was five," Colin helpfully added.

Brody ignored him. "We used to joke around, pretend we weren't as close as we really are. You see, when you're new to falling in love, it's scary to let yourself be vulnerable with another person."

J.T. gaped. "This from the same guy who shoved his passed-out brother's finger up his nose and took pictures he shared at the last family picnic?"

Abby grinned. "Therapy has helped Brody get in touch with his inner common sense."

"Very inner, I'll bet," Hope murmured.

"So anyway, we just wanted to see this special new romance blossom. Close up."

Colin narrowed his eyes from J.T. to Hope. "Wait. They're dating? Like, for real?"

"You saw them both at the bowling alley."

J.T. frowned. "You're pretty well informed, Brody."

"Mike has a big mouth."

"He does." Colin sighed. "We have a hard time keeping secrets with Dad around."

Hope laughed. "That's funny. Landon is the same way. A real stick in the mud about everything."

"You got that right." J.T. still didn't much care for the way her older brother had treated him. As if J.T. would do something to hurt Hope. Just thinking about her ever crying over something he'd done turned his stomach upside down.

"So have you met the parents yet, J.T.?"

"Yeah. It was great. Her dad cooked, then Hope and her mom yelled at each other while her brothers gave me the third degree. I can't wait to do it again," he added with a large amount of sarcasm.

Abby bit her lip. "Um, wow. Sounds like an…interesting…night. I've only met your parents a few times, Hope, but they were super nice to me."

"Aunt Linda is intense." Brody shook his head. "I once slipped a whoopee cushion on her seat when I was kid. She sat on it and freaked out. Then she chased me around the house with a wooden spoon to instill some much-needed discipline."

Colin laughed. "Awesome."

Brody grinned. "It was, actually. I would have gotten away if Landon hadn't sat on me. The killjoy."

"Yeah, I can see that." J.T. certainly understood the dynamic of bossy mother and bossy son.

Colin kept squirming in his seat.

"Okay, buddy." Abby stood and rubbed her tummy. She had a tiny bump where her baby was growing. "Time to use the bathroom. No more putting it off."

"But I want to talk to J.T."

"What am I?" Hope asked, biting back a smile. "Chopped liver?"

"Hope too." Colin nodded with enthusiasm.

Abby tugged him toward the restrooms. "I need to go, so we'll go together."

"Aw. I don't want to use the ladies' room. That's for girls."

They left, and Brody turned serious. "Okay, gimme the scoop on this stalker that's bothering Hope." Hope opened her mouth, but before she could talk, Brody said, "Cam told Flynn, who told me. Any leads yet?"

"Not yet." Hope sighed. "And it's not like I can call the cops. There's no crime against sending flowers or a cinnamon bun."

J.T. reached across the table to hold her hand. "Her brothers are looking into an ex of hers. But other than that, nothing. There was no way to tell where the flowers came from."

"Hope? You okay, sweetie?" Brody asked.

She nodded. "It's a little weird, but nothing's happened other than getting little gifts. Probably some kid with a crush. I feel silly for making too big a deal and—"

"Don't." J.T. squeezed her hand again, lending her his strength. He could see the worry darkening her pretty eyes, and he didn't like it. "You're smart not to ignore this. Until we find the guy, I'll stick close." He drew her hand to his mouth and kissed it. "Super close. Like glue. The sexy kind." He noticed Brody watching with fascination and let go of her hand.

"Glue can be sexy?" She smiled.

Feeling good for banishing her worry, J.T. chuckled. "Oh yeah. Glue and me. We're tight, we don't let go, and we're—"

"White and sticky?" Brody added. "Not seeing the resemblance, guy."

J.T.'s thoughts took a dive, remembering a part of him that was indeed white and sticky, and that Hope had been particularly good at lapping it up. He met her gaze with his own and gave her a naughty smile.

She turned beet-red. *Ah, great minds think alike.*

"Well, actually, Brody, the similarity is in my—"

Hope stood. "Oh good. Abby's back."

Brody, apparently as depraved as J.T., mouthed *Nice one*, and welcomed his wife and nephew back. "Good news, guys."

"Oh?" Abby ruffled the boy's hair.

"J.T.'s buying us pizza!"

"Yeah! J.T. is the best," Colin exclaimed.

J.T. shot Brody a dirty look.

"What? Something I said, sticky man?"

When Colin asked Brody what the *sticky man* reference meant, Hope hurried to ask the boy about his summer plans. Colin blathered on about camp, his best friend, and a summer soccer league.

Brody leaned close to J.T. while Colin held the ladies' attention. "You need anything for Hope, just ask. Take care of her."

"Will do, man. Nothing gets to her."

He'd die before he let that happen.

Sunday afternoon, after having spent an hour arguing about what constituted a decent gym—the one they'd attended was all the way in Green Lake but had nice floor mats and good-looking instructors, excluding her brothers—Hope and J.T. were enjoying smoothies from Sofa's, a popular coffee shop near the lake. Hope apparently had some connection to the place due to an in-law of a cousin of an owner, or six degrees of Donnigan, as J.T. liked to say. They sat inside since the wind had kicked up. The place had a decent crowd and killer cookies. With any luck, they could have a date without interruption from a family member.

Unfortunately, they ran into an even bigger mouth than Brody.

"Hey, guys. Don't you look all sweaty and bothered." Del grinned at him, and he groaned when he spotted Rena not far behind. "Well, well. What have you two been up to?"

Hope lowered her head to the table and groaned. "God. Our family is *everywhere*."

"No shit." Glaring into his annoying sister's smirking face, J.T. scooted over in his chair, leaving no room at the two-person table for guests. "We were working out."

"*Really?*" A lot of innuendo in that one word.

"At the gym," Hope snapped.

"Hey, Rena," Del said, ignoring their irritation, "let's pull up some chairs."

J.T. shared a sigh with Hope.

"Hey, guys." Rena's smile brightened the day. "What's going on?" She glanced from him to Hope. "Oh. We're interrupting. We should go."

"No, no." Del gave an emphatic headshake. "Rena, we both know that J.T. and Hope are just *pretending* to be involved. This is all an elaborate scheme—"

"Wow, big words, Del." J.T. wondered if shoving her off her seat would be considered rude. Then he remembered the baby she carried and figured it would be safer to keep his hands to himself.

She talked over him. "—to make Hope's mom mad. They're not really dating. Remember? You told me that's what he said."

Rena nodded, her innocent expression overdone. "Oh, right. Now I remember." She smiled at Hope, who couldn't help smiling back. Rena was like a puppy that way. You couldn't look into the girl's big, brown eyes without losing your will to argue.

J.T. blew out a breath. "Okay, what do you two want? Why are you here, bothering us poor pretenders?"

Hope shot him a frown, which he returned. As if it was his fault his sister and cousin had broadsided them.

Del sipped from her drink. "Oh, this hits the spot. Rena and I decided to spend our Sunday walking around Green Lake. Want to come?"

J.T. stared at his sister. "Wait. You're telling me you wanted to exercise? Voluntarily?"

Rena laughed. "Yeah, that sounds pretty weird to me too."

"Hey, I keep in shape."

J.T. shrugged. "Luck of the genes. Pretty much the only thing I've ever seen you run is your mouth."

"Seriously? When's the last time your fat ass got up on a treadmill?"

He snarled, "My fat ass is *amazing*. Tell her, Hope."

Hope nodded. "It's amazing."

"Any number of women would die to get a shot at this ass."

"Any number," Hope repeated.

Rena snorted.

"I mean, Hope can barely look away, and we're just playacting this relationship. Imagine if we were really dating? Hope, you'd be glued to my ass."

"Glued," she said, then snickered.

"Why does she keep repeating you?" Del asked. "What are you two drinking, anyway?" She sniffed at his drink, and J.T. gently pushed her back by her forehead. Well, mostly gently.

"Easy, Del. Don't want to scar the baby, you know, by making me spank your ass. So how's the seed? Did the doctor say it's germinating yet?"

"It's officially a kid." Del grinned. "A real one. I mean, we need to wait a few more weeks to make sure it's all smooth sailing, but after three months, barring any complications, it's safe to tell people. So consider yourself told."

"So cool! And don't worry. You're too mean to let a kid slip away. Unless Mike scares him with that wimpy voice."

She shook her head. "Really? Would you please get off my husband?"

"Shouldn't I be the one saying that? Seems to me you wouldn't be pregnant if *you'd* get off the poor guy."

Hope watched brother and sister argue.

"I find them almost as entertaining as my books." Rena sipped from an iced coffee. "And I live to read."

Hope grinned. "So what are you guys doing out here? Are you really walking around the lake, or did you somehow track us down to torture us?"

"That would have been a nice plan, but no." Rena's

eyes clouded. "We've been wandering, checking out retail spaces."

"Why?"

"Well, I work at Ray's Bar. I think you know that. But I'm actually a hair stylist. I've been slaving away for years to get enough money to open my own shop."

"Oh, that's great. But no luck on finding a space?"

"One that won't cost me a kidney and my firstborn? No." Rena looked depressed. "I had the perfect spot all picked out. Even talked to the landlady about it and got her okay. Then she gave it away before I could come up with the rest of the money."

"Are you trying to buy it or lease it?" Hope didn't think the woman would need that much money to rent, even for a year. And if she didn't have the funds for just a year, it might be prudent to wait a bit longer.

"Oh, I'm leasing. But I have a set amount I wanted to have before I enter into any contracts. It's all planned out, has been for years." She sighed. "And trust me, I looked for a long, long time. I found the perfect space. Close to home, close to the garage, to places I feel comfortable being near and where I'll get great foot traffic. Then, she rented it right out from under me."

Hope felt for her. "Tell me what you're looking for, and I'll get someone to help you." Her mother was a massive pain, but she was a good woman. And she loved helping independent businesses get started whenever possible. "I know a big-wig real estate guru. She normally sells houses, but she'll know if something comes up you could rent for a great price. What area are you looking at?"

They talked for a bit before Hope realized she and Rena had become entertainment for the Websters.

She looked up to see J.T. and Del staring at her. "What?"

J.T. leaned over the table and kissed her. On the mouth, *with tongue*, in front of his sister and cousin.

"What was that for?" He'd scrambled her brain.

"For being you."

She didn't understand, but Del looked like the cat that had eaten the canary, and Rena soon mirrored her. "What are you two smiling at?"

"Oh my gosh. She's even starting to sound like him," Del said and slapped her leg.

Rena snorted coffee out her nose, then clamped a hand over her face.

Soon all of them were laughing and making fun of each other. And Hope realized she never had a bad time when she was with J.T.

Chapter 16

HOPE WAITED ALL WEEK AT WORK FOR SOMETHING TO HAPPEN. When nothing did, she felt both glad and annoyed. Sure, it would be great if her secret admirer problem would just go away, but she'd rather she knew the identity of the gift giver, to allay her fears she'd attracted the attentions of some psycho.

Bad enough she had her own psycho to deal with… in bed.

She smiled to herself, still unsure where she stood with J.T. but having too much fun to call things off. He constantly made her laugh. He'd convinced her to sit still so he could draw her. Then he showed her pictures of herself looking ridiculous. Her face on a shark's body. Her as a cartoon with a huge head and butt. Hope as an anime character dressed in a slutty Sailor Moon outfit. But her favorite was Hope as Wonder Woman, which had been very cool, especially because he'd made her tall and curvy instead of vertically challenged and simply cute.

Either he or Cam walked her to her car after work, and Cam had started arriving earlier in the mornings so she didn't have to walk up the stairs to the office by herself. She hadn't received any flowers, treats, or notes. Just blessed quiet.

Today she'd turned thirty, yet she couldn't say she felt any differently than she had yesterday. The day had been mostly uneventful, with the exception of Cam's surprise birthday cake for her during lunch and his gift certificate to a trendy dining spot she'd had her eye on for a while.

"Any plans for tonight?" Cam asked as they wrapped up for the day.

"Noelle and I are going out on the town."

"Nothing with J.T.?"

She shrugged, swallowing her disappointment. Again. "We're not joined at the hip."

"Ah. Well, happy birthday. Just one more appointment today, and you're free to be thirty."

"Gee, thanks, Cam."

He laughed.

"Joe Gregory should be here in another twenty minutes."

He nodded and went back to his office, humming "Happy Birthday" along the way.

No, Hope and J.T. didn't need to spend every waking moment together. It had surprised her that he hadn't mentioned doing anything tonight. They'd spent the last two weekends together. And though they hadn't seen each other every night this week, on those evenings he had a late appointment, they talked before bed.

She'd gotten used to her *pretend* relationship, which J.T. continued to tease her about. She didn't know how to handle him, exactly. As they both well knew, the reason for them coming together had been to convince her mother that Hope wasn't as immature as she knew herself to be. Her lame rationalization to stay together afterward, to make it convincing when they broke up, was embarrassing. But that didn't explain why he'd agreed to remain an item. Or why he called her more on the phone than she called him.

Yet on her birthday, he hadn't said a thing other than for her to have a great day. He knew she and Noelle were going out, but not where. Noelle hadn't told her, wanting it to be a surprise. And J.T. hadn't even asked if he could come.

"Hope, you should celebrate with family, with your best friend. I'd only be in the way, and we're keeping it casual, right?" he'd said while getting ready for work. "I mean, me hanging with you on your special day feels a little off for what we have."

"Good points." She'd faked a smile, waved goodbye, and left for the day.

She tried not to feel hurt about it, but she couldn't help it.

Even her family was doing something nice, everyone congregating on Sunday for brunch to celebrate. With that in mind, Hope needed to get her act together. No time to freak out on her mother again, not when it did no good to try to convince Linda that Hope had her own mind.

Ten minutes later, she looked up when the door chimed.

"Hi, Hope. I have an appointment with Cam at four thirty."

She smiled and buzzed Cam to let him know Joe had arrived a few minutes early. The owner of a small IT firm making its mark had been smart to get Cam to help invest for his personal retirement. Slender, funny, and a nice-looking man in his mid-thirties, Joe had been someone her mother had talked about setting her up with. Fortunately, Cam had intervened before Linda had all his single male clients lined up to take Hope out for a test drive.

"We've been looking forward to seeing you again, Joe. How was Hawaii?" They made small talk as she walked him back to Cam's office.

As she left him, she caught Joe looking at her breasts before he glanced at her face and smiled. "Thank you." He turned to meet Cam, who extended his hand in greeting.

Hope shut the door behind them and went back down the hall, confused. Joe had never before given her any kind of weird looks, but he'd for sure been staring at her chest.

Perhaps…he was her admirer.

She had a mini freak-out, then did the math. Joe had never been anything but pleasant yet aloof in the six months he'd been a client. Cam really liked him. Plus Joe had been in Hawaii when she'd received the flowers. True, he could have ordered those, but a man had ordered her a pastry in person. Unless he'd hired someone to order it at the store?

What kind of man could look a woman in the eye, yet not admit he was leaving her gifts? Following her around, knowing her routine?

Hurrying off to the bathroom, Hope did her business and was washing her hands when she caught sight of herself in the mirror. A piece of pink fuzz from her sweater sat smack-dab in the middle of her chest. She plucked it off and threw it away.

She had to laugh at herself. "I am such a moron." Just because she liked her looks, and J.T. happened to feel the same, didn't mean every man wanted to do her. *Or buy me flowers.*

The rest of the day passed quickly, and before she knew it, she'd gone home, changed, and met with Noelle at a popular nightclub downtown. Dressed in a slinky black skirt, a dark-red top with a plunging neckline, and risky black heels, Hope felt pretty, sexy, and thirty.

She sighed, toying with her drink.

Noelle looked fabulous, dressed to kill in a short green dress that made her already long legs look even longer. "Isn't this dress great? I got it at a consignment shop for twenty bucks. Go, me."

Hope laughed. "You truly are the bargain shopper."

Noelle held up her glass. "A toast to my dress and your birthday. To us."

Hope clinked it and took a sip of a cosmopolitan done just right. "So what's the plan?" Noelle had told Hope to do nothing but enjoy herself. Hope had taken the bus so as not to have to drive home, and had shown up content to let her best friend make magic happen with the rest of her night.

"I have a private room reserved for us in the back."

"Oh?"

"Yeah. You're going to love this." Noelle grabbed her by the arm and took her back down a hallway. "This is just for you, Hope. Happy birthday."

Noelle pushed them through a door and closed it behind her. A raised platform had been set up at one end of the small room. A minibar sat at the other end, and small tables and chairs faced the stage. On the table closest to the stage, a cake with candles sat. A glance over the doorway showed a HAPPY BIRTHDAY, HOPE banner.

"Aw, Noelle. This is so nice." Hope teared up.

"Stop! You'll ruin your mascara."

Hope laughed.

The door opened, and a bunch of her friends filed in. Amber, Sarah, Collette, more buddies from the gym and a few of her past jobs. They made small talk before the girls grabbed some seats. Ava and Zoe arrived soon after, looking around with wide eyes.

"Happy birthday, Hope." Zoe hugged her.

Ava grinned. "Wow. Thirty. Welcome to the big leagues."

They chatted a bit. Then her cousins' wives entered, along with Del and Rena.

"Wow. You really did invite everyone." There had to be close to twenty women filling the room.

When a buff, shirtless man dressed in black dress pants, dress shoes, and a bow tie entered and took position behind the bar, Hope blinked in surprise. The club wasn't a strip joint, and it didn't employ half-dressed, gorgeous men either. Her friends immediately surged to buy drinks. Enough cocktails, and they'd be filling his tip jar with more than bills. Knowing her friends, the bartender would get a fair amount of phone numbers.

Yep. Collette hadn't waited for the drinks. A business card already sat in his tip jar.

Hope had a feeling the night was about to get wild. "Ah, Noelle, did the bartender lose his shirt or what?"

"Eye candy, milady." Noelle laughed. "Wait until you get a look at tonight's entertainment."

"Oh my God. This *is* a strip show!"

"Hell yeah. You only turn thirty once."

Hope had a scandalous thought. "Please tell me J.T. isn't going to strut his stuff onstage taking off his clothes." Not that she wouldn't mind seeing that—at all—but she didn't want him naked around other women. And certainly not Collette.

"Now that's one heck of an idea. I met him, you know, when we put this party plan together." Noelle sighed. "If I wasn't so into Jean-Luc, I'd fight you for him." She checked her phone, then grabbed Hope and dragged her to their table. "Wait here. Cosmo, right?" She pointed at the drink Hope had set at the table.

"Yeah, but—"

Noelle left, and Rena arrived to take the unoccupied chair at the table. "Hi, Hope. Happy birthday." Rena had put her hair back in a clip, and she looked different. Less cute and wholesome and more dangerous and seductive.

Hope blinked. "Holy cow. You look vampy."

Rena grinned. "Thanks. I can do a look besides sweet. I'm trying it out here before I put it to good use later."

"Oh? On who?"

"It's whom, and I bet I know," came a deep voice from behind her.

Hope whirled around to see J.T. standing there, in pants *and* a shirt, thank God. "Oh good. You're wearing more than a tie."

He raised a brow as he leaned in to kiss the breath out of her. A ton of whistles and catcalls from her friends made Hope blush. He handed her a single long-stemmed red rose, minus the thorns.

So sweet. "Aw, that's so nice." She blinked again, telling herself to stop getting so emotional over the simplest things.

"Have fun, baby. I'll see you when you get home." He left before she could ask him what exactly he meant by that. But the fact he'd shown up to wish her a happy birthday, with a flower, no less, made her so very happy.

Music started pumping from overhead speakers, and the lights flickered. A low male voice announced, "Everyone, the show's about to start. If you could all please take your seats."

Hope sat. Noelle hurried back, put drinks on the table, and rubbed her hands together. Multicolored lights flashed on the small stage, and the room around them darkened except for the slight glow back by the minibar.

"Noelle, seriously, tell me this isn't some cheesy stripper show," Hope whispered.

Rena nodded. "They stuff their bikinis with socks. So I hear."

"Nothing cheesy about it or their bikinis." Noelle grinned. "Shh. Enjoy the drink." She put a stack of ones in front of Hope. "Happy birthday."

Hope groaned.

"Ladies, may I present Turf. He's a landscaper who likes to dance. And he's crazy good at trimming bush." The women groaned. "He's also found that sometimes wetting down the bush makes it that much easier to care for." The groans soon turned to cheers.

"That was horrible," Hope murmured to Noelle.

Rena laughed along with several others.

When six and a half feet of oiled Turf walked onto the stage, those cheers became shouts. Nothing cheesy about the handsome guy with muscles to spare who smiled and asked for the birthday girl.

No, not so cheesy at all.

Hope caught a ride home with Noelle, having spent all of Noelle's money. Fifteen ones, but it had been worth it. She'd gone to exactly one stripper show about five years ago, and it had been nothing like the one she'd seen tonight. The guys had been fun, could dance, and seemed to really enjoy the evening. It helped that her crowd hadn't been too obnoxious; thankfully, Collette and the bartender had found a quiet place to enjoy themselves on his break.

The company had been grand, the show more than enjoyable, and the booze flowing freely, which had gone nicely with the cake.

Hope was still singing that last number Guns—*Oh my God, his ass, and I'm not an ass girl*—had been dancing to when Noelle parked in front of her apartment.

"You are the best friend ever." Hope gave her a tight hug, only slightly buzzed since she'd spent more time dancing than drinking. The show had turned into a dance party at the end, with everyone laughing it up.

"I am. And I have a secret for you." Noelle grinned wide. "Guns is Jean-Luc."

"*What?*"

"I know. Well, I have to go. He's giving me my own private show in half an hour. Au revoir."

Hope left the car and waved to Noelle. Best. Friend. Ever. But as she turned, a large figure loomed near the entry.

"About time you got home," J.T. said as he walked into the light.

She let out the breath she'd been holding. "You scared me."

"Good. From what I hear, I should be scared.

How many ones did you shove down those manly G-strings, anyway?" But instead of scowling, he was smiling at her.

She laughed. "Oh my gosh. What a night. That was so much fun." She squealed when he lifted her in his arms and swung her around. "I was afraid you might show up onstage."

"Nah. I didn't want to make Turf look bad." He laughed. "That was my guy Grim in there. Did you see him?"

"Wait. Your guy?"

"He works at the studio. Hell of an artist. I had no idea he could dance until Noelle stopped by to mention her great idea for a gift for you." He snorted. "I still say you only needed me up there, but since she was bringing family, no way I could shake my thing for you."

Hope laughed harder, wondering if she maybe was tipsier than she'd thought. "Did you know Noelle's guy was there? He danced at the end. What an ass."

"I hope you mean he was really obnoxious." He finally set her down and gave her a look.

"Oh, um, yeah. So rude. I can't believe she's dating that guy." She giggled. "I think I'm a little loopy."

His smile made the night brighter. "I think you are too. Come on, old lady. Let's get you inside so I can give you my present."

She sighed. "I'm so happy right now. I was really bummed out earlier when I thought you didn't care."

They walked in together, and she told him all about the party, especially about her friends' antics, as well as the McCauleys in attendance drinking and dancing with abandon.

"I had no idea Vanessa could move like that. She's normally pretty tight-assed. She tight-asses all over the place. Hmm. Is that a verb?"

"It is tonight." He helped her inside and locked up after her. Then he led her down the hallway to her bedroom, where he'd decorated with candles and flowers. A wrapped package the size of a magazine lay in the middle of her bed. "Happy birthday, Hope."

She couldn't help it. She teared up. "Oh, I'm trying not to make my mascara run."

"Too late."

She hugged and kissed him, but before things got too steamy, he gently moved her back. "Not yet." He cleared his throat. "Tonight is about you. Not me sexing you up, unless you want that, of course." He grinned. "Open your present."

She fetched it off the bed, wobbled, and realized she had yet to take off her heels. She would have, except that she wanted J.T. to see her in them, looking sexy, before she fell on her face. Carefully balanced, she started to open the present when she looked at J.T. and saw him frowning.

"What's wrong?" she asked.

"I hope you like it."

He seemed nervous, the cutie. So big, strong, and unsure that she'd like his gift. "I'll love it, no matter what it is." *Like I love you.*

She nearly dropped the gift.

"What's wrong? You're not going to be sick, are you?"

Doing her best not to hyperventilate and chalking up her amorous thoughts to her cosmopolitans, she shook her head. "Nope. Fine. I'm just so excited to see it." It felt like a frame, like a picture.

He relaxed somewhat and stuffed his hands in his pockets. She stared, having never seen him so worried. "Open it already," he growled.

Even more curious now, she tore open the paper. A framed picture looked back at her.

"It's you," he stated, as if she couldn't tell.

He'd drawn her in the middle of an artistic explosion of color, beauty, and wonder. She marveled at his talent, that anyone could make her look so magnificent. Her eyes sparkled in the picture, and in them she saw images. Small pictures of so many things. Hearts, butterflies, flowers. In the background of her image he'd drawn a seascape and a deep-blue sky, the sun casting a glow over everything, especially her hair.

"This is…" She couldn't believe he'd done this for her.

"I can do something else, if you want. Get you a necklace or something. I know you liked that sapphire one at that Green Lake jeweler last weekend."

"No. This… It's absolutely incredible. I love it." She couldn't stop staring at it. "How did you get so much detail into my eyes? And the images all over the place. They should be too much, but they aren't." She raised her gaze to his and saw him blushing. "I *love* this. Thank you so much." She kissed him, deeply affected by the thoughtfulness of the gift.

Because in the drawing she saw that he'd listened to her. He'd put things into it that meant something to Hope. A fun trip to an aquarium she'd taken with family as a teenager. Her preference for summer and spring, flowers and butterflies, which she loved. She'd actually considered a butterfly for a tattoo, not that she'd ever followed through on it. All the tiny details came from things Hope had shared with J.T. during their many talks.

"This is the best present I've ever received."

He seemed embarrassed at her admiration, which served to make it even better. He hadn't drawn the art for praise, but for her. "I'm glad you like it, honey."

"You know what would make my night perfect?" She carefully set the picture on her dresser and returned to him, placing her hands on his waist.

He put his hands on hers as well. "What's that?"

"If my boyfriend made love to me in a room filled with flowers and candlelight."

"Your wish is my command." He stared into her eyes. "You get prettier every time I see you. How's that possible?"

She grinned. "It's magic."

"Yeah. Magic." He kissed her.

Lost in his taste, in his touch, Hope felt her dress slide down her body, followed by her bra and panties. Left in nothing but heels, she was at least a few inches taller and better able to meet J.T.'s mouth so he didn't have to bend so much.

"You're fucking gorgeous," he said as he stood back to see her, his chest rising and falling, his body rigid. When his gaze met hers again, she was taken aback by the hunger there. "It's so much more than your looks, Hope. It's all of you. Man, you make me so happy."

"I'm glad." She reached for his shirt and tugged it up. He helped her take it off, and she ran her hands over his chest to his massive shoulders. "I love the way we look together." Her lighter-colored hand over his darker skin.

J.T. could have been up on that stage tonight raking in the money. Or modeling for any fitness magazine. Heck, he could model for any vanity magazine as well. "You're so pretty."

"Hope, men are handsome. Not pretty." He took her hands in his, lacing their fingers together. "You're pretty. All over pretty."

How could a girl not fall in love with a man who said things like that?

"My girl is hot and built like a goddess. You sure this is your birthday wish and not mine?" He looked her over with a smile.

She'd had enough. "Kiss me."

Seeing her desire, he stopped teasing. J.T. drew her in to his body, their chests brushing, skin to skin.

She opened her mouth in a sigh, and he plundered. The kiss turned scorching from one heartbeat to the next. She followed where he led, her heart as much affected as her body. J.T. stroked her with tenderness and lust, and the emotional climax hit her well before her physical one.

Such feeling for this man in her arms. Hers. She'd claimed him, and even if he'd never know, she'd treasure tonight forever. She gave as good as she got, and by the time they were both naked on the bed, she wanted nothing more than him inside her.

While he sucked her nipples and ran a hand down her belly, thumbing her clit and sliding his fingers between her legs, rubbing that slick desire over her sex, she was losing herself in him.

"So good, baby. So right."

She nipped his neck, felt him jerk against her, and grabbed his cock. He felt slick, and she loved knowing he wanted her with the same desperation she felt. "Inside me."

He shook his head, his entire body taut. "No. Not without a condom. I'll come in you tonight. I want you too much."

"Then put one on, or I'll take the choice from you." She pumped him and saw his dark eyes narrow.

"Keep it up, I'll come all over you."

"Talk is cheap."

He yanked her hands up and put them on either side of her head. "Keep 'em there." Then he sheathed himself in a condom faster than anyone she'd ever seen do that. He returned, grabbed her hands to hold them pinned, and nudged her legs wider.

"In me," she whispered and watched him watching her.

"I'm gonna fuck you hard. Balls deep. And I mean deep." He sucked on her lower lip, and she arched up, brushing her erect nipples against his chest. "Oh, you're asking for it."

So saying, he positioned himself between her legs and gave her a tiny bit of him.

"Please," she begged, nearly going over the edge.

J.T. stared into her eyes and shoved hard and fast.

She came on a gasp, her entire body one live wire of feeling, while he took her like a man possessed. He swore and told her how much he loved her while he sawed in and out of her, the fierceness of his taking matched only by the violence of her never-ending orgasm.

When he finally stilled inside her, she'd come to her end. His hands gripped her wrists so hard, but she didn't give a damn, trembling under the man still jerking inside her.

They lay joined, connected in a way they'd never been before. Hope nuzzled his throat, planting soft kisses, and he released her wrists and propped himself on his elbows to see her.

"God, Hope. You get to me. You really do." He didn't smile. Didn't look pleased. In fact, he looked a little angry.

"J.T.?"

He withdrew and left for the bathroom, then returned with a…paddle? "Don't even think of falling asleep yet, birthday girl. Someone needs some birthday spankings. And not just one, but at least, say, fifteen. That is the number of ones you shoved down those strippers' thongs, isn't it?"

She blinked. "More?" Her gaze wouldn't leave the paddle, because when she met his hard stare, she felt another climax promising to build.

"Oh yeah." He chuckled, slapping the cloth-covered paddle against his hand. "So much more."

Chapter 17

"You going to marry the ointment, or can I get a tube?" Grim stood behind J.T., his hand out, waiting.

"Oh, sure." He tossed a bottle to the guy and had to start over counting. He'd volunteered to do the inventory on supplies to keep his mind busy Monday afternoon, because fuck if he could focus on anything but Hope Donnigan.

His new archenemy, the woman knocking down his last defense against ever settling down. He still didn't know how it had happened. It was a fake relationship. They hadn't exactly committed to each other.

"Hey, J.T. Tell your girl thanks for the bills." Grim chuckled, and it sounded like the rasp of a chain saw coming to life. And just as rusty as one left out in the rain.

"Funny." J.T. turned to see Grim leaning against the door, a shit-eating grin on his bearded face. "So how was it?"

Of all the guys J.T. knew, Grim was the last one he'd have expected to volunteer to dance, nearly naked, for a gaggle of women. But his go-to artist apparently had an even more colorful past than J.T. had assumed. Some of the other strippers he'd known for years, and they danced professionally, so he'd given Noelle their contact info.

"Good. Surprisingly fun." Grim turned to go and threw over his shoulder, "Your sister's hot. So weird." He walked away.

Weird that he found Del attractive? Or that Del was weird? Both applied to his sister, and frankly, J.T. didn't want to know. He had his own problems trying to grapple with feelings he shouldn't be having.

Suke stuck her head in. "How come I wasn't invited to the party?"

"You met Hope one time. And the guys were getting naked. Not the women."

"Yeah, but I'm bi."

"Since when?"

She sighed. "I'm not, but Hope is cute, and I bet her friends were too."

"Go ask Grim. He can tell you."

She frowned. "Fine. I will." She left.

He had a moment's peace. Then Vargas had to mouth off, joining him in the closet. "Yo, J.T. I heard your woman liked Grim best."

"Says who? Oh right. Grim."

Vargas laughed. "I would have paid to see that. Grim shaking his moneymaker. Dude never smiles, but I bet you he was smiling a lot Friday night. Nao still doesn't believe it."

"Liar," he heard Nao shout. "Grim, no way in hell you took your clothes off for a hen party."

"A chick party, dickhead," Grim rumbled. "They were hot. And they all wanted me. Oh, hey, I think I saw your sister there too. And you know, she likes to get dirty..."

"Fuck you."

"That's what she said."

He heard Suke laughing like a loon.

J.T. sighed. "Go play referee, would you? I keep having to count the same shit over and over again."

Vargas studied him. “Have Daisy do it.”

“She’s taking her lunch.”

“Have her do it when she gets back.”

“I got this,” he growled.

“Need some space?”

“Yeah. No. Fuck. I don’t know.”

Vargas grinned. “I’m sensing it’s a woman.”

“Well, it sure isn’t Grim and his hairy ass.”

Vargas snorted. “Okay. I’ll let you get back to counting.” He left, and a minute later J.T. heard Nao laughing and agreeing with Vargas that Grim probably did have a hairy ass.

When Grim asked if they wanted to see, even Suke said yes.

“I don’t want to know.” J.T. forced himself to remain sequestered. He finally got the ointment tubes accounted for, the bandages, cleaning supplies, water cups and bottles. The other stuff on the shelf to his left could keep for Daisy.

When he’d finally had enough time to decompress, he went back to his station to check on his own supplies. Daisy stuck her head in to let him know Suke was in the back room conferring with a potential new customer.

Nao and Grim were working on clients, and Vargas had an Out to Lunch sign on his table. All was organized, functional, profitable. Normally, the notion that J.T. was succeeding was enough to make him smile. Not today.

“Guys, you okay if I get us some more upbeat music?” The chill techno wasn’t working for him today.

“Please,” Nao said. And his client agreed.

J.T. left to switch the music and returned, ready to work.

But his mind remained on Hope.

He was still a little fuzzy about some details, like how they'd gone from clothed to fucking. That had been a pleasurable blur. After seeing her in nothing but those black heels, all the blood had pooled to his dick, leaving his brain unable to function past knowing he needed to get inside her.

They'd done more than just make love with their bodies. He'd always been a bit fanciful, poetic. He had the soul of an artist, his father liked to say. And he straight up knew he'd connected with Hope on another plane. Fuck, but he might have said he loved her in the heat of the moment. And he'd swear she'd said it back to him.

But maybe that was just wishful thinking, which was crazy. They still hadn't officially claimed each other, sticking to the idea of their *pretend* dating status. Every damn time Hope called it that, he wanted to hit something. For all that they'd begun as something fake, their relationship had for sure turned into the real deal.

I fucking love her.

Well, hell.

Everything she did mattered. He knew so much about her, and drawing her had been easy, a true pleasure because his art spoke to all of him. He never had a problem expressing himself artistically. And when his subject was someone as clear and lovely as Hope, he could lose himself in the pleasure of its creation.

When she'd seemed so touched by his work, understanding he'd given her more than the drawing, but something of himself, she'd breached that last part of him shielding against sharing and taking that final step.

Watching his father, a man he respected and tried to emulate, lose his shit *for decades* over love, J.T. had vowed to go in the opposite direction. Lots of girlfriends, lots of fun, and he kept everyone at a distance. No pain. Not like the kind his aunt felt when she chose the wrong men to trust. Or the kind his cousin felt after putting her heart out there only to have it stomped on by guys not worthy.

Or his sister, who'd nearly died once, then felt even worse when the man she loved supposedly didn't love her back. Yeah, she'd made a muck of that one, because Mike was clearly whipped, but whatever. His sister had experienced real hurt.

He was the smart one. The Webster who learned from other people's mistakes. And for thirty-two freakin' years, he'd been successful.

Hope Donnigan had ruined him.

He loved everything about her, and J.T. wasn't a guy who had ever thought falling in love would be good for him. He didn't know what to do about it either. The smart thing would be to take a break and get some distance.

Except that some asshole was stalking Hope, and until they found the guy, J.T. didn't want her on her own. If he could keep his dick in his pants around her, he'd suggest they back off the sex wagon. Unfortunately, when they were together, he wanted more. Sadly, it wasn't always about being physical. He'd been with women where the attraction was out-of-this-world hot. When he sank inside Hope, though, his orgasm didn't seem as important as being as humanly close to her as possible did.

He rubbed his eyes, wondering where to turn for help. Sure as shit, he couldn't ask Del. The McCauleys were out, because lately they all wanted nothing more than to procreate. His cousin and his aunt had no clue how to have a stable relationship with the opposite sex. His dad, maybe?

Thinking it to death wasn't helping, so he told himself to sac up and do his job.

"Yo, J.T. Note stuck on your car for you." Vargas handed him a folded note, then went back to his station to work.

J.T. opened it, curious who might have left him a note instead of coming inside to talk to him. The note had been typed on fancy white paper.

> *Meet me at Ray's at nine. Don't be late. Don't call—this is your only invitation. I'll be toward the back by the tree, where it's PRIVATE. I'll be wearing my black heels…and nothing else. Hope.*

So she wanted to be kinky? Some lovin' out in public? He was game. She'd loved the paddle, as he'd anticipated. Hope had been a naughty girl.

He felt himself smiling and groaned. *So gone over this girl. What to do?*

Meeting her at Ray's sounded like a good place to start.

Suke appeared. "J.T., Melissa is here."

He sighed. "Send her back."

At nine o'clock on the dot, J.T. stood by the tree in the back of the lot. Ray's wouldn't be too crowded on a

Monday. So she'd picked a good day to try this. The large tree that stood by itself at the end of the gravel parking lot was thick enough to hide a pair of lovers using it as leverage. And the overhead lamplight from the property adjacent to Ray's didn't filter through the leaves, giving them plenty of shadow to work with.

He looked around, suspicious that Hope had yet to show. Where could she be hiding?

He heard the snap of a stick on the ground and turned just as the blow to his side took him to his knees and had him sucking wind.

"Fucker. Here's a message for you. Stay away from Hope."

Before he could get hit a second time, J.T. scooted away and turned to see a stranger coming at him. No, *two* strangers. He hurried to stand. The one who'd punched him was carrying a bat. Before he could get hit again, J.T. feinted a step at the unarmed one before knocking into the bat guy. He grabbed the bat and tossed it far away, striking someone's car.

He felt another punch, this one to his back but below his kidney, fortunately.

Angry and needing to hurt someone, J.T. put Bat Guy down without too much issue. But the one behind him had found time to grab a big, fucking rock.

"Asshole, drop it before I drop you." J.T. wanted to hurt him. Badly. "So you think you can have Hope, is that it?"

"I don't know the bitch. I was paid to pass on a message." He grinned. "Actually, all three of us were."

Three…?

The next tackle took J.T. off his feet into a face-plant

that would have made his father proud. A brief spate of sports in high school had shown he had a proclivity for athletics. Of course, back then J.T. had been the one doing the tackling.

He could still take a hit, though. He elbowed the load on top of him and heard a grunt, then rolled them over in time to see that rock land where his head used to be. Unfortunately, the load, who had to weigh nearly half again as much as J.T., was a big fucker, and strong. He rolled them back so that he straddled J.T., gaining leverage.

"Shit, man. He said to hurt him, not kill him," the load said to his buddy as he punched J.T. in the mouth. J.T. blocked the next hit but took the third on the cheek. Pain blossomed on the left side of his face while he fought to focus his next punch.

"There's a bonus if he's hurt bad but still breathing."

"Seriously? Oh, I... *Oof.*" The load went down, J.T.'s fist to his nuts a definite grounder.

Before the guy with a rock could bring it down on J.T.'s face, Heller was there. He took one look at J.T. on the ground, Bat Guy unconscious, and the other two assholes, and smiled.

His scary, I-am-your-personal-hell-on-earth smile.

He hit Rock Guy once and dropped him like a bag of dirt. Load stood, shaking off his groin shot. Being a decent bruiser, Heller waited for the guy to strike first.

He did, and Heller beat the shit out of him, only stopping when the guy pleaded for mercy. Bat Guy, now waking and woozy from J.T.'s punch, saw Heller and ran.

Doing his best to breathe shallowly—because, hell

if he didn't worry he'd maybe cracked a rib—J.T. just lay there.

Heller crouched, frowning down at him. "You good?"

"Oh sure. Just enjoying the sight of this beautiful tree."

Heller laughed. "It is a nice tree. Ah, J.T. You always make me smile. Thanks for this."

"Yeah, because I planned to get sucker punched so I could get you in on a fight."

Heller helped him to his feet, then half carried him to the bar while J.T. told him about the note he'd received. "But not one word about this to anyone, okay? I need to figure this out."

"Sure." Heller wouldn't say a word. Not like he talked all that much as it was.

The bouncers took one look at J.T. and demanded to know what had happened, because Earl and Big J. were like that, friends of his who didn't play when it came to policing Ray's. Heller explained because J.T. knew if he opened his mouth, he'd moan.

Big J. took off to grab the guys.

No one mentioned calling the police, because folks at Ray's handled their own business. J.T. agreed. Well, he normally would have. But he knew Hope hadn't set him up to be hurt. He had a bad feeling her secret admirer had, and escalating to violence took the guy's creepiness to a new, scary playing field.

He coughed and moaned. "Shit. Earl, see if you can find out who hired the guys."

"I'll watch the bar while you go," Heller offered, still holding J.T. up as if he weighed nothing.

Earl nodded and went after Big J.

"Let's get you settled." Heller dragged J.T. to a nearby table, while the few patrons inside muttered to themselves.

Just his dumb luck that his cousin happened to be working tonight.

"Oh no. J.T., what happened?" Rena rushed over to them, took one look at his face, and left. Only to return with a first aid kit, some ice, and a cloth. "Put this on his face," she ordered Heller, who did as he was told without question.

While they worked, Heller told her all he knew. J.T. added a little, but nothing about the note he'd received until he talked to Hope about it.

After getting his face wiped down, his cheek iced, and his ribs prodded by Heller, J.T. felt ready to fight again. "I said I'm *fine*."

"*Nein*. They may be broken. I think a doctor would be good." Heller's accent deepened, his worry clear.

"What the heck?" Rena glared at J.T.—her favorite cousin.

"What did I do?"

"That's my question. Why would someone just attack you like that?"

"The world is full of asshats. I don't know for sure. But maybe Earl or Big J. will get something out of them."

Earl walked over, shaking his head. "Big J. said one of them took off. The other was just coming around when we talked to him. He said someone hired him over the phone. Gave him a grand to break your face. An extra five hundred if it hurt a lot."

"Nice of him." J.T. winced when Rena cooed over him, putting that damn ice over his cheek again.

"Dropped off the cash in an agreed-upon spot. He didn't see the guy, but he told me that one of the ones who rabbited did. Guy's name is Paulie."

"I know him." Heller nodded. "I'll find out." He stood.

Rena stood with him, finally leaving that damn ice alone.

"Be careful." She grabbed Heller by the hand and squeezed. "You hear me? Don't get hurt."

Heller's soft smile made J.T. want to groan. Didn't the man know better than to show such weakness around his cousin? She already had the guy wrapped around her little finger. She didn't need to know it.

He glanced at Earl and saw the guy straight-up grinning at the pair. "J.T., want to talk to him?" In other words, want to beat his ass?

"Nah. I think Heller did enough damage."

Earl grunted. "Yeah. Big J. said the two guys looked like they'd been clobbered by a hammer. Didn't see the third one."

"He ran after watching Heller work."

"Smart guy."

Rena must have realized she had a hold on Heller, because she flushed and quickly released him. Turning to J.T., she shook her head. "You're a mess."

"You know, I think Heller's right. I should see a doctor. Heller, can you take me?"

"*Ja*. Come." He lifted J.T. to his feet and, when J.T. hissed, moved to carry him.

"Stop. I will *not* be carried out of Ray's, for God's sake. Just gimme some space." He took a shallow breath and walked slowly toward the door.

"I'm telling Uncle Liam, so you'd better not be lying about the doctor," Rena called after him.

"Shit."

Next to him, Heller chuckled. "That Rena, she's such a smart one. And so pretty." The big guy sighed.

"Sucker."

Heller didn't argue.

With Heller's help, J.T. made it back to his car. "How'd you know to come back here? It's well away from the rest of the cars."

"I saw something not right. So I thought I'd investigate. You're welcome."

"*Danke*." J.T. grinned, and winced. "Teeth are okay. But my lip is split."

"So no kissing for a while, hmm?" Heller sure picked a fine night to have a sense of humor. "Do you need me to take you to the doctor? Or did you say that to get your cousin to stop hovering?"

"The second thing you said." J.T. painfully lowered himself into his car, swearing up a storm. "At least they left my hands alone. I might have a bruise or two, but nothing to impede movement." He flexed his fingers and hands, relieved. Since he was used to hitting a bag at the gym, his hands didn't feel strained from punching.

"Yes, but sitting might be painful. Then how will you work?"

"Damn it." He really would need to take a trip to the hospital. "Thanks, man. I owe you one."

"Be well. And remember that favor when I come courting your cousin."

Courting? What century was Heller living in? J.T.

snorted. "Yeah? When's that going to be? You've been humming around her for months."

Heller flipped him off, making J.T. laugh again. Which in turn made him groan.

Heller smirked, said something in German, then swaggered away.

The trip to the hospital took a while, because J.T. took his time getting out of the car and walking. The aches had settled in, and he wasn't pleased. What a waste. He could have been spending time with Hope.

No. That's the problem. I need to just relax and get back into my usual routine—and stop *focusing on one particular blond.*

If only he could.

Once he'd signed in, it didn't take him long to be seen. Though the X-ray and results took a while. A few different nurses came in to check on him, and he did his requisite flirting, but his heart wasn't in it. He took the two phone numbers he'd been given and threw them away when the nurses left.

J.T. groaned. So many pretty women. Even the doctor was attractive. But he didn't care. He only wanted Hope.

"Are you in pain?" the doctor asked, hearing him groan.

"Yeah, from stupidity." He blew out a breath. "It hurts to breathe when I move, and when I don't move, but it's manageable." He didn't do drugs. Didn't want any.

She looked at the X-rays, then studied his face. "You're going to have swelling, obviously. But nothing too major on your face. You have two fractured ribs, however. And your intercostal muscles are bound to be bruised, causing pain. I imagine when you say it's a 'manageable' pain, you're gritting your teeth and trying to act tough. But it hurts like a bitch."

He bit back a grin, not wanting to pull at the cut on his lip.

She sighed. "As I thought. On a scale of one to ten, what are you right now?"

"A seven."

"And that's *after* the medicine we've already given you. You're only going to be sorer tomorrow."

He thought about it, knew he had some tattoos scheduled, and accepted the prescription for Tylenol 3, which would give him some codeine, but not too much. "Okay."

"You get one refill, and then we'll see you back for an evaluation, okay?"

"Sure." He'd be fine with what they gave him now. "How long to heal?"

"Everyone's different, but I'd guess, with your physical health prior to the incident and the extent of your injuries, anywhere from three to five weeks."

"Great. Thanks, Doc." He wanted to sit up but didn't want to sound weak when he did. "Ah, could you give me a hand?"

"No. I don't want you moving, Mr. Webster. You sit there and wait for the nurses to come back." She stood and shook her head. "I've got two of them asking after you as it is. You're a pretty popular guy."

"It's the smile. The ladies love a split lip."

"I see." She shook her head and laughed as she left.

It took another hour for him to get discharged. He felt tired and hurt, and it took forever to walk to his car. Once there, he just stared at the low seat. "Crap."

His phone vibrated in his pocket, and he saw he had

several missed calls. He answered the one ringing—Hope. "Hello?"

"Rena called me. Oh my gosh. Are you okay? Are you at the hospital? Where are you? I'll be right there."

He chuckled and wished he hadn't. "I'm leaving. But I'm not great company. Can I see you tomorrow?"

"No. You come over here right now. You're staying with me until you heal. Take your time, but I swear, if you go home, I will hit you right where they did." She disconnected.

Huh.

So J.T. found himself driving to Hope's apartment building. He parked in a visitor spot in the garage, cautious because if he'd been attacked once, he could be attacked again if the stalker knew where she lived.

But he saw no movement, and the lighting made it easy enough to spot a potential threat. He carried a heavy flashlight with him toward the building, enough to protect himself, should he have need.

He used the lame elevator instead of the stairs, and once at her door, it took him one knock before Hope whipped it open. She took one look at his face and burst into tears.

"Hope."

"I've been so worried." She gently tugged him inside, locked the door behind him, then pulled him in for the lightest hug they'd ever shared. "I'm so sorry. This is all my fault. Oh, J.T."

He frowned. "How is this your fault? I got jumped by some assholes. It happens."

She moved back, anger replacing her worry. "So you're telling me the guys who did this didn't have anything to do with me and my secret admirer?"

"Why would you think that?"

She just stared at him.

"What?"

"I'm blond, not stupid." *Not a great time for a blond joke, then.* "I know this has something to do with me. Rena knows too. Heller told her."

"Bastard."

"Well?"

Ah, what the hell? He could use her tender care. "So maybe your guy hired some muscle to make me go away. Not permanently, just hurt enough that I'd leave you alone."

"I knew it." She glared at him and wiped her eyes. And he realized she was wearing a pair of boy shorts and a tank top with no bra. And him too tired to do anything about it. What a crying shame—because he literally felt like crying the longer he looked at those shorts.

"Can you take care of me for a day or two, until I get used to being sore?"

"Yes. In fact, I was going to demand you stay here. So that works for me."

She led him back to her bedroom, where she stripped him down and sighed over every little bruise on him. He wasn't too stubborn to admit he liked her fussing over him. Liked it a lot.

Hope planted tiny kisses on the cuts on his face, and the butterfly-light pressure did nothing but relax him. The affection in those kisses made him feel ten times better. He started to drift off and fought sleep.

"No, sweetie. You rest your eyes. I'll make sure your work gets handled. Is Suke's number in your phone?"

He felt her stroking his head, and the touch was

sublime—a word he'd only heard used on some BBC baking show, which Sophie and Liam had forced him to watch once. "Suke's number is in the phone under *S*," he slurred.

"Okay. I got it." A soft hand stroked his scalp and cupped his uninjured cheek. He felt the press of another kiss and let himself go. Hope was there. Everything would be just fine.

Chapter 18

Early Wednesday evening, Hope glared at her patient, amazed at how bad he was at being taken care of. Tuesday had gone smoothly. He hadn't minded her calling Suke to cancel the day's appointments, because he'd found it hard to sit upright and breathe without wincing. He continued to take his medication, though she'd had to prod him the last time. Nice to know J.T. didn't like drugs.

His father, sister, cousin, and the guys from work had come to see him. And he'd acted fine, shrugging off their concern, smiling. But as soon as they'd left, he'd showed her his pain. The poor guy. Then he'd spent a lot of time sleeping, and she'd gone and reaffirmed to Suke to cancel his appointments until Friday. J.T. could say what he wanted, but he didn't look well at all.

She felt so bad for him. Earlier today she'd taken off at lunch. Since Cam knew why she'd wanted to be home, he'd given her Thursday off as well. At the moment, she thought she might need it.

To hide the body.

"Take a pill."

He scowled. "No. I'm good."

"You're nearly as white as I am." She didn't find his groaning laughter amusing. "Look. You're hurting. And my brothers are coming over in about"—she checked her phone—"twenty minutes. So unless you want them to see a complete wuss moaning when he so much as farts, you'll take a freakin' pill."

He stared at her, wide-eyed. "You said 'farts.'"

"Yes, I did."

"So…is this a turning point in our fake relationship? Where we can say 'farts' but not do it in front of each other?"

"You are such a pain in the ass."

"That's a yes, then?" He grinned and moaned again, touching his sore lip. "Sorry, baby. I don't like hurting. I don't like being weak. And I sure the hell don't like you seeing it."

"Why? If I was in pain, you'd help me, wouldn't you?"

"Of course."

She shrugged. "So why is this different?"

"It just is."

She watched him down the pain pill. "I am *so* glad I wasn't born with a penis. Having one makes you stupid."

"Tell me about it."

She stared at him on her couch, the ashen man propped up on a pillow, turned to watch some car chase on television. He was so handsome, even beaten and battered, wearing sweatpants and a Jethro Tull T-shirt his father had brought him that for some reason had him cursing his father's name.

Sophie and Liam had tried babying him. Hope had to admit she'd loved watching J.T. grow embarrassed at all the attention, especially his father's. But he'd acted as if he could manage the pain well enough, and they'd left with a promise to return tomorrow. On the way out, Liam had taken her aside and warned her J.T. didn't do pain well. Boy, was he right.

Apparently her boyfriend could only take so much pampering.

And yeah, she meant *boyfriend*, not preceded by *fake* or *pretend*. Tired of trying to lie to herself about what he meant to her, she accepted that she wanted him. The man gave her orgasms, treated her like gold, and had taken a beating he still didn't blame her for. His family and friends loved him, and he treated people like they mattered. Even ex-girlfriends like Trish who were too pushy to know better. What wasn't to love?

Hope had dated a lot of men in her thirty years. And not one had ever been so sweet, sexy, or caring. Or made her feel so much so fast. Taking care of him soothed her. It wasn't a chore or a need of his to fulfill.

Now she had to figure out a way to get him to stay and make it seem like his idea. Not one of her better moves, but it beat pining for the doofus for the rest of her life.

Since he'd taken the pill, she confessed. "I was kidding. My brothers aren't coming over tonight. They're coming over tomorrow."

J.T. gave her a narrow-eyed stare.

"Is that supposed to scare me?"

The glare grew icier. He was turning her on with that attitude. Sadly for him, the bruises made him look more badass.

She put her hands on her hips and waited.

He sighed. "You win. Happy now?"

"No. I'll be happy when they find the guy responsible for all this."

"Stop."

She sat on the coffee table and stared at his bruised cheek. "Stop what?"

"Stop blaming yourself. I should have known not to go."

"But you thought it was me."

"Well, I should have wondered if it was really you. The note was kind of weird."

She sat up straighter. "What do you mean? What exactly did the note say?" He hadn't been specific before, so she'd thought it a simple case of misdirection.

"The person claiming to be you might have hinted that you wanted to have sex in the parking lot of Ray's."

"I'm sorry. What?"

He covered his eyes. "This is embarrassing."

"Oh, now I *have* to know what that note said."

"Well, basically it told me not to call, because the note was my only invitation. And that you'd give me a private show, wearing only your black heels."

"You thought I'd write something like that?"

He eased his head back and stared at the ceiling, not meeting her eyes. "Actually, you typed it."

"Wait. You thought I'd *type* up a note telling you to meet me in the parking lot at Ray's—where I'd only be wearing heels?"

He groaned. "I know. It makes no sense now. But the note mentioned your black heels, so I thought for sure it was you."

She laughed so hard she cried.

"It's not that funny," he snapped. She continued, lost in the hilarity, and he grumbled, "I am injured, you know."

When she could contain herself, she wiped her eyes. "Thanks. I needed that. You're a moron, you know that?"

"Yes." He gave her a pitiful look.

"First of all, if I was going to write a note like that, I'd write it out by hand. Like, jotting you a note. I wouldn't go back to my computer to type and print it out. Second, I wouldn't leave it on your car, where anyone could find it. God knows what Suke would do with something like that."

He snorted.

"Third, every woman I know has black heels. It's a standard thing, like a guy owning a pair of sneakers. But if you're thinking my 'admirer' knew because he saw me wearing them, I guess that's possible. He would've had to see me leaving my apartment or meeting Noelle for my birthday. And since the dance club isn't one of our regular haunts, he would have had to follow us. I don't buy it."

"Me neither. Maybe he guessed on the shoes."

She stared at him, bemused. "So you got jumped because you wanted to meet me for outdoor sex."

"Yes. But I was all for the sex because you initiated, not about doing it outside."

"Are you sure?"

"Yes."

She thought about that. "I initiate sex. Or I would. I just never get a chance because you beat me to it."

He gave her a slow smile. "That's good to know, because I—"

His phone rang. She handed it to him, and after a moment, he set it on the table. "Okay, Heller. Tell us both. You're on speaker."

"I found your Paulie. He tells me of a man—medium height, slender. Dark hair, dark eyes maybe. This man gives him money. Paulie thought he was probably the actual person behind it, because he was bossy, rude, and adamant about not giving any more until the deed was done. Apparently the bonus for making you feel much pain was to be given after proof of you being broken. Paulie didn't plan to kill you, but he did think about taking a few of your teeth as proof of a job well done."

"Thanks. I think."

Heller hung up.

Nice to know J.T.'s molars were worth a pretty penny. He did have straight white teeth, Hope noticed. "The description Heller gave us could fit a few of Cam's clients, actually. Brad, Joe, and Steven come to mind. They've been in during the period this has been going on. What did my brothers say about Greg?" He'd told her that her brothers would look into her ex.

"I don't know. Why don't you call them...since they aren't coming over until *tomorrow*?"

She smiled. "Yes, dear."

He laughed and gave her a sly smile. "Man, you are like your mom."

"Sticks and stones, big guy. Sticks and stones." She called Landon.

"Hope? You okay?"

"Yes. Have you talked to Greg?"

"Yeah."

She put him on speaker. "Okay, now J.T. and I can hear you."

"Hey, Landon." J.T. looked more animated. "What about Greg?"

"J.T., how are you feeling? I heard you look like shit."

"He does," Hope told him. "Now—Greg?"

"Right. So Numbnuts had no idea what the hell was going on. He says about a month ago, somebody busts his windshield and leaves a note telling him to leave you alone. So he assumed it was us and came to talk to you. That's when you kicked his ass at the park."

"It had to be my admirer."

"Yep. But it's odd. The inconsistency of when the guy is sending you gifts and having J.T. beat down. I mean, it's not happening often enough to tie this guy to an actual suspect. Like, if every time the pizza guy showed up, you got flowers, we'd know it's him."

"According to J.T.'s. friend, who talked to one of the guys who beat up J.T., he—"

J.T. interrupted. "Okay, hold on. I was not beaten up. I was sucker punched, managed to kick two guys' asses, then Heller helped. Okay?"

"Sure, man." Landon sounded amused.

J.T. heard it, because he glared at the phone. "Asshole."

Landon laughed.

"The point," Hope reiterated, "is that the person who hired them could match the description of a few of Cam's clients."

"If we could get the guy to see some pictures, maybe he could confirm who it was. Think he'd tell us?"

J.T. nodded. "Yeah, if Heller asks, Paulie will tell him anything my boy wants to know."

"Great. But I think at this point we want the police in on this," Landon said. "J.T., you've got broken ribs. Yeah, okay, you can take care of yourself. If that had happened to Hope…"

"I know." J.T. looked at her, and she saw fear in his

eyes. "I know someone who can help. At this point, if I go the cops, they'll want details. And I can tell you no one at Ray's saw anything. Heller sure won't talk to the cops. Not with all the dirt on him."

Hope blinked. "On Heller?"

"Nothing that could stick," he tried to reassure her. "Anyway, it's probably best we handle this ourselves. Catch the guy in the act so we have proof, not just what we think he did. It'll play better for the cops."

"Well, let me know if you need help," Landon said. "I know some people too."

"Yeah, but your people would be more interested in putting my kind of people in jail."

Landon growled, "Somehow, that doesn't inspire confidence in your ability to protect my sister, Webster."

"It should," Hope said. "His friends carry all sorts of illegal weapons."

"What—"

"Gotta go." Hope hung up. "He's such a brat. Born first and thinks he knows everything." She saw J.T. trying not to grin.

"Stop making me laugh. My mouth hurts."

She leaned over to kiss it better. And he turned and took the kiss full on the mouth when she'd meant to kiss the cut on the side. She kept it light and stroked his uninjured cheek. "I really am sorry you got hurt."

"I know." He sighed. "You smell good."

Staring down at him, she thought about what might have happened if Heller hadn't stopped by when he had. What if the guys had permanently injured J.T.? Or, worse, killed him? Yes, she wanted to keep J.T. To marry him and live out her own happily ever after.

But she knew better than most that the fantasy never lived up to the reality. And how fair was it to coerce the guy into being not only her fake boyfriend, but a real fiancé? One who might not make it to an *I do* because of *her* problem?

Guilt didn't feel good, and neither did the notion she'd been really selfish with J.T.

"Hey, what's that look?"

She didn't want to give him up. But didn't real love mean sacrifice? If she truly wanted what was best for him, maybe being safe, far away from her, was better. And she'd start by distancing herself emotionally, so that after he'd healed, he could go his own way.

"You should rest." She smiled, and before she could tear up, she stood. "I've got a few things to email to Cam since I'm not going in tomorrow. I'll be in the office getting it done, okay?" She grabbed him a bowl of ice cream, then kissed him on the forehead.

"What, am I two?" he joked.

Man, she didn't want to let him go. No more teasing, no more J.T. smiles. No more holding hands or hot, sweaty sex all over the place. Most of all, she'd miss his laughter and the way he made her feel perfect just as she was.

"Ha. Funny. Okay, work to do." She raced down the hall and darted into the bathroom to dry her eyes. She forced herself to stay by her computer for an hour, looking through emails and Facebook.

Hearing nothing but the TV, she looked in on him and found him asleep. She just watched him, seeing him relaxed. So masculine, so big and present, there on her couch.

She adjusted the pillow behind his head to make him more comfortable, and he sighed her name.

She bit her lip and told herself to keep it together. Then she arranged the blanket over him, turned off the television and the lights, and left him alone. She went back to her big bed and slid between the sheets. Alone. Where she belonged.

J.T. didn't know what the hell had happened, but Hope was acting differently. She was almost manic in her desire to clean the place, keep busy, and generally ignore him.

Realizing she probably did have a lot to do, and babysitting a grown-ass man had to be low on her list of priorities, he let her be. The guys from Webster's rolled in a few at a time, and she made herself scarce. Lou raised a brow, looking from her to him, and J.T. shrugged.

Johnny grinned. J.T. hadn't seen the guy in forever, since Johnny was apparently too busy with his sexy girlfriend to care about his single friends.

Wait. Single? Is that what I am? He didn't feel single. He felt like part of a couple—him and Hope. Committed, monogamous. He tested out the sensation of being locked tight to another person. But not just any person. Hope.

"Those meds must be good. He's ignoring me," Johnny said dryly.

Lou grinned. "What they got you on? Vicodin? Morphine?"

"Try Tylenol 3," J.T. said.

"Bummer."

Johnny stared at J.T.'s face. "Lara is itching to come see you. My pretty little nurse thinks she can help you get better."

"You hear that, Hope?" J.T. called out, seeing her pass into the kitchen in one of her mad dashes to "stay out of the way." "Johnny's woman wants me."

"She can have you," Hope said as she passed. "You're not a good patient," she called from the hallway.

Lou laughed. "You all high-maintenance, J.T.?"

"Nah. Not me." In a lower voice, he told them, "She's been acting weird since last night. I don't know why."

Johnny looked around, made sure she wasn't near, and said, "Maybe she's just worried about you. You could have been seriously hurt."

"I know."

"Or she could be PMSing. Is she?"

J.T. blinked. "I, uh, don't know." He should know that, shouldn't he? With as much as he and Hope had been going at it before Monday, he should be aware of her cycle. The timing seemed right…

Lou gave him a sly grin. "Maybe our friend here isn't as tight with Hope as he'd like us to think he is. You know, I have a few friends who would seriously like to get to know her better. Good guys who—"

"Fuck off. You're giving me a headache."

Lou and Johnny shared a grin.

"Well, we'd better go." Johnny stood. "Del let us out of the garage because we were coming to check on you. She wants a full report when we get back."

Lou nodded. "Yeah, and I have a Chevy to handle. Bastard won't turn over, and I can't figure out why."

Johnny rolled his eyes. "I swear, you spend a few

days with Heller painting, and it's like you forget how to be a mechanic."

"You're an asshole, you know that?"

They continued to bicker out the door.

Hope hurried to the closet and grabbed her purse while stepping into some sandals. "While they're still here, I'll walk out with them. So no worries about safety, okay? I'm going to get more ice cream and some milk. We're out."

"Let me give you some money so you—"

The door slammed. He heard the lock turn.

Well, then.

Something was definitely up with Hope. She'd spent more time avoiding talking, looking at, or being near him since last night than she had in the month they'd been dating. As much as he kept trying to remind himself that they were pretend, he knew—in his heart—they weren't. At least, not on his end.

But maybe she wanted to cut ties and didn't know how to tell him. So she started distancing herself now?

Hope wouldn't do that, would she? She wasn't the type to play games. She'd been honest with him from the beginning. She could have led him on and used him to get back at her mom. Instead, she'd asked him for help, then told him to just be himself. No, she liked him. She more than liked him.

She gave him her trust, her body, her fucking smiles that lit up the room. Special ones she didn't share with other people. God, he had it so bad for her that even the panic he should have felt at falling for a woman refused to come. Only the notion that he might lose her to some psycho terrified him. He could work out everything else.

He hoped.

And the pun wasn't lost on him.

He forced himself to get up and walk around, letting his lungs fill and dealing with the pain. He didn't want to chance an infection setting in, and he refused to be short of breath.

As he did slow laps in her apartment, feeling like a big hamster in a tiny maze, he wondered at his father's choice in clothing. Three Jethro Tull T-shirts—that belonged to his father—and sweatpants. How was he supposed to impress Hope looking like a slob with a hankering for the seventies? Like J.T. didn't know his father was teasing him. Hope hadn't asked about his fascination with the rock band, though. She'd been doing her best not to look at him.

He needed to talk to her.

She knocked at the door.

Finally. "Hold on." He moved slowly but with a steady gait. When he looked through the peephole, though, he saw his father. "Dad?" He opened it.

Liam had come alone this time. "Sophie wanted to come, but she had something come up at the gallery needing her attention." His father coughed, emotion bright in his eyes.

"No problem, Dad. Come on in." He stepped back and let his father enter.

Liam walked in, looked around, then ordered J.T. to sit. Considering J.T. had just seen his father and Sophie the other day when they'd brought him some clothes, he didn't understand what his dad was doing here again. Had Hope asked him to come check on him? "Dad, what's up?"

Frowning, Liam ran a hand through his closely cropped hair. He glared at J.T., then exploded. "Jesus, boy. I taught you better than that!"

J.T. blinked. "Dad?"

"You're getting soft. Letting them punch you from behind? Taking you down? I talked to Heller, who saw some of it. You could have been killed."

Stupid Heller. "I'm fine. I held my own."

"Barely."

"Hey."

"*Damn it*." Liam paced, and J.T. watched his father lose it. The old man swore up and down, not making much sense.

"You okay?"

"No, I'm *not* okay. My son was nearly killed." Liam's voice cracked, and he cleared his throat, his gaze murderous. "You don't *ever* let them do that again. Get your ass back in the gym. Once you're healed up, you're getting some extra training. If I have to get Sam and Foley to knock some defensive moves into you, I will. And don't think Heller won't help as well. We talked about you, and we're both concerned." The fire of anger burned bright in his dad's eyes.

"Aw, Dad. It was a freak thing."

Liam shook his head. "When I lost your mother, something broke inside me." He sat in the chair near J.T., his gaze honest, furious, his voice anxious. "But I had you, and I had Del. You two were a huge pain in my ass for years."

"I tried," J.T. said drily.

"Little shit." Liam managed a watery smile, and J.T. worried about his father's mental state. He'd never seen his dad so rattled. Even when they'd heard that Del had been hit by a car, his father had kept his shit together. "Life is good. So good I keep waiting for something to take it all away. When your sister was injured, I was scared, but I knew, deep down, that she'd be okay. She's always had a hard head, and truth be told, by the time I knew she'd been hit, I'd already heard from Beth that she was recovering just fine. But you." His father leaned over and slugged him in the arm.

"*Ow,* damn it. That hurt."

"You scared the hell out of me. You're smart, smarter than I ever was. You have a gift, son. A magic in the way you see the world. And wondering if you'd be alive to share it after they put a beating on you, that shook me. J.T., I love you, boy."

"Aw, Dad. I know." Shit. Now his vision was starting to get blurry. "Damn. Got some dust in my eyes." He blinked to clear his tears.

"Then you should also know Paulie and I had a chat." At that moment, Liam looked like a man not even J.T. would mess with. "I'll be talking to his friends soon enough. No one messes with a Webster and gets away with it. You're mine. And you always will be. I protect what's mine."

Liam stared at J.T., who stared back, not sure what to say.

"Um, okay."

With a grunt, Liam nodded, looked at him, then stood. He expelled a heavy breath, turned, and walked to the door. He paused with his hand on the knob. "Hope. Is she taking good care of you?"

"Yeah." J.T. sighed. "She's...she's good."

Liam glanced over his shoulder, no longer looking so stressed. "That she is. Sophie thinks the world of her. I like her too." He nodded, and J.T. realized he'd just gotten his father's seal of approval concerning Hope. "She's the type of woman who'll love a man for who he is deep inside. Even when he's too much of a jackass to let her know, she'll wait and be patient. Because at some point, even a jackass has to know when he's got a good thing."

J.T. frowned. "Hold on. I'm the jackass?"

His father just stared at him.

"What happened to you loving me, and me having a gift?"

"Not a damn thing. But it's worth nothing if you don't share it. Remember that." And that said, Liam left.

J.T. sat in quiet speculation, not sure what to make of his father's compliments and insults uttered in the same breath. All that emotion expelled in a matter of minutes. Shaken yet pleased that his father cared enough to check on him again, J.T. sat and thought about things.

He sat unmoving for several minutes before a knock at the door interrupted him.

"Christ. Now what?" He lumbered to his feet once more, groaning, and moved to the door. Only to look through the peephole and see Hope's mother.

She knocked again.

He had to let her in, right? J.T. unlocked the door and opened it, stepping back. "Hi, Linda."

She looked him over, from top to bottom, and shook her head. "You look awful."

"Thanks." He closed the door behind her and joined her in the living room. "Hope went to the store. She'll be back soon."

"Yes, I know. I called her."

"Ah, okay." He walked with her to the couch, watched her sit, and knew he should sit as well to be polite.

It took him a minute and a few muttered curses, but he eased his way into the plush chair by the couch. "So how are you?"

"Better than you." She looked him over, and in her mannerisms he saw hints of her daughter. The way Linda held her head, the way she looked at him with such intensity. Hell, the way she looked, pretty and classy—a mature version of Hope. "We need to talk."

"Funny, that's the line I was going to use on your daughter when she gets home."

Linda pursed her lips. "What exactly is going on between you and my daughter?"

"That's between us, don't you think?"

"You don't like me, do you?"

"I don't know you." He paused. "But I could turn that right around. You don't know me either, but you don't like me, do you?"

"I do."

"Exactly, so—wait. What?"

"I think you are exactly what my daughter needs."

"Say that again? Aren't you the same woman who was going on and on about money and men and Hope being too lame to know her own mind?"

"Yes and no. J.T., I've done a good bit of thinking about you and Hope since I met you. And don't even pretend you two were dating weeks ago. I knew from the start she was using you to teach me a lesson."

"Then why didn't you call her on it?"

"Because, believe it or not, I care about my daughter."

She crossed her legs, and J.T. cringed, seeing her black heels. Hope had been right about every woman having a pair. "Hope and I are a lot alike. I think she'd die before admitting it, but she's competitive, bossy—if gentler going about it—and smart. She also has her own set of priorities in life, and sadly, those haven't included having a decent job or finding a man of worth." She paused. "Until you."

"I really do tattoo people for a living."

She smirked. "I know. I saw your website. I listened to my husband and sons talking about you."

"Well, ignore everything Landon said."

"Why? He's your biggest fan."

"Yeah right." This conversation was nothing like what he might have imagined having with Linda Donnigan.

She laughed. "I'm also close to my sister Beth, who thinks you and your sister are just amazing, by the way."

He flushed. "Aw. Beth is a great lady. She keeps Del in line. My sister needs it. Liam was way too easy on her growing up."

"So she says about you." Linda leaned forward, resting her elbows on her chic red skirt. Her black jacket parted, revealing a silk blouse and a string of pearls around her neck. The woman screamed sophistication with every breath she took. "Hope needs a strong man in her life. She's been searching for a long time, and part of it's my fault. In my attempts to make her strong and independent, I've managed to make her think she can never live up to my expectations. Which couldn't be further from the truth. Hope is a sensitive girl with a big heart. But she has so much untapped potential."

"I disagree."

"Oh?"

A lot of disdain in that one syllable. "Your daughter is one of the kindest, sweetest, most wonderful women I've ever met. She's got a great sense of humor, works hard, and is always trying to please you. She loves her family and friends. She's living up to what she needs to be—herself. She isn't you. Money doesn't mean much to her, and she has no desire to be king of the castle."

"You mean 'queen.'"

Humor, from Linda?

"Yeah, well, queen, then. She likes working for Cam, and she's good at it. She could have any guy she wants."

"Yet she chose you."

"To screw with you, yeah."

"Ah, but there's the rub. I knew who you were when she brought you. All I ever wanted was for my daughter to find someone to love her as much as her father and I love each other. And yes, I want her taken care of. Hope has no thoughts for money. But if you want to live more than paycheck to paycheck and enjoy a day or two not focused on bills, someone has to care about the almighty dollar. You're not poor. Not rich either, but you're no pauper."

"Thanks."

"Yes, I checked up on you. And someday when you have a daughter, you'll do the same. I'm a bit of a throwback, I'm afraid. I don't worry for my sons the way I do Hope. She's just vulnerable in a way they aren't. I've seen her cry when her relationships fall apart, and I know she's heartbroken when yet another decision of hers turns out to be bad. I don't want to be right all the time, you know. I just am." Linda blew out a breath.

"But I have to tell you, I've never seen her look at a man or talk about him the way she does you. I saw you two at dinner together, and you fit. According to your sister and Mike, Sophie, Beth, Liam, and my sons, you and Hope are involved in more than a scam. You're a real couple."

"We are." No point in lying about it, even to himself.

"Do you love her?"

He wished to hell he hadn't opened the door.

"Never mind. You will if you don't already, because my daughter is amazing and lovable and perfect." Linda touched her hair. "Just like her mother." She winked. "So I'm going to do you a favor. I'm going to give you some advice."

Linda stood and walked to the door. After a moment, J.T. straightened, holding his ribs, and joined her.

"What's the advice?"

"Don't tell her I like you. That girl will cut off her nose to spite her face. If she thinks I don't like you, she'll find you that much more attractive. But if I approve, there must be something wrong with you. We have a weird dynamic, and I know it. But I love my daughter more than anything. And I want what's best for her." She stepped closer and cupped his cheek, like Hope did.

He froze, weirded out. Especially when Linda teared up. *Hell.*

"I heard all about what you've been doing to watch over my daughter. And I know you got hurt because of it. I wanted to say thank you. And keep doing what you're doing—only be safer."

He smiled, and she patted his cheek before turning away.

"I was never here."

He repeated, "You were never here."

She put her hand on the doorknob. "I still don't think you'll suit my daughter."

"Nope, not suiting."

"If you have a daughter, I want you to slip Linda into her name somewhere."

"When we—What?"

She laughed and stepped outside. "Funny you said 'when' and not 'if.' Have a lovely day, and I'll see you two for brunch next week."

He watched her walk down the hallway toward the stairs. A ping sounded, signaling the elevator, and Hope stepped out carrying two bags, just missing her mother.

She saw him in the open doorway and started. "You should be lying down."

When, not if.

"We need to talk."

Chapter 19

Hope nodded. "You're right. Let's talk while I put these groceries away." She needed more distance. J.T. should have looked like a gym leftover in sweatpants and yet another Jethro Tull tee. Instead he appeared sexy, rumpled, and doable.

She concentrated on unbagging the groceries, determined to go through with this. She'd thought about nothing else since last night. Though it would kill her to let him go, it would be better for him in the long run. And hey, if he did come back to her, then she could keep him, right?

"J.T., I think you should go home."

"Hope, I think we should—*what?*"

She nodded, putting the milk in the fridge. "It's not safe for you to be here. I don't want you hurt again. And let's face it, this whole thing was just a scam to get my mother off my back. You've gone above and beyond the call of duty for a friend."

"For a *friend*?" He yanked her around to face him, angrier than she'd ever seen him. They'd had their fair share of minor disagreements, but not major fights. Until now, it seemed. "What the fuck are you talking about?"

He stood close, enraged, but she didn't feel threatened. The realization she could trust him to that level shook her. She didn't want him to go.

"I like you, J.T. A lot." She swallowed. "I just think it's not fair to ask you to—"

"Who the hell is asking me anything?" he huffed, and she stared in fascination as Mr. Easygoing turned into a rager. His ribs had to be hurting with all the chest heaving, but he didn't so much as groan or hold his ribs. "I'm your friend, your lover, your goddamn *boyfriend*. We're together now, damn it. You don't ditch a guy because it's not safe. You stay with each other to get through rough times." He glared at her, but beneath the anger she saw a glimmer of hurt, and it shocked her.

"But I—"

"But nothing," he roared. "When two people hit it off like we do, they stick. They don't toss over the other because it's hard or uncomfortable. Christ. When you love somebody, you make it work."

She gaped. *Love?*

"I mean, we like each other, right?" The words tumbled over one another as he rushed to explain himself. His eyes looked a little wild, and he leaned against the wall, away from her, now grabbing his injured side. "We're smokin' in bed. We joke, we laugh. We have fucking fun together. It's not like I'm stopping you from dating. You told me yourself you were done with those losers."

"But you—"

"And I have no intention of hooking up with some other chick after getting to hold on to you for a while. No way," he hissed, still annoyed, apparently. His voice rose once more. "I don't care about other women. I want *you*."

He grabbed her by the shoulders and yanked her close

for a punishing kiss that had to hurt his lip. Yet she could only hold on, enthralled with the man she hadn't been with in days.

"Now quit talking shit, and settle the hell down. There's no walking away from us. Not now, not later. Jesus." He stormed away, not quite as effective in showcasing his rage when he slowed down, but the angry intent was clear.

Hope grinned like an idiot at the empty bag on the counter.

"And put the damn ice cream away before it melts," he shouted. "I'm taking a nap. If you want me, I'll be in *your bed*, where I should have been last night."

Wow. She felt his anger all the way in the kitchen.

And it was glorious.

The sincere fury and pain and affection he felt had poured out, and Hope forgot all about doing the "right" thing and went back to plan A. Making the man realize that being together was the only way to go—and all his idea.

She laughed and hummed while she put the rest of the food away and cleaned up the tiny mess in the kitchen. Then she puttered, doing odd chores around the house.

An hour later, Hope decided to try to make nice with J.T. Except he'd fallen asleep, the poor, angry angel. She laughed to herself and tucked the blanket around him, thinking that even in sleep the man seemed solid, unbreakable.

Yet she knew all too well how he could be hurt. The bruise on his cheekbone looked painful, and his cut lip had to be sore. From what the hospital had told him, he'd have a few weeks until he healed properly. She guessed she'd need to stay close, then, because people who *loved* each other stuck.

She stared down at him, a curious warmth in her heart. He'd meant what he'd said. He loved her. She felt it, and she treasured the knowledge. She also knew he'd nearly had a panic attack after letting that slip, so she'd be damned if she'd bring it up and chance scaring him again.

I love him. I love him. I love him. Saying it to herself turned her giddy with joy. But until she knew he wouldn't run from open confessions of affection, she'd hold it tight to her chest. It meant a lot to her that he hadn't liked the thought of her sending him away. They could have broken it off right then. She'd clearly given him an out he hadn't taken.

A long road lay ahead of them, though. Hope with her mother issues and need for acceptance, and J.T. with his fear of abandonment and the pain that came with loving someone. She wondered if he'd listened to himself, because he'd been spot-on about lovers who stuck with each other through thick and thin.

J.T. felt groggy. He'd gone to sleep annoyed with Hope. Hurt and, yes, angry that she could think to end things "for his protection." What bullshit. That's what guys said to women to get out of relationships. The whole "It's not you, it's me" crap. Well, this time, he was laying down the law.

She was either with him, or he'd spend the next few months convincing her they belonged together.

He shifted and groaned, pulling his sore ribs.

"Here, hold on."

He opened his eyes to see Hope there, stuffing pillows under his back and neck, letting him sit semi-propped in the middle of the bed.

"J.T., I'm sorry."

He grunted. *Good. She apologized.*

"I just felt guilty for all you suffered, and I wasn't there with you when you needed help."

"You're here now."

She nodded and smiled, and he felt as if the sun had risen, the light of her smile covering him better than her blanket did. She must have covered him up, because he'd been hot when he'd fallen asleep. Now he felt comfortable under the covers.

Hope lay down next to him and leaned up on her elbow, on her side. She shifted the blanket down to his waist and drew light circles over his chest. He swore her fingertip sank through cotton, muscle, and bone, touching the heart of him.

"I'm here now." She nodded. "I should also admit I don't feel like a very good girlfriend. And no, I'm not calling us fake or pretend anymore. I'm sorry if that bothers you, but I've felt really close to you for a while now. You're right. We do have fun together. You make me laugh, and you make me smile. I like you a lot."

He swallowed. "You said that." A much better thing to confess than "People who love each other stick together." What the hell was wrong with him? Telling a woman you loved her before she said it was a recipe for disaster.

Although she didn't seem upset. Maybe she'd ignored it, thinking he said it in the heat of the moment. But he meant it. Every word. Again, instead of running—or in his case, wheezing—for the hills, he wanted to hug Hope close and show her how much he loved her.

She eased her hand under his shirt and teased his belly with gentle, barely there touches. He had the urge to really *show her* what he felt.

It had been four days since they'd made love. Not a long stretch of time, but with Hope, it felt like forever. With her, he could always rise to the occasion. Even now. Despite his injuries, he started responding.

It didn't help that her clever fingers kept brushing under the waist of his pants. She untied them and pushed them down a little, scratching his lower abdomen with her kitten-sharp nails.

His dick spiked. From semi-aroused to a brick between his thighs in seconds. He tried to exert some control and got nowhere. Fuck, it felt good to have her hands on him. He wouldn't worry about his erection. It just was. She could ignore it.

"Yes," Hope was saying as she *pushed his pants down*. He hadn't bothered with underwear, not wanting the hassle of dealing with too many clothes when he had to take care of business. The loose sweatpants were easier to work with. She slid them under his ass to mid-thigh, the blanket suddenly gone as well.

He had to clear his throat to speak. His heart raced, and his entire body felt sensitive to the slightest breeze. "Hope?"

"I'm so sorry. A good girlfriend would help her man. Make him comfortable."

Comfortable? He ached in more than just his ribs now.

She kept apologizing and leaned over to kiss his stomach. He tensed as if turned to granite. Then she moved lower still, to his pelvis. Then his inner thighs.

He couldn't part his legs because his lowered pants held him in place. But Hope's hot little hands and even hotter mouth showed she didn't seem to mind.

"I'm just so incredibly sorry," she whispered over his dick. Semi-propped up, he had a front-row seat, watching that silky blond head go down over him while her lips threatened to suck him dry.

"*Shit*. Hope, honey." He groaned and reached for her head. Instead of pulling her off, as he'd intended, he urged her to continue, threading his fingers through the golden glow of her hair. "Yeah, that's it. Oh fuck. You feel so good."

She moaned, and to his pleased shock, he saw her put a hand down her own pants, fingering herself while she blew him. It was the hottest thing ever, and despite the pain that came from an increase in his breathing, the ecstasy of her mouth centered him on nothing but Hope.

Her small hands cupped his balls, and he jerked in her mouth, the movement hurting oh so good.

"Gonna come, honey. So fucking hard," he rasped and would have pumped faster. But Hope suddenly held him down by a hip and bobbed faster. Up and down, sucking like she couldn't get enough of him.

He wanted to hold on, to let her quick fingers draw out her enjoyment, but he couldn't wait.

"I'm coming," he moaned and felt the pleasure curl in his limbs, his torso, then flow from his balls out his body. He filled her mouth, continuing to thrust until he was spent. When she sucked harder, groaning and coming under her own finger, he pushed deeper, wanting to give her the last of him.

She sucked him all down and pulled her mouth away, her lips swollen and rosy from working him over. After righting his clothes, she pulled the blanket back to his waist and laid her head on his uninjured side, by his shoulder. She gently hugged him.

He felt no discomfort at all, awash in the endorphins flooding his body. Screw Tylenol 3. All he needed was a little bit of Hope to keep him floating free of pain.

"That was..." He didn't have the right words. "Thank you."

She smiled against his arm; he could feel it. "You're welcome."

They stayed like that for a while, the joy in just being together enough to soothe him.

"We never did talk about your past lovers," Hope said out of the blue.

"We really need to work on your after-sex talk."

She laughed. "Well, since we're now an official couple, we might as well get to know each other's dirty secrets." She seemed to tense against him.

He waited for the claustrophobia to set in, that feeling of being tied down to one woman stirring an itch to take off and be free. But it didn't come. Just more proof he'd fallen for her.

"Okay, Hope. You go first."

"Wait. I told you about my exes."

"You told me some about them. But I'd like to know more. And besides, you brought it up. You go first."

"Fine." She sighed and ran her fingers over his chest. He'd have purred if he'd been a cat. "I've dated a lot of guys who didn't fit me. You met Greg. He was cute but too controlling. At the end, he'd gone from verbally abusive to scary. I was afraid it might escalate, so I left. Well, that and I found out he'd been cheating on me."

"Ouch." He kissed the top of her head.

"Yeah. Before him, I dated men I thought would give me what I needed."

"Oh? What's that?"

"Someone strong. I wanted a confident type of character, but I kept finding dominant personalities with little give. And they were handsome, muscular men. At least I picked good-looking assholes. Count yourself included."

He frowned at the ceiling. "Thanks so much."

She snickered. "I'm kidding. You're the first guy in a long time to treat me like I have a brain in my head and like my opinions matter. But you're not a pushover." She sounded shy when she added, "And I like how you take charge in bed. We're good together."

"You got that right." He smiled. "You're a strong personality yourself. You can't deal with a wimp, and an alpha type is just going to piss you off. Me? I'm the best of both worlds. Laid-back, a beast at work and in the gym. Oh, and in bed, but you knew that. So is that all you got? No dark secrets?"

"Well, if you must know, when it comes to the prank wars, I usually beat everybody. I pretend it's my brothers doing all the mean stuff, but it's really me."

"Prank wars?"

"Oh yeah. Every year, one of us starts messing with someone else in the family. Fake dog poop in your yard, one shoe missing from each pair in your closet, short-sheeted bedsheets, you name it. Well, back when Ava and Landon first started dating, I'm the one who put the blow-up doll in his bed."

"What's this?"

"Theo took the credit, but he and I both know it was me." She smiled down at him. "I found this blow-up doll at a sex shop, and she looked like Ava. It was weird."

"Wait. What were you doing at a sex shop?"

"Birthday gag gift for a friend. So I bought the doll and dressed it in Jameson's Gym clothes. I left it in Landon's bed, and when he was showing Ava around his place for the first time, she found it." They both started laughing. "It was classic. I'll never forget the shock and embarrassment on Landon's face."

"Yeah, that's a keeper. Your brother..." J.T. shook his head. "I get that he loves you, but he's kind of annoying."

"They all are. I'm the only girl among all my cousins and siblings. I get coddled way too much, except for Theo, who's a good nine years younger than me. It was so I couldn't breathe when I was a kid, my brothers constantly making sure other kids treated me nice. I mean, I was thankful to have a tight family. But geez, it was hard to date."

He grinned. "I tried to help Del, but she pretty much kicked my tail if I got too close. She was always a hardass. Rena, now, she was a sweet thing. Still is. So I took out my defensive frustration on her. Safest girl at school, aside from Del."

"I can see that. You're actually a lot like my brothers. And my dad." Hope frowned. "Is that a good thing?"

"It is if we share positive qualities. Anything annoying and no, you must be wrong."

She grinned. "Okay. Your turn. What are your deep,

dark secrets?" She paused, and he wondered if she'd ask about Trish and the others. Instead she said, "Can you tell me about your mom?"

He'd known she might ask something that personal. To his surprise, he wanted to share. "Bridget Webster was an angel, according to my dad. Now you talk to Aunt Caroline, and you get a reality check. Yeah, Mom was a hottie. She was kind, loving, and stubborn as all get-out. Dad tends to forget that part.

"I don't remember too much of her, and that used to make me feel bad. But hell, I was three when she died of cancer. I sincerely think she was the love of Dad's life. He just faded after that. It was hard the next few years. I remember bad times, like constant sadness, darkness. Not literal dark, but—"

"I understand." She kissed his shoulder, and he sighed, feeling her care to his toes.

"Dad met Penelope, Del's mom, right after Mom passed. She was a diversion, I think, and then she got pregnant. That woke him up. Things were better for a while, until she had Del. But I think Dad was always kind of down, even when married to her.

"She was so pretty, but she wasn't all that nice. Especially when Dad wasn't around. He used to work his ass off with the shop, and we had some lean times where he worried it would go under. But it didn't. Anyhow, so Penelope wanted a better life than that of a mechanic's wife. She did a lot of stuff I think I know but I'm not sure about. Even to this day, Dad won't talk about it."

"Must have been rough."

"It was. I didn't make it any easier, and I was just

a kid. Penelope died in a car accident, high, no doubt, with her lover. Then it was just Liam, Del, and me. And Rena and Aunt Caroline too. I used to push my dad to see when he'd snap. All jokes and skirting the edge of the law. I got into fights. I was a punk, and I admit it. But the old man kicked my ass into gear. I only did a little bit of juvie, and maybe a stint or two in jail after high school. Nothing serious. A fight, that shoplifting gag gone wrong. I told you about that."

"I can't imagine."

"I bet you can't, Goody Two-Shoes."

"Hey." She frowned. "I wasn't that good. I didn't get nearly straight A's like you did, Poindexter."

"I should have never told you that." He laughed at the mischief in her big, brown eyes. "So that's all me."

"Oh, heck no. What about all the broken hearts trailing behind you?"

Now he felt a moment's unease. "Not that many."

"What about Trish? All those nurses at the hospital?" Oh yeah, that smile had a lot of teeth.

"There are a few facts in life I'm sure of. One, I got my looks from Mom, my build from my dad. Both good things when it comes to women. Two, I'm a heck of a guy. I'm gonna straight-out admit I've never had a problem charming women."

"Aha."

"But, I was never a player. I learned early on to treat women with respect. Liam don't play when it comes to the ladies," he teased.

"Good man, your dad."

"Yeah, he is." J.T. smiled. "I'm so glad he's got Sophie now. I've never seen him so happy."

"It took him a long time to find someone to love. What about you? Did you ever come close to getting married? Engaged?"

"Nah."

"Why not?"

"The truth?" At her nod, he bared it all. "Because my dad fucked me up. I've never told him, but seeing how half-alive he was after my mom died, then how Penelope fucked him over, well, it got to me. It didn't help that the only other relationships I witnessed came from my aunt. Have I told you she divorced her fifth husband?"

"You might have mentioned it."

"That's right. And no, you're nothing like her. You're smart and loving."

"Then why did I pick such terrible guys to date? Seriously, my streak before you was like two years of dating duds."

"I think maybe you wanted love too much to wait for the right guy—that'd be me. Hell, I'm not a shrink. Who knows why you picked the wrong guys? Why did it take me this long to get in your bed? I should have been here months ago."

"J.T."

He laughed. "I'm not kidding. I knew you were sexy and pretty, and I wanted a piece of you bad. But dumb Del made me promise to keep my distance. I'm never listening to her again."

Hope kissed him. "Good." Then she asked point-blank, "Do you think you'll ever get married?" She didn't look away, piercing him with that stare.

"Are you proposing?"

The pause before she adamantly denied it took him

aback. Imagine him and Hope married. That was moving way too fast…wasn't it? Next thing he'd be thinking about… "Hey, you ever think about having kids?"

"Sure." She shrugged. "I know I will someday. I'm not set on how many, but I'd like to be a mom. I want to be married and have babies and be crazy in love." She laughed. "But have no fear, I'm not pushing for a ring, J.T. It's like I can see your skin crawling when the m-word comes up. It's kind of fun."

"Not true." To his surprise, it wasn't. It used to be, but for some reason, he liked Hope imagining a future in which she had a family, love, and security. "Can I tell you something else?"

"Oh. Another secret?"

"Kind of." He stroked her arm. "That picture I gave you for your birthday." They both glanced at the frame directly next to her dresser, prominently positioned near her mirror, where she looked at it every day. "That was only part of your present. The other part is a real tattoo. I can do it or have one of the guys at the shop do it. I think you'd look good with one."

"Really?" Her lips parted, then curled into a smile. "Where would you put it, if you were me?"

"Hmm. I was thinking something here." He grazed her upper chest. "Or maybe here." He dragged his hand to her left hip.

"Not a tramp stamp?" She put her hand on the small of her back.

"I *love* those. The trampier the better."

She laughed, but the look she gave him. It filled him full. Her eyes cheerful, her cheeks rosy. Her mouth curled into a smile. She was a picture he'd take to his grave. The ultimate fantasy of what he wanted his future to be.

"Hope..." *I love you.*

She put her head back on his shoulder. "Yeah, me too."

If only.

Chapter 20

Nearly a week had passed, and Hope was no closer to finding her stalker, as she now thought of him. The florist had nothing for her. Her brothers had made some calls, looked into her exes' whereabouts, and turned up nothing. She didn't know what else she could do.

Wednesday afternoon, she sat at lunch with Steven, having finally found a day that worked for both their schedules.

"I've been meaning to try this pizza place for a while."

"I like their Caesar salads." She smiled. J.T. had converted her.

"No need to watch your figure with me." Steven chuckled. "And before you tell me you have a boyfriend, I know. I happened to catch a very large man with you the other day when I drove by on my way to a friend's. Even if I wanted to try my luck, I don't think I'd like him to catch me trying."

She smiled, wondering if this would be a lead-in to a confession, maybe? Would Steven admit to being her stalker? Let something drop to clue her in?

Unfortunately, the guy who'd fractured J.T.'s ribs had been a bust. She'd found some photos of Brad, Joe, and Steven online and sent them to Heller. When Heller had shown them to Paulie, he had denied that any of them was his contact. But the man—and it had been a man—who'd given him the money had worn a hat and sweatshirt. A lot like the description of her cinnamon-bun buyer.

They paused to order their food, then sat down with a number to wait.

She spent an entertaining forty minutes with Steven, enjoying being with a man without the pressure of a date. Steven told her about a woman he'd met in the neighborhood he planned to ask out. They talked about Hope's mother, and Steven told her some funny stories about his house-hunting experiences. Especially the one about finding the owners unexpectedly home for one viewing.

"Yes, the husband and his nanny weren't expecting anyone to be walking around his almost-empty house. How convenient he'd left a bed behind."

"Oh boy."

"Your mom was a champ." Steven laughed. "Calmly, as if we weren't watching the man's bare ass waving in the wind as he frantically tried to cover up, she starts asking him about the house. Square footage, improvements, his favorite selling point. I'm doing my best not to burst out laughing. The woman's hiding under the covers, and the guy is bright red. But he's answering your mother. I kept waiting for him to ask us to leave. He never did."

"That's the magic of Linda. But I have to say, I heard what you got your house for, and it's a steal."

"I told friends moving to the city about her. She'll be getting more clients in no time." He paused. "You never thought about working with her? She mentioned it."

"Oh my God. No. One nightmare of a summer was all either of us could stand."

"Ah. Probably for the same reasons I refused to work at the same hospital as my mother. Chief neurosurgeon makes for a lousy boss and mother."

"Amen." They toasted glasses. "Oh boy. I'd better get back."

"Shoot. Me too. It was a pleasure. And I hope it's not too pushy, but I'd like to have you—and your boyfriend—over for dinner some time. I'm new to the city and making friends, and hell, I like you. Cam too." He paused. "Vanessa..."

"Say no more. She's magnificent. Beautiful. And deadly with a calculator."

He laughed. "I was going to say she sold me on her firm in less time than it took to say hello. She's intimidating."

"And very good at her job. Between Cam helping you manage your money and Vanessa making sure the IRS doesn't take it all away, you're in good hands."

They left the restaurant and returned to their cars, parked next to each other.

Steven frowned and bent over the hood of his car. "Damn it."

"What's wrong?"

"Someone keyed my car. Son of a bitch."

"Will your insurance cover that?"

"I hope so. Man." He looked around, but his car seemed to be the only one affected. "Just my luck."

Hope felt the odd sensation of being watched, and when she turned around, she saw a familiar figure in a sweatshirt and ball cap rounding the corner across the street.

She trembled, forced a smile for Steven, and left to

head back to work. In her car, she called J.T. and got his voicemail.

"Hey, it's me. I had lunch with Steven, and it's not him. My stalker keyed his car. I saw him, J.T. I saw the guy from a distance, in a blue sweatshirt and hat. I couldn't make out much more than that, but I saw him. Call me when you get this."

She had just walked into her office when J.T. returned her call. "You somewhere safe?" he asked.

"Yes. I'm in the office." She heard Cam on the phone in the back. "Cam's here."

"All right. This shit ends now. I'm coming to get you."

"No. We need to let this play out. So far, this person hasn't hurt me. He's hurting people who have any interest in me."

"Steven's interested?" J.T.'s voice lowered. "I thought it was a friendly, I-have-a-boyfriend lunch."

"It was. He was really nice. Even invited both of us—you and me—to get together with him sometime. He's new and looking for friends."

"Yeah, well, he can find his own *friends*."

"Stop." J.T.'s jealousy secretly thrilled her, because it showed he cared. "You know I"—Cam walked in—"can't talk now. My boss is here. I have to go."

"I'll swing by to get you at six. Stay there until I'm in your office, looking at you."

"Yes, Landon. I mean, J.T. Funny how you guys sound alike, all authoritative and all."

"Smart-ass." He hung up.

Cam sat on the corner of her desk. "So, how's the fake boyfriend?"

"What? Does everyone know about my attempt to annoy my mother?"

"You told me about your clever little ruse, remember?"

Only Cam used words like *ruse* in everyday conversation. "Oh, right." She'd forgotten.

"Of course, your behemoth of a boyfriend has been coming here all week, sucking face with you and basically pounding his chest if anyone not a male relative gets near."

"Isn't he sweet?" She batted her lashes.

Cam grinned. "All good, then?"

"With J.T., yes." She told Cam about the incident at lunch.

"Damn. Hope, I don't like any of this."

"Me neither. But J.T. had a friend of his consult with a policeman they know. Basically, he said what we all know. They can't do anything unless we can prove it's all related, and we can't. But at least now we can take Steven off the list."

"Are you doing okay?"

"I am." Because of J.T. in her life. Otherwise, she'd be a basket case. "I admit I'm freaked out. It helps that I have a really hunky bodyguard." And if anything else happened, she'd go to the police. Hope had had enough of it all.

Cam rolled his eyes. "Women. Vanessa seems to think he's sexy. I don't see it, but whatever."

"Tell your greedy wife he's mine. And I'll fight her for him."

"Yes, I'll do that." Cam shook his head and walked back to his office.

The day passed quickly, and Wednesday turned into

Thursday without much fanfare. J.T. had driven her to work in the morning, adamant that he be the one to pick her up and take her home, to his place tonight. They'd been going back and forth, and she loved how each night spent in his arms brought them closer.

He'd shown her a picture of his mother. Bridget Webster had been a knockout, no question. Back at her apartment, Hope had cooked for him, showing him what he'd be getting if they remained together. He'd gobbled up her sweet basil chicken and had not only seconds, but thirds.

Life kept getting better…except for her pesky stalker.

At nine fifty Thursday morning, Brad Wheeler walked in carrying flowers. "Hi, Hope. I found these outside your door, and your name is on the envelope. Pretty."

She took them from him, dreading what she'd find inside. The card said:

> *You can do so much better than him. Roses trump pizza, milady fair.*

"From your boyfriend?" Brad asked.

She frowned. "No. You didn't see anyone put them there, did you?"

"No. They were sitting in front of the door."

If it was Brad, best he know right now she was calling the cops on his sorry butt. "I've been getting small gifts. Flowers, a treat at a bakery, and some unexpected violence."

Brad's eyes grew wide. "What?"

"Two friends of mine have been affected. One got seriously hurt. The other had his car keyed. I don't like it, and I think whoever did this has a serious problem." She couldn't believe it when Brad paled.

"What did the note say?"

Why? Do you want to see if you spelled my name right? "Here."

She showed him the card. His brows shot up as he read, clearly concerned and surprised. She might have read him wrong.

He looked up, even paler. "Wow. I'm so sorry." He handed the card back to her. "No one should have to be harassed like that."

"No." She sighed. "I'm sorry for sharing my problems. It's got nothing to do with you."

"How long has this been going on?"

"A few weeks." A glance at Brad's several-thousand-dollar suit and expensive watch, and she wondered how she could have thought him her sweatshirt and baseball cap stalker.

"Again, I'm sorry."

"It's not your fault."

Cam appeared and welcomed Brad back. He spied the flowers but said nothing. Once Brad left, Cam took the flowers back to his office. "Hope. Go home. I'm serious. I'm going to call the police, and I don't give a crap what we can or can't prove. This has gone on long enough."

"But—"

"No buts. I only have a few more clients, and Alex will be in at two. He can help catch us up."

"Cam, I'm not hurt or incapable of doing my job."

"I know, but I'm feeling protective. Humor me, would you?"

"Fine." She paused. "But I don't have a ride."

"I'll call you a cab."

Ten minutes later, she stood downstairs in broad daylight, in the safety of a wide sidewalk with a minimal crowd, waiting for the cab to pull up.

A dark-gray BMW sidled to the curb. A window rolled down. "Hope, get in." Brad Wheeler looked worried. "I need to talk to you."

"Um, I don't think so." She fiddled with her purse, and her phone fell out. *Damn*.

"I know who's been bothering you."

She froze in the process of picking it up. "Brad, you're a nice man, but you're married. Remember? Jennifer?" Though had anyone ever seen his wife in person? Or had he made her up?

"Hell. It's not me. Hope, get in the car." He was staring over her shoulder.

She turned to see a slender figure in a ball cap and sweatshirt standing by the building, just steps away. He had his right hand tucked into his sweatshirt pocket, his features hidden from her by his brim. She still didn't recognize him.

"Get in," Brad insisted. "You don't want to talk to him. Trust me."

She noted the stranger's height at close to six feet. Several inches taller than Hope, at least. Then the man pulled what looked like the hilt of a hunting knife from his sweatshirt pocket and started toward her.

Brad insisted. "Hope, *please*."

Torn between wanting to get to sure safety and away from the stalker almost upon her, she did the only thing that made sense and darted into Brad's car. And left her friggin' phone behind.

J.T. had a bad feeling. He couldn't pinpoint the reason why, but something was wrong. He called Hope's phone, but she didn't answer. Uncaring of Cam's business hours, he dialed the man's number.

"Hello?"

"It's J.T. Is Hope there?"

Cam grunted. "She got more flowers, so I told her to go home and called her a cab."

"Oh." J.T. let out a relieved breath. "Okay." Pleased to know she was all right, he still would have liked to talk to her. He worked on some touch-ups for a client, cleaned up his station, then did some mock-ups for the woman coming in at one.

Twice more he tried to call Hope, and she still hadn't answered.

What the hell?

Then he received a text. *Am fine. But I need to talk to you. Come to my apartment when done work.*

Will do, he answered.

Now able to get back to work, J.T. turned to the dragon eating the demons plaguing Margery Salton. *Therapy through skin and ink. Go figure*. The artwork looked fantastic, but it needed some tweaking before he could go over it with her. But not today.

By eleven thirty, he couldn't stand it anymore. He called Margery and rescheduled her for tomorrow during his lunch hour, which she was able to make.

"Yo, Grim. I need to bail. I'll be back later, maybe."

Grim nodded and continued inking an amazing rendition of the client's mother in black and gray.

J.T. needed to see Hope. Now. His ribs had been protesting all morning, and he missed her.

After sitting in craptastic traffic, as usual, he arrived at her apartment complex in half an hour. A pretty brunette held open the door and gave him a come-hither once-over.

"Thanks," he said absently and hurried, as best he was able, to Hope's apartment. Just as he put his hand on the doorknob, he sensed someone behind him.

Acting on instinct, he ducked and missed getting knifed in the back by inches. Instead, a large hunting knife stuck to her door.

"Hope," he yelled. "Call the police."

A slender man in a blue sweatshirt and hat came at him again, the knife once again in his possession. J.T. felt like shit. His ribs protested, adrenaline flooded his body, and a headache blossomed out of nowhere.

"You're done here." It was the only warning J.T. would give him. He ignored his ribs and lunged at the guy, tackling him to the floor and pinning the hand with the knife. The door opened behind him, and he yelled at Hope to close it.

"J.T.!" she cried.

"I'll help him," came an unfamiliar voice, followed by a woman saying, "I called the police."

A man in a suit joined J.T. to help hold down the thrashing attacker, who started yelling.

"Jennifer, you're mean. I'm going to tell Mom and Dad what you did." His words and high-pitched tone suggested someone much younger than a grown man, a dose of crazy that unnerved J.T.

"Who the fuck are you people?" He turned his head

to the man in the suit. Glimpsing Hope, he was relieved to see her healthy and scared, but unharmed.

She nodded at the suit. "Brad Wheeler is a client of Cam's, and he's a friend. He's helping you hold his brother-in-law, Jennifer's brother. This is Jennifer." J.T. saw an older woman regarding the scene with concern. She wore a dress and heels in addition to diamonds on her ears, fingers, and throat. She screamed money, as did the suit next to him.

"Brad, huh?"

"Yes." He stared down at his brother-in-law, who had stopped struggling. "Casey, Hope is her own person. She has her own friends, and you can't keep her."

"I can if I want." The guy shot Hope a sly look. "Especially if she's a whore, just like the one you married."

J.T. pulled back and slugged him. Broke his damn nose and knocked the guy senseless.

"Watch who you call a whore, asshole." He turned to Hope. "Grab me something to tie him up with, would you?" His ribs started protesting. Big time.

Hope darted away and returned with some duct tape.

"Perfect." He and Brad rolled the psycho over and tied his wrists, then his ankles. J.T. left him on his belly, then slowly stood, with Hope's help, and glared at her. "Can you *please* tell me what the hell is going on?"

She nodded. "I was waiting for a cab when Brad pulled up looking nervous. He acted kind of weird when he found out I'd been getting flowers."

"When she gave me the note to read, I knew. Casey likes the phrase 'milady fair.'" Brad shook his head. "I wish I had known about this. It's all my fault."

"No, it's not," Jennifer said.

"It's not," Hope agreed.

"Would someone get on with the explanation and save the blame game for later?" *Before my brain explodes?* The fact that a man with a knife lay outside Hope's door freaked him the hell out. He wanted to end the guy, to permanently get rid of the threat. But there were witnesses, and he didn't know if Hope could handle that much violence.

A darkly amused thought struck. Where was Grim when you needed to make a body disappear?

The suit extended a hand toward him. "I'm Brad Wheeler, a client of Cameron's."

"Yes, I know. I'm J.T., Hope's boyfriend."

"What you don't know is that Jennifer's brother, Casey"—he nodded to the trussed-up creep—"doesn't think the way normal people do. He's been institutionalized for much of his life, but he's been doing so much better lately. He was recently released to us with prescribed medications, under our supervision. He's always been a little obsessive, but never with a person. And never to the extent that he'd try to hurt someone." Brad looked on the verge of tears. Jennifer was already crying.

Casey muttered something against the floor.

Jennifer wiped her eyes, clearly distraught. "The medication helps. It leaves him groggy but less destructive. God, he was doing so well I probably didn't pay close enough attention to his meds. Casey, have you been taking your pills?"

"Hate the pills. No more pills."

Jennifer shook her head. "Oh, Casey, you know

you need them. They help regulate your moods so this doesn't happen." She shot Hope a sad, apologetic look.

"Wait. Why me?" Hope asked.

A good question. J.T. wanted to know how Hope tied into this as well.

"It's my fault," Jennifer said. "Casey's been living with us, so he overhears a lot. I asked Brad if he knew someone we could set my brother *Wyatt* up with. Brad mentioned you. Then one day he took Casey with him to the office. You don't remember seeing him?"

Hope frowned. "I… Wait. I think I remember a young man waiting for Brad. But he was buttoned up and so quiet."

"Sometimes Casey is lucid and calm." Brad studied his brother-in-law with grief and resignation.

Jennifer said, "Casey doesn't understand that just because he wants something, that doesn't mean he can have it. But like I said, this is the first time he's ever considered *a person* his."

Brad left Casey to hug his wife. "It's not your fault, honey. He's got to go back where they can monitor him."

"I know. Perhaps that facility in Switzerland. It's quiet and aboveboard."

"And secure," Brad added with a nod to J.T.

"I'm not going. Mom won't make me," Casey bragged. "Hope wants me to stay. Pretty Hope. She can be my girlfriend."

"I'm sorry, Casey. But I have a boyfriend. J.T. loves me, and I love him. We're getting married and having babies."

"Yeah, all the works," J.T. added, pity warring with

the need to do this grown man violence. Yet he didn't know if the guy would really understand why he was so pissed. What a sad mess.

"Wait. Really?" Casey stared at Hope. "But I thought you were Wyatt's."

Hope shook her head. "I'm not anybody's. I don't even know Wyatt. I *choose* to be with J.T."

J.T. frowned, something still bothering him. "Hold on. You're telling me this guy hired those jerks at Ray's to beat on me?"

"Yes." Jennifer studied her brother. "Like I said, Casey can function well on his meds. He was doing so well, we never noticed when he went off them. And that gradual degeneration obviously affected his ability to rationalize right from wrong." She leaned down to wipe a tear that had trickled down Casey's cheek. "Don't worry. We'll help you, Casey. Won't we, Brad?"

"We will." Brad nodded. To Hope, he said, "We're so very, very sorry about all this. Honestly, had we any idea, we'd have taken steps to stop him. I can't believe he turned so aggressive. God, he could have killed someone."

The police arrived. They took a full statement and carted a subdued Casey away. Brad and Jennifer continued to apologize until Hope promised them she'd be all right, and they left to join Casey at the station.

A sad circumstance all around, but at least now Hope would be safe.

Finally alone together, J.T. grabbed Hope and dragged her with him to her bedroom.

"Are you all right?" she asked.

"No." Realizing she'd been in real danger, knowing

she could have been hurt by that knife-wielding maniac, had him thinking of all he might have lost.

He didn't know how to handle what he was feeling. So he pulled her in bed, hugged her, and held on.

Hope sighed. "I love you too."

Chapter 21

A DAY AND A HALF LATER, J.T. CONTINUED TO REPLAY Hope's words. She'd said it. *I love you too*. What the hell did he do now?

When she'd mentioned marriage and babies to Casey, J.T. had realized she'd said it to show the guy she had zero interest in him. But saying the love stuff to J.T. while in bed, just the two of them?

He hadn't mentioned it again. She hadn't either, and for the last thirty-six hours, he'd been stressing about how to handle the situation. Since desperate times called for desperate measures, he'd finally called his father.

Now, Saturday afternoon, sitting at Ray's and watching a baseball game on the new television Ray had mounted to the lone clean wall in the joint, J.T. toyed with his beer.

"How are the ribs?" his dad asked.

"Fine."

"Uh-huh. How's Hope?"

"Good." Perky, sweet, sexy. She'd blown his mind yet again last night, her enthusiasm for making love matching his. He'd swear she'd been slipping him something, because he'd been so damn hungry for her that they'd hit it for hours.

Or maybe she too had understood what they might have lost. He didn't know anymore. He just knew he needed to do *something*. To make a statement.

"So she's not having nightmares or anything because of that creepy guy?"

"No. She's good. In a weird way, she was always safe. He targeted everyone but her. But he's going away for a long time." Brad had called early that morning, confirming that Casey was leaving the country.

"Glad to hear it." Liam cleared his throat. "Now things can get back to normal, right?"

"Maybe." *Shit*. His palms were sweaty. "Dad, can I ask you something?"

"Sure."

He looked into Liam's light-gray eyes and saw the happiness there, that emotion that had come and gone but never stayed. For years his father had been existing, but not living. Sure, he loved his children, his garage, his friends, but he'd been alone and lonely. And they all knew it.

"Do you think I'm lonely?"

Liam didn't blink. He studied J.T. and shook his head.

"What?"

"Let's stop avoiding what you really want to know. You want me to tell you how you feel about Hope."

"I do?"

"Yes." Liam slugged back his beer and waved to Rena for another. "You saw me all fucked up for years about your mother and Del's mother. You've watched your aunt fall for dickheads, finding them everywhere. Yeah, she picks 'em like ripe fruit from asshole bushes."

"Great imagery there, Dad."

"Hush. I'm talking." Liam took the beer from Rena and handed her a ten. "Keep it, honey."

"Thanks." She winked at J.T. "Let me know how the Hope engagement thing works."

He swallowed the ball suddenly lodged in his throat.

"Ignore her." Yet Liam was smiling. "Son, I've watched you your whole life, and I can honestly say I've never seen you as whole and happy and satisfied as you've been with Hope. Same way I am with Sophie." Liam sighed. "She fits me. We're getting married, you know. I finally got the stones to ask her, and she said yes."

"Seriously?" J.T.'s issues could wait. He leaned closer to hug his dad. "That's *awesome*. When are you tying the knot?"

"At Christmas this year. We want to do a white wedding."

"Wow."

Liam blinked, and J.T. wondered if he was seeing things, because his dad looked about to cry. "Wanted to know if you'd be my best man."

"Oh. Wow. Heck, yeah."

Liam nodded and wiped his cheeks. "Something in my eyes."

"Sure." J.T. had something in his too.

"Now about Hope. Sophie and I talked about this. We both see what's happening. And you've got to shit or get off the pot, boy."

"Somehow I don't see Sophie saying that."

"Hope Donnigan is a gem. She's sweet and lovely, and Sophie just adores her. Her words, not mine. The girl wants nothing more than love and a happily-ever-after. Much as I'm having a tough time fathoming it, the girl wants you."

"Thanks, Dad."

Liam's grin faded. "Point is, don't make the same mistakes I made. Don't live afraid of every day, wondering who else you're gonna lose. Because with that thinking, you're already lost. Just think of it this way. Imagine your life without Hope."

"I can't."

"Then it's too late for you. Now get out of here and go make it right with her."

"What does that mean?" J.T. wanted to know. "Marriage? Kids? Moving in together?"

"I'd say take it one step at a time, but at the very least, let her know what she means to you."

I love you too.

"She might already know."

"Maybe if you'd stop being a pussy and just tell her, all this mysterious miscommunication crap would go away," Liam suggested in a voice sweet enough to melt sugar. "For God's sake, boy, don't be like your sister. She almost ended it with Mike over a simple misunderstanding. I thought you were smarter than that."

"I am." He was. "Fine. I'm going. Thanks for the pep talk, if you could call it that."

Liam held up a glass in toast. "To fools rushing in."

"Huh?"

"'Can't Help Falling in Love.' Elvis Presley. Listen to it, and learn a thing or two."

"How old are you again? A hundred?"

His father flipped him off, and all was again right with the world. J.T. headed to his *real* girlfriend's apartment for a meeting of hearts and minds.

Back at home after an intense workout at the gym, Hope finally had a minute to herself. Having been nearly attached at the hip to J.T. for weeks on end, it was nice—and not lonely—to be by herself again. The relief of knowing who had been giving her presents actually eclipsed having him put away. As creepy as he'd been, Casey deserved her pity, not her animosity.

After all, without him, she might not have had J.T. to lean on so much.

And that was the crux of it. She loved the big oaf. She knew he loved her. So where did that leave them? Where did that leave *her*? In another relationship going nowhere?

She knew they hadn't been together all that long, though it felt like forever. She'd never felt like this about anyone. What should she do? Continue to pretend everything was fine? Make him—and them—deal with it? Or start over with someone else?

As if I can let him go that easily. The big jerk is addictive.

She sighed and decided to shower off the grime from her workout.

Since she and J.T. had grown close, she'd given him a spare key. Sadly, she wished it wasn't just a matter of time before he returned it.

Letting the hot water slide over her body, she saw a future so close, there for the taking, if only she could reach out and grab it. A life with a funny, artistic man and a few kids on the side, gorgeous babies with caramel skin and light-brown eyes. They'd look like a perfect blend of Hope and J.T.

She sighed. Babies on the brain couldn't be a good thing.

A scuff on the floor told her she was no longer alone.

"It's just me. Don't freak out."

"Too late." She hadn't expected him home. No, not *home*. *Back*. Hadn't expected him back. "What's wrong?"

"Everything." He stepped into the shower still wearing his jeans and T-shirt.

"Okay, I have to know. What is with you and Jethro Tull?"

He appeared pained. "You still don't get it? Jethro Tull?" At her look, he sighed. "J.T.?"

"No." She gaped. "Are you serious? Your name is Jethro Tull Webster?" She paused. "Jethro?" Hope laughed. And laughed.

And laughed some more.

"Yeah, my name sucks. You done yet?"

"Jethro!" she hooted. "Oh, thanks, I needed that." She took some time to catch her breath, saw his annoyance, his Jethro Tull shirt, and laughed again.

He knocked his head back against the shower wall. "Why me?"

"Sorry."

His attention span easily diverted, he soon turned his gaze from the ceiling to her breasts. "I have problems."

"Jethro. Tull."

"Stop it." He tried not to grin and couldn't help it. "You're such a shit."

"Oh, that's nice."

"That's one of the many reasons I love you."

Hope forgot what she wanted to say.

"I figured it's about time I acted like I have a pair and admitted it. You already know anyway."

She'd known, but it never hurt to hear it again.

"You're sexy and smart. I love your body, your obnoxious mouth, the way you make me laugh. I've never felt this way about anyone before, and to be honest, it scares the shit out of me."

"Oh. Me too." She smiled.

"Hey. Let me say this."

She didn't point out that he was soaked now. Or that he had a habit of looking her over while talking, as if unable to stop himself from staring at her body. She liked that.

"When I gave you that speech about people who love each other staying together, it just came out of nowhere. I panicked that you might leave me. I don't want that. Fuck, Hope. I want you. Like, I think about us together in the future. I watch you with Colin and think about what you'd be like with your own kid. With our kid."

She wanted to pinch herself. Was this real?

"But it feels fast to think like that. We're new. I've never had a relationship last more than six months, tops. And your mother—"

"Will come around. Don't worry." The need to convince her mother of his worth burned. "I'll make her see the light."

He smiled. "That mean spark in your eyes worries me and turns me on. What am I going to do with you?"

"I know. I think I'd like a tattoo, sir. A butterfly right down here." She brought his hand to her lower right belly. "And maybe you can tattoo a *J*. on one wing and a *T*. on the other."

He looked horrified.

"What did I say?"

"Tattooing a girl's or guy's name on your body is the

kiss of death for a relationship. Trust me, I've seen it too many times."

"Fine. Then how about something magical on my body?"

"Honey, your body *is* magical. My dick has never been so hard all the time. Hell, I'm hard now, and I'm still confused about how I can feel this way. But I do."

"So go with it. We don't have to rush into anything, you know."

"Well, okay. But I was thinking. Maybe we can ease us into things with a fake engagement. Like, we can plan things and pick out rings and shit."

"And shit." She grinned.

"You know my dad and your aunt are getting married this Christmas."

"Oh, that's so great." She let him pull her into his arms.

"But we can do them one better. How about we think about next year? Like, Valentine's Day?"

"Too clichéd."

He kissed her. "First day of spring?"

"Nah." She pulled his shirt off. Then she took his nipple between her lips.

"Damn." He blew out a breath. "What was I saying?"

"You were going to take off your pants and get naked first."

"Right."

She helped him strip to nothing—carefully, which took some effort.

He frowned. "I probably need to hold you up to make this work."

"You will not. Your ribs are healing." She reached

around him and turned off the shower. They dried off, then she moved into her room and bent over the bed. "The pill is safe now, so we don't need a—" She shrieked as he pounced, which couldn't have been good for his ribs.

But later, after they'd both been well pleasured, he lay with her in bed, each of them hugging the other tightly.

He yawned. "Let me get some rest so we can go again."

"*Nooo*."

He laughed. "So keep thinking about a good date for us."

"Already have one."

"Oh?"

She dragged his head down and whispered, "April first."

He pulled back and smiled at her. "That sounds about right. So are we going to have a pretend engagement to go with our pretend relationship?"

"Whatever you want. You're in charge."

He nodded. "I can work with that."

Yep, let him think it's his own idea to keep you. "Man, I really am the queen."

He laughed. "I love you, you crazy woman."

"I love you too." A pause. "Jethro."

Don't miss *Test Drive*, the first book in Marie Harte's Body Shop Bad Boys series!

Chapter 1

The opening riff of an old-school AC/DC song echoed through the garage. Johnny Devlin bit back a curse when he scraped his knuckles on the pump of the piece of crap Cadillac he was working on.

The smell of motor oil, sweat, and grease warmed the interior of Johnny's favorite place in the world. Webster's Garage boasted a double set of bay doors and a roomy interior complete with a cement floor and red-and-brown brick walls, a holdover from the original Tooley's Auto Shop.

"Hey, asshole," he heard Foley snarl. "We talked about this. Hands off my stuff."

Best buds Foley and Sam were squared off, staring holes through each other. When it came to order—and pretty much everything related to cleanliness—the two thugs sat on opposite ends of the spectrum. Foley—Mr. Tall, Dangerous, and Arrogant—was compulsively neat, while Sam might as well have had the word *chaos* tattooed on his forehead. Covered in tattoos, Sam was a walking billboard for badassery.

Lou stepped over to the radio near his work station, and soon loud classic rock drowned out the rest of the argument.

Just another day at the office.

A cool breeze made Johnny sigh. Seattle's unseasonably warm autumn temps continued to be a pleasant surprise this year, and they kept the garage doors open to let the air circulate through the sticky auto repair shop. Even at nine thirty in the morning, he had worked himself into a sweat.

Johnny cranked his wrench and stared at a stubborn pump assembly that refused to cooperate. He loosened it, got to the fan belt, then glared down at the problematic power steering pump.

After glancing over his shoulder to make sure he was in the clear, he softly muttered, "Shitty Cadillac."

The sound of someone shaking a familiar glass jar of coins made him tense. He heard it again, even over the blast of AC/DC. Ducking deeper under the Cadillac's hood, Johnny wondered who his sexy-scary boss was going to call out for cursing now. He was sure he hadn't been that loud.

"Seriously, guys?" Delilah Webster held the newly purposed amber glass growler out to Sam and Foley. The woman had a hard-on for swearwords lately.

Such a sad waste of a perfectly good beer container. Once the half-gallon jar had been home to a killer IPA flavored with hops and a hint of citrus. Now, it was nothing but a no-swearing jar filled with goddamn quarters.

As if the shop going clean would prevent Del from slipping up at her wedding.

He imagined her dolled up in a white gown, tats, piercings, and her hair all done up in some funky twist, looking like a million bucks. She'd be glowing at her behemoth of a fiancé before letting loose with an "I *fucking* do." With a snort, he buried himself back under the hood of the bastard of a car and did his best to calm his frustration. He never had anything pleasant to say before ten a.m. anyway. God knew he needed a jolt of caffeine, and soon, before he took a tire iron to the gray piece of crap he just *knew* was laughing at him.

Sam and Foley bitched about the new no-swear policy even as he heard them drop change into what Johnny had taken to calling the "Rattle of Oppression—ROP." A few clinks of change against glass and everyone seemed to sink into themselves, anxious that their fearsome boss would come storming back in, demanding a quarter for a "hell," "shit," or "damn."

Johnny knew better. Dubbed the smart one of the crew, he kept his nose out of trouble and everyone else on the straight and narrow. Mostly.

He heard Del step in his direction, grazed his already sore knuckle against the frame as he removed the assembly, and let it rip. "*Fudge*."

"See?" Del yelled to be heard above a man on the radio screeching about shaking all night long. "At least *someone* can keep his friggin' mouth clean." She patted him on the shoulder, and he did his best not to flinch. Woman had hands like rocks. "Thanks, Johnny."

He kept his head down and continued to tinker, listening as her footsteps gradually faded. Then an office door closed, and he found it safe to look up.

"You are *such* a kiss ass." Sam frowned. Then again, Sam did nothing but frown.

Next to him, Foley crossed massive arms over a broad

chest and made kissy noises. A glance across the garage showed Lou shaking his head, looking disappointed.

"What?" Johnny tossed up his hands. "Am I the *only* one smart enough to know you catch more bees with honey?" He smirked at the many middle fingers shot his way. "Thought so. Dumbasses."

Of the four of them currently in the shop, Sam was the one whose temper could turn on a dime. He'd gotten better over the years, but everyone knew to avoid the brute when he sank into a rage. Only Foley could talk him down, the pair closer than most brothers. Lou had a sense of humor like Johnny's, but without the quick wit—or so Johnny liked to constantly tell him.

Keeping on Sam's good side would be the smart thing to do.

So of course, Johnny had to prod him. "Hey, McSteroid, you and your boyfriend got plans for tonight?"

Foley sighed. Lou grinned.

Sam's frown darkened. "Why? You got a death wish, stick boy?"

Johnny flexed a greasy arm. "Seriously? Stick boy? Man, I'm ripped. And it's all natural." He raised a brow at Sam and pushed his bicep up from the back, trying to appear bigger.

Even Sam couldn't withstand the Devlin charm. A rare smiled appeared on his face. "Whatever. No, I don't have plans. And Foley—not my boyfriend, dickhead—has his own life."

"So." Lou looked Foley up and down. "No plans for you then?"

"Suck it."

Lou grinned. It took a lot to push the guy's buttons. "Back at you, hombre."

"I thought we'd hang at Ray's if you losers have nothing better to do. Darts rematch?" Johnny offered.

The others agreed.

"You're on." Lou looked eager. The only one of the group who gave Johnny a serious run for his money at the game. Intelligent, a real ladies' man, and he had a steady hand. A useful trait for a guy who painted with great attention to detail.

"Cool." Johnny gave them a thumbs-up. "Winner doesn't pay for drinks. So make sure you idiots bring your wallets."

"Dream on, motherfu—"

"*Foley*," Del snarled from the office door. "What the hell did I say about swearing?" The ROP had returned.

Johnny buried his head back under the hood of the car. He was pretty sure the others did the same. Survival of the fittest worked only if you let the weaker ones, like Foley, take one for the team.

A few hours later, he lounged outside on a picnic table, eating a sandwich Dale, their service writer, had picked up from their favorite shop two doors down. The rare sunshine, not marred by a single cloud, added to the perfection of the moment. A few birds chirped, cars buzzed down Rainier, and only Foley crunching on a huge bag of chips interrupted Johnny's peace.

Foley glanced at Johnny's third sandwich. "Where do you put all that food? You should be really fat."

"You should talk. And just because I don't spend my leisure time jerking off with weights doesn't mean I'm not in shape. I like running."

"From the law," Foley muttered and crunched some more, a sly grin on his face.

"Nah. That's in the past. The trick now is not to get caught." He wiggled his brows, and Foley laughed. "I run after work, if you're interested."

"Nope. I'd rather 'jerk off with weights,'" Foley sneered. "You know, with that smart mouth, it's a wonder no one's rearranged your face lately."

"It's been a few months," Johnny admitted. He had a hard time going without a fight, cursed with an inability to keep his mouth shut around less intelligent, ill-humored people. "I'm not a half-bad boxer. Hence my ability to still breathe on my own."

"I know. That's the only reason Sam and I tolerate you. That and if we're in a fight, we'll throw them the runt and mosey off."

Johnny laughed. Foley and Sam weren't known to *mosey* away from anything. The badass bros, as he and the others called them behind their backs, ended more shit than Johnny ever started. That weird moral code the pair insisted on keeping often had them interfering when a smarter man would steer clear.

"You still dating Alicia?" Foley asked out of the blue.

"Nah. She got a little clingy."

Foley sighed. "They all do."

"I take it you and Sue are quits then."

"Yep."

"Should make tonight at Ray's interesting." Johnny grinned. Sue waitressed at Ray's, and though he'd been curious, he'd been too intimidated by her rough edges to try her on for size. A sweetheart underneath the heavy kohl, many piercings, and fierce tats, Sue nevertheless didn't tolerate horny fools. Fuck with her and meet a bad end. Period.

Granted, Johnny wouldn't typically let a little thing like a woman kicking his ass stop him if he really wanted her. He'd charmed harder cases than Sue. But he didn't want to break her heart, then have to deal with her when he went back to the bar.

"It wasn't like we were serious."

"A little defensive, hoss?"

"Shut up. I am not."

"Uh-huh."

Foley groaned. "It was just supposed to be sex. Then she's texting me all the time. Can I help it if I'm damn good in bed? I mean, Jesus. A little oral foreplay, and the chick's hinting at wedding bells."

"Really?"

"Okay, so I'm exaggerating. But she wanted to go exclusive, so I backed out quick." Foley's ended relationship apparently hadn't dulled his appetite, because he finished the chips and started on a few cookies. Carrying around so much muscle obviously expended energy. "She said she's cool with it, but I haven't been face-to-face with her since Saturday night."

Johnny did the math. "That's nearly a week. Hey, with any luck, she'll be too slammed with orders tonight to notice you. You know how Fridays at Ray's can get." Johnny gave him a fake smile. "Good luck, friend."

Foley frowned at him. "You don't sound all that sincere."

"I'm not. I'll be placing bets on you leaving Ray's with at least one or two darts in your ass. You know Sue holds the bar record, right?"

"Hell."

Johnny snickered. Liam Webster, Del's old man and the other owner of the garage, approached alongside Sam. Before either could sit, Johnny announced the bet. "Okay, gentlemen—and I use that term loosely—ten bucks says Sue tries to attack Foley before we leave Ray's tonight."

Sam considered Foley. "I'll take that bet." To Foley he said, "I told you not to date the chicks at Ray's. You bonehead."

"We're going to Ray's, if you're interested," Johnny told Liam, the rational half of his employers.

Del's father had to be in his late fifties but looked years younger. He had height and muscle on him that Johnny, no matter how hard he worked, would never have. Liam also had an easygoing attitude and knowledge of mechanics that put most auto-thugs to shame. Del was his pride and joy, and J.T., his bruiser of a son, was always good for a laugh when he dropped by.

Liam had grown up poor, worked his tail off to make something of himself, and had raised two fine if aggressive kids. A terrific boss, he didn't judge, knew how difficult it could be to get a second chance, and always gave a guy the benefit of the doubt. Hell, he'd hired Johnny, and Johnny would never claim to be a saint. Not after that pesky felony. Friggin' cops refused to let a guy joyride without making it a huge deal.

Ah, but life at eighteen had seemed so simple back then.

"I'd love to join you boys at Ray's, but I have a date with a lady."

Johnny said kindly, "Blow-up dolls don't count, Liam."

Foley and Sam chuckled.

"Shut it, Son, before I shut it for you." Liam made a fist at Johnny, but his amusement was plain to see.

They all knew he'd scored big time a few months ago, and ever since, he and Sophie, his lady friend, had been acting like a pair of lovebirds.

Sam shrugged and sat next to Foley, stealing the rest of his cookies.

"Hey."

Sam put an open hand on Foley's face and shoved while inhaling a cookie whole. He talked around his food, opening his mouth to Johnny, especially because the bastard knew it grossed Johnny out. "Still can't believe you got a classy lady like that to give you the time of day, Liam," he said around expelled cookie crumbs.

They all looked at Liam, who puffed up. "I know. Boggles the mind."

They shared a laugh, though Johnny knew they'd all been beyond pleased to see the boss finally get lucky. For thirty years the guy had mourned his true love, raised two hellions, and somehow run a successful garage. Johnny looked up to Liam. Hell, he wanted to *be* Liam, someday. Especially since Liam had scored a fine woman. A mystery to them all.

"So what are your plans? Going to take her ballroom dancing?" Johnny teased.

The whole garage had given Liam shit for the dancing date a month ago.

Liam frowned. "As a matter of fact, we're going fine dining."

Sam stuffed the last cookie in his mouth and mumbled "Good luck" while chewing.

"Sam, close your mouth." Johnny cringed, pushed past his limit. "Just…gross."

Foley snorted. "Hey, at least he's dressed and not

scratching his ass, drinking straight from the milk carton, and busting into your room when you're trying to get lucky."

"With a girl?" Lou asked from behind them. "What happened to Sue?"

Foley growled, "Sue's a girl."

"Yeah, but you already got lucky, right?" Lou shrugged. "Once you're in, you're in. Unless you're doing it wrong." And Lou would know. The guy never hurt for women.

Liam sighed. "You guys are pitiful. Now get back to work."

"Yeah, yeah." Johnny stood with the others and filled Lou in on Foley's dilemma.

"Cool. I'm down for ten. I say she ignores him completely. Kind of the way Lara treats *you*, Johnny."

His face heated, but he pretended not to hear the other guys razzing him and hightailed it back into the garage.

Lara Valley—the lust of his life. He'd been going to Ray's forever, and the first time he'd seen her, four-plus years ago, he'd fallen hard. But his reputation had preceded him: a player and proud of it. He'd teased and flirted his way to learning her name and a few details about the stunning brunette, but little more.

Currently twenty-seven years old and still single, she had her mom, dad, and sister, two nieces she helped care for, and took classes at the community college. For nursing, if he wasn't mistaken. Man, she could help him heal up anytime.

He'd spent many a night at Ray's, discreetly watching her. Long brown hair, deep, chocolate-brown eyes, a slender body curved in all the right places. She worked hard, didn't take shit from anyone, and had a genuinely kind heart for the poor souls sobbing heartache into their beers.

He preferred when she tended bar, because it kept her fine ass away from grabby customers, unlike when she waitressed.

Just the thought of seeing her again made his heart leap, but he knew better. A smart guy didn't shit where he ate. Look at poor Foley and his breakup with Sue. Guaranteed the woman would make him pay in some way tonight. Johnny knew women. He knew what they liked and didn't like. And Sue would be gunning for the guy who'd dumped her, even if she claimed the breakup was no big deal.

He snorted, wondering how Foley could appear so together and be so clueless.

Now take Lara. Johnny wanted her, no question. For a night, a week, a month. Hell, he'd been obsessed with her for a while, and he knew it would take time to get her out of his system. First he had to get her to go out with him.

But Lara? She had a thing about not dating the guys who hung out at Ray's. A smart choice, actually. Johnny loved the joint, but Ray's catered to a rough crowd.

The perfect place for his kind of people, he thought with a grin.

Hours later and a dollar in quarters poorer, having been goaded into a few f-bombs though Sam had *sworn* Del was outside the garage, Johnny sat with his buddies near the darts at Ray's, drinking and preparing for his weekend.

"No plans, guys. For once, I'm a free man for two whole days." He kicked back and sighed with pleasure.

"So no work at your dad's club for you, huh?" Foley asked. "Too bad. I was going to offer to help."

"Me too," Sam added, his voice like the growl of a wounded bear. "Damn. I was hoping to talk to Candy again."

"Sorry, sport. Dear old Dad is Candy's new squeeze."

"Bummer." Sam shrugged. "But the guy's got good taste."

He always had. Johnny had grown up without his mother, but with a bevy of maternal support. His father had a thing for strippers, so it made sense Jack Devlin had finally ponied up and bought his own strip club a few years back. Johnny had never faulted his father's fascination with tits and ass. But it would have been nice to have just *one* set around while growing up, and getting to know more than the girl's stage name before she squirreled.

"So have you seen Sue yet?" he asked Foley.

The others waited. Lou seemed especially amused. Johnny knew that gleam in his friend's eyes.

"Ah, not yet."

Sam snorted. "He's been either hiding in the bathroom or ducking behind Earl."

Earl—a huge-ass bouncer Johnny had no intention of annoying. Ever. And the same went for the other guy, Big J, whom everyone said looked like Mr. Clean.

Foley flushed. "First off, I had to piss. Second, I wasn't ducking behind Earl. I said hi to the guy, and he asked me what I thought about Dodge trucks."

"Uh-huh. Sure you weren't asking him about Sue's

frame of mind?" Johnny teased. Over Foley's shoulder, he saw Lara smiling at a woman over the bar. His heart stuttered, and he did his best to act cool, collected. *She's not interested. She's a nice girl. Leave her alone.*

Like clockwork, his perverse, inner loudmouth had him offering to order the next round. "Be right back. And remember, don't hate the player, hate the game—when *I win*. Suckers."

Grinning, he left the guys at the table swearing, and nabbed a free place at the crowded bar. Lara, Sue, and a few others were hopping, grabbing drinks, and pouring like mad. Behind him he heard a scuffle break out, and he turned to see two guys who used to be friends hammering on each other.

"That's rough," a biker covered in tats next to him said. "But then, Jim should have known better than to hit up Sheila with her new guy right there."

"He really needs to lay off the tequila." Lara sounded exasperated. "I told Earl to keep an eye on him."

Johnny turned and locked gazes with her. She had her long brown hair pulled back in a familiar ponytail. The silky mass reached her lower back, and he was dying to see her hair down just once. She wore minimal makeup, a bit of liner and some thicker mascara. Growing up around women who glammed up for a living, he'd learned early on about a woman's trade secrets. But he doubted the red in her cheeks came from blush. More like from the heat in the place. And damn, it would have been nice if everyone around him cared about personal hygiene as much as he did.

He wrinkled his nose when a new guy replaced the one next to him and leaned toward Lara, wafting his less-than-pleasant scent. Lara wiped her hand over her nose and pretended a cough.

He and she shared a grin, and his pulse galloped like a racehorse. The sight of her smile, and that heart-stopping dimple, always made it hard for him to breathe. More than physical beauty, Lara possessed a warm inner core that got him hazy and drunk faster than a hometown IPA.

"So, you the bartender?" Smelly drunk guy wanted to know.

She glanced at her black T-shirt that read "Bartender" in bold white letters. "Um, yeah." Lara gave smelly guy a fake smile. "Another beer?"

"Yep. And keep the change." He slid a grimy twenty her way.

She poured his beer and handed him back a few bills. "You gave me a twenty. You sure about me keeping all that change?" She was so sweet, so honest.

Way too good for you, Devlin. Leave her alone.

The guy belched, then pulled back ten, giving her a few bucks. "Thanks, honey. I'll be back." He stumbled from the barstool, which was quickly occupied by a new customer. Thankfully, this one a woman who smelled like cheap perfume instead of BO.

"What can I get you, Johnny?"

He loved hearing his name on Lara's lips. She had a husky quality to her voice, and he could too easily imagine it whispering her pleasure while he showed her why she should take a chance on him. Foley thought he had oral foreplay down to a science, but Johnny could have written a book on how to please women, a virtual connoisseur by age sixteen.

He cleared his throat and tried to will away his lecherous thoughts. "A pitcher for the crew." He nodded to the guys across the bar then leaned closer to her, to be heard above the crowd. "So what's with Sue? I hear she and Foley split."

Lara rolled her eyes. Of all the staff at Ray's, she and Rena seemed the most levelheaded. No drama for them. "She's pining for the guy. I warned her about him, but did she listen to me?"

"Foley's a good guy." He felt the need to defend his friend.

"Sure, but he's not a *permanent* guy. None of you are," she said with a direct gaze that aroused and annoyed him at the same time.

"Maybe we just need to find the right woman." He gave her the Devlin smile.

For a second it looked like he might have connected with her, but then she laughed and shoved his pitcher at him. "For you guys, there's a right woman, and a left woman, and a woman on the side..."

The woman next to him laughed. "Seems like she's got you pegged, sexy."

He gave her the Devlin smile and winked, and she stared at him, her lips parted. So at least he hadn't lost his magic. He took the pitcher from Lara, and their fingers brushed. He felt the tingle all the way to his cock and swallowed a groan. Pasting on a sly grin, he said, "But, Lara, if I had *you*, I wouldn't need any of those others." He drew her hand to his mouth and kissed the back of it. "See you later, gorgeous. And you know, you ever change your mind about mixing pleasure with pleasure, you have my number."

"You mean business with pleasure," she corrected.

"Do I?" He grinned and left, doing his best not to look over his shoulder at her, but it was damn hard. Especially when she laughed. The sound carried like wind chimes, and he felt a shiver start from his toes and work its way up his body. That hollow in his gut hit him, because he had a crazy urge to go back to the bar just to stare at her. Take in her joy with life.

I am such an asswipe.

An *erect* asswipe. *Hell.* Time to cool off before he rejoined the crew.

"Jesus, what were you doing up there?" Foley bitched when he returned. "Waiting for the hops to grow?"

Lou snickered. "More like dying for a smile from sexy Lara." He moaned and patted his heart. "What I wouldn't give for some alone time with that gorgeous woman."

Sam had to add, "She can tend my bar anytime."

"Shut up, dickheads." Johnny glared. "Drink your beer, and let's throw a few darts."

He waited until Foley stepped to the line before he added, "Oh, and guess what Lara told me about Sue?" When Foley hit a lousy one *outside* the ring, Johnny smiled wide.

Foley rattled. Mission accomplished. Now to get in Lou's headspace and win the game. He shot a glance at the bar, saw his favorite brunette laugh, and thought about strategy. About his endgame.

Because Johnny always played to win.

Acknowledgments

A huge thanks to Edward Kehoe at Monolith Tattoo Studio. Your information was invaluable. Any mistakes in the story are mine alone.

And to the talented folks at Sourcebooks, thanks for all that you do.

About the Author

Caffeine addict, boy referee, and romance aficionado, *New York Times* and *USA Today* bestselling author Marie Harte is a self-confessed bibliophile and devotee of action movies. Whether hiking in Central Oregon, biking around town, or hanging at the local tea shop, she's constantly plotting to give everyone a happily ever after. Visit marieharte.com and fall in love.

BODY SHOP BAD BOYS

These rough-and-tumble mechanics live fast and love hard.

By Marie Harte, *New York Times* and *USA Today* Bestselling Author

Test Drive
Johnny Devlin's a charmer with a checkered past. He's had his eye on bartender Lara Valley for ages, but she's rejected him more than once. That doesn't mean he won't come to her aid when some dirtbag mauls her.

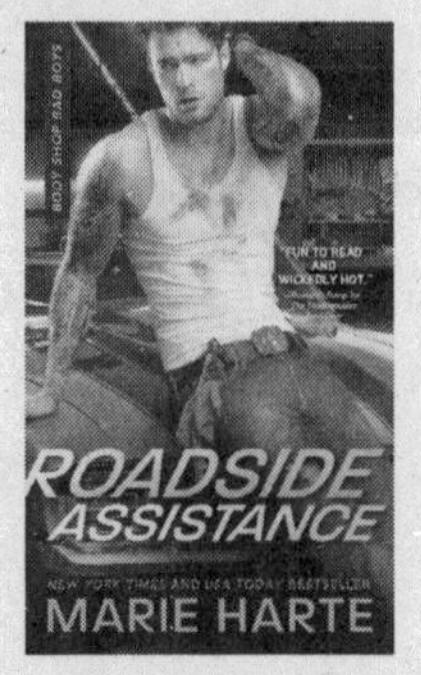

Roadside Assistance
Foley might look like a bad idea, but underneath, he's all gentleman. Too bad Cyn Nichols isn't buying it. What's a bad boy to do when the goddess of his dreams won't give him the time of day?